"A spectacular writer. He makes SF seem all fresh and new again."
– Robert J Sawyer

"What lifts this novel far above the norm is that Blackthorne is such a fine writer. Cumberland leaps off the page, a trained killer whose anger and grief at his daughter's condition is brilliantly portrayed; the depiction of his simmering rage, barely held in check, and how he channels it, provides a masterclass in characterisation."
– *The Guardian*

"A dark, believable vision of a (near) future Britain, but more importantly an intelligent, slick and brilliantly executed novel with a quite unexpected but superbly scripted ending."
– *Science Fiction & Fantasy UK*

"One of the best authors of hard SF in the world…"
– *SFX*

"One of British science fiction's most original and exciting practitioners."
– *Barnes & Noble*

"A wonderful writer who deserves worldwide recognition."
– Cheryl Morgan, *Emerald City*

"Fast paced, very entertaining and out of the ordinary… both haunting and engaging."
– *SFFWorld.com*

THOMAS BLACKTHORNE

Edge

ANGRY
ROBOT

ANGRY ROBOT
A member of the Osprey Group

Lace Market House,
54-56 High Pavement,
Nottingham
NG1 1HW, UK

www.angryrobotbooks.com
Kiss the blade

Originally published in the UK by Angry Robot 2010
First American paperback printing 2010

ISBN 978-0-85766-040-4

Printed in the United States of America

9 8 7 6 5 4 3 2 1

[EDGE]

[ONE]

They drove through the Wiltshire night not saying the name of Sophie. He at the wheel, she in the front passenger seat, tension clamping her mouth. Over and over, not saying it aloud. The insistent thought of her was a black transformation, joy into pain, the sundering of reconciliation; while from over the trees, a golden butter moon watched as it had in the centuries before humans, the eras before primates, aeons before vertebrates, never commenting on what it saw. For Josh and Maria, the suddenness of loss was everything.

Headlights floated in the mirror: call them company. Josh was in no mood for anything but darkness; but perhaps that was wrong. He reached halfway to the dash, needing music to slow down by, then changed his mind. With her name inside his skull, mantra-like – *Sophie, oh, sweet Sophie* – he fastened his hands back on the wheel, 10 and 2 o'clock, the way they had drummed into him, then hammered the engine, the gear too low if he wanted the car to maintain its value, but on ops they always thrashed the things because you did the business now or there was no later.

"What a *twat*."

The headlights from behind were incandescent, almost on them.

"What is it?" Maria's first words for hours. "What's wrong?"

"Besides the obvious, some arsehole coming up our rear."

And a blind bend ahead. Shadows like ink, the road twisting to one side and out of sight.

"So drop your speed and—"

A blaze in the mirror, a suddenness of black then massive light in front – *lorry coming at us* – white paintwork flashing as the arseholemobile swung across – Audi – fighting to pull in before colliding, while the lorry driver yelled unheard, his face a glimpse of onrushing death as Josh reacted.

"Fuck!"

Magnetic brakes are supposed to be quiet but the car howled and shuddered as he slammed down, the car bucking, then the oncoming lorry and the maniac who'd come from behind to squeeze between them were past. The Audi's driver had cut in fast enough to save them all, the innocents whose lives he risked. Josh had done worse but always with good cause, and this wasn't it. At his hip – he grew conscious of it now – was the feel of hardness clipped to his belt: the mark of citizenship, his with the royal coat of arms because that's what you got for military service: *William Rex, Dieu et mon droit*. Kill the foreign bastards for the sake of the state; except that if you'd been born in their country, you'd have done the same as them; and that was how it always was, had always been since tribal groups of primates fought, because even the most peaceful apes kill on occasion.

"Jesus. Jesus *fuck*."

He'd stopped the car. Silence was an invitation. Maria looked vulnerable in a way she rarely did these days – when had she become so strong, developed that strength? – and if he found the right words he might perhaps fix everything (*everything but Sophie*) here and now, repair the damage he had done, that the world and random cruelty brought on. Build a bridge; bring her back; and make things whole.

But all he said was, "Motherfucker."

"Josh?"

"Stupid mother*fucker*."

He shifted gear and pushed the accelerator down, needing the pressure against his back, the kinaesthetic analogue of computation: inertia, vectors of velocity, the tactics of the chase; as he drove his lips were curling back. They call *Homo sapiens sapiens* the smiling ape, and while we're fangless like prey, we have eyes in the front of our heads, for we are hunters too; and when there's a target we need to track it, focus hard and close the distance, all the way until it's dead, and we have bones to crunch between our teeth. As Lofty Young used to have it: "*Identify target. Take 'em out. Repeat until done.*"

He forced the car, accelerating harder.

"*Till every bastard is down.*"

Harder still.

"*Every last one of 'em.*"

And the engine's scream was cutting through Maria's command: "Stop the car!"

His response was visceral, muscles tensing and releasing as he hauled the car through a turn, increasing speed all the way through the arc, hammering down as the road straightened. Red tail lights beckoned like targets on the firing range.

"Josh. Stop now."

Her words were in the air but meaningless because Sophie's name was howling in his blood while the reptile brain that lives in all of us was locked on now, targeting its prey. A lizard might not know the way to stop a speeding car but Josh Cumberland did. His own car was juddering as he drew alongside the white Audi – the driver looking over, eyes wide – and then Josh was past, fingers curled around the handbrake lever – "Dear God, no, Josh!" – and ripping up, the car slewing sideways on to block the road, the burning-rubber stink immediate, smoke-clouds rising from the tyres as he halted and the chassis rocked.

If the Audi failed to stop he'd hit the passenger side, right where Maria was sitting – *shit* – and for a fifth of a second sickness filled Josh. Then the idiot *was* screaming to a halt; and Josh was already out on the road, like some quantum effect, with no memory of unfastening of the seat belt or opening the door. The bulk of his car was between him and his target, and he did it the quick way, a half step back for the plyometric spring, then throwing himself across the front, shoulder-rolling, dropping feet-first on the roadway, then four sprinting paces to the moron's door.

The guy's mouth was working like a goldfish which has leaped from the tank into a new and deadly world. Josh's hand went for the thermoplastic sheath on his belt – he could hammer the hilt into the window – and then he had a thought. Grinning, he pulled at the Audi's door – and it came open.

Idiot. No idea.

A suicide jockey, with none of the most basic precautions.

No fucking idea.

He unsnapped the guy's seat belt, clamped hands on jaw and the crown of the head, digging in his thumbs and fingers as he twisted, hooked, and pulled. With a squeak, the guy came out of the car headfirst. Still controlling the head, Josh hauled him half upright, then let go.

"Formal challenge." He pointed to the man's hip. "Citizens' confrontation."

"Jesus Christ."

"You're a voting citizen," said Josh. "Aren't you?"

The sheath was shiny with polish, not with use. Likewise the too-smooth hilt.

"Th-that's all. To vote, I mean. I've never... You know. Never."

"Always a first time."

Josh hardly seemed to move, but his blade was in his hand. Tau-bar, military, balanced for throwing in addition to slash and thrust: it had everything, including the memory of blood, and God but he wanted to use it now.

"I can't." The man was shaking. "I can't. I'm not... Not like..."

His whimper accompanied a rising pungent aroma. In the headlight beams reflected from bodywork, Josh saw the spreading dark patch at the man's crotch.

"Draw or die, motherfucker."

Go on. Draw and come at me.

Trembling, the man fumbled at his sheath. There was a narrow safety strip around the hilt, and it took him three attempts to fumble the clip open. Then he held up the knife, shaking, tears like rain-streaks down his face. The blade was polished and unmarked.

Yes. Do it.

"Josh, no."

Maria's voice was commanding... through the car's open window. She knew better than to climb out of the car, understanding the danger, for in extremis the amygdala takes over, the brain's emergency response bypassing conscious thought, our civilised selves that are far too slow for deadly action. And that was the risk, because there was no rational thought, not here and now – only the need to act.

"Now!" yelled Josh.

He leaped forward, sheathing his tau-bar as he moved, slamming down with his left hand, tension in the elbow, keeping it bent, while his right hand punched – throat – pulling his aim down – no – hitting the collarbone, not the neck, hitting twice more, then ripping the bastard's knife from his clammy, slackening fingers. And the man was on the ground, propped on one knee, holding up a useless hand, every limb shaking. Josh grabbed a wrist, twisted, and pressed the knife against soft inner flesh.

"Radial artery, motherfucker." This was the Timetable of Death which Josh could recite in his sleep (and had, according to Maria). "Penetration to one-quarter inch, unconscious after thirty seconds. Dead in two minutes."

He slid the blade to the inside of the man's biceps.

"Brachial artery. Half inch penetration, fourteen seconds then unconscious, ninety seconds to death." Then the side of the neck, pricking the point against the skin. "Carotid, one and a half inches. Five seconds and unconscious, twelve seconds dead."

"Please..."

"Josh, I'm calling the police."

Carefully, he placed the tau-bar's point against the man's shirt, feeling for ribs beneath the fat. Here you needed to position carefully before you rammed the point in.

"Heart. Three and a half inches." Josh moved the point, and the man squealed. "Loss of consciousness: instantaneous. Time to death: three seconds."

There were other arteries, other places to cut and to stab, each with their own triplet of figures – penetration depth, time to unconsciousness, time to death – and Josh could enumerate them all. *For King and country.* He looked at the man's sweat-covered face – the wide eyes, the gasping, drooling mouth – and inhaled the urine scent of fear. Then something changed, for as he pushed the breath out, he also pushed back the rage, and took a retreating step from the violence that so wanted to blossom forth, to manifest itself in surging aggression, filling the moment and drowning the memories of Sophie, but not for long.

"Sometimes you get to live."

Josh twisted away, and hurled the man's knife into the darkness, over a high hedge and into darkness. Field and woodland lay beyond. Then he reached into the Audi, grabbed hold of the key – shouldn't do this – and yanked it out – better than killing the bastard – and held it in front of Moron Features' face as the engine shuddering to stillness, quiet now. Josh waited for the moron to speak; but he was too afraid or had learned his lesson, or both. His eyes were very wide.

"Wise man."

Josh snarled as he threw the key into the night, following the knife. There was a glint, and then it was gone; then a faint, grass-softened thud. Gone forever, and he so wanted to hew the bastard's head from his shoulders, rip that aloft – see the lolling tongue and shocked, dead eyes – and throw it likewise into the wilderness; and that was when he wondered, whimsical yet serious, at the primal origins of basketball – and suddenly he barked a laugh, then stopped.

Won't bring Sophie back.

Nothing would, that was the point.

Sophie, Sophie, Sophie.

He climbed back inside his car and pulled the door shut. Maria's expression was clamped down, silent, her eyes filled with fear and anger and something more, a mixture he could not decompose or analyse. But he had his own concerns, because Sophie was gone, in every way that mattered.

Oh, my beautiful girl.

The car started forward, and he accelerated gently, keeping control, his attention on the road ahead, refusing to look back at the devastated man and his useless car.

One hour later, in the hotel reception area – all silvery fluorescent lights and stained carpet squares – Josh put down their bags and stood next to Maria before the desk. The young receptionist looked up. Josh wanted to smash that soft face, but the feeling was irrational and the night had been wild enough already, so he forced the feeling down and made his voice soften.

"Cumberland. We've got a reservation."

"Uh, sure, Mr Cumberland. Would you care to–?"

"And a separate room for me," said Maria.

The receptionist blinked and stared at her.

"Not necessary," Josh found himself saying. "I'm not hanging around."

He picked up his black gym bag, leaving her case where it was. Then he stopped, giving her time to speak, to change her mind if she was going to, to fix everything, if only she could.

Nothing.

I'm sorry, Sophie.

He went back out to the car, tossed the gym bag onto the passenger seat, climbed in and shut the door. There was a moment – he closed his eyes – of total lucidity, a deep knowledge of just how stupid and painful everything was, including his own actions. Then he pressed in the key and pushed the gear lever, and rolled the car forward on crunching gravel, out onto the night-shrouded road, a T-junction ahead. There, he turned right for no good reason, not bothering to read the signs, because everything was cloaked beneath darkness and all roads led to the same location: exactly nowhere.

He drove on at steady speed.

[TWO]

The carriage was warm, the air-con half working, as it rattled along the Circle and District line. Suzanne, from her seat, watched the other passengers reading the news or watching movies on their phones, or bobbing their heads in time to music in their earbeads. Some of the businessmen and women wore the new lightweight suits with trousers ending mid-calf. Her own outfit was dark grey with a silvery sheen, a long-sleeved top and longish skirt; professional, expensive, looking good against her chocolatté-coloured skin.

The man on her left was reading the news on his phone. Hers was switched off – not realising you could go offline was a modern malaise, had been for decades – but she couldn't help reading the headline: ITALY RIOTS AGAIN, 200 DEAD. How else to start the day than by dwelling on the worst that had happened? The rioters would be African camp-dwellers, some with skins as light as hers, railing at the country that had taken them in before failing to deliver the water-rich paradise they had imagined. In her mind she wrote another headline. BILLIONS TRAVEL TO WORK OK, HAVE ORDINARY DAY. Because geopolitical trends might be bad, but the truth was that half the world prospered, while the majority survived through every day.

As the train pulled in to Embankment she sighed, thumbed on her phone, and put it to her ear. *"Four messages waiting, one urgent. Listen to urgent message first?"* She tapped an acknowledgment. *"From Peter Hall."* It was a synthetic voice, reading out stored text. *"Sorry, Dr Duchesne, but I've got a problem at work, and I can't make our appointment. I'm doing really well. Sorry."*

Shit. She'd have to invoice him anyway because she'd booked the room in Elliptical House for the session. Billing a client for a no-show was necessary but might create a setback. Damn it. The voicemail gave few clues to Hall's mood. She listened to her other messages, all trivial, then put her phone away as the train slid into Westminster. She followed the other passengers off, filing past the kevlar-armoured guards, onto the escalator.

Out on the Embankment proper she watched the stately vanes of wind-turbines. Sailing boats moved along the steel-coloured Thames, the Houses of Parliament glittered in the hot sun, while somewhere a vendor was selling roast nuts and cicadas – she caught the smell, and then it was gone.

"Peter Hall," she told her phone. "Ring him."

She waited.

"Unavailable. Would you like to leave a message?"

Whether he was offline to her specifically or to the world, there was no way to tell. She formed a gesture with her fingers, a simple neurophysiological trigger to create a resourceful mood. Then she held up her phone, smiling at the beady lens.

"Hello, Peter. How much better are you doing? I feel confident that now you'll make the changes you want to make, and it doesn't matter whether you ring me this morning or tonight, because you'll feel better when we talk. Go well, Peter."

Good enough. Through careful tonality, some of her words were covert hypnotic suggestions, combining with the results of the previous sessions to give him a confidence boost as soon as he watched her message, or so she hoped. It was funny because, as a little girl, she had dreamed of being an actress, except when she imagined herself as a scientist or doctor; and now she got to be all three. At least that was the way she saw her life now, so much better – I'm lucky, really lucky – than the old days. As she walked, her fingers touched the inside of her opposite sleeve: always long sleeves, not just for her clients' sake. But it was mostly fine, not a case of "Physician, heal thyself," for in many respects she'd done just that.

Keeping the phone on, she set off parallel to the stone balustrade. The glass barrier beyond was translucent turquoise, the finest of Dutch engineering to keep the capital dry, to ensure that everyone was safe.

So enjoy the day, right?

She made herself smile as she walked.

Stag Place was a plaza in Victoria, its shape irregular, surrounded by sweeping glass buildings. The wind tugged at Suzanne as she stopped near a tall steel sculpture, a shining tree whose leaves were big, bright plastic panels: tomato red, egg-yolk yellow, apple green. Elliptical House was another five minutes away, but there were coffee shops inside the mall, and where better to relax and prepare her–

A ripping sound preceded a woman's scream and the shocking twang of steel cable parting; then came momentary silence, as if something had sucked away the air. And then a maelstrom of dust and flying shards – red, yellow, green, all with edges like knives – filled the world, became the world, while all around were people were throwing themselves down, trying to escape, some plucked upward by the air, levitating for a second, then flung aside like old socks.

Vortex.

This was a snap whirlwind, and dangerous. Suzanne dropped to the pavement, holding her head in her hands, imagining all that glass in flying pieces, sharp and deadly, and even as she had the thought, windows shattered overhead. Then percussive wind was beating on her, slamming her down – *no, please no* – and was gone.

Just gone.

She was on elbows and knees, head hanging, gasping. Was this the centre, the stillness at the whirlwind's heart, or had the whole thing passed? She dared to look up, then squeezed her eyes shut at the awfulness – no, deal with it – and forced them open. One person was a butchered mess: man or woman, she could not tell, only that the carcass was ripped open and all was soft and slick and glistening, bathed in redness, and none of this was helping. Act professional. As Suzanne hauled herself up, she focused on the ones who needed help: here a blood-soaked face, there a white-haired man, supine and groaning, his arm twisted beneath him. Off to one side, a woman whimpered, trembling, in the throes of seizure. Someone, calm-voiced, spoke into his phone, calling for medics. Others got into motion, crossing to the fallen. One man gave orders: "I'm a nurse. You, press here on his shoulder – yes, there, you've got it, keep pressing – while I help this person over here." All around, like snow in the aftermath of blizzard, shards of glass reflected sunlight, almost pretty if you had not seen the blood. They crunched beneath Suzanne's shoes as she made her way to the shaking woman.

"Look at me."

But the woman's attention remained locked on the bloody mess that had been a person just a few breaths earlier, a living person thinking about the day ahead, a thousand small concerns and perhaps the meaningful events of life, images of lovers, children, parents, all of it shut down in an instant. Suzanne stepped between her and the corpse, blocking the view.

"Are you hurt?"

The woman couldn't speak, but she was flapping her hands, staring through Suzanne as if the body were still in focus; and in a very real way it was, but Suzanne dared not deal with that until she was sure the woman was not bleeding. She ran her fingertips down the fragile neck, the narrow torso, while checking by sight. Physically, everything seemed intact.

"Let me help," said a man's voice.

"We need to get her inside." Suzanne reached under the woman's armpit. "Come on."

With the man's help – she had a glimpse of blonde hair, a suit: a thin, thirtyish man – she got the woman moving slowly towards the mall. The entrance was mostly undamaged. *All I wanted was a coffee.* They led the woman into Seattle's Finest, then Suzanne sat her down while the man fetched bottled water.

"I'm Adam," he said.

The woman did not respond.

"And I'm Suzanne." To the woman: "What's your name?"

"You saw him?"

Her eyes focused on a point in space, seeing the same thing in her mind, over and over. From the pupil dilation and involuntary twitch, she was recreating the mental picture in vivid, moving colours. It was a textbook precursor to post-traumatic stress, but this wasn't a case study – it was a suffering person, in need of help. *So help her.* Usually Suzanne met clients long after the traumatic event when the memories had been laid down – and replayed over and over before finally seeking help. This should be even easier to deal with, except that she herself was shaking in reaction. Or perhaps she could help herself and the woman at the same time: the point wasn't to kill the flooding emotions, just dampen them enough to prevent future nightmares.

"Just breathe," she said. "Concentrate on blowing the breath out."

The man, Adam, looked at her, then slowly put down the unwanted water. He gave a nod, seeming to recognise that Suzanne knew what she was doing. At least *I'm supposed to know.*

Synchronising her breathing with the woman's, Suzanne began to alter her mental state. In a coffee shop at normal times, you would see friends chatting, their gestures tending to phase-lock, performing a subliminal dance, its intricacy obvious only to trained watchers. Now, Suzanne was using the process deliberately, entering physiological rapport, before leading the way to a different neurological state. She raised her hand before the woman's eyes.

"Look at my hand," she said, her voice a living thing, every nuance of pitch and rhythm and timbre keyed to some aspect of the woman's physiology. "See the changing focus of your eyes and in a moment you

might blink, that's right, and before you enter trance
now" – the woman's eyelids fluttered – "you can hear
the silence between sounds like time to sleep and my
voice will go with you as you close your eyes... now...
and sink deeper... and deeper... into a soft relaxing
daydream state... That's right."

The woman slid into trance.

She went fast and deep, while Adam's jaw dropped.
In Suzanne's office, the portable fMRI would have
shown the brain's activity profoundly altered: the an-
terior cingulate diminished, the precuneus nucleus in
spectacular, multicoloured overdrive on the monitor
display. Even to an untrained observer like Adam, the
effect was obvious. He remained riveted as Suzanne
completed the induction, taking the woman back in
time, inside her mind, to situations where she felt secure; and each time the state was at its deepest,
Suzanne touched the woman's shoulder.

"Now in the whirlwind, step outside yourself, like
watching a screen, then drain the colour out and push
the image off into the distance–"

Recoding the recent memory to remove trauma, then
using the shoulder pressure to trigger confidence and
calm, she left an instruction for ongoing improvement
in the woman's life – *"Just fixing the problem isn't good
enough,"* her teachers used to say, *"so leave them better
than before, better than they thought possible"* – before leading her back to normal consciousness.

"And you can come awake as I count backwards. Ten,
nine..."

Finally she snapped her fingers, and the woman's
eyes snapped open.

"My God."

"Bloody hell," said Adam.

"I…" The woman stopped, then: "I remember that poor man, but I'm not terrified by it. How can I–? That was amazing, thank you."

Blinking, she pulled out her phone and checked the time.

"You have to go," said Suzanne. "You've a life to lead, after all."

"Yes." The woman stood up. "I don't–"

"You're welcome."

"Oh. Thank you. Just… thank you."

Suzanne hugged her. Then the woman turned and walked out, her posture straight.

"Did she just grow six inches taller?" asked Adam. "Or is that an illusion?"

"Illusion," said Suzanne. "A natural one."

"So can I get you a cappuccino or something?"

"Perhaps I should check whether–"

She was intending to say, whether anyone else needed help, for she had already checked his hand and seen that he was married. The ring was white gold.

"I know someone who should see you," said Adam. "You're a professional therapist, I take it?"

"Yes, but my client list is…"

"My friend is very rich." Adam grinned. "If that helps."

A vision of her bank balance swam before Suzanne.

"I'd love a cappuccino."

Seven hours later she was back in the same Seattle's Finest, having passed through a cleaned-up piazza – the sculpture bare of colourful plastic, but still standing – to find the same seat as this morning. Her last session had finished at four, and this was a good time to wind down and review the day. Over the counter, a thin monitor displayed a weather map, with today's statistics scrolling down one side. Nine flash whirlwinds around the country, four fatalities in all. British summer at its finest.

"Suzanne."

"Hi, Adam."

"And this is Philip Broomhall."

Obviously Broomhall liked gold, from the four rings on each hand to the glimpsed knife hilt as he unbuttoned his jacket. When he shook hands, she noted the way he turned his hand palm-down, seeking to dominate. Alpha male, primate behaviour. No challenge at all for someone with a brain who kept calm.

He's a potential client, that's all.

Adam fetched drinks while Broomhall sat down and told Suzanne that she had a good reputation, with several respected clients recommending her. He'd obviously trawled the Web to check her out. In contrast to Broomhall, Suzanne noticed the lack of a bulge at Adam's hip as he rejoined them. Weaponless but confident.

"It's my son Richard," said Broomhall. "He's scared of everything."

"How old is Richard?"

"Fourteen. And a damned sight softer than I was at that age."

Adam's mouth made a stretched sideways S. "That's what all the old guys say."

"Well, in this case it's true. Anyhow, your clients, Dr Duchesne, say you make phobias disappear like that. A few minutes, and bang, it's gone."

"That's right," said Suzanne. "I maintain total confidentiality. Some clients post open reviews regardless, which is very kind of them."

She had her own downloadable statistics, digitally verified, identifying no one by name, to show the effectiveness of her work. For phobic behaviours, it was ninety-seven percent success in one short session. Broomhall had either read the results, she guessed, or employed someone to do it.

"My son needs help. From someone like you."

Adam's grimace was outside Broomhall's peripheral vision.

So the boy needs saving from his father too.

Perhaps there was something worthwhile here, more worthwhile than the fee.

"So what's his problem specifically?" She didn't believe people were broken like damaged toys – disliking the word *problem* and hating *cure* – but she framed her questions on Broomhall's terms. "You say he's afraid?"

"He's…" Broomhall's eyes shifted to the side. "He's hoplophobic, for God's sake."

"Hoplophobic?"

I so don't want this.

"Yes. It's embarrassing." Broomhall wiped his sweating face. "Excuse me."

What's embarrassing? His condition or your prejudice?

But she said "You can feel confident it's OK to talk about this. It really is all right."

"OK."

Adam leaned forward. "You want me to go?"

"No, no." Broomhall took a swig of iced coffee. "It's fine."

"So what happens to trigger his reaction? How does he do his fear?"

"What do you mean?"

"I know it's a strange question." One she'd anticipated. "If you were about to draw your knife, at what point would he look fearful?"

"The second I walk into the room, if I'm wearing it. He cringes if someone just mentions the word *blade*."

Suzanne understood that reaction. "I guess that is a problem, but I'm really not comfortable with–"

"I'll offer you ten thousand if you can fix him up. Another ten if he improves in school."

"Then I'll do it," she said.

If you couldn't accept the need to pay the rent, you were hardly an integrated personality, not as a grown-up. She helped people for free at times – like the woman this morning – so perhaps it was her turn to get rich, doing what she loved to do. Maybe with a wealthier level of clientele, starting now.

She wondered what young Richard Broomhall was like.

"Glad to have you on board, Dr Duchesne."

They shook hands.

Marvellous.

Had she joined Broomhall's non-nautical crew voluntarily or been press-ganged? Was this a mistake, the arrangement she'd just committed to?

"It would be good to see Richard the day after tomorrow, if that's possible."

"I'll bloody well make sure it is."

[THREE]

The turrets and courtyards of St Michael's Academy were two centuries old and looked much older. Some of the boys lived in, but Richard's father wanted a "normal" upbringing for his only son, so a chauffeur-driven car took him home every evening, to their enclosed manor house in deepest, richest Surrey.

Grandfather Jack had been a merchant marine and an East End trader. There was an old family story about a dinner party when someone, hearing Jack was a trader, asked whether he was in bonds or derivatives, and Jack said: "Nah, mate. A barrow in the market." But that barrow had carried imported Japanese calculators, and over the next decade the barrow became a store on Tottenham Court Road, then half a dozen more around the country with an expanding mail-order business, before flourishing on the Web and diversifying into a dozen different sectors, from fashion to phones, continuing to boom.

Richard missed his grandfather, while knowing he himself was nothing like the tough old man. At the funeral, Richard had cried – his father called it *blubbing* – which caused embarrassment among the business associates at the graveside, and earned him more disapproval from Mother and Father. They dealt with the matter afterwards in the usual way: getting drunk on port from the cellar and shouting at each other. Mutual blame for their son's softness and other failings.

"Broomhall, you done your maths assignment?" It was Zajac who called out, coming across the quadrangle, swinging his bulky arms. "You have, haven't you?"

He made it sound as if Richard had been up to something dirty, whereas he was really after a copy-and-paste of Richard's work.

"I can't help you, Zajac."

"Help? Why would I need your bastard help? Just for that, I'm going to–"

But Richard had taken another step, into view of the courtyard cameras. Mr Dutton, the Head of Geography, was across the way, looking at him and Zajac, frowning. Zajac muttered something in Slovakian, then walked off.

This was not a good start to the day.

Within minutes, Richard was at his desk, and the big flatscreen monitor at the front of the class was displaying stacked panes of images: tropical cyclones with white surf smashing over palm trees and single-storey buildings; arid reddish dust bowls where verdant savannah once lay; concrete tower blocks in the outer banlieues of Paris where armoured cars of the Police Judiciaire patrolled; the three year-old steel border wall separating CalOrWashington – the Left Coast Republic – from Arizona and the rest of the US; the latest bomb atrocities in Amsterdam, Harare, and Jakarta; the cumulative death toll of the Adelaide Flu.

Beijing was threatening sanctions against the US if President Brand didn't stop the arms build up on the

Mexican border where *"At least the wetbacks are Christian,"* according to one right-wing pundit who was trying to explain why the Left Coast was Sodom and Gomorrah – the true Obama legacy requiring destruction – while South America was a land where the real US could expand, bringing freedom to repressed citizens. They might have said the same about Canada; but the Canadians had nukes.

The first lesson was supposed to be psychology. News displays that got the adults stressed – maybe that was what Mr Keele was going to talk about. Richard rubbed his forehead. He didn't care about adults. It seemed they'd all forgotten what it was like to be at school – logically, they must have been children once, every last one of them – and he told himself that he'd remember, if he lived long enough.

"So, everyone." Mr Keele worked his phone, causing a new window to appear on the big wallscreen, filled with a graph and tabular figures. "What we're looking at is the Factorial Aggregate Social Tension Score as a function of increasing average temperature, for several capital cities. Even though there are peaceful hot countries, what we'll see is that the increase in temperature correlates to a FASTS index tending to–"

And so on.

To be fair, the lesson became more interesting when Mr Keele stilled the displays and got the class talking, but Richard found it hard to join in because he knew that Zajac was going to try to grab him during the break. Maybe more than grabbing, unless he could stay in full view of security cams. But that was just going to build up Zajac's anger, so that when they did finally meet where no one could see–

"Master Broomhall?"

"Uh, sorry, sir."

"Not enough, but we'll change that. Unless you can answer the question."

"Sir…"

And that was how it went, until the lesson's end.

At the start of break time, heading along the parquet-floored corridor, Mal James matched pace with Richard, and asked if he'd like to come to the boarders' study instead of going outside.

"Uh – why?"

"Cause Zajac looks bloody mad, old mate. Keeps staring at you."

"Oh. Right."

So two minutes later, Richard was in the broadly octagonal study reserved for the older boarders – Mal James was in Year 11 – and occasional guests. Richard stood by himself while James went to talk with his real friends. Being charitable had limits.

Some of the boys were playing telephone poker on their linked phones. Others were reading or just chatting. Several were watching *Knife Edge* on the big wallscreen.

"It'll be Blades this year. The new Bloods suck."

"They're still training. Wait till they've had another month with Fireman Carlsen."

"Hey, Broomhall. What do you think?"

"Er… About what?"

"You think the Bloods will do good again, or what?"

"Um, I don't really know. Maybe."

Someone made a disgusted noise, then the group returned their attention to the screen. The view was a dormitory in the fighters' training camp. Richard had no idea which team it was, but he knew that the annual series was still in its early weeks, and that the hopeful fighters would be talking to the cameras about their families and their fears, and the money they hoped to make from the tournament if they survived.

He felt vomit rise up inside as the screen blurred along with the entire room, and he rubbed his face as he turned away. Mal James might have said something, but Richard was already at the door, and then he was through, heading down the corridor to the toilets, where he could find a cubicle to hide inside, or at least a sink to swill cold water on his face. But there were teachers approaching, and he was on his own without a boarder to vouch for him, so he turned left instead, and went out into the quadrangle, where a mild spring rain had begun to fall, forming threads of white and silver in the sunlight.

Zajac stood in one corner, arms folded, like a statue in the rain. He looked at Richard but made no move. Perhaps it was going to be OK.

He went inside, and survived through the next lesson – History – telling himself that Zajac had abandoned his resentment. It had to be true, so Richard acted as if it were, until it was lunchtime and he was walking to the school restaurant, remembering something Mr Keele said earlier: *"People don't like holding contradictory views – it's called cognitive dissonance, see chapter 24 in Gross – and they'll do anything to blind themselves to the inner conflict."*

Richard was fooling himself. If Zajac was acting un-aggressive, that didn't mean he'd stopped planning violence. This was awful. While not eating his lunch, Richard looked around for Zajac, and saw him sitting at a table by himself, with some glass object by his plate. Maybe it was a paperweight. Father had some at home, and was old-fashioned enough to browse hardcopy at his study desk, but Richard had never seen the ornaments used to hold down pages.

Zajac turned, and Richard dropped his attention to the food on his plate.

Nothing happened until the end of lunch break, when everyone was milling out the doors, heading back via the rear courtyard. Richard was swept along as always. Suddenly a hard thump took him in the back of the shoulder and glass smashed at his foot, spraying outward from the impact.

"Broomhall, look what you've fucking done."

Other boys drew back, but Zajac had a grip on Richard's skin, through his sleeve.

"You'll accept the challenge" – his voice was low – "or I'll just shank you on the street. Big time."

"N-no."

No one had heard Zajac's threat, but everyone heard now as he stepped back saying: "That was Waterford crystal, and I'm issuing challenge. Now."

Several older boys pushed their way forward, Mal James among them.

"What the hell are you playing at, Zajac?"

"I'm arranging to meet little Broomhall in the gym. And I did it all formal. Right, Broomhall?"

Richard was about to throw up.

"R-right."

"No," said James. "You're not going to do it."

But Zajac just smiled, and Richard knew he meant it: either fight in the gym half-armoured, or feel a blade slide into his guts out on the street. Sooner or later they'd meet where there were no witnesses or cameras, and it would happen.

"I accept."

The words just came, materialising in his vocal cords as if transmitted from some distant continent.

"No." James closed his eyes, and shook his head. "You idiot, Broomhall."

"He's done it now." Zajac was grinning.

"And when it's done–" began James.

"You don't want to challenge me. But you're worried about your soft bum-boy, I'll give him eight weeks."

James looked disgusted.

"Night of the final," continued Zajac. "I'll give you till then."

"Final?" said Richard.

"*Knife Edge*." James looked at his friends. "On the twentieth, right?"

"Yeah."

"It'll be final, all right," said Zajac.

Then he pushed his way through the stationary crowd of boys, ignoring the smashed detritus of his excuse for the challenge, and the reactions of those who'd witnessed it.

Or Richard's vomiting on the ground: hot, spattering, and full of stink.

[FOUR]

Pre-dawn was an avocado glimmer in the east. Josh
scrunched up his face, shivering as he came awake in
the car, the reclined driver's seat his bed. He liked this,
experiencing conditions most people never knew; and
he had slept in worse places, far removed from the soft,
over-regulated conditions of ordinary lives, lacking danger. And keeping their marriages intact.

Sophie.

By reflex he scanned the world outside, the dark-
ness-within-darkness of sloping field and surrounding
trees. He was parked on a muddy track that meandered
off the road. Flicking off the interior light – old habit –
he cracked open the door and rolled out, coming down
into mud in a deep crouch. All his attention went outward, for this was the Zen of survival, allowing the
animal brain to sniff the environment, listen for danger. Nothing, so it was safe to pee – execute a slash-ex,
they said in the Regiment – and he crossed to the trees.
Afterwards, he pulled out a carryall from the back of
the car, extracted a bottle of cold water – only the concentration on physical details, the chill feel of the
plastic, the sloshing of liquid inside, the faint smell of

woodiness and grass, kept the rage trapped inside him, coiling round like a snake in a vortex – then he stripped down, pulled on tracksuit and Nikes, and got to work.

Deep breathing and abdominal contractions took the place of sit-ups, then he ran up and down the sloping field, easy at first, then sprinting uphill at fast intervals, sucking in dawn air. Breathless, he returned to the car and took out a black kettlebell, like a cannonball with handle attached, ripped the weight skyward and performed swings and snatches and presses, feeling every sinew, because you have to push the fitness all the way or the fuckers will get you, for somewhere an enemy lies in wait, while the sounds he heard were not the waking birds but the crash of frag grenades, the screams of limbless men.

"What's that?" Maria had asked, the first time she saw one of his kettlebells.

"Oh, I call it Maria," he'd said. "Because it's gorgeous and I can't keep my hands off it."

"Uh-huh."

"Or because it's dangerous as fuck, and flies off the handle if you don't watch out."

They had laughed, both of them, so long ago.

Sophie.

The susurrating machines that did the breathing for her, the shining green tubes festooning her pale body, the beep of monitors which–

"Oy, you!"

Anger in the voice. Josh hunched over, slumping as if afraid, knowing he should not play these games. The approaching man was a licensed farmer, no doubt, for he carried a long taser rifle, while at his side a lean black-and-white collie bared teeth. Blood rush washed in Josh's ears, obscuring the unfriendly words. Then he straightened up, kettlebell in hand – quite a weapon – and the farmer stopped dead, confusion sizzling in his eyes, voice croaking to stillness, and in that moment he might have died, if Josh had wanted it.

Man and dog stayed back, swallowing, as Josh heaved his things into the car, got in and started the engine. He bumped his way in reverse along the track, swung a reverse-one-eighty manoeuvre, and accelerated onto the road.

Behind him, the farmer had not moved.

From outside the café was blue and white, the Zak's Kaff sign bright yellow, like every other ZK in the country. Each parking space had sockets to plug into, the recharge "free", meaning it was factored into the cost of food. Three other cars were parked. Josh pulled in, hooked up the cable, and lugged his carryall inside.

"Table for one, dear?" The waitress didn't glance at his sodden tracksuit. "Where would you like to sit? There's always plenty of room at this hour, specially Saturdays."

"I'll pop to the loo first. Can I sit there, against the wall? And I'll have a large cappuccino."

"All right. It'll be a few–"

He went through to the disabled toilet, because there was plenty of room and no one who might need to use it. He took out his washbag, everything neatly in place – a symptom of military OCD, Maria called his neatness, not knowing how seconds late for a rendezvous could spell death, how equipment organised and to hand made all the difference, and if that was obsessive-compulsive then he could live with it. Sponging himself in front of the sink, he remembered how quickly he had learned these habits, for every soldier – not just special forces – can wash and dress in eight minutes flat.

Refreshed, enjoying the clean clothes against his skin, he sat down at the table and sipped from the waiting cappuccino. Scalding, even though it had been sitting there.

"You ready to order food, love?"

"Large OJ, beans on toast, another large cappuccino."

"Blimey, you'll have the wind behind you."

Josh looked up at her and she stepped back, raising her touchpad like a shield. *Shit.* What was wrong with him?

"Sorry. Bit of a family situation, and I'm in a mood, you know?"

"Oh." A near-laugh. "I know how that goes."

"And I feel better already, with the coffee. Thanks."

She smiled, meaning it now, and went back behind the counter.

Lofty Young used to advise against life-changing decisions made on an empty stomach, saying: *"Low blood sugar equals suspect thinking."* Good advice, hard to follow given the missions Ghost Force often faced, yet based on sound understanding. Last night seemed to signal a sundering from Maria, a severing with no going back, and he pulled out his phone but did not call her, for Lofty was always right. As he waited, he watched the waitress bring food to another table, a family of three looking up startled when she put the first plate down, because they had not seen or heard her coming. How could people be so unaware and yet survive?

Perhaps because others fought their wars for them, keeping the place safe and peaceful and far too soft, but that was an old thought and far too simplistic, and wasn't it time he put it out of his head? Encircling his neck with a narrow cord – a throat mic for subvocal speech – he plugged it into his phone, thumbed through his contacts and chose Tony Gore. He pushed a bead into his ear as Tony's face came to life.

"Hey, Josh. It's a bit early to call. You all right, mate?"

"Flying green, and I knew you'd be awake. Everything still on for next week?"

"Uh-huh. Hang on." The phone showed Tony turning away. "Hey, Am? You hear the kids screaming?" A distant answer sounded, then he turned face-on again. "Sorry, yeah, the course is on plan. You sure you're OK to teach?"

"Definitely. So is the basha free tonight, by any chance?"

"I didn't expect anyone before tomorrow, but yeah, it's booked since the beginning of the month, because of the programme."

It was an eight-week training programme for Quantal Bank, and Tony had booked a Docklands apartment, cheaper and more homely than a hotel. Most of the trainers called it a basha, because Tony hired only ex-military.

"Thought I'd settle in, get my bearings. Same entrance code?"

"Sure. You're OK with the mentoring aspect? You're not primary teach until week three. Next week, the big thing will be getting them fired up for the old board breaking."

Bankers wanting SpecOps mystique to give them confidence, deal with the deadly stress of meetings, bureaucracy, and back-stabbing. It was the security-and-crypto modules for the IT guys that Josh was looking forward to.

"No change with Sophie?" added Tony.

"No miracles, no."

Giggles sounded in the background.

"Listen, Am could look after the kids, and I'll meet you in the basha tonight."

"No, enjoy your weekend," – he looked up as the waitress appeared, beans on toast in hand – "and give Amber my love. Hi to the kids. Cheers."

"Cheers, mate. Take it easy."

He flicked the phone to GPS, ready to slot into the car's dash, and placed it face up on the table as the waitress put down his food.

"Enjoy, love."

"I will, thanks."

The map displayed his long and lat, his position a glowing yellow dot, while in subterranean data centres beneath the Cotswolds, massively parallel networked clusters tracked the movements of every phone and car in Britain, DNA-tagged and ID-registered, everyone known to the system, even as the most important parts of their lives, the millions of thoughts and feelings, everyday and profound, remained unknowable, un-trackable, beyond governance.

Josh could drop off the grid if he had to. If only he could pull his daughter into health and freedom with the same kind of ease.

He stared at his food, feeling dreadful.

[FIVE]

Nine minutes before the Broomhall boy's appointment, Suzanne's phone beeped. She turned her chair away from the window, and picked the phone up from her desktop, checking the caller's picture. It was a client, Rosa, so she pressed the Accept symbol, pointing the phone at the wallscreen, transferring the image.

Rosa's face sharpened, larger than life-sized.

"Hey. Just wanted to call and say thank you."

"Rosa, does that mean you've good news?"

"The hospital confirms what you thought. The consultant's nice."

"And there's a treatment?"

"Uh-huh. They can't believe I'm breathing so easily, what with the micro-scarring they found. Both lungs. I told them you work miracles."

"A very scientific kind of miracle, and I'm glad you're so much better."

"The medium that I go to see, she's impressed with all I've told her about you. She'd love to meet you sometime."

"Uh-huh. Well, right now, I've someone to see. You go well, Rosa."

"And you. See ya!"

The wallscreen blanked out.

Miracles. Right.

When Rosa had seen her own brain activity pulsing in sheets of colour on that same screen, she had been in awe, sitting beneath the silver tree that was Suzanne's fMRI scanner, set on castors so you could roll it across the floor, like a hairdryer from a salon. "It's kind of a sacred moment, Doc," she had said, for to her science was magic.

Therapists focusing on the mind too often treated every illness as psychosomatic – Rosa had seen hypnotherapists before – but in her case Suzanne had been right to suggest another medical opinion, despite the two medics who had given the all-clear, suggesting that the tightness in Rosa's breathing was her own fault, caused by stress.

If only it were ethical for Suzanne to change New Age irrationality as easily as she removed the other limiting beliefs of Rosa's mental world.

"Dr Duchesne?" The image went straight up on the wallscreen. "Your appointment is here. With his, um, driver."

"Thanks, Colin. Send them up, would you?"

She disengaged her phone from the wallscreen, muted it and blocked incoming calls, then walked out into the lobby and waited in front of the lift. Soft sounds carried from the other firms on this floor – freight consultants and a marketing agency – deadened by soft carpeting and fibre-covered walls. The lift door dinged open.

Richard Broomhall was fourteen, looked a year or two younger, and did not move until a big woman – she stood behind him – touched his shoulder. Then he stepped out, followed by the woman.

"I'm Richard's driver," she said. "You won't want me inside, I assume?"

"There's a coffee machine round there."

"I'm good, thanks. Right here is fine."

Suzanne nodded, then focused every sense on the boy, excluding the world. His eyes widened.

"Come inside, Richard." Direct commands are unambiguous. "And sit down."

Some teenagers respond to *Would you like to sit down?* as if it might be a question, not an instruction, so she needed to set the tone. But there was no surliness in Richard's manner as he took the client seat, glancing at the fMRI in the corner.

"You know what that is?"

"Atomic magnetometer," he said. "You're going to look inside my brain?"

"I'm surprised you know that, so well done. But no scanning today. So do you like science?"

"Uh, sure." His tone said: *Doesn't everyone?*

"Any field in particular?"

"Astrophysics. Galaxy formation. Dark matter strut formation. And I'm an atheist."

From dark matter to religion was a leap, therefore interesting.

"I'm curious. Tell me more about that."

"You can't see dark matter but you can see its effects. And it doesn't matter where you were brought up, physics is the same, and anyone can do experiments to false, um, falsify theories, right? But you're supposed to believe in the same God as your father wherever you are, even though every country has different religions, because – well … they just do."

He blinked as if surprised at the way his words had spilled out.

"And your father?"

"He knows… He's so, er, certain."

"What kind of thing is he certain about?"

"Everything."

She could challenge that for exceptions, because there must be times when Broomhall senior looked or acted uncertain, but she chose a different route. "Is there any specific belief of his that bothers you?"

"I… don't know."

The hesitation told her everything.

"If you did know, what would the answer be? And if you still don't know, just guess."

"Knives." The word popped out. Richard blinked again, then stared at her. "He thinks it's good to carry knives."

"Do all adults carry them?"

"Yes." A pause, then: "Um, no. But lots do."

"Is there anyone you know who doesn't?"

"Mr Dutton, at school. He's brilliant and he doesn't carry."

Good for Mr Dutton.

"Imagine someone with a knife were about to walk in now."

Richard's gaze flicked down and right, his face whitening.

"Tell me," she continued, "how you would feel."

"Sick. Like… like throwing up."

"How would you like to feel around knives?"

"I…" His left hand made an unconscious gesture over his stomach. "I dunno."

Knives brought on a roiling sensation, and he would rather feel settled. That much he had told her without words.

"If you felt calm inside yourself, what would that do for you?"

"I... I'd be safer? Able to work at school without worrying about... things."

There was something there, something to uncover that was school-related, but going for it now would be confrontational. For the moment, she needed rapport; and with four sessions already booked, she could afford to postpone this line of questioning.

And she wanted to know about his father.

For a while she continued with gentle questions, learning about the death of Richard's mother three years ago, the loneliness of a Surrey mansion, and the way his father smelled of whisky at the breakfast table, far too often. And then there were exams, the pressure to do well, and Richard's increasing difficulty in revision. The reason for revision is that revisiting a memory strengthens it, and the principle applies universally. She wondered what bad memories Broomhall senior kept replaying and so strengthening inside his head, what pictures, sounds, and feelings needed the deadening effect of booze to let him sleep.

But there were practical things she could do for Richard now, beginning by instructing him in the fourteen-minutes-study, five-minutes-rest cycle for optimum revising. Then she raised his hand and dropped him into trance.

Limb catalepsy is unknown in the conscious state, an extra convincer to Richard that something new was going on: his hand would feel suspended by wires, held in place by invisible force. While the hand remained poised level with his head, Suzanne talked him down into deep relaxation. "Think back to a time when everything was all right, all was well..."

She showed him how to bring feelings of confidence back into play when needed, and finally instructed his hand to lower – "with honest unconscious movement only as fast as your unconscious agrees to integrate these understandings" – and told a metaphorical tale, as the hand inched downward, of a novice monk graduating via the dark, fear-filled, final chamber to reach the light, only to look back and see flimsy paper dragons hanging from the ceiling: a metaphor which, in Richard's current neurophysiological state, might have profound effects. Beneath his eyelids, tears welled.

"And you can awaken now…"

He rubbed his eyes and smiled.

The next client was a ten year-old bedwetter, accompanied by her mother. Here Suzanne's work was subtle, directed more toward mother than daughter, changing the source of the behaviour. Next up was a webmovie scriptwriter, blocked for months because of a single cutting remark at a vulnerable time. That was straightforward, and by the session's end he was almost dancing as he stood – with ideas, he said, bursting inside his head, desperate to pour out.

Freud said that words were once magic, while Dawkins called even birdsong "barcodes on the air", causing the state of listeners' brains to change. Suzanne wondered, as her writer client left, if he had any clue how her use of language patterns had changed the way he–

"Dr Duchesne." This was a security override, popping up on her wallscreen. "Richard Broomhall's driver is on her way up. I couldn't stop her."

Suzanne blinked, then exhaled, centring herself like a dancer.

"I'll deal with her. That's fine."

Clearly there was a problem. Forestalling the woman's actions, Suzanne pulled her office door open.

The big woman from earlier was storming out of the lift.

"Something's wrong," said Suzanne. "Tell me what it is."

"Richard—"

"But I don't know your name, so what is it?"

"Lexa Armstrong, and I want to know what you did to him. Before the plod come asking."

"Excuse me? Plod?"

"The little bugger slid out of the car when I was distracted, when we were stopped, right? And of course I've told the police, but that doesn't get him back necessarily, so where the hell has he gone?"

"This is awful—" Suzanne spoke fast, matching Lexa Armstrong's scared-and-angry voice, and whether that was professional voice-rapport or because of the sudden coldness dropping inside her own belly, she could not tell – "so you need to slow down and tell me more, because I don't know what happened and we need to find out."

The long sentence, phrases run together, was deliberate, lulling, far better than staccato questions.

"We'd just gone past the Gherkin, stopped at the lights, and there was a crowd crossing the road, some rowdy lads, some a bit suspect, kind of leery, you know?"

"What happened?"

"Richard must have – I just caught like a whisper, a glimpse – but he slipped his arm between the front seats – he was in back – and switched the central locking off, and then he slipped out and that was it. Gone."

This was awful.

"What did you do next?"

"Left the car where it was – that's an automatic fine

– and went to look for him, calling the cops while I did it. No sign of him. He's never done anything like it, too pulled in on himself, if you know what I mean. What did you do to him, Doc?"

"Taught him confidence too soon, or maybe that's nothing to do with it. Where was this? Near the Gherkin building, you said?"

"Heading up Bishopsgate. You think that's maybe significant?"

"I don't know of anything relevant, no locations that would trigger a reaction. You don't know any?"

"No. Shit." Lexa Armstrong rubbed her face. "He's fourteen years old and soft, you know? Anything could happen to him."

"You've told his father?"

"Yeah, and there was a lot of yelling, but I think he's scared, too."

What Broomhall would do to the driver who had let his son disappear in the middle of crowded London, Suzanne had no idea. And as for what action he might take against the therapist who'd seen the boy just minutes before this radical new behaviour shattered everything–

Lexa Armstrong had probably just lost her job; Suzanne's entire career was crashing down.

"You've got the car downstairs?"

"Another fine, and yeah."

"So let's go look for Richard."

The Merc whispered to a halt on Bishopsgate. Suzanne sat up front, shivering a little from the air-con or from worry. At red lights they stopped – the delays seemed longer these days – allowing Lexa to point out a stall selling caps and T-shirts.

"After Richard ran out, he might have gone past that – shit, not that guy, it's someone else. Claimed he hadn't just sold a veil-cap to a white kid."

"He was lying?"

"Telling the truth, I thought, but you'd know for sure. Point is, there's a bunch of other sellers just the – oh, here we go." Lexa put the car into drive. "If Richard got the idea of picking up a veil-cap, the streetcams probably lost him in the crowds."

They passed a turning on the left. Farther down Threadneedle Street, blood pooled on the pavement outside a bar. Bankers' duel, a lunchtime foolishness, or perhaps a disgruntled client calling out a bank employee.

"High price to pay for voting, don't you think, Doc?"

Lexa had noticed Suzanne looking down the street. It confirmed Suzanne's impression of Lexa: observant, her perceptions trustworthy.

"So where would you guess Richard went? And I mean, just take a guess."

"Could be anywhere." Lexa shrugged, betraying no unconscious gestures to suggest otherwise. "Any direction takes you into crowds around stations, overground or Tube or just on foot."

They were passing a steel-and-glass side entrance to Liverpool Street station.

"But that means more streetcams, doesn't it?"

"With a harder job to do."

"Good point," said Suzanne. "If you were Richard, what would you be running away from?"

"His entire life, maybe? Posh house, absolutely lovely, but it don't make up for the rest. I'm not talking actual abuse, mind."

"Of course not."

Suzanne wondered if Richard might be running toward something, rather than away; but it seemed unlikely. In the throng surrounding the car – they had stopped yet again – it seemed impossible to track a single figure. Thirty years of being the most surveilled city on Earth had not stopped London from being a Mecca for runaways. The blur of moving faces brought home the impossibility of their task.

"Which way shall I go?"

"Just drive by instinct."

"You think that will help?"

Maybe I'm just trying to avoid calling Philip Broomhall.

"It's the best we can do," said Suzanne.

"Shit. I was hoping for a miracle."

Suzanne rubbed the inside of her arm.

"There's no such thing, I'm afraid."

[SIX]

End of day one, 6pm and everyone going home. Beside Josh, Vikram alternately fiddled with his beard or folded his arms across the swell of his belly. From the edge of the piazza, they watched the crowds stream toward Dockland station, while high overhead, tethered to the pointed apex of Canary Wharf, a dark-green trizep swayed in the crossdraught. The airship was a symbol of eco-economic trade, the *Global Eco^{2}nomy* legend in distorted yellow characters on its side.

"You actually believe in carbon derivatives and all that shit?" asked Vikram.

"No, but the grads in my group do."

"Silly buggers. How did the team building go?"

"They were supposed to plan an outdoor corporate bash for fictitious foreign customers, VIPs. Themed event, venue hire, catering, the lot. You know what their risk analysis listed as the one thing that might go wrong? It might rain."

"Poor little sods. Too much time in classrooms." Vikram tugged at his sweat-patched shirt. "It's hot. You reckon the others already hit Bar Aleph?"

"Probably."

"So this'll be a good time for you to get shit-faced, right?"

"Don't touch the stuff, you know that."

"Sometimes you need to let rip. That's what I say."

Josh stared up at the airship.

Letting rip is what I'm afraid of.

"I'll get my head back together in time for week three."

The first two weeks were a wandering role, mentoring, and helping out, because the groups were large enough to need more than the lead instructor, at least in the bank's opinion, and they were paying the bills. The third week was when he would come into his own, teaching the stuff he knew best.

"Can you afford to take time off?" asked Vikram. "Money-wise, I mean."

As with all freelancers, no work meant no money.

"Probably not. And I need to keep busy."

"Well, that makes sense. Or we could just get normal jobs like normal people. So what would you do?"

"God knows."

"How about running a pig farm? Or a brothel? Hey, you could combine the two."

"Say what?"

"You know, like the two Welsh farmers talking. One says, 'How do you find a sheep in long grass?' The other says, 'Irresistible, boyo.' You could do a piggy version. All those plump porky arses with their cute curly tails."

"Vikram Vivekananda, I am seriously concerned for your mental health."

"Then you can turn 'em into rashers when they're all used up. Might taste kinda salty."

"You're sick, man. Very, very sick."

Tony and the other trainers were approaching.

"What are you two chuckling about?"

"Believe me, mate," said Josh. "You so don't want to know."

As a group, seven of them, they headed into Bar Aleph and took seats among the old-fashioned chrome fittings, surrounded by colourful liquid crystal lighting, the air bouncing with the kind of rap Josh heard as a little kid.

"I've got to teach a bit of crypto to my lot," said Vikram. "Just an intro. I was gonna start with Alice and Bob sending signals to each other."

"Like every other example since World War II." Tony raised his dark beer. "Cheers, everyone."

"Cheers."

"Yeah." Vikram sipped from a fluorescent blue cocktail. "That's my theme, like. You know, how Alice has been sending signals for fucking ever, and Bob ain't taking the hint. Either the relationship evolves or she's got to find someone else, you know? Maybe Charlie."

"No, that's not it." Sheena, with the bronze earrings like ninja weapons, gave a jangling shake of her head. "Bob and Charlie are gay, you see. What you need to say is–"

"Or Bob's the father of her love child." This was Alan, getting into the act. "And her encrypted signal reads: Little Davey keeps asking where Daddy is. Or should that be little Tony?"

Josh's phone vibrated.

"No offence, everyone, but thank God I've got a call."

He went outside, though he could have used the noise-cancelling earbeads tucked in his pocket. The caller was Kath Gleason, and she was Sophie's teacher, or had been. Everything about Sophie was inching into past tense, detail by detail.

"Mr Cumberland, I'm sorry to call you in the evening, but I thought you might be working."

"I was, yes. There's no change in Sophie."

"Mostly I was wondering if I can help. The hospital staff don't tell us everything, but Eileen" – she meant Eileen O'Donoghue, the headmistress – "has been keeping in touch. How are you and Mrs Cumberland doing?"

"You've talked to Maria?"

"No, I tried you first."

"Look, Ms Gleason–"

"Kath, please."

"All right, thanks, but I don't think talking about it helps."

For a second he thought the call had ended, then:

"I'm going to see the Brezhinski boy on Saturday. Would it help if you came along?"

"Brezhinski?"

"The boy the other two set upon."

"Shit. How is he?"

"At home, still months away from returning to school. His parents asked me to pass on their regrets, say how sorry they were about Sophie. I think they'd like to tell you in person."

"I'm in London at the moment."

"Oh. Yes – I think I knew that you travel a lot."

Too much. So many hours spent in airports and railway stations, driving on motorways and highways. And that was after the years of active service, months at a time anywhere on the bloody planet. Maybe if he'd taken a more sensible path, they might have moved house to suit a settled career, put Sophie in a different school, and she'd still be all right instead of–

"Perhaps I shouldn't have called."

"No, it's all right."

"Call me, please, if you decide to come. And I'm so sorry, Mr Cumberland."

"Josh."

"All right. Bye-bye."

"Bye."

Thumbing his phone display, he scrolled through the contacts list until he reached *those* entries: **Sophie**, the mobile he would never ring again; and **Sophie2**, which he chose now. It took a second to contact the URI and form the connection, so that her image brightened in the phone. She's so small. The picture was realtime video but might almost have been a photo: white sheets, stacked monitors, child-sized mask like some toy biowarfare kit, and her small chest scarcely moving in response to the machines, for they performed the breathing.

All unchanging, until the day when she would leave that place; and while they had not begun to discuss the matter yet, he expected the coffin would be white.

My baby girl.

She'd say to that: "Dad, I'm ten and a half, you know."

Ten and a half forever.

High above the plaza, lightning flashed, white and purple; and then the rain came down. At the pointed apex of the tower, the trizep airship was bucking in the wind. Everyone else at ground level stopped to look up as a *crump* sounded. The airship had struck the building and bounced off.

"They'd better let it go. Unhitch it, or whatever." It was a young woman who spoke: twenty years old, short skirt, violet lipstick. "Gonna be a right smash-up otherwise."

There was another thump, then something cracked, and the trizep's cable dropped away like a flying tree snake, making S-shaped curves as it fell.

"A kite in the wind." She raised her eyebrows at Josh. "Wouldn't like to be on board that thing."

"Er, yeah."

"So you looking for some friendship?"

"Is that what you call it?" But his blood was flowing downward, stirring. "Why not?"

Christ, I'm going with her.

Just like that, she slipped her arm through his. He forced away the voice inside his head asking how many times a night she did this.

"I have got a nice place we can go."

"Good. Er... How much?"

"Thirty all the way, dirty sex is fifty."

He wondered what the difference was.

"I, er, need to go via a cash machine."

She tossed her head, tightening her hold on his arm.

"This way, lover."

As they walked, she took hold of his hand, and rubbed it across her buttock like a promise. Nothing beneath the thin skirt save warm flesh.

Bloody hell.

"You're beautiful," he told her.

The kind of beauty he could purchase by the hour. He could pay phone-to-phone but that would leave a traceable transaction. By the time they reached the lobby of ATMs, he felt shaky. His fingers trembled as he withdrew the fifty.

Don't do this.

He had the money, the opportunity, and no one to stop him.

Don't.

He pushed out a breath and handed over twenty. "Sorry, I can't. But that's for you."

Then he kissed her on the cheek.

"What is wrong? We can do whatever you want. I like you very much."

"That's nice, but no, thank you."

She raised her hands, then let them flop as Josh walked away. Trembling, he decided to walk back to the flat, get changed, and go out for a run; otherwise he would eat first and end up running the streets at one in the morning, which would at least be quiet. But here, as he turned into an old residential street, the atmosphere was already muted, while at the corner, next to an abandoned mini-supermarket, three youths were leaning against the wall, watching everything, their jackets unzipped to allow access to sheathed blades.

There was rain now, soft as a mother's tears.

He crossed the empty road, continuing along the other side, checking behind him; but the youths had not moved. His nerves relaxed a fraction, then came sounds of scuffling. There was an alleyway behind the disused supermarket, and that was probably where the–

A female yelp, followed by: "Back here, ya cunt."

"Leave me alone!"

The thud of bone against bone, fist on flesh. Josh broke into a run, but the three youths were closer, spilling into the alley ahead of him. By the time he reached them, two of the youths had hauled the woman clear, while the third, arm outstretched, was sighting along his blade as if aiming a lance, his target the attacker's vulnerable throat.

"You want formal duel, motherfucker?"

There was blood on the attacker's face. Two neat slices: the youth was fast.

"N-no, mate. No trouble."

"You go hitting women again, mate, there'll be plenty of trouble. Know what I mean?"

"Yeah, sure. Sorry."

Josh stood, hands loose, while the attacker backed away, then stumbled into a broken jog.

"You need a hand?" One of the youths still held the woman's sleeve. "Or can you manage?"

"I'm just there." She pointed to a front door. "Thank you. You're very brave."

"Any time."

They watched her go in. Then they shrugged, went back to the corner, and resumed their leaning against the wall.

"Nice work, guys," called Josh.

Nods all round, then he walked on.

You watching this, Dad?

Police Sergeant Jeff Cumberland died at the boots of a teenage gang while a hundred shoppers watched and did not help. Times had changed in the decades since; not everything was worse.

Only the weather–

Lightning, silver-white, lit up the streets.

[SEVEN]

Tuesday lunchtime, and Suzanne sat opposite Carol Klugmann in a coffee shop, the remains of lunch on the table between them. Carol was from Austin, Texas, weighing in at double Suzanne's body weight, and still she had success with clients – using behavioural repatterning and hypnosis – who needed to get thin.

"If they look at me funny," she would tell her colleagues, "I say I'm fat cause I don't give a shit, and I don't mean constipation."

Her clothes were expensive, her presence imposing, every word and gesture a masterclass in effectiveness.

"You look terrific," Suzanne told her. "On the phone you said you needed cheering up."

"I lied, sugar. Just wanted your company. Plus… you know I'm on the Council complaint committee, right?"

"*Merde*."

"Exactly. We had some lawyers asking us about complaint procedures. A big City firm with an outlying office in Guildford. Philip Broomhall's solicitors, or I'll eat my Stetson."

"You don't have a Stetson. And you used to think solicitors were door-to-door salesfolk."

"And that barristers worked in coffee shops, not law courts, cause I'm a simple cowgirl."

Suzanne first saw her at a conference in York. Carol's voluminous pink sweatshirt had borne the slogan Keep Austin Weird. Surrounding her, a group of male therapists had been rocking with laughter. The next morning, the slimmest, best-looking of their number had shared a breakfast table with Carol, looking dazed.

"I played the mother figure," she'd said. "For someone with naughty Freudian desires."

Now, Suzanne squeezed the bridge of her nose. Tears were beginning to form, and there was no point in masking her expression, because Carol noticed everything.

"Maybe I don't deserve to hold a licence. A fourteen year-old has run away."

"You've not talked to Broomhall, the father?"

"I listened to him shout at me, then ended the call. It didn't help anyone, and I didn't handle it well."

"What do you know that he doesn't?"

"I don't understand."

"Come on, Suzanne. You spend a few minutes with anyone, you find out things they've kept to themselves for life. So what did you learn about young Richard?"

"Nothing besides…"

"Uh-huh?"

"Bullying at school. There was something specific there. We had four sessions booked, you see. I thought I could address it later."

"Shit."

"So maybe I did exactly what Philip Broomhall thinks I did. Gave the boy confidence enough to look at his situation and make a desperate move to change everything. Just enough of a boost to drop him into deep, deep trouble. Think how scared he must be."

"At least you gave him some confidence," said Carol. "Maybe more than you think."

"Which means you accept it's my fault?"

"Would it help you if I did?"

"Oh, sod off."

"You've lived in London too long, girlfriend. You and me both."

Suzanne rubbed her face, using her imagination to push troubling mental images – a frowning disciplinary board, a terse letter revoking her licence – off into the distance: in view but tractable.

"You ever going back?" she asked Carol.

"Not likely. You seen Brand's antics in Geneva?"

"Uh, no." Suzanne had not browsed the news. "What's he done now?"

"Refused to sit near the other two prime ministers. Least he didn't call 'em godless Commies this time."

Brand and the others were supposed to be a triumvirate, three prime ministers, one serving as president for the tripartite commonwealth of the US. But Brand was the voice of mid-America, his worldview myopic and threatening, so that Left and Right Coast commentators now called their country the Theoretically United States or worse.

"He's such a – oh." Suzanne's phone was sounding *dit-dit-dit, dit-dit-dit*. "Oh, no."

Other customers were glancing over, because this was the police ringtone, sounding only on receipt of an official call.

"Answer it, hon."

"Yes." She thumbed the phone. "Dr Suzanne Duchesne. Can I help you, officer?"

A lean-faced man, real not virtual, showed in the small screen.

"It would be better in person, Dr Duchesne. If you could accompany me to the station, please."

"Accompany you?"

"I'm outside the coffee shop, on the corner. It's more discreet that way."

Not with that ringtone, but never mind, because if she didn't obey she could be arrested on suspicion of being unhelpful to a police officer. The law had been passed after an online referendum – with knife-holders wielding four votes each – a hardline decision that was consistent with normal trends. Even before the Blade Acts, higher knife crime meant lower crime overall (perhaps for the same reason that American towns with 100% gun ownership suffered zero burglaries, an observation that continued to cause shudders), a fact whose implications came into focus when the blade generation grew up.

"I'll be right there, officer."

"And I'm coming with you," said Carol.

"There's no need."

"Sure there is. Have you any idea how dull my day was till now?"

"I'm scared."

"And it's OK because–" Carol clasped Suzanne's upper arm – "it will work out all right."

A small boost but that was fine, with Suzanne needing all the help she could get.

Inside the interrogation room, the armchair was comfortable. Suzanne sank back in it. With the big wallscreens all round, currently blank, it was like some corporate conference room. To get here, they had passed through the equally corporate-looking interior of Covent Garden Police Station, a contrast to the creamy Georgian exterior she had often walked past.

"If you could keep your palms on the arms, please." The nameless officer sat across from her. "It gives clearer readings that way."

"Readings? Oh."

There was a wallscreen directly behind her, set to display the scanner output, assuming this worked like the movies.

"You saw Richard Broomhall the day before yesterday, Doctor, is that right?"

"Yes. 11 o'clock. His father wanted him to lose the hoplophobic behaviours he'd been exhibiting."

"The son's afraid of knives?"

"Right," said Suzanne. "He was and probably still is, because we didn't get into specific behaviour change in that session."

"And what did take place during the session?"

"My phone has the full recording." She started to reach for it.

"Hands on the armrests, please."

"Sorry. Um… I questioned Richard about his life and goals."

"He's fourteen, is that right?"

"Yes. You could call it the age when the adult personality begins to emerge. It's a delicate time, so the final part of operant change is what we call an 'ecology check'. For example, if I cured someone of a fear of heights, I wouldn't want them dangling one-handed off a roof."

"And a fourteen year-old running away from home is appropriate?"

"Of course not. It's terrible. That's sort of my point. I didn't notice any precursors to that shift, and I did check."

"All right." The officer was stone-faced. "Did Richard give any indication of people he might know in London? Any places he might go?"

"No indication. If you review the session recording, you'll–"

"Thank you, I will. Any family member he might visit, anywhere?"

"From what Richard said, there's just him and his widower father. Plus staff at the family home."

"You've been there?"

"Uh, no. I met Philip Broomhall in Victoria," she said. "Just the once. And the only time I met Richard was during that session."

"In Elliptical House," said the officer.

"Yes, that's right."

"What about the driver?"

"Lexa?"

"You know her?"

"Not before, er, beforehand. Is she under suspicion?"

"Is there any reason she ought to be?"

"I don't… Let me think." Closing her eyes, Suzanne was able to picture Lexa in the consulting room, her expression as she broke the news. "She wasn't lying, I'm almost sure of it. She was scared for Richard's sake, as I am."

"You can tell if someone is lying, Doctor?"

"Not really. If someone stares up and to their right, that may indicate visual imagination, but not necessarily falsehood. Some people navigate their memories by mental imagery. The other common mistake, made by people with too little training, is to assume that signs of stress, like hand-wringing or crossing ankles, mean someone is lying. It only means the person is stressed."

There had been far too many miscarriages of justice, innocent people pressurised by the interrogating officers, forced into giving false confessions, because officers misinterpreted stress or visualisation signals as guilt. Suzanne had been an expert witness in a retrial – an innocent man walking free after seven years in a cell – and the officer probably knew that already.

"Are you stressed right now?" he asked.

"Of course I am. If I could give you any hint about where Richard might be, then I would. He was under pressure at school, and I don't know the specifics, because I'd intended to follow up on that in the next session. You might look for evidence of bullying, probably from peers."

"Meaning possibly from teachers?"

"Possibly, but there was no evidence for that. But you need to know where he's headed, not what he's running from, and I can't help. You must know more about homeless kids on the street than I do. Where would he go?"

The officer looked over Suzanne's shoulder, presumably reading the screen.

"Is there anything else you can think of, Doctor?"

"No, I'm sorry. And I've thought about it, over and over again."

"I'm sure you have. If you could hand over your phone, please."

"My…? Oh. Sure."

She put it on the table, just as he slid a handset toward to her.

"This is your replacement, from us. You can keep it."

"Really? It looks expensive."

"That's all right. It will register to you by the time you've left the building. Any cached files will be copied during the procedure."

"But my contact list and–"

"It's all online." The officer waved his hand. "Cloud computing, the web all around us. Only the most recent changes are in the handset, in cache, and we'll make sure they're copied to you."

"Well…" She picked up the new phone, its TCC logo embossed in gold on black: *Tyndall Cloud Communications.* "Thank you."

"Thanks for your help, Dr Duchesne." He popped her old phone into a clear plastic bag and sealed it. "Nice talking with you."

"Yes. I hope you find Richard."

The door clicked open.

"We'll do our best, Doctor. Mind how you go."

There were fire-eaters and clowns on stilts, jugglers and acrobats clowns performing flick-flack somersaults across the cobblestones. The piazza of Covent Garden was busy, usual for a summer evening. Suzanne and Carol watched the performers, flames and movement serving as distraction for the eyes, while thought followed its own path, however dark.

"At least I got a new phone out of it."

"While they do forensics on the old."

"I don't even know what's on it. The officer said it's all out in the clouds, the data."

"Probably records all your sexual encounters." Carol nudged her. "So when was the last time you got laid?"

Despite her age and her training, Suzanne's cheeks warmed. "You are a bad person, Dr Klugmann."

"And you've not yet answered my question, Dr

Duchesne. So are you going to answer me now or in a couple of minutes?"

"No. You want smut, check your own phone."

"You think there's room on one itty-bitty handset for all my sensual encounters?"

"Probably not."

One of the jugglers dropped his clubs, apparently by accident as another cartwheeled across him; but when the second juggler was standing, everyone could see that he now had the clubs arcing through the air. Onlookers clapped, as the duo began to toss clubs between them.

"For your sake, hon, we need to do something about this investigation."

"What do you mean?" Suzanne forgot the performers. "The investigation?"

"If CCTV was going to provide a quick result, they'd have found Richard already. So it's not happening, is it?"

"You're not suggesting we track him down ourselves?"

"Right." Carol slapped her belly. Everything jiggled, voluptuous and rippling. "Running around the streets is so what I do."

Men glanced in her direction.

"Broomhall needs to hire someone," Carol went on. "A specialist, working full-time on finding Richard. And you see that blonde guy over there?"

"Uh–"

"You think he's staring at my breasts?"

"Of course he is. But you can't tell Broomhall to hire an investigator."

"He's rich, so he can afford it."

"But–"

"And after I've talked to him he'll be pleased to have thought of the idea for himself. Because that's what he'll think has happened."

"You're marvellous." Suzanne squeezed Carol's upper arm. "Thank you."

"It's still early."

"And you've a blonde guy to seduce, which you won't while I'm hanging around."

"There's another nice-looking man over there. We could double d–"

"Good night, Carol."

"'Night, sweetie. We'll catch up tomorrow."

"Catch yourself a good one tonight."

"Count on it."

Suzanne watched as Carol moved among the spectators, exuding charisma and sex, gaze fastened on her prey.

"Be good."

She turned and crossed the cobblestones, heading for the Tube.

[EIGHT]

The first night was awful. Then things got worse.

The world was cold, that was the obvious thing. During the sweltering daytime, Richard's white shirt had been enough; but evening had been a warning, and when darkness fell, he was in trouble. Plus, a white shirt stands out in shadows. Why hadn't anyone told him that?

Because it never mattered before.

In the real world, where fear came from Father shouting and the stink of whisky on his breath, or being alone in a house with eight or ten people, depending on which staff were on duty… in that world, the colour of your clothes didn't mark you out, transform you into a target. Now he was alone in a city of five million people, all of them bigger and more violent than him; but the thing was, he could go anywhere, not trapped inside school boundaries with a maniac like Zajac intending to kill him.

A year ago, he was trailing his father into Selfridges and found his gaze hooked by a dirty blanket on the ground. On it, a young girl-woman slumped, a stained medical dressing on her hand, her features delicate beneath grime, and redness in her eyes that spoke of recent tears. Father had not stopped, so neither did he; but inside, riding up on the escalator, he'd said: "Did you see that girl?"

"What girl?"

"Outside by the doorway. Begging, I guess."

"No, nothing worth noticing."

Later, at home over dinner, he'd tried to ask about her again, explaining about the blanket and the gauze bandage. Father had explained that he hadn't seen a girl as such, but he might have glimpsed a beggar, an example of a generic type; and that her kind were an infestation, and would Richard pass the chocolate sauce, and how were the crêpes tonight?

Today, a few people had asked if Richard had any spare change. Mostly he'd walked past. But now, a youth of his own age with weeping sores on neck and forearm was standing in front of him, asking the same thing: *Spare any change?* Richard reached into his pocket, thinking he could pay phone-to-phone, maybe get to an ATM... but the only thing he found was a used tissue. No phone meant no bank account, meant everything was gone. Bumping through the crowds in Leicester Square, that was when it must have happened.

"I'm sorry. I've got... nothing."

"Christ, mate." The youth wiped away snot-dribble with his sleeve. "You one of us?"

"I... think so. You mean beg... uh... homeless."

Runaway. That's what I am.

It was a frightening word, conjuring up stone-faced police officers chasing him down with dogs and stunguns. But it was hard to maintain the fright, because the hunger that had begun as deepening stomach pains had slowly metamorphosed into listlessness, a feeling of sleepiness despite the cold. Standing in front of the youth, he began to sway.

"I'm Jayce. Who are you?"

"Huh?"

"Jayce. What's your name?"

"Rich–, er, Richie. Hall."

"No surnames, mate, not round here. You ain't eaten today, huh?"

"Not since… No."

His mouth began to salivate.

"Well, Richie, you'll get used to it."

His stomach felt like a stone.

"Jee-zus," added Jayce after a moment. "All right, come with me."

He struggled to his feet, slung his blanket over his shoulder, and emptied a few coins out of a plastic cup. "Fuckin' poor day today. You'd think they'd have a heart."

As Jayce moved closer to Richard, a wave of sweet stink came from his mouth – the teeth were tinged with greyish green, speckled with black. His clothes smelled ripe.

"Who would?" Richard took a step back. "Who'd have a heart?"

"The rich ones with the money, who else?"

Father said that no one gave anything for nothing, and without money there'd be savagery. All you had to do was earn your living; and what else was life for?

"Come on," added Jayce. "You can do me a favour later."

"Favour?"

"Like I'm doing you. What, you want to eat, don't you?"

"Er... Yeah. Please."

"Well, ain't you polite. Come on, we're going to see Greaser Khan."

"Who's that?"

"Someone who'll like you for a messenger-boy, 'cause you still look clean. Won't last, mind."

"Being a messenger?" Richard trembled, not knowing why.

"Looking clean. You're respectable, see. So you'll be able to go inside, like, department stores and things, with no one noticing. Drop off little deliveries for old Greaser."

"Deliveries."

"Little ones. Not heavy."

"But–" Richard stopped.

"You want to eat or not?"

"Well, yeah."

"So this way. Oh, yeah... Fuck's sake, don't go calling him Greaser."

"I wouldn't–"

"Or if he asks if you'd like to go with him into the stockroom round back," said Jayce, "tell him no thanks, Mr Khan, I'd prefer to wait out here if that's OK. Trust me on this one."

They were walking along broken pavement, beneath a streetlamp that was fizzing dull scarlet instead of orange. Up ahead was the brightness of an all-night store. Several people slouched outside.

"Out where?" said Richard.

"Huh?"

"You said, wait out here. Where?"

"In the shop, where else? And here's me thinking you weren't a tosser."

"I–"

Better to keep his mouth shut. Blabbermouths at school suffered; and this world was even harder. When Jayce removed his cap outside the shop, Richard did the same. Jayce nodded: "He don't like it, not seeing faces, like."

When they went in, a plump Asian lady smiled at them from behind the counter. From the rear of the shop, two men watched, hard-faced.

"Is Mr Khan in?" Jayce bobbed up and down, almost on tiptoe. "Got someone to meet him, like."

The lady remained smiling. One of the men turned and went through a bead curtain.

"Let's look at the mags," said Jayce.

"I–Right."

There was food and it was calling to him. He still had a little change; perhaps he could buy a Twix bar. But Jayce was tugging his sleeve, so he followed. A youth with dreadlocks and a steel chain spiralling around one arm was flicking through *Blade Warriors*, then holding open a double spread: two fighters clad in trunks, streaked with scarlet, blades wet and bloody.

Richard squeezed his eyes shut.

"So who's this?"

"This is Richie, Mr Khan."

Khan had high, square shoulders and a trimmed beard. The woman was no longer in sight. Behind Richard, the guy with dreadlocks placed the magazine back on the shelf and scurried out of the shop. Meanwhile music started playing: something old and fast, about Illuminati.

"You're not local, are you, Richie?"

"Er, no, sir."

"You know your way around?"

"I could help him, Mr Khan."

"Why would you do that, Jayce?"

"Look after a mate, like."

"Uh-huh." Khan rubbed his knuckles against his beard. "Since you ask, there's a little something needs to go to the Adult Education College. Bit of extra study material. So, you're in?"

"He's in, Mr Khan."

"All right." Khan fished a small red box from his pocket. "Mr Maxwell, teaching Chinese, class starts at eight. Be there ten minutes early."

Richard swallowed salty saliva – maybe tears? – as the world blurred.

I have to do this.

He didn't know what his reward was going to be, but there was a commitment now.

"You like the music, Richie?"

"Uh, sir?"

"Sir." Khan looked at Jayce, then at the hard-faced men behind the counter. "He called me 'sir'. I like this boy. I asked" – his eyes became large, focused on Richard – "if you like Fatboy Slim. We're talking classic here. None of your modern din."

"Um, yes. I do. Like it."

"Good."

The red box, when Khan handed it over, fitted in Richard's palm.

"And I'll pay you now, since I trust you." Khan gave Jayce a boiled sweet wrapped in cellophane: that was what it looked like. "You know what would happen if – you know, don't you?"

"Yes, Mr Khan. Thank you."

The music changed to Kids in Glass Houses, who Mrs Kovac liked to play in the kitchen while she was cooking, except that she was in his old life, where everything was clean and rich, taken for granted until now.

I'm so hungry.

But Jayce was leaving the shop. Richard hurried after, clutching the box, feeling acid pain inside. Could a stomach dissolve itself for lack of food?

This was so hard.

Out on the street, beyond the next corner, they stopped. Jayce took the "sweet" out of his pocket, and undid the cellophane a little, revealing caked green powder. It reminded Richard of the orange ammonium dichromate used in class to build a volcano, turning green and spewing everywhere when set alight. He thought about trying to explain chemical volcanoes to Jayce; instead he asked about the powder.

"You don't want to be trying this." Jayce dabbed some onto his tongue, and his eyes darkened. "Not till you need to."

"What do you mean?"

"Nothing. Let's get you fed."

"We have to be at this college by ten to eight."

"Plenty of time. What time is it now?"

"I don't… I lost my phone."

"Probably why the Bill ain't picked you up. Come on."

Soon they were at a ramshackle establishment, once a furniture store, from the faded signs. From round back, the aroma of tomato soup and toast was overwhelming. Cracked doors, horizontal across piles of bricks, served as tables. Plastic chairs, with the frozen bubbles of burn marks, were set out in the yard. Some fifteen or twenty people, shabby-looking, were queuing for soup.

"No one asks no questions," said Jayce. "Why we come, ain't it?"

There were ham sandwiches and Bovril crisps as well as soup and toast, an explosion of taste and sensation in Richard's mouth. Nothing had ever been like this: flavour-filled, urgent, seeping into his body through his tongue.

"Am I supposed to be getting paid?" The words just came out. "For the... you know."

"Would you have found this place by yourself?"

"Uh..."

"So, you've been paid, intya?"

Richard shook his head, then wiped the last of his bread round inside the soup cup, soaking up the last of it.

"All right, look," continued Jayce. "I'll see you all right afterward. We... never mind."

A big woman was standing next to Richard. "Did anyone explain that we don't ask questions?"

Richard nodded.

"So we don't, but if someone wants to talk, we listen. And you" – she thrust out a green sweatshirt – "need to put on an extra layer. Sorry we've no blankets tonight."

"Er... thank you."

"Uh-huh." She watched him a moment, gave a mouth movement that might have been anything, then walked away.

"Do-gooders," muttered Jayce.

"What?" Richard pulled on the sweatshirt. "What do you mean?"

"Feel sorry for you one minute, suck you into the machine the next."

"Machine?"

"The system. The *thing*, man."

"Oh. Right."

"Like teachers, like bosses, like yer fat cats in banks, telling you what to do."

"So what if we don't go to the college tonight, like Mr Khan said?"

"You crazy, Richie-boy? You don't let him down."

There was a contradiction there, invisible to Jayce. But so far being smart had not helped Richard at all; while Jayce with his teeth that looked covered in lichen, his breath stinking, survived.

"How long have you been here? On the streets?"

Some of the others were looking at them.

"Come on." Jayce kicked Richard's ankle. "Let's get gone."

Some time later, walking along a street of graffiti-tagged houses, Richard felt his bowels shifting.

"Uh… Jayce?"

"Yeah, man?"

"How far is the college? I mean, how long will it take to get there?"

"I dunno. Twenty minutes? Maybe a bit more."

"Are there any, uh, toilets closer than that?"

Jayce stared at him. "You're something else, intya?"

"What do you–?"

"'Sakes, lookit the street. No one here. Pick a doorway. I won't tell."

"What?" Desperate enough to cry, Richard looked around. There was nowhere else.

"And I ain't gonna watch, neither. See you at the next corner."

"Shit." Not the kind of language he used.

"Do whatever you like, Richie-boy."

"I–I'll see you in a bit."

• • •

There were three visible cameras – one on each pillar of the big gateway leading to the yard in front, the other beyond the yard, inside the main entrance – and all three were coated in a blackened mess.

"Been bubbled," said Jayce. "Know what I mean?"

"Sort of."

"Like a spray kind of thing. Shoots upward real high, sticks real well. Hard to clean off."

"So I just go straight in?" Richard felt the small box in his pocket. "Cap on?"

"Take the cap off until you're inside. Most of these dozy buggers" – Jayce pointed at the people, all adults, crossing the yard – "won't have noticed the cameras are screwed. You'll look more normal, like, with no cap."

"But I put it on inside? With the veil?"

"Of course, unless you're sure every cam's been fucked. Anyway, you'll do great."

"You're not coming in?"

"Your gig, not mine. I don't look like a student, or someone's kid."

And I do?

Not if he carried on living like this. He wanted to think there was something inside him that made him different; but he knew that if he stayed on the streets he would change.

"You're going to wait?"

"Sure. Fuck's sake go in, willya?"

Taking off his cap, Richard rubbed his face several times, wanting to hide his features as he passed through the gate, not trusting that the cameras were dead. His skin felt prickled as if by tiny ants migrating across him. Then, as he entered the foyer, someone coughed and his heart punched inside his chest. But he had to keep going.

A wall display showed a multicoloured list, including *Intermediate Mandarin, 20:00, Room 17, instructor: T. Maxwell, M.A. (Oxon)*, which was what Mr Khan had said. The room was upstairs, so he climbed polished steps, pulling his cap on and tipping it low as he passed beneath a camera, his feet moving by themselves – *sua sponte*, Mr Robbins would have said, but Latin lessons were a world away, even though he was inside a college – taking him to Room 17.

"Uh, hello?" This must be T Maxwell. "Are you in this class?"

"No, sir."

"Well, it is for adults." A sick brightness rose in his eyes. "I don't suppose you're looking for me?"

"I've got… something. From, er…"

"Shall we call him Mr K?"

Both their hands were shaking, Richard's as he handed over the box, Maxwell's as he took hold of it.

"OK." Maxwell pushed out a shaky breath that smelled of mint. "OK. And I've paid already, you know that, right?"

"Er…"

What to do next? Blankness floated in Richard's mind.

"Did you want to see me later on?" The voice was slick, like grease-stained silk. "Perhaps outside?"

"Um. No."

Fear sluiced down through Richard's body, then he was stumbling from the room, along the corridor and down the grimy stairs, forgetting the cap that was clutched in his hand, his head filled with images of wide-shouldered police with stun-batons and gauntlets, smashing his face before they snapped on magnetic cuffs, dragging him across the floor without regard for bloodstains, for he was a criminal now.

They'll arrest me. Father will kill me.

The world had changed.

I'm a criminal.

Last term, Ms Simms had talked about "phase tran-sitions", the change from ice to liquid water to gas, the same molecules involved, their relationships snapping into new and different configurations. While some changes, like a broken egg, can never be reversed; and you can state the Second Law of Thermodynamics like this: You can't ever go back.

He had destroyed his life.

Someone was talking to Jayce outside the college. Had the police had found him already? But the man's sil-houette was a little familiar – one of the men from Khan's shop. Maybe he was only a shop assistant; but the look that swivelled in Jayce's direction was dark and cold, then the man was stalking away, not looking back.

"Do me a favour, man." Jayce's hand trembled, hold-ing out a pen. "Write this, will ya?"

The pen was a felt-tip, chewed and sticky. Jayce pulled up his sleeve and offered the pale inside of his forearm.

"Write, uh…" Jayce's eyes jiggled, dancing to ghost music. "Arches, Wandsworth, 9 o'clock Thursday."

A discarded sweet wrapper lay curled on the ground, containing no trace of green powder.

"Uh, how do you spell Wandsworth?"

"Shit, man. How it sounds."

Richard wrote: **ARCHES WONZWORTH 9**, thought for a moment, then added: **PM THURSDAY**.

"Great." Jayce pushed down his sleeve. "Yeah. Wow. Oh, wow."

He tilted his head to one side, eyes like slits.

"What?" Richard looked round. "What is it?"

"That light, man." Jayce pointed at a streetlamp. "You gotta squeeze your eyes nearly shut. See the pattern? In like your eyelashes?"

"Diffraction."

"Say what? You're mad in the head, pal."

But when Richard started to walk on, Jayce followed, his gait bouncing. Chemical springs in his heels.

"So where we going, man?"

"You tell me," said Richard.

Adrenalised fear was seeping away from him, his body staring to slump in on itself. The surrounding night was chill.

"Let's go up the West End. See what happens, right?"

"I was thinking of somewhere to sleep." Standing upright was becoming hard.

"Man, you want to sleep in the dark? Around here?"

A spurt of fear came back, a short-lived boost of energy. But if he didn't find someplace, he would end up sliding down and closing his eyes, fatigued, with no other options.

"I know a doorway." Jayce flicked his fingers at Richard's sleeve. "Come on."

"A doorway?"

"Better than it sounds. And look." Jayce pointed to a wheelie-bin in front of a house, filled with black bags for tomorrow's collection. "Take that."

"The bin?"

"That cardboard box beside it."

"Oh, right."

Insulation. Thermal insulation using cardboard.

Hey, Ms Simms. Physics can save your life.

"Tip the rubbish out, you moron. Quietly."

"Uh. Right."

He did what he was told.

There was a doorway in shadow, part of some old building, not a house. Tucked in the corner of a cold porch,
he was invisible from the road. Opposite him, Jayce
spread his blanket on concrete.

"You really going to sleep, man?"

"Yeah." Invisible fingers were pushing down on
Richard's eyelids. "Sorry."

"I'll keep watch, like. You're safe."

His chin dipped. It was too cold to sleep, but Richard
slipped into a grey dream regardless, shivering but no
longer fully conscious, while some minutes passed...
until he trembled into wakefulness, and saw the dark
green edge to the night sky. This was pre-dawn, and
hours had slipped by, while Jayce must have gone, taking his blanket, for the porch was empty.

Richard slipped back into pseudo-sleep, trying to
dream of a warm world and luxury, where enemies did
not lurk in the night, and reality was no longer alien
and hard.

[NINE]

Josh clapped and cheered along with the others.

"Come on, Paula. You can do it!"

She adjusted her hair, tugged at the jacket of her trouser suit, then settled her stance. Not bad, on the basis of ten minutes' instruction. The cheering filled the corporate classroom: twenty-two delegates and four instructors, including Josh, while Vikram and Pete held the smooth plastic "board" ready for breaking. A vertical hair's-breadth line bisected the plastic, almost invisible, for it was designed to split apart under the same force as one-inch pine, all very traditional.

Paula twisted and thrust out her palm–

"*Ha!*"

–while the two halves clunked apart and fell as the guys let go.

"Yes!"

"Way to go, Paula!"

Whoops and backslapping, fists pumped in the air. Paula's face flushed beneath a shining lamina of sweat.

"Good work." Tony raised his thumb, nodding to Josh as well as Paula. "Well done, team. So, let's sit down for the wrap-up."

The delegates had filled in their online feedback forms after the afternoon break, when they were re-laxed, not rushing to get home. Tony was a professional, and knew exactly how to direct corporate training.

"So." He spoke as they took their seats, and a list of checked-off bullet-points appeared on the wallscreen. "There's our objectives from the start of the week and, well... those ticks or check-marks might be a little hint" – he smiled at the delegates' laughter – "that we've achieved them all. So this is like the finale of special forces selection, and I hereby declare you all special operatives in systems development. Well done, everyone!"

There was applause, the pushing back of chairs on carpet, then the shaking of hands and the delegates slipping out, chatting and laughing as they went. Tony, Vikram, and Pete went with them, saying final farewells in the corridor. At last there was quiet, as Josh turned to regard the empty room. A last tidy-up, and they were done.

"Fuck it."

He had wanted the training to finish. Now there was an empty weekend to face. Going forward felt awful; going back in time was impossible.

Sophie. I could have saved you, if I'd been there.

There were six board-halves lying on the floor, the relics of three teams breaking simultaneously, boosting their self-belief, the confidence they could achieve any-thing they wanted. (*Like Sophie, whole and well.*) Slotting pieces together, he created three unbroken boards, then tossed them into the air. Lightning flew through his nerves as his fists cracked *one, one-two* and the shards were down once more.

"Not bad." Tony had returned. "Braced at the edges is one thing, but boards in the air? Good focus in those punches, well done."

Josh did his best Bruce Lee voice: "Boards... don't fight back."

"Uh-huh. So you're OK, then?"

"Sure am."

"Lying sod."

"Sure am."

"You know," said Tony, "Vikram could teach your course next week."

"I thought he was teaching genetic algorithms."

"Sylvie can do that."

"I don't know..."

"If it's the money, we can come to some arrangement. You bill me for next week as course development, and I'll pay you. You can actually write a course later. What do you say?"

In the end Tony would probably want more than five days' effort for the money, but this was still was a favour, and a big one.

"When do you need to know?" asked Josh.

He really didn't feel like teaching next week, but what else could he do?

"Sunday lunchtime, latest."

In the Regiment, before a mission, you came clean about any weakness, told the commander in private necessary, because the boss needed accurate information to obey the Seven-P Principle: Proper Prior Planning Prevents Piss-Poor Performance.

"OK. Good."

"So what are you up to this weekend, mate?"

Josh found himself wincing. He stared out the window over Docklands.

"Going to Hereford."

"If there'd been a change, you'd have told me, right?"

"Sophie's the same. I'm going to see her teacher, not sure why. Other than she asked."

"A good-looking lady teacher?"

Josh, not knowing the answer – Kath was female but he had no opinion about her looks – ignored the question.

"She wants me to meet the parents of another boy injured in the… When it happened. I think she's trying create a mutual support group."

"Maybe she's got the right idea. You ring me anytime, all right?"

"Yeah. Thanks."

"And call me lunchtime Sunday for sure."

"You got it."

Josh arrived twenty minutes early, but Kath Gleason was already sitting there, at a clean aluminium table in front of a café, at one end of a colonnade.

"Hello." She looked up from her milky tea. "I thought I'd get here in plenty of time."

"In case I came early, then changed my mind?"

"No, I just thought… you'd be super-punctual, and all."

Most often, Josh had missed parent-teacher evenings, while Maria had attended. Had she and Kath Gleason talked about his military service, and the itin-erant life of a corporate trainer? Or perhaps, since this was Hereford, Kath had drawn independent conclu-sions, for many of the ex-Regiment guys continued to live in the area, unable to tear themselves away from the life.

"You need another coffee, Ms Gleason? I mean Kath."

Lightning cracked somewhere in the distance.

"Jesus."

"Are you all right?" asked Josh.

"Electric storms worry me. Do you know we've had more this month already than the whole of last year? Which was more than the whole decade before that."

"Really?"

"Yes, and I–I'm sorry. Did you see Sophie last night?"

"This morning." He had driven from London before dawn. "Still the same."

"I'm so sorry."

"Drinks," said Josh. "I'll just be a minute."

This was such a bad idea.

Twenty minutes later, in Kath's car, they drove into a plain residential street, and pulled up before a house coated in pink pebbledash, the front door inset with amber glass. No sign of an alarm system; trusting to the high-mounted neighbourhood watchcams.

"Don't worry about what to say." Kath switched off the engine. "I'm sure they'll be nervous too."

The doorbell had no fingerprint recognition, but the door opened straightaway, pulled back by a blank-faced man.

"This is Carl, Marek's father." Kath gestured. "This is Josh."

Entering the front room, Josh scanned from near to far, and above, checking the overstuffed furniture and cluttered ornaments, the photographs on shelves. Then a thick-waisted woman came through from the rear, holding out her hand.

"Hello, I'm Irina. Good to meet you." She looked at her husband. "Carl, you want to offer our guests drinks?"

"Um, would you like something? Beer, vodka, tea?"

"I just made a pot," said Irina.

Josh and Kath chose tea; Carl, head down, went out back.

"I'm sorry about Carl." Irina gestured. "Please sit."

The placement was not tactical, but ordinary people had no thought of preventing clear shots in through their living-room window. Not liking it, Josh sat down. Kath blinked at him, then turned back to Irina.

"Marek's at home, I presume."

"In his bedroom. He spends his time there."

"Is he seeing someone?"

"The GP, every Thursday." Irina turned to Josh. "I'm sorry about your daughter. So sorry."

"Thank you."

Kath said, "Everyone's devastated. And our safety record is good, had been so good."

"So." Irina's expression closed in. "The boy who started it, from St Joseph's, not even the same school, but he was hanging around and no one cared."

"The pupils have siblings who attend other schools. At the start or end of a day, it's not unusual–"

Carl came in with a laden tea tray: mugs, teapot, milk in an open carton, a packet of plain chocolate McVities. Irina shook her head. Perhaps she had expected a milk jug and nicer cups. After Carl handed around the mugs, he stood looking down at his own tea, then walked out saying nothing, closing the door behind him. A clink sounded, and everyone waited, Josh expecting the crash of shattered crockery or glass; instead, there was nothing.

"Would you like to meet Marek?" said Irina finally. "I mean, if it would help."

"Sure." Josh put down his mug. "Are you going to call him down or–?"

"You could go up." Irina pointed to the hallway. "Upstairs on the right. You'll see."

"Just me?"

"Better than all of us." Kath tucked in her lower lip. "Don't want to look like a delegation."

Josh breathed with conscious control, getting ready.

"Upstairs. Right."

He felt disengaged from his body, almost floating on automatic up the stairs, not knowing how he felt about meeting the boy – the other victim of the incident that turned Sophie, his beautiful Sophie, into a small warm body with no mind. Beneath a bright graffiti notice – Marek's Room – he knocked.

"Hey, my name's Josh. Can I come in?"

Nothing.

"I'm Sophie Cumberland's father."

There was a reply that sounded like "Ugh", which was enough. He turned the handle.

Inside, on the wall behind the boy's chair was a poster of Fireman Carlsen in half armour, blade in hand. A white blanket covered the boy's lap. These were the things Josh noticed first, before he processed the too-pale, almost blue complexion, the bruise-purple hollowness of the eyes.

"Hi, Marek."

It took a second, but then Marek nodded, then he pushed PAUSE on the unfolded control pad attached to his phone, freezing the wallscreen display.

"What are you watching?"

"*Firefly*," he said.

"The old Joss Whedon thing, or the remake?"

"Huh? It's just out."

"The remake. Any good?"

"Still on the first chapter. There's no way out of Serenity Valley, no third-level choice till later."

"Uh, right."

When he'd been Marek's age, games, novels and movies had been separate things. Phone accounts had not been bank accounts; and phones were not computers.

Marek's gaze returned to the stilled image on screen. *This is stupid.*

They had nothing to say to each other. He should leave the poor kid alone, let him immerse himself in imagination, forget the reality of what occurred. Up on the wall, the flat muscularity of Fireman Carlsen – motto: *Sh*t hot with a blade* – was a mockery. It was the end-of-fight shot from the rematch against Slicer Stross, the Fireman's comeback from defeat, a classic fight. Why had no one taken the poster down?

"I just wanted to say I'm sorry about… everything."

"Sure." Marek's lower lip seemed to be swelling.

"Look, I can–"

Then Marek was sobbing. "He sliced me." He pulled the white blanket aside, pulled up his pyjama shirt, revealing white plastic, an abdominal shell. "They were slipping out, my things, my insides. They're soft and, and… wet."

"Yes."

"You don't know. Nobody–"

Josh's voice dropped. "I know."

Marek stopped. His eyes went wide as Josh touched the plastic with one finger.

"This is bad," Josh went on. "Real bad, and you can get through it. You ever heard of Ironman?"

With a sniff: "The remake?"

That was promising, the slyness of his humour.

"I mean the event. Run, bike, swim. You ever seen it on screen?"

"I guess."

"Friend of mine competes, fittest man I know. Had one of these" – Josh tapped the plastic – "for nearly two years."

"He's… all right?"

"Oh, yeah." Apart from rippling scars, the hollow curvature of skin and missing muscle. "Super, super fit."

"Oh."

Josh stood up. For some reason, the movement brought back his memory of the movie – game, what-ever – that Marek was watching, and the military disaster it began with.

"You know, if the events at the start hadn't hap-pened, there'd have been no story. They survived the hard times, got through them."

"Oh."

"Take it easy, my friend."

He let himself out of the room and went downstairs, not quite smiling, but aware that he might have done some good.

Sophie. Oh, Jesus, Sophie. Some good, but not enough.

Tears like acid came from nowhere.

Finally, Irina showed them out, her smile sad but her eyes bright; and she watched them until they reached the car, then closed the door. Josh reached for the door handle, but Kath stood unmoving. Then tipped her head back toward the house.

"Take a look at this."

She walked back to the wheelie bin out front, and pointed to one of the recycling boxes behind it. Then she raised the lid.

Vodka bottles filled the box.

Josh said, "He's having a hard time of it."

"Not Carl. He doesn't drink."

"But–"

The brightness in Irina's eyes. The near-permanent sad smile.

"Shit."

"I wish I could help, but I don't know how. Eileen would kill me if I tried."

As headmistress, Eileen O'Donoghue would be worried about legal implications.

"I don't know how, either."

Kath opened the car door. "Maybe you need someone to look after you."

This feels wrong. "You go on. I'm all right."

"What do you mean?"

"I'll walk back. Be glad of the exercise."

"It must be five kilometres."

"Right."

He turned away and began walking. After a minute, he heard Kath's car hum into life, then roll past him. She continued to the road's end, then sped up, and was gone from sight.

Just trying to help.

Maybe. Or maybe she was a vulnerable woman looking for a vulnerable man to connect with, which made sense only if the Cumberland marriage was over, which half of him couldn't accept while the other half took it as read.

Both halves felt awful.

• • •

He was in his own car when a call came through. The image was of Haresh Riley, known to everyone in the Regiment as Raghead Mick and seeming not to mind. Josh pressed to accept.

"Did Tony tell you to call me?"

"Tony who?"

"Shit."

"Oh yeah, Tony Shit. He did ring, come to think of it. Said you were a miserable fucker who wasn't going to see his mates unless they called him first."

Josh had no idea what to say.

"So the RV is the Bunch of Grapes, seventeen hundred precisely. Be there, or we'll have your nuts."

"You'll eat all the peanuts in the pub?"

"See? You're better already. Out."

The phone blanked out.

"Tony, Tony, Tony."

Silly bastard, trying to be helpful. And then there was Kath Gleason, and her *Maybe you need someone to look after you*. They were wrong, all of them; for the person who needed help was Sophie, but no one was doing anything, achieving anything, while she was trapped in a hell whose entranceway read Persistent Vegetative State, the abandonment of hope, a sentence no one seemed capable of commuting.

Bad, bad, bad.

At 5pm on a Saturday, the Bunch of Grapes was packed. By the bar, a huge wallscreen was showing the opening credits of *Knife Edge*, the thirteenth season. Regulars were seated at small round tables, on the bench seats near the walls, and at the counter, beer in hand, their attention on the screen. At the back, five quiet men were gathered around a table.

You're here. Thanks, lads.

He was on time, because if you agree to a rendezvous you keep it. With a glass-tipping signal to Haresh, he established that they had drinks already, and there was a drink waiting for him. It would be Diet Coke, and he could trust them not to spike it without telling him. Threading his way among the crowd, he checked the environment – harmless, cheerful, and noisy – and the five guys: Haresh, Kev, Vinnie, and Del, plus a wide-shouldered man he didn't know.

Haresh pointed: "Josh Cumberland, Matt Klugmann. Now drink."

"Hey," said Josh.

"Likewise." Matt's accent was American Southwest. He raised his beer. "Bottoms up, old chap."

"Jesus, don't let these buggers teach you how we speak."

"You mean, they might be less than truthful? Heaven forfend."

"Hey," said someone nearby. "Who are these fuckers?"

On the wallscreen, the picture changed to a news report. Two overweight men in suits were sitting at the bar counter, and one of them had the screen's remote in hand. It didn't take massive awareness to notice the tensing body language around the room, or the scowls as *Knife Edge* was replaced by pictures of President Brand failing to return Premier Han Lei's bow at the Geneva Conference.

"Asshole," muttered Matt.

"The guy who changed the picture?" asked Del. "Or your duly elected president?"

"Either one." Matt stared toward the screen, and a muscle at the side of his mouth jumped. "There."

The image changed back to *Knife Edge*.

"Er, we like to be more discreet," said Haresh. "Ghosts in the night, remember?"

"Shit, have I got cowflap on my boots again?"

"When don't you, good buddy?" said Del. To Josh: "Epsilon Force, been here four months, poor bastard."

The barman took the remote from the guy in the suit, shook it as though to demonstrate that it was broken, then put it below the counter. He made no attempt to change the image back.

"So who'd you piss off," asked Josh, "to end up among this lot?"

"Truth to tell, I can't rightly remember, there bein' so many."

"See?" said Del. "Fits right in."

"Too bad it's not a compliment," said Josh. "What have you been–?"

"Hush," said Haresh. "They're going back to the House after training. Should be interesting."

Everyone was looking at the screen, besides the businessmen finishing off their drinks, looking ready to leave.

"Why interesting?" asked Josh.

"Shit," said Del. "You missed the previous episode?"

"Well, yeah."

More important things to worry about.

"Two of the lightweights, André and Lynwood, had a little contretemps."

Matt mouthed the word: *contretemps*.

"Oh," said Josh. "OK."

Haresh leaned forward. "What he means is, Lynwood pissed down André's leg, standing at the urinal. In the training centre."

"And the cameras were there? Jesus."

"They're both on Fireman Carlsen's team," said Del, "so they're not likely to have to fight each other until much later. If they make it that far."

"Unless they go for it on their own time."

"Right. Exactly."

Knives and booze were banned from the Knife Edge House. But so were phones and wallscreens – only a few hardcopy fight mags allowed – which meant close confinement for sixteen semi-pro fighters, most from troubled childhoods or they wouldn't be there, although three fighters over the years had been PhDs, and a handful of pros in the Knifefight Challenge Federation held master's degrees.

A grudge match with its extra excitement accounted for the leaning forward in seats, anticipation as the drinkers focused on the wallscreen. Under other circumstances, Josh would have resonated with the mood.

"Come on, mate," said Haresh. "Let's check out the beer garden."

"All right."

On screen, two of the fighters, in the kitchen of the training house, were having at it with rolled-up hardcopy mags. Half of the regulars were laughing at the sight, but Del and Kev held still, along with several older men sitting quietly here and there. To some people, the use of improvised weapons to shatter a cheekbone or take out an eye was as basic as polymorphism and delegation in software design, or the inverse-power law of adaptive networks. Or perhaps Ghost Force thinking was a form of insanity, far removed from the thoughts of ordinary people.

Josh followed Haresh out into the garden. There were plenty of seats free, in contrast to the crowded indoor lounge.

"You remember Lofty getting us to read the *Go Rin No Sho*?" Haresh put his beer down on a table.

The *Go Rin No Sho*, or Book of Five Rings, was written by master strategist Miyamoto Musashi, the Japanese counterpart to Sun Tzu and von Clausewitz. Josh was never sure whether the three of them were geniuses or psychopaths. Musashi, unbeaten swordsman, stank with body odour, his skin scrofulous – after assassins tried to cut him down in the bath, he developed a phobia of bath-houses – and led an isolated, friendless life.

"That thing Musashi wrote" – Haresh sat down, scanning the environment – "about mastering one discipline gives you mastery of all? But then Lofty said, no matter how many times he hit the punchbag, he still couldn't play the fucking piano, because of specificity in training."

"And you said: Maybe you ought to take the gloves off, Lofty. Make it easier to hit the keys."

"Right."

"And Lofty made us do a hundred push-ups for laughing, as I recall."

"Yeah. So, look." As Haresh sipped beer, he maintained a clear view of their surroundings. "Marriages are casualties of war. Always have been."

"Except that I'm out of the life. Should've made things different."

"Civvie street. I have no idea how to cope with that. Not sure I'd want to."

"It's not so bad."

"Backstabbing shits for co-workers" – Haresh scowled – "and no sense of camaraderie."

"And no one trying to kill you."

"Good point. Look, you know software and combat. I'm wondering," said Haresh, "if you need a job.

Something you're good at, cause like Lofty said, training is specific."

"I'm doing stuff for Tony."

"He seemed to think you need a break. Something different from teaching corporates."

"Like what?"

"I notice you didn't say he was wrong."

Josh rubbed his chin with his thumb, and stared up at the sky. It was empty of inspiration.

"I got something," Haresh went on, "from our Epsilon Force pal in there."

"You mean Captain Implant?"

"Yeah. They don't travel commercial, not those guys."

Joining the SAS had been a huge challenge of physicality and mental toughness; joining Ghost Force, the Service-inside-the-Regiment, had stretched his intellect in unexpected ways; and their missions lay within MI6 as much as Army territory. Josh, along with Haresh and the rest, had worked espionage/sabotage ops, looking like civilians, sometimes just sitting in a coffee shop or railway station, running infiltration code from a covert phone.

The Americans had travelled a different route, and Epsilon Force owed as much to the Marine Corps as to their parent Delta Force, their troops armed with as much implanted tech as they could operate. Storming military installations guarded with smart weapons was their forte, and they could take down enemy AI-drones in the field; but subtle they were not. This Matt Klugmann might be able to crash the systems at Heathrow, but to walk through the airport scanners like an ordinary person would be impossible.

"So what, is this a job in the States?"

"No." Haresh nodded back toward the lounge. "Our friend has a cousin, lived here for ages. She asked Matt about a missing person job, and he put her onto Geordie Biggs."

"Geordie's got guys who can do that."

"Sure, and he'd like you to be one of them. Freelance basis, like your training gig with Tony." Haresh raised his glass. "You know Geordie. Always looking out for new opportunities."

"I wouldn't know where to start."

"Missing kid in London? It's a systems problem."

"The police might have official access to surveillance, but I don't. And won't they be looking for the kid?"

"Like they say in movies, you can work the case full-time, the cops can't. Also, you're better. Plus, you remember Andy's sister? Petra Osbourne?"

"Er, yeah."

He hadn't seen Petra since Andy's memorial service. There'd been no funeral, on the basis that Andy's body had been vaporised during a hostage rescue on the Ivory Coast, with nothing left to bury. Not unless you shipped a few tonnes of soil and rubble home, for whatever organic traces remained mixed up inside.

"She's still with the Met. Always seemed to have a thing for you."

"As I recall, she's a lesbian."

"So what does that say about your girlish charms, mate? Anyway, she's bound to help, provided you ask nicely."

"Fuck."

"Uh-huh." Haresh held up his phone. "Is that 'fuck' as in 'loadsa-fuckin-thanks-to-all-my-mates-for-doing-me-a-good-turn'? The kind of thanks I can pass on to Geordie?"

Josh rolled his shoulder muscles as if loosening up for a fight. Then he blew out a breath.

"Yeah. That kind. Thank you."

"Any time."

[TEN]

From the time he parked in front of the gate and waved to the camera, to sitting down in a leather armchair in what the maid – yes, a maid – called the drawing room, he felt out of his depth. But taking in the cream and pale-yellow walls, polished wooden floor and expensive fittings, it felt more and more impersonal, like a hotel, not a home. And for all that Philip Broomhall might be rich, he commanded fewer resources than senior military officers, the best of whom were always approachable.

He waited, something he was good at, comparing this to the cramped, messy flat in Brixton where Mum and Dad had raised him: overflowing with cushions and tattered books, housework readily put aside in favour of a chat or reading. The military had drilled neatness into him; otherwise Josh was his parents' son, and they had raised him in a warmer place than this.

"Mr Cumberland? Josh? I'm Philip."

"Sir." Josh controlled his grip as they shook. "Good to meet you."

"What I want is simple. My son is missing and I need him back."

"Understood. Clearly the police haven't got any-where, or I wouldn't be here."

"I'm told you're an expert."

"I can construct specific searches, use profiling, and talk to people who might avoid the police." ELINT and HUMINT, electronic intelligence and human intelli-gence, were grist to the mill; and he had access to algorithms and bots undreamt of by Scotland Yard's Se-rious Systems Crimes Unit. "Is there any specific person who'd want to do you harm?"

"No, and there's not been any kind of ransom de-mand. Richard slipped out of the car by himself, you know."

"I'd like to speak to the driver."

"Lexa's here. You'll be able to talk to her."

"Thank you. I don't suppose there were cameras in the car?"

"Absolutely not. I'm often on the phone discussing confidential matters, or riding with business partners I'm negotiating with. No recordings permitted, ever."

Broomhall headed for a cabinet, picked up a whisky glass, and raised an eyebrow.

"Not for me, thanks," said Josh. "I'll read the file, but are there any friends of Richard's that spring to mind?"

"He was in the chess club at school." Broomhall poured dark rum. "Dropped the science club because he preferred just to read by himself, he said."

Clubs, not individuals.

"It would help if I can go through his room. Have the police done that?"

"No, they bloody well have not."

"You're worried about him. About Richard."

"He's soft." Broomhall's left hand rested on his own heavy abdomen. "Not tough like... I work to keep my

family. Since his mother... I'm a widower, you see."
Swirling rum in his glass, he stared into the liquid.
"He's important to me. Understand that. I'm not sure
Richard does."

"I get it. Was there anything troubling Richard particularly?"

If there had been, Broomhall probably hadn't noticed.

"He was normal, except for going to see that bloody
shrink, and then he didn't even make it home. What
do you make of that? Bitch is still practicing, still screwing other patients' minds."

"I'll need details of that as well."

"So I hope you're a damn sight better than she
turned out to be."

"Why do you say that?"

"Obviously because–Well, because the same person
recommended you both, but in your case he checked
more carefully. So he's assured me."

"Who's that, if you don't mind me asking?"

"More of a second opinion. I came up with the idea
originally, got the name of Biggs' company from someone. But I passed your name to a friend who works in
the DTI, and he tells me you're good."

"Me personally?"

"That's what I mean."

There were civil servants who could check special
forces records, but not in the Department of Trade and
Industry. Broomhall knew less about his friend than he
realised.

"Is there anyone I should be talking to besides the
driver, Lexa?"

"The rest of the staff, I guess. Lexa can show you
round." Broomhall took his phone from his pocket, and
said into it: "Mr Cumberland is ready."

"Thank you. What about Richard's school? I don't know for sure yet, but a visit might help."

"I'll let the headmaster know. He should be helpful, the amount we pay each year. I pay."

Then a broad-shouldered woman walked through an archway, and nodded to Josh.

"Where would you like to start?" She had a Birmingham accent.

"Richard's room, I guess."

"I'll see you later." Broomhall gestured with his phone, and intricate tables and graphs of data lit up on the wallscreens. "Let me know if there's a problem."

But his attention was already lost in the world of corporate finance.

In the hallway, Josh shook hands with Lexa. Her grip was stronger than Broomhall's. Then she led the way upstairs, along a corridor with panelled walls and ugly expensive paintings, to a door that opened onto a massive tidy bedroom.

"Like a big hotel suite, ain't it?" She pointed at the neat shelves. "That's not the maids. Richard keeps everything organised himself."

"Maids."

"Yeah. It's a far cry from Selly Oak, where I started."

"I was thinking the same kind of thing. Brixton, in my case."

"Your old man a drunk, or anything like that?"

"No. Good family."

"Then you probably had it better than young Richard, for all the old man's money."

A Navajo rug lay on the floor. No posters on the walls. Nothing left scattered around.

"I'm just going to poke about for a bit." He slid open

a drawer. "Christ, that's neat."

Folded underwear, squared off. Everything was right angles.

"He's a bright kid." Lexa looked at him. "You want me to leave you alone?"

"No, you're all right there. Is this why he was seeing the shrink? Obsessive-compulsive?"

"That wasn't it." Lexa raised her eyebrows. "Hoplo-phobia, allegedly."

"Why allegedly?"

"How many people do you know that aren't afraid of a blade?"

"Good point."

"You saw the weapon on Broomhall's belt?"

"Yeah. Nice hilt."

"Any idea how many times he's duelled with it?"

Josh did, but said: "Tell me."

"Exactly none. But he has issued challenge, twice. Both times, to guys even less likely than him to fight. They have enough money, they can afford the fines."

"So you think Richard's not really a weapon hater?"

"Oh, he hates them all right," said Lexa. "I'm just not sure it's a problem. You know Birmingham? Selly Oak and King's Heath?"

"Sure." Josh smiled. "Ansells Mild and pork scratch-ings."

"And burglary and drugs, when I was young. Before the Blade Acts. In some ways it's better now."

"Huh." Josh was checking the wardrobe and cup-boards. "No sports kit."

"Not Richard."

Intellectual, physically soft, alone on the streets of London. Poor combination.

"So, are you done?"

In his pocket, he thumbed his phone. Wallscreen and processor stacks winked blue then shut down.

"All done," he said.

"So that's why the old man called you in."

"What do you mean?"

"I served in Tibet. 3 Mercian." Lexa nodded toward the wallscreen. "Came across quiet guys with eyes like yours, could do things like that."

"Like what?"

"Uh-huh. You just downloaded the entire system logs. And they got firewalls, firebreaks, shields. Crypto up the wazoo."

"Is that going to be a problem?"

"Christ, no." She grinned. "Means you stand a chance of finding the poor little bugger."

He parked in a multi-storey in Guildford. The hourly rate was ridiculous, double if you recharged your vehicle, but the batteries were running low. Sitting in the car, he called Petra Osbourne, directing her image to the windscreen heads-up display.

"Hey, lover." Her image was ghostly. "Haven't seen you for a long time."

"Too long. Sorry."

"For what? Hang on." She looked away. "Will you guys slow down? Control, with your partner. Save your power for the bags."

There were muffled sounds.

"Sorry," she went on. "It's hard for them to understand the difference, when to be a partner and when to be an opponent. So, what favour are you ringing up to ask?"

"Who are you teaching? Cops or kids?"

"Kids. I'm not on duty till twenty hundred. Here, take a look." A translucent image washed across the windscreen: children, aged from maybe eight to fifteen, with sparring gloves and headgear. "Doing some good."

"Yes, you are."

Some of the kids needed self-esteem, properly earned. Others needed to physically defend themselves. Petra and her friends taught for free.

"Huh. Mark, take over, willya?" The image shifted, her face filling the windscreen. "So you're after a favour. If it's a blowjob you want, the answer's no."

"Jesus, Petra."

"But I know some nice guys who wouldn't mind–"

"It's a missing kid."

"Official police case?"

"Uh-huh. Along with all the thousands of others on file."

"And you're taking a special interest?"

"Yeah. I'm putting together a ghost search, gait analysis, the whole thing."

Anyone who watched crime dramas knew how to use wigs, cap-veils, and changes of clothing to slip through surveilled crowds. Fewer would change the way they walked.

"And you want me to slip your little querybot into the London Transport net."

"You have authority to do that, Sergeant Osbourne?"

"Let's say it's not impossible. When's the code going to be ready?"

"A first cut tonight, if you let me have two attempts. Otherwise, I'm still gathering info. I'll have version two ready in the morning."

"Send that to me tomorrow, then."

A rough search tonight might save Richard a night on the streets. But this was her deal.

"Done."

"All right. Daniel! I said control, not miss by a mile–"

Her image flickered out, leaving only the sight of concrete and shadow, an anonymous urban car park that could have been anywhere, impersonal as Richard Broomhall's bedroom.

Hey, kid. Where the hell are you?

Yet in his mind's eye was not a teenage youth on London's streets, but a ten year-old girl with rice-paper skin, body intubated, surrounded by relentless machines that kept her organs working, however much they yearned to stop.

Where was the sense in any of it?

Silver sheets of rain were washing from the sky as he pulled in to the lay-by. Other cars hissed past on the dual carriageway, and good luck to them. He was going to stay parked until the worst was past. This was yet another flash storm in a year of storms and whirlwinds, the worst of driving conditions. No problem for Josh: with a few commands, he turned his windscreen into a full-on display, cranking up a programming environment with debugging and simulation panes, the lot. Unfurling a keyboard and coding glove, he set up his querybot as nested shells, and began with the inference engine. Soon he was in programming Zen, absorbed in the code, sketching in prototypes and test harnesses, working fast because he knew these frameworks and face it, he was good.

Finally he paused, considered calling the shrink that Richard had seen, rejected the idea – it would take a minimum of fifteen minutes to restore his thoughts afterwards, to get back in the zone – then changed his mind again, and placed the call.

"Hello. My name's Josh Cumberland. I'm working on behalf of Philip Broomhall."

On the windscreen, her coffee-coloured skin was translucent, the eyes somewhere between nut-brown and honey. She nodded, both smiling and serious.

"I've been expecting someone to call."

"Well, I'm not with the police, but I am investigating on Philip Broomhall's behalf. If you'd like to verify, I'm happy to wait offline."

"But would he accept a call from me? Tell me the name of the agent you're working through."

"You mean Geordie Biggs?"

"All right, Mr Cumberland. Now I don't know where Richard went, nor do I know the specific trigger that set him off. I do know there was an issue to be explored, bullying at school, and the more I think about it, the more relevant it feels."

"That's the kind of thing I hoped you could enlighten me with."

"You could step through the recording of our session, assuming that will be a help."

"Um, yes, please. Transmit via any archiving format you like."

Her eyes seemed to keep growing larger.

"I'd rather meet face to face. There are nuances to pay attention to in the recording, behavioural signals to highlight, that kind of thing."

"OK. You're in Elliptical House, is that right?"

"Not this afternoon. I live in what some people call the smart end of Kilburn."

"I can meet you there." He looked at the side windows, rippling with water but no longer awash, as the storm lessened. "Your place, or a bar?"

"How about a restaurant? Do you like Jamaican

food? Later, say at seven?"

"Perfect."

"OK, I'm appending details. There's a red star on the map, highlights the place."

"Works for me."

"Look forward to meeting you."

The attachment pinged and opened as the comm pane closed.

Wow.

Broomhall blamed her, so she would want to deflect that, get Josh on her side. If she was genuine in wanting to help him find Richard, then the rest was irrelevant.

He realised he was staring where her image had been, as if trying to summon her back.

Bad idea. Concentrate.

But she was the first good thing to distract him for a long time.

Browns and oranges dominated the restaurant. Each table bore a bonsai palm tree. Josh smiled as Suzanne Duchesne addressed the staff by their first names, and they responded likewise. A Jamaican waiter called Clyde seated them next to the wall, away from the other diners, giving them a quiet zone.

From her shoulder bag, Suzanne drew a portable screen and unrolled it, spreading it across the table. While they waited for drinks to arrive – some kind of tea – they made small talk: how long she had lived in Kilburn (four years), where he was staying (a budget Travelodge off the M4), and who would win the general election.

"Let's see." Josh looked down at the lifeless screen. "Sharon Caldwell is female, lesbian, an atheist-rationalist with two PhDs. Then there's Billy Church, aka Fat Billy, man of the people, beer lover and fight fan, already in office, and he's just announced tax cuts."

"You think there's no contest?"

"I wish there were."

Clyde brought the tea, then left them alone. Breathing in warm scents from the kitchen, Josh watched as Suzanne brought the portable screen to life. Then she tapped her phone, and the unfurled screen showed a room interior, Suzanne sitting at an angle to Richard Broomhall. Josh put his own phone on the table; both handsets winked amber, establishing a sharespace. In the image, she was putting young Richard at ease; in reality, she was tugging down her sleeve which had pulled up, just by centimetres.

Few people would have noticed; but Josh needed only a glimpse to take in the silver scarring.

"You want audio?" Suzanne took out her earbeads. "Or just transcription for now?"

Printed text – her words in red, Richard's in white – scrolled down a side pane.

"Hmm. Can we get rid of both for the moment?"

"All right."

"This will help the automated search." As he tapped his phone, dots sprinkled themselves across Richard's moving image, then lines joined the dots, like moving wire frames. "Improve the motion analysis."

"On CCTV, you mean? Like on the Tube?"

"Uh-huh. My bots can look for subtle things like – see that? The way he rubbed his nose? If that's a habit, we've just increased our chances."

"Interesting." Her polished-chestnut eyes contained golden flecks. "Emphasising process over content.

That's close to the way I work, because I'm as interested in his posture and voice tone as in the actual words."

"But if he'd said anything about where he might go, you would have picked it up. And the police have seen this?"

"Yes, so they should have picked up any local references I missed."

When she focused on him, it was like the total universe concentrating its attention; when she looked at the screen, she was absorbed in the images. To Josh, this was extraordinary.

"Here we are." Clyde bore plates of spicy bean stew with rice and bread. "Enjoy, enjoy."

"We will."

"Smells terrific," said Josh.

And the taste burst into his mouth, slowing him right down. Suzanne blanked the screen – now it was the food she concentrated on – and they made little conversation until their plates were mostly empty. She pushed her plate aside just moments before he finished too.

"I don't understand–" he would have liked to enjoy the warm feeling a while longer, but they were here for a reason – "what you mean by process over content. In your work, that is."

"Look at this interaction." She worked her phone, bringing the screen back to life and skipping to a time-stamped moment. "Here, we're discussing Richard's reaction to blades."

The words scrolled down the transcript pane.

"See here?" Suzanne slowed the movie down. "That gesture with his left hand, cupped toward his stomach? An unconscious reaction to my question, in parallel to the words he spoke, telling its own story."

Josh frowned. "Gestures like that mean something?"

"Movement and timing are most important. Here, his left hand – under control of his right cerebral hemisphere – indicates he gets an automatic feeling in his stomach at the thought or sight of knives. It's an internal reaction, call it gut feeling, and it's real because every major organ has receptors for neuropeptides, almost like another nervous system."

"Really?"

"When people say something is *heartfelt*, it's often more literal than they think. Figures of speech have to come from somewhere."

Josh had felt his guts roiling in circumstances most people would never know. Visceral feelings were intense; he knew they were real.

"So how does that help you?"

"Everything is mental modelling. Even a black shirt in the open air reflects less light than a white shirt indoors, so something as basic as colour is a neural process."

"Computation," he said.

"Exactly. By using Richard's imagination, I could have got him to focus on the fear-feeling, experience it as a loop... See, you haven't noticed the feeling of your sock on your left foot until I mentioned it, because a constant sensation just fades away. So a gut feeling doesn't literally keep looping around, but while it's strong it feels that way."

"All right." Josh was smiling, still aware of his foot.

"In his imagination, I could've got him to spin the feeling in the opposite way, add some visualisation, and his fear reaction would be gone. Sounds too simple to work, yet it does."

"But you didn't do that."

"No, look. I taught him something else, but not for blades specifically." She flicked through thumbnail stills, then jumped the main pane to another part of the session. "Here, Richard is imagining something, and see how his eyes focus on a point in space? Even though he's seeing a picture in his mind? The entorhinal cortex has a component called the spatiotemporal grid which— Well, I'll save the neurology lecture for later, shall I?"

"If you like." The idea of a later was appealing to Josh. "So what happened next?"

"I taught him to experience the picture differently. Push it off to a different location and imagine it flaring bright, then washing out."

Josh started blinking, very fast.

Gun coming up, half the face exploding and my God he's just a kid—

"—out now, breathe in, let the feeling out, Josh, that's right, and you're fine now."

"Jesus." He rubbed his face, sweat-slick as if in a sauna. "Sorry."

Clyde started to approach. "Sir? Are you all right?"

"He's fine." Suzanne waved him back. "We're doing OK."

"Shit." Not the language he would normally use over dinner, not with someone like this. "I don't know what happened. Something took me back—"

"You've had counselling, after battlefield trauma."

"I guess that's what you'd call it. Sure."

"And they used similar techniques with you, working successfully almost all of the time, is that right?"

"Sure." He rubbed his mouth. "Most of the time."

"So you had a little resonance of memory, and it's all gone now."

"It… it has gone. I feel OK."

"Good."

"How did you do that?"

"Well." Her smile and gaze hummed with mystery, deep as voodoo. "Call it magic if you like."

Casting some kind of spell, for sure.

Suzanne noted, as they walked, the way Josh cast his attention outward, in what looked like a trained pattern: left-right-left, starting close and extending to the distance. He made a soft humming noise as he spotted something about a building, then continued scanning.

"What did you notice?" she had to ask.

"Huh? Oh, those flats, how the building went from stables to warehouse to homes over the centuries."

"You're kidding." She saw the black iron crosses, part of the supports that held swelling brickwork in place. "I guess the place is old."

"Look how the place used to be mercantile, and before that rural, because the roads follow the natural contours. See?"

"Hmm. Interesting."

So he could overlay mental pictures across reality, make deductions that were not obvious; and if he was the kind of software expert she thought, he could wrap himself in highly abstract, creative visualisations of complex systems she could not imagine. This was not how she had imagined an ex-soldier would be.

"Where is your car?" she asked.

"Not far."

From a tiny motion of his head, she realised it was behind them somewhere, and that his walking her home took him further from the vehicle. It was good that she could read these nuances, because in some ways Josh Cumberland was unknowable, his physicality breathtaking, diverting her from the reason for their meeting.

"Have you thought what's going to happen once you find Richard?"

"Er, taking him home seems like a good idea."

"It wasn't me he was running from."

"No." Josh stopped and scanned in all directions, before turning to her. "I won't take him back into danger."

"I believe the physical danger comes from his school. The home environment is stressful in other ways."

"Yeah, I got that. Doesn't make Broomhall a bad man. I mean, he's money-grabbing and corporate, but I've met worse."

"We agree. He's just different from his son."

"Ah. Right."

Again, he scanned the street. Did he ever stop?

"I'm going to ask you a favour." Her heart, warm in her chest, reminded her of their conversation, the neuropeptide basis of emotion. "Let me help you look for Richard."

Was it for Richard's sake she was asking? Or to spend more time with this man?

Doesn't matter to Richard. We just need to get him back.

"I'll call you," he said.

They walked on, reaching the door to her apartment house too soon. She went inside, stopped in the hallway, and looked back out. Josh gave a little fingertip wave, an informal salute, and slipped away. It felt as if something had been pulled out of her.

Part of her awareness, throughout the meal, had observed the natural matching of their body language, the interlocking rhythm of microgesture, and the subliminal courting dance of pheromones, their effect surfacing in the dilation of eyes, the flaring of nostrils, the inability of either person to look away.

Josh Cumberland.

The name rolled around in her brain, warming her, threatening her equilibrium. Perhaps he was good news, perhaps he was bad; what she could not do was ignore him.

[ELEVEN]

A plain budget hotel room at five in the morning. How often had Josh woken up in places like this? Sometimes – when rich corporates paid his expenses – he slept in five-star elegance; other times it was hard soil or rock beneath his sleeping bag, the Brecon Beacons or Tibetan Alps or the expanding Sahara, snow or heat, always different. But like a turtle in its shell, he was always at home, because of the discipline, the routines he carried everywhere.

Drinking tap water from a plastic cup, he unrolled his screen and keypad, thumbed his phone to life, and began amending his search arguments, changing his choice of algorithms based on the new patterns he had to look for. Most of the framework remained unaltered, while his coding changes had more to do with the London Transport network, an environment he had not hacked before. Soon his more-than-querybot – call it a stealthbot – was ready to ship.

"Hey, Petra," he dictated, his phone turning speech into text, "if you could load this inside the interface shield, we might save a missing kid."

He sent the message, his stealthbot attached inside an

anonymous archive file, along with a manifest that made it look like an ordinary in-house complex written by the Transport Police.

For a few minutes he waited, on the off-chance that Petra was awake at this hour, then he shut everything down. What he needed was to keep fit and maintain his reflexes, so he pulled a pillow from the bed and a cheap soccer ball from his bag. It would not look like a fight gym to most people; but it was enough.

A cat-stretch press-up, slow at first, then fluid and fast: two hundred and fifty Hindu push-ups in fifteen minutes. It was deep knee-bends for the next quarter hour, five hundred Hindu squats. Then, putting the pillow on the floor, he arched backward, weight on his feet and the top of his head at first, before stretching to press forehead and nose into the pillow. He held position for four minutes, following it with a forward bridge and ab crunches to finish.

Then he was ready to fight.

When a struggle goes to the ground and you're on top, the guy underneath is squirming – which was what the football reproduced. Josh worked rolls and flips and reversals, grappling manoeuvres on the floor with the ball twisting beneath him. On his feet, he practiced rapid-fire hand drills, adding elbows, knees and powerful kicks. Finally, he drew his knife, and worked the combos with blade in hand, over and over on imaginary enemies; and at last he was done, taking huge breaths to slow down, his body encased in warm, slick sweat. Then he spun, a half-second before a thump rocked the door.

He checked through the spyhole, then opened up in silence.

"It's 6.30 in the morning." The guy in the corridor was round and soft-bodied. "You could have some consider–"

Then his eyes triangulated on Josh's blade.

"I like to keep sharp." Josh smiled. "Stay a cut above the rest."

"Er... Look..." A swallow. "I... Um."

"My apologies."

Josh closed the door, shutting the guy out. There was a long pause, then stumbling footsteps receded.

Before going to bed, he had filled two canteens with water from the bathroom tap, and mixed in purifying powder, because you could never trust a hotel to have clean filters. Now he drank, half a litre at first, then another half with powdered peas and milk mixed in, before checking his messages. Petra had responded, but not in the way he wanted.

"Sorry, Josh. You've obviously worked hard on this one. But there's been a couple of, well, questionable uses of privileges recently. Internal Investigations are looking motivated. Sorry again."

And that was it. No help from Petra.

"Bollocks."

Then he felt chill. It might have been the sudden cooling-off, his body still inside its layer of sweat; or perhaps it was something else.

She changed her mind overnight.

Not only that, but the message was way too polite for her. Had someone warned her off?

Sluicing off in the shower was a simple pleasure, always enhanced by a workout beforehand; but now that his plans were derailed, he could have scheduled exercise for later and got something else going instead. However wonderfully his querybot was crafted, if he couldn't insert it inside the official surveillance systems, its functionality was useless.

There was another way in, but he did not want to try it yet, not without knowing why Petra had backed off from helping him. What he wanted – as though he needed an excuse – was to talk to Suzanne Duchesne again. And he had promised to call her; but she probably thought that meant at a civilised hour.

So hurry up and wait.

He cranked up text-only and read from the autobiography of Lyoto Machida, a Japanese-Brazilian fighter from the civilised days of MMA cage fights. The samurai mindset was admirable, except for the daily drink-your-own-urine ritual, allegedly traditional. Josh glanced at the dregs of his pea-and-milk shake, and shook his head.

Then, hoping that Suzanne was an early riser, he placed the call.

"Hey. How are you this morning?"

"A little surprised that you're calling."

"You mean, at this hour. I don't have any news."

"All right."

"You must be busy. Can I buy you lunch later on?"

"I'll be at Elliptical House working with clients. Is two pm too late?"

"Perfect."

"Then I'll see you."

"See you. Cheers."

Outside the window a silver summer rain began to fall, rippling with sunlight, like magic. Probably it was there all the time, the wonder, but people were too busy to see it.

Two o'clock. Lunch.

"Oh, yeah."

Good news. He could almost forget Sophie lying comatose, the beeping life support, or the wreckage of his marriage to Maria, testament to a decade or more of bad decisions.

Like hell he could forget.

The Tube carriage rocked, half full, as Josh checked the hidden and not-so-hidden cameras. They were potential routes into the surveillance net – most transmitted realtime to relays and servers outside – but too restricted for what he needed. At the far end of the carriage, two men bumped into each other, hands going for hilts, then stopping as they rethought their situation. An abbreviated apology, a delayed nod, and they moved away from each other, eye contact broken.

Josh's phone gave a characteristic vibration.

Who's sending this?

There were people looking relaxed or bored or hacked off by their jobs; none looked away suddenly at his gaze. Someone professional then, who had redfanged a short-range message while his attention was on the two guys. There was no easy way of telling who it was; and besides the train was slowing. This was his intended stop.

"Victoria Station. Mind the gap."

He could have played tag games, trying to flush out the message sender, but instead he got out as planned, keeping in the midst of other passengers as he ascended to the mainline station. Far outside rush hour, the concourse was still busy. Hunching his shoulders, he pulled out his phone, tilting it so no surveillance cams could see the screen.

TELL YOUR GIRLFRIEND

Slipping the phone into his pocket, he headed

outside, walked the single block to the red brick cathedral, and went inside. Heavy darkness seemed a permanent denizen in here. In a pew at the back, he sat down, then knelt, cupping his phone again to read the words in full.

TELL YOUR GIRLFRIEND TO LEAVE HER PHONE AT HOME. BIG EARS EVERYWHERE.

Getting to his feet, he crossed to one of the shadowed side-chapels, and stopped at a metal stand bearing rows of candle holders, some two-thirds in use. He used cash, bought a candle and lit it, then pressed it into place. Call it cover, acting like the real worshippers. Or call it a prayer to an imaginary entity he had no belief in: a plea to the universe for a miracle, for Sophie's sake.

Get out of here.

Leaving, he kept his head down, using natural movement to disguise the way he scanned the environment, checking everyone, detecting no patterns, knowing that the real watchers were everywhere: lenses ranging in size from pinholes to golf balls, overtly on posts and hidden in nooks, outside and inside the buildings, reporting every second of every day on the ant-like behaviour sweeping through their fields of view. A camera does not blink; a server does not sleep.

Why was someone eavesdropping on Suzanne? And who was the helpful message from, if it was real?

He wandered into Stag Place, buffeted by wind – some kind of tunnel effect produced by the glass buildings – and found Elliptical House, its outline living up to its name. Inside, a receptionist with weightlifter muscles nodded at Josh's name, and said he was on the visitor's list.

"Fourth floor. Lift is over there."

"Thanks."

There was a mutual nod, a recognition of physical potential; then Josh made his way to the lift, wondering what Richard Broomhall had thought as he made this journey, and what had flipped inside his head to make him act so differently afterwards. On the fourth floor, he found a mother-and-daughter pair just leaving Suzanne's office. Consulting room. Whatever.

"Hey," he said.

"Hey." Suzanne watched her clients go, then: "Come in while I grab my things."

A smart remark rose up inside him, about grabbing her things, and he pushed it back down. As he followed her inside, he checked the observation vectors – the placement of the four internal office cameras was obvious – then turned his phone towards her, its screen hidden from surveillance.

LEAVE YOUR PHONE HERE

A blink of polished-chestnut eyes; a raised eyebrow.

"Least I can do is buy you a sandwich," he said.

"A sandwich? Is that all you're offering?"

"I could have made cheese sarnies in my hotel, brought them along in a plastic box."

"Lucky escape for me, then."

By this time they were out in the fourth-floor lobby, and Suzanne was checking that her door was shut, while her phone remained inside atop her desk. She looked at Josh; he dipped his chin, then asked her about the rubbish strike, whether she thought the dustbin collections might restart any time soon, and if she had seen any rats around where she lived.

"Not as yet, but I'm hoping," she said inside the lift. "Think of all those phobic patients I'll be gaining."

"All coughing at you and spreading their bubonic plague."

"There is that."

Outside, they strolled past the mall, then Josh pointed as if suggesting a place to eat, and led her between a glass pillar and the main exterior wall.

"Dead zone," he said. "Your phone is compromised, or so I've been told."

"Compromised?" Her expression looked like the beginning of a smile; then she glanced to her left. "The police gave me a replacement handset."

"We're on the same side."

Except that my search methods are illegal.

"So what now?"

"We go to lunch. I'm going to ask you to come somewhere with me tonight, and we can talk about that openly. If you do say yes, can you remember to forget your phone?"

Her smile was unrestrained.

"Josh Cumberland, you have a way with hypnotic language."

"Er..."

Some ninety minutes later, in another dead zone free from surveillance, Josh made a call.

"Tony? How're you doing?"

"OK. Just on a break."

"Good guess on my part."

"Guess, my arse. Some of us are organised, stick to a timetable."

"Uh-huh. Does Terry B still have his black cab?"

"Big Tel? Course he does. Want me to have a word with him?"

"I was hoping to book a taxi for, say, six tonight."

"Christ, leave things till the last minute, why don't you? This job working out, is it?"

"Keeping me busy."

"And you need Tel? It's that sort of gig?"

"Just for the wheels."

"Huh. Call you right back."

"OK."

At twenty past six, Suzanne stepped from a doorway in a Bloomsbury sidestreet, and slid into the black cab that had just pulled up. Josh, on the bench-seat beside her, smiled at her.

"We can talk." He pointed at the ceiling-mounted cam. "We won't be recorded."

"Is that legal?"

"Not in the slightest."

From the driver's seat in front of the plexiglass partition, a big hand waved in greeting.

"He's a friend," Josh added.

"If the police check his video log," said Suzanne, "he'll be in trouble."

"Actually, there'll be a perfectly good-looking record of someone making this journey, with the correct background showing through the windows and all, but it won't be us. Two other people, having a harmless conversation, and the lighting on their faces just right, matching the light from outside."

She did not really know this man. Perhaps it was worth remembering that.

"So are we going to see someone called Petra, or is that more subterfuge?"

"That's real. She's a police officer, and she can help us. But not by staying inside the rules."

"Oh."

"Her being a career police officer and all, she might be reluctant. Maybe someone who understands people really well can persuade her to slip a querybot into the system."

"Was that *persuade* as in *manipulate*?"

"Surely you wouldn't act unethically, Dr Duchesne."

"Huh. So that's the only reason you wanted me along."

"Well." There was something about the muscles in Josh's face that made his smile compelling. "What other reason could there be?"

She smiled back.

It was half an hour and one traffic jam later when they stood outside the railway arches, watching the taxi drive off. Rain from an earlier shower was dripping from Victorian archways; their brickwork thrumming with the sound of electromag trains sliding overhead. Broken furniture, rusted junk, and dark-stained weeds were prevalent. Welcome to Wandsworth: so near to MI6 HQ, that severe and glistening fortress, and yet a world away.

Perhaps it was Josh's past that had her thinking about the intelligence services; in any case, when he knocked four times on a metal door – thump, thump-thump, thump – she had to fight down a giggle.

"Don't tell me it's a secret signal."

"Just don't knock it."

Was that a pun? She might have asked, but a small hatch scraped back, something silver shone – checking out with a mirror, not exposing an eyeball – then the hatch clunked shut, and the door swung inward.

"Petra teaches paranoia." Josh's tone lightened, but not in humour. "The kind that keeps you alive when they're really out to get you."

"Oh. That kind."

Inside, old khaki mats stretched across a stone floor. Battered-looking punchbags hung from chains. In front of the class stood a lean, fit-looking woman wearing old sweats, her hands wrapped in stained pink bandages.

"See Petra's hand wraps?" Josh kept his voice low. "As dainty she gets."

The stains looked to be old blood. *Petra's, or other people's?* Two rows of men and women in pyjama-like white outfits stood ready, intent on Petra.

"Why isn't she dressed like her students?"

"Actually" – Josh pointed to one corner where a smaller number waited, in tattered shorts and T-shirts – "they're the regulars."

Also, they were smiling. In front of the others, Petra was talking with hands clasped behind her back.

"So in your dojo" – she nodded to the black belts in the group – "you teach, what do you call it, focused awareness."

"*Zanshin.*"

"Right. While on the street, awareness is your first weapon. Run if you can, fight if you have to, in which case fight to win."

The black belts nodded first, then the others. Beside Suzanne, Josh was failing to stop his grin widening.

"And then there's distancing and timing, right? What do you guys call them?"

"*Ma-ai* and–"

"YAAHHH!" She whipped something silver against a black belt's throat. "You're fucking dead."

Then she had spun away and was standing beyond kicking range, blade held high.

Baise-moi.

It was rare for Suzanne's thinking to be shocked back into French.

"Ah, Petra." Josh shook his head, teeth bared in a fighter's smile. "You're good."

The karate guys looked pale.

"We do street shotokan," said Petra. "No white *gis*, no tag-you're-it play-sparring. This is the real tradition, people." She threw the knife – *thunk* – into pockmarked chipboard. "And next time someone's holding a weapon and giving you the soothing verbals, you'll know precisely what they're fucking up to, won't you?"

Nods, and acknowledgements sounding like "*Uss.*" Another Japanese word.

"All right, partner up." Petra pointed. "Every visitor with one of my gang. One-step drills, coming up. And... go."

The karate guys started to drop into fighting stances – then froze as the others started spitting, waving their arms and yelling: "You fucking want this?" "Who you fuckin' lookin' at?" "Come on then. Come on."

Then the gesticulating fighters leaped into the attack, and the defenders fell back with clumsy blocks. Only two of the karate guys – one black belt, one brown – roared into the onslaught and slammed their opponents back with heavy punches.

"Good." Petra nodded to the pair. "Everyone else, shape up."

Josh was chuckling.

I'm cold and sweating, about to pee myself, and he finds this funny? My God.

For the rest of the session, Petra dropped the disorienting antics but kept the pressure on. By the end, the visitors were responding well, their previous fighting reflexes now operating under conditions of adrenal overload, laid down in the amygdala, the brain's emergency response system. The old training would now kick in under circumstances where they might have frozen before. It wasn't any kind of cognitive strategy that Suzanne had instilled in her clients; but the mechanism was clear enough... and still, even now as they wrapped up the training session, touching fists or bowing to each other, frightening to observe.

"Can one of you close the place up?" Petra pulled off her sweat-soaked T-shirt – her sports bra was black – then pulled on a sweatshirt bearing the words: I FIGHT LIKE A GIRL – SAY GOODBYE TO YOUR BALLS. "I've got an old buddy here to beat up."

"Or I could buy you a drink," called Josh.

"Guess I'll let him off." Petra winked at her students. "Nice work tonight."

In a pub called the Thin Stiletto, Suzanne sat with Petra while Josh went up to the bar.

"Your students are impressive," said Suzanne.

"The visitors did all right."

"Now that their conditioned reflexes are triggered by appropriate cues, in the context of massive adrenaline dump."

"They just needed to field-strip what they knew, and take control."

"And you like empowering people."

"Uh-huh. You're good, aren't you, Dr Duchesne? Plus, you understood what was going on, even though you're not a fighter."

Josh came back with Petra's blackcurrant-and-lemonade and Suzanne's coffee.

"You girls are such boozers. By the way, Suzanne left her phone at home."

"Good." Petra saluted him with her glass. "And yes, it was one of my officers that redfanged you that little warning."

"Thanks. Back in a mo."

While Josh was paying and fetching his drink – it looked like Coke – Petra checked her own phone, then nodded.

"No one's listening here and now."

"What about Josh's phone?"

"Oh, he's secure, except when he's talking to you. He and his mates use PFUC crypto among themselves."

"What's that? You did say pea-fuck, didn't you?"

"There's a polite version, but the truth is it stands for Pretty Fucking Unbreakable Code."

Suzanne realised that she had missed something.

"When you say someone's listening in, you mean the police, right?"

"Official authorities, let's say."

"So why is that a problem? We all want Richard back."

"And some of us might bend the regs to do so. In management circles, that's called breaking the law."

"Oh."

When Josh returned, he toasted them both.

"Your health. Tell me, you still run ShieldIx 3 for security?"

Petra said, "You're really not supposed to know that."

"So let's say, hypothetically, you were logged on. You'd be running a session pool with its own flows, processes, and threads. Marked with your user ID."

"Hypothetically, I'm a grandma and I know how to suck eggs."

"Uh-huh. So if you kick off a querybot – hypothetically – that would create a second session pool for it to execute in. Right?"

"Sure." Petra looked at Suzanne. "You following this?"

"I only speak French and English."

"You hang around with buddy boy long enough, you'll get fluent in Geek for sure."

"For God's sake," said Josh. "Now, a second pool with whose user ID?"

"Same as the first session pool. I log on, create a new pool, it picks up my user ID automatically."

Josh smiled. "*Automatically* is the keyword du jour. Substitute a subclass instance for the controller, and you can adopt chief security officer privileges."

"You're joking."

"If someone's installed a monitor, like some old Observer pattern – distributed across the net and with heavy use of proxies – then you're effectively screwing with its Observers list." Josh pushed a memory flake across the table. "That's all you need. There's another copy of the bot code, too."

"Good, cause I deleted the one you sent me. Just as well, since we had an internal audit including full phone scan today. Bastards."

Suzanne took a sip of air, realised she had finished her coffee, and put the cup down.

"Have you changed your mind, Petra? Before, you didn't want to help Josh with the search, and now you do, is that right?"

"Kind of. This monitoring shit doesn't add up."

"I don't really follow what you've been saying."

"That's just shooting the breeze about the security design and how to slip past it. You asked who's observing, and I said official authorities, but I really mean Five, or someone like them."

"Five?"

"MI5, sweetheart. The big boys, and the reason that doesn't add up is that if they were looking for young Richard, they'd have found him by now." Petra's cheekbones appeared to sharpen as her mouth tensed. "In whatever condition."

Oh, God.

"They've got a monitor on anything to do with Broomhall," said Josh. "He's flagged as need-to-watch. It's got all the signs, hasn't it?"

"Looks that way. Either he's been a naughty boy or he's crossed people in the corridors of power."

Suzanne did not see how this prevented people doing everything they could to search for one missing boy. Or perhaps she did. People saw intricate fictions all around them in the workplace, exactly as real and exactly as imaginary as the airborne chemicals in an ant nest that drove the behaviour of every member, including the so-called queen, who was a captive breeder more than a ruler, every ant existing in its place, carrying out its role in the emergent behaviour of the nest-as-a-whole.

"What are you thinking?" asked Josh.

"About ant nests, and the way people behave."

"Whoo." Petra raised her glass towards Josh. "She's too deep for you, mate."

"We're just... Never mind."

"So, you two are OK getting back by yourselves?"

"Sure."

"Then I'll see you."

Petra stood, tugging down her I FIGHT LIKE A GIRL sweatshirt, outlining her breasts. Perhaps it was a distraction for the men in the bar, because the memory flake was gone from the tabletop, though Suzanne had not seen Petra pocket it. Then Petra turned, revealing the back of her sweatshirt – another friendly message:

CASTRATION? IT'S JUST LIKE SHELLING PEAS – and left.

"That was abrupt," said Suzanne.

"Just her way."

"But she's going to help."

"Because she likes my hack. First, it's elegant. Second, it exploits a ShieldIx feature she didn't know about. Hardly anyone knows."

"Really." Suzanne put her fingertips on the back of his hand, felt an electric fizz, and withdrew. "That's not why she's helping you. The word, I think, is *smitten*."

"Jesus, not you as well." Josh stared at the exit Petra had left by. "She happens to be gay, you know."

"Actually, I got that. I stand by smitten."

"Oh, please. Isn't there anyone who can rescue me?"

Suzanne tried not to think too much about the meaning of her response, knowing she could shut up, but saying it anyway.

"Maybe there is."

[TWELVE]

Trafalgar Square, early. Quite why he had walked here, Richard did not know. The atmosphere around the fountains was odd, just a few homeless people – *people like me* – sleeping on the benches, roused and rousted by cleaning staff. Commuters were waiting at the bus stops and streaming toward their offices; down here it was too early for tourists. It was as if the old statues and monument had a viscosity that slowed their passage through time, as if their awakening came later than the streets. Wanting to be different from the others groaning awake on the benches, Richard pulled off his garish sweatshirt, quickly replacing his cap on his head. With luck, he looked like someone on his way to school, not a vagrant. But he wondered, as he saw the grime on the clothes of those who had slept here overnight, how long he could pass himself off as normal, how long before he became invisible like these others.

"I'm sorry," a turbaned worker was saying to someone, no, two people, "but you have to move on. Here, this'll get you breakfast."

"You're very kind, young man."

"Why don't you pop over to the station for a cuppa? They'll let you sit a while."

The vagrants he was addressing were a white-haired couple, their clothes frayed but not stained, fragile faces clean but not fresh. They were rosy-cheeked from sunlight, and they smiled at the man for his kindness. Richard could only stand and watch them walk away toward Charing Cross, where they might have an hour or two sitting on hard metal seats before someone moved them on. As they walked, the woman slipped her hand into the man's, and they continued on with the delicate, heartbreaking sweetness of aged love.

It's not supposed to be like this.

There are no comfortable places to sit – or lie down – in the external world of stone and concrete buildings. Indoors, there are few places of refuge for someone who has no money to pay. Already he was learning the hardness of the world. He felt like a swimmer far from shore, face dipped beneath the surface for longer and longer periods of time; soon enough he would be under and sinking.

"It's not right, is it?" It was the man in the turban, addressing him. "An old couple like that."

"Er… No, sir."

"Which is why you work hard in school, isn't it? My daughter is top of her class."

"Oh. Good."

The man's smile was disconcerting in its warmth, shaming Richard for not revealing his true nature: a runaway, and worse. *I'm a criminal now.* Inside that college, he'd handed over contraband – drugs or who knew what – and if he hadn't dodged the cameras as well as he'd intended, then the police would be hunting him down. Maybe he should try to get away from

London. But nowhere was under tighter surveillance than the railways.

"Hallo, Richie-boy," said a familiar voice.

"Jayce!"

"Vodka Mary saw you head across Vauxhall Bridge. Thought I'd follow."

"Who's–? Never mind."

The expression on the turbaned man's face seemed to be melting downward. Richard's stomach lurched with shame.

"I get ya," said Jayce. "Come on."

They moved through well-dressed crowds, heading along the Strand. In shop doorways, the destitute sat awake or still slept, under shabby blankets or cardboard boxes. Soon they would have to move as the businesses opened. At least one form was so still that it could be dead; but no one was checking. Richard felt sick as he kept pace with Jayce, because he was like the rest, doing nothing to help. From some doorways came "Spare any change?" – directed to those who had money, not toward two homeless youths encroaching on choice territory. Hard looks sent a message even Richard could read, however confusing he found this new world.

In the shops, glowglass windows doubled as display screens, reporting the morning's headlines: WEST MID-LANDS FLASH FLOODS, 22 DEAD; VIOLENT CLASHES BETWEEN CHINESE CONGLOMERATES IN AFRICA; PM BILLY CHURCH GAINS 43% LEAD IN POLLS… He tuned it out, for they were meaningless signals, no more relevant to finding something to eat than the weather on Jupiter or the beating of pulsars beyond the galactic rim.

He missed his books.

"Sod this," said Jayce. "It's better south of the river."

Everywhere people were hurrying to work. What did people actually do all day in offices? What did Father do? He was on the boards of companies, but for the first time Richard realised he had no idea what that meant.

"Is it always like this?"

Jayce might have shrugged, but Richard's attention shifted to the other side of the street, a couple with two children, well-dressed and laughing as they paused before the Apollo Theatre, pointing at the animated poster over the doors. Sourness rotated in his stomach. He watched as the parents hugged their kids, continuing their saunter down the Strand.

"Fuckin' plod's all over the place." Jayce nodded toward three police officers further down the street, and another trio beyond. "See what I mean?"

Before he became a criminal, Richard had thought of police as reassuring. Now he wanted to break into a run, but that would catch their attention.

"Can we get out of here?"

"Down this way."

Old steps sloped between two centuries-old buildings. At the bottom, Jayce turned left and Richard followed, continuing toward Waterloo Bridge. They climbed up to bridge level, made the long walk across – an ache throbbed in the back of Richard's legs – and descended an underpass to a round area below ground level, open to the sky, containing the black, shattered cylinder of the Imax Ruin. In the ramps and underpasses all around, Cardboard City was a packed confusion of makeshift shelters, grime-caked faces, tattered clothes, and a pervasive, heavy sourness that entered the nose and lungs and would not leave.

"'S crowded 'ere." Jayce had begun slurring. "Innit?"
Is he sick?

Or perhaps it was something to do with the green
powder he'd taken last night. Whatever happened,
Richard knew he had to steer clear of that stuff. Was
there something he should do to help Jayce? The
thought made his arms tremble, helplessness spreading
inside him. And then Jayce was gone. Rubbing his eyes,
Richard wove his gaze among the shabby figures, trying
to spot… There. Jayce was wobbling his way through
another underpass tunnel. What else could Richard do
but follow? Among the fragrant stench of the lost, he
made his way as best he could, only catching up Jayce
when they were above ground, heading for the South
Bank where the buildings shone and clean air blew off
the Thames, the turbine vanes circling, and everything
in its place.

Around the pillars and blocky sculptures, in the profusion of concrete architecture – Festival Hall, ramps,
and walkways – were brightly-dressed figures who took
Richard's breath away. Despite the early hour, they ran
and vaulted over stairwells, rolled across concrete outdoor tables, threw themselves cartwheeling from walls,
hit flagstones with a shoulder roll and came to their
feet. Some used slideshoes, while others with boots and
gauntlets spidered up buildings and took urban gymnastics to a level Richard had never seen.

"Who are they, Jayce?"

"Huh? Spidermen. Gekrunners."

"Will they talk to us?"

"Dunno, man. Tired."

"Jayce?"

But Jayce was sliding to the ground. He curled up
sideways on the paving stones, shivered in hot

sunlight, and fell into sleep.

What can I do?

He was too heavy to carry. Should he go to hospital? There were few pedestrians here – not so many offices for the commuters to rush to – and the whatsits, the gekrunners, were intent on their own thing. But a trio of police officers, bulky in their body armour, was heading this way. Trembling, Richard shook his head as if in disgust at the sight of Jayce, then walked on, head down, as if he had places to go, classes to attend. The more he realised this was a dream, the slower his paces became; and then there was a tap on his shoulder, and his bladder almost let go.

"You're his friend?" It was a girl's voice. "Jayce's friend?"

She was thin, about his height, wearing a helmet, gauntlets, and boots. Her sweatshirt flickered between two messages – Born to Jump and Head over Heels – beneath a moving graphic, a cartwheeling silhouette.

"Uh, yeah."

"You look straight. I'm Opal."

She held out her hand like an adult. It took Richard a moment to react.

"R-Richie."

The gauntlet, as he shook her hand, felt tough.

"You ain't been on the streets long."

"No." There was a crack of sound overhead. "Bloody hell."

A young man with dreadlocks clung spiderlike to sheer concrete, after a spectacular spinning leap from a table. He grinned at Opal and Richard, then twisted off and dropped, shoulder-rolling as he hit the ground, coming up into a skating motion, sliding away as if the flagstones were slick as ice.

"That's Kyle, and he's nuts. Good, though."

It was impossible to look away as Kyle vaulted over a stone plinth, cartwheeled, then skated onward.

"How does he do that?"

"Practice every day and you'll find out."

"But–" He stared up at the concrete wall. "I don't see how it's possible."

"Oh, that. Watch, and don't move a muscle." Opal curled the middle and ring fingers of her right hand, then opened them. "Totally still, now. Don't want to tear your skin."

She placed the palms of both gauntleted hands on his shoulders, then raised her arms a little. The fabric of Richard's shirt pulled upward. Then she crimped her fingers and the shirt dropped free.

"Gekkomere strips." She turned over her hand. "See? Sticks like magic."

"Fractal microtendrils." Richard peered at the strips. "Tap into the van der Waals forces between the molecules, the covalent bonds."

Opal looked at him.

"You so gotta talk to Brian. He's a right tech-head, too."

"Brian?" Then Richard remembered Jayce. "Oh, shit."

Looking back, he saw that the officers had hauled a wobbling Jayce to his feet.

"Let's hope they'll take him in this time," said Opal.

"You want them to arrest Jayce?"

"Stick him in a cell, inject him with anti-whatsit to clear his veins? Too right. It zaps the cravings for days. Give him another chance to go cold turkey."

Two of the officers, hands in Jayce's armpits, pretty much carried him along as they walked. The other

officer was scanning everyone in sight. Richard turned
away, feeling as if he were about to cry.

"Hey, what is it?"

"I just… don't know what to do. Where to go."

"Why don't you come with us?"

"Who's 'us'?"

"We are the Vauxhall Spidermen." Opal grinned.
"Except I'm more Spidergirl myself."

Richard's eyes were blurring. He gave one sob, then
caught himself. "Sorry."

"Come on. This way."

Technically the Spidermen lived in a squat, or a sequence of squats joined together. The street was
part-derelict, but the local council had refurbished some
of the houses: outer walls coated with cheap ceramic,
rooftops shining with photoplastic. The gekrunners had
possession of houses that were on the council's to-do
list – or according to Opal, the won't-ever-get-around-
to list. The interiors were plain-painted, scraped back
to brick in some places, decorated with movie posters
looping through five-second clips. Several showed
gekrunners performing daredevil acrobatics. Through
the rear windows, Richard could see rows of photob-
ulbs, soaking up sunlight. Inside, he counted
twenty-eight different people before he gave up keeping track. Most were thin, some with lean muscle. Was
everyone a gekrunner?

Laughter sounded from upstairs.

"Do all these people live here?" Richard looked at the
varicoloured cushions scattered around the floor. "I
mean, here or the other houses?"

Opal was about to answer, but a male voice
forestalled her.

"Most do." The speaker was tall and white. "Me, I sleep over the shop most times."

"This is Brian," said Opal. "And this is Richie."

"Hey."

"Hey."

"Richie's a tech head. Richie, tell Brian about the Van Vols. You know."

"Say what?"

"In the gloves. Tell him."

"Uh…" Richard shook his head. "She means gekkomere tapping into van der Waals forces."

"Cool. You've got it."

"But Kyle's skating, how does that work?"

Brian gestured. "Show him your boot soles, Opal."

"OK." She put on hand on Richard's shoulder for balance, then raised one foot. "See?"

"Hyperglace gel strips." Brian pointed. "Like the gekkomere, flips between two modes. Just apply a tiny potential."

"And they're frictionless?"

"Coefficient damn near close to zero."

"At ambient temperature?"

"Unless the weather is–"

"You two." Opal lowered her foot, releasing Richard's shoulder. "Tech heads."

The absence of her hand felt… strange. Warm and strange.

"You hack code?" asked Brian. "Course you do. If you want to work, come over to the shop in the morning."

"Er…" Richard looked at Opal. "Work?"

"We aren't losers." Brian nodded toward the seated people. "Apart from maybe Kenny over there. He's a doctoral student at King's, and a total waste of space."

"I love you too, man." Kenny raised a hand to Richard. "Hey."

"Hey."

Richard looked down at the floor. It was cleaner than he'd expected. Of course he had to work, because that was what people did, or at least grown-ups. Fourteen year-olds did not pay tax, were outside the system that adults lived in, so whatever Brian meant it was surely illegal.

"It's what they call cash in hand," said Opal. "No ID required. No phone. Good place."

"Oh. And it's a shop?"

"You'll like it." Brian tapped Opal's gauntlet. "We sell stuff like this. Gekrunner tech, bikes with graphite memories, you name it. At least until July twentieth."

Richard's guts clenched. *Knife blade, coming at me.* But there was no knife, and he was safe, because Zajac was in school and that was another world. July twentieth was the day of the *Knife Edge* final, when Zajac had said he'd come for him. But he was away from that, and safe.

Safe from Zajac, anyhow.

"He's talking about the general election." Opal shrugged, distorting the cartwheeling logo on her shirt. "Politics."

"Matters more than you think, kid." Brian waved his phone. "If Fat Billy Church stays in office, they're threatening to make cash illegal. Pure phone-to-phone economy."

"That's impossible," said Opal.

"All they got to do is stop making coins and notes, then announce a cut-off date. Bring your cash into a bank for credit, or it drops to zero value, and you have bugger all."

Richard's stomach made a noise. He felt stricken; but Opal smiled.

"He needs feeding. Smell that? They're cooking chilli."

"Right," said Brian. "Let's get him fed."

But the food wasn't ready yet. It hurt to leave the steamy kitchen and step out into the back yard, where old mattresses lay in neat rows, plastic crates stood in a pyramid, and rusted poles supported a web of clothes-lines. Eight or nine teenagers were practicing flips and rolls around the makeshift outdoor gym.

"He's going to mess that up," said Opal. "See?"

One of the youths rolled off a mattress, hitting the ground hard. He stood up, rubbing his ribs.

"Ouch," he said.

"You nearly nailed it," Opal told him.

From their left, a canine yap sounded. A Jack Russell on a lead formed of braided string wagged his tail. His owner was a girl around Richard's age; her sweatshirt was pink, bearing a picture of a flat-chested muscular man holding a knife. The heading read CARLSEN: THE FIREMAN RETURNS, while his blade dripped moving blood, animated droplets sliding down the sweatshirt fabric.

"That's Zoe," said Opal. "And this–"

Everything faded as Richard's hearing filled with the hiss of non-existent surf.

Blades and the whirring machines, peeling back the skin and slicing the skull, glistening folds of fatty brain, trickles of blood and no one noticing.

Richard felt choked by hands that did not exist, punched by invisible fists inside his chest.

"Jeez," said Zoe. "What's with the fucking kid?"

"I don't– Richie? You all right?"

A cramp pulled him over. Hot fluid spewed from his mouth.

"Oh, gross."

"Richie…"

"Sorry." He wiped his mouth. "I'm really sorry."

Zoe picked up her Jack Russell.

"Hey, Opal. You keep a pet, you gotta clean up after it, y'know?"

"Fuck you." Opal put her arm around Richard. "Just go away."

His world lurched again.

She's hugging me.

The world was so strange.

Next morning he walked with Brian through Brixton, past blocks of flats with piles of bin-bags stacked outside. Rotting rubbish emanated a stink; it felt as if the air had thickened, becoming heavier, and you had to push through it to get anywhere.

"No pick-ups for six weeks," said Brian. "And that shit Fat Billy is making like it's not his fault."

"Oh," said Richard.

"And like, the weird thing is people believe him. Like if he had more powers, he'd be able to sort out the mess."

Back in the squat, there had been a couple of people with shirts whose logos were the A-on-pentagram symbol of New Anarchism.

"You're an NAer?"

"Shit, no. They're stupid. OK, through here."

They passed along an alleyway, skirting more rotting refuse, and came out onto a grimy road. Opposite was a shop with a handpainted sign – Cal's Cycles – and ceramic sheeting protecting the window. The metal door was guarded by three locks; Brian pressed his thumb against one, and extended his keychain from his belt to open the others.

"Give us a hand with these, will you?"

"What do I do?"

There was a trick to jerking the ceramic shutters open. Richard tried to helpe push them up, into the slots over the windows, but Brian did all the work.

"Cal won't be in till ten, most likely. You'll recognise him by the tats."

"Tats?"

"Bare arms and tattoos, kind of old-fashioned, but at least the designs move."

Inside, the shop smelled of sawdust and oil, and the floorboards were grey with age, iron-hard. Racks hung from the ceiling; from them bicycles were suspended, looking insectile, like praying mantises, in the vertical position. Gauntlets and boots filled shelves and two glass display cases, one of which doubled as a sales counter. There was a phone pad for taking payments, and a stained coffee mug which someone had left standing overnight.

"If we don't clean that," said Brian, "it'll just stay there growing fungus, maybe evolve intelligence. Could do with the conversation round here."

"You want me to work on software?"

"Got a bunch of gauntlets out back. Whole batch has buggy controlware. You up for sorting it out?"

"I... don't know."

"So let's find out."

The workshop-storeroom was cluttered with electronics and mechanical components, the air tangy with oil and metal dust, sharper than out front. A large scratched wallscreen would serve as Richard's display, and a small graphite processor pad for the actual programming, instead of a phone. On one wall, triggered by Richard and Brian's entrance, a movie poster brightened into animation: a grey-haired man performing gekrunner-style moves but with bare hands and ordinary shoes, and beneath him the words: *Le Mouvement, C'est Moi.*

"Early parkour guy," said Brian. "French, coming to London to talk about the Tao of free-running. Old school, before your actual gekrunning, cause they didn't have these little doodads."

He handed over a gauntlet with a cracked-open casing.

"Looks like a car motive cell." Richard followed weblines with his finger. "Viral engineering, viruses carrying the electronic–You know."

Pain rotated inside his forehead.

"You all right, Richie?"

"Sorry, yeah." Richard rubbed his forehead. "No problem."

"OK, good. See, that control web is the kind of thing NAers don't get. Actually, just the fastenings on your clothes need a technical civilisation, stuff dug out of the ground with machinery, trucks for transport, factories, and shops, right? They don't get how complicated it all is."

Richard looked around the workshop, remembering the redwood-panelled rooms at home, clean and elegant but never welcoming, not comfortable like here.

"You're not rich, though. You, Opal, Jayce, and all the–"

"Him."Brian's expression closed down. "You want to stay with us, you do not nick from your friends."

"I wouldn't–Oh. Is that what Jayce did?"

"Uh-huh. Now, you know the first rule of hacking, right?"

"Er…"

"You start with a cup of coffee, refill every twenty minutes, repeat until task finished. I'll put the kettle on while you crank up the display. Give us a shout if nothing's in English."

Richard popped the service interface onto the wallscreen – the text was Korean – but he found a ReadMe and babelled the contents. By the time Brian put coffee down beside him, he was already deep in the code, sketching diagrams in the side panes as Mr Stanier had taught at school. When he surfaced back into day-to-day reality, his coffee was cold. He sipped from it anyway.

Mr Keele periodically said that optimum cognition requires frequent breaks, so Richard flipped open another pane to browse the news. Unable to help himself, he murmured a query into a bead microphone, and watched as the results blossomed inside the new pane, with FRIENDLY ENEMIES? as the headline, a picture of Father and someone else – someone familiar – dressed in tuxedos, and the caption: *Philip Broomhall greets Zebediah Tyndall at City dinner.*

He thumbed on the audio…

"*Despite the hard-fought takeover battle between Tyndall Industries and BroomCon regarding Hixon Media, the corporate rivals appeared to put aside their differences before the Lady Mayor of London. However, appearances can be deceptive, since both men–*"

…then silenced it.

Hands shaking, he made the pane disappear, then continued to stare at the screen where it had been.

After some time, his attention drifted as if on gentle currents into the coding panes, and then he was back at work, forgetting everything, at home with himself once more.

[THIRTEEN]

Josh walked along the Embankment south of the river, watching the solar barges drift past. There was no reason to be in this part of London particularly – there were other places that Richard Broomhall could be – but this was central, with hostels and more: an entire ecology of homelessness, a bleak, pervasive undersea of living that was easy to fall into and hard to escape. Every few minutes, he checked his phone display. At 10:01am, finally, output appeared: *Entry OK.* Thirty seconds later, an appended message brightened: *1st gen replication successful, 53 processes spawned.*

Although Petra had slipped the querybot inside the net's defences, she did not know how subtle and pervasive it could be, and he had not told her. Most of his spawned code would suicide quietly in a kind of controlled apoptosis, deliberate suicide just like human cells, for the sake of the body's health. The risk of being traced back to Petra was low. He would have liked more detailed progress reports from the burrowing code, but more traffic meant greater likelihood of monitors noticing and–

His phone buzzed, and for a moment was too blurred

to make out. *They've found me.* But he blinked and refocused, to identify the caller as Kath Gleason, from Sophie's school.

"Hello, Josh."

"Miss Gleason."

"Kath, please. I just thought I should check in with you."

"There's no news."

"I didn't think there was." In the phone image, she shook her head. "Your, er, Mrs Cumberland came in to see Eileen. Asked for Sophie to be taken off the school roll."

Eileen was the headmistress.

"The school roll...?"

"Mrs Cumberland said that regardless of the outcome, Sophie would never return."

Josh rubbed his face. *There's only one outcome.*

"I'm sure Maria's right."

"Probably. It's just– We asked about you, for confirmation, and she said you're out of the picture."

"Out of the picture."

"That's what she said."

He looked up at the rotating wind-turbines, the long row stretching past the Houses of Parliament, and said again, without knowing why: "I'm sure she's right."

"Oh, then... Are you in Swindon at the moment?"

"Nowhere near."

"I just wondered if you were going to be around."

Josh stared at her in the phone.

Christ, she's hitting on me.

Sometimes a woman was interested and he didn't get it – in fact, he still didn't believe that Petra could fancy him – but this was blatant. With Sophie worse than comatose – persistent vegetative state meant there was nothing left to awaken – and Maria filled with confusion, hating him… How did that equate with him being available?

"The Brezhinskis aren't doing too well," Kath went on. "The father's still bottling things up inside, the mother's still drinking, and Marek… We'd like to see him back in school."

"It sounds as if the family needs help. Would the school pay for counselling?"

"I… don't know."

"There's someone who could help, so long as she does get paid. I can put her in touch with the family directly. You can vouch for her, if Mr Brezhinski asks you."

"Vouch for whom, exactly?"

"Dr Suzanne Duchesne. I'll send you her details."

"Well, I–"

"Thank you, Kath. It's good to meet a teacher who really cares."

"Oh. Thanks."

He killed the call.

Christ, what a bitch.

After some ten seconds, the phone buzzed again – She's calling back, for God's sake – but it was his querybot, returning initial results. Only one instance showed an above-fifty-percent match: some three seconds of unfocused footage, a youth in white shirt and veil-cap ascending a staircase. The location was a college, so it should be filled with young people, and for a moment Josh did not understand how the probability rating could be so high – it was his own algorithm, after all. But the timestamp was 19.57, far too late for normal classes.

Two nights ago. Even if it's him, he could be dead.

Bad thinking. Useless pessimism.

The college was within walking distance – another reason for the high probability – and at close range he could redfang querybots into the building system without going through the Web. And the physical movement would help him forget about Kath Gleason, and the images she invoked in his mind, with a montage backdrop of Sophie-memories: playing in school, playing in the garden, giggling at a worm, lying in a bed surrounded by monitors.

He walked fast.

Perhaps it looked better at night, but in daylight the college exterior showed cracked paintwork and dull windows. Someone had smeared black goo over the spycams, which did not bode well for trawling through the surveillance logs. Josh decided to make the college's problems worse, just for the time being, by slipping interference bots into the building system and blanking out recordings for the yard and corridors he passed through. Once inside, a garish display screen showed adverts – salsa classes every Wednesday, homemade cakes for sale tomorrow lunchtime – and a searchable timetable.

In the brief footage of Richard Broomhall, this noticeboard appeared in the background, so the staircase over there must be where he ascended. But where had he been going? Josh flicked through the timetable. If Richard went up a floor, there would have been just one class about to start: *Intermediate Mandarin, room 17, instructor T. Maxwell*. A trivial hack popped up a fragment of low-level data:

    <instructor>
    <name>

```
<firstname>Tarquin</firstname>
<surname>Maxwell</surname>
</name>
<citizenID>100087TQ3598ML</citizenID>
<address><a1>84a Gladwell Court</a1><a2>Lon-
don</a2>
<pc>W349 8AQ1</pc>
</address>
<empType>PT</empType>
</instructor>
```

Josh could have accessed the relevant schema to check, but PT clearly designated part-time employees. Maxwell could be anywhere, so rather than stake out the home address or manually search the college premises, a realtime GPSID hack was called for.

On resigning from Ghost Force and the Army in one go, Josh went through a series of exit interviews, including one with Lofty Young. They had sat inside the quartermaster's office next to Pre-Deployment Stores, and shot the breeze for a few minutes. Then Lofty had reached into a drawer, and pulled out a shoulder-holstered handgun, a black phone, and three iridescent memory flakes. Leaving them on the desktop, he stood up.

"Ah, the old bladder. Must go for a slash-ex." *Ex* meant military exercise, and what he meant was, he needed to pee. "All part of getting old, like noticing how every little thing needs thumbprint and vocal confirmation these days. There's still shedloads of stuff floating around, mind, that's impossible to track."

"That's what quartermasters are for."

"Yeah." At the door, Lofty gave a half grin. "I'll be a few minutes. Too bad it's so hard to keep the inventory straight."

After he had gone, Josh had stared at the desktop.

Message received, boss.

The shoulder holster felt snug, the phone and memory flakes disappeared into his pockets, and the desk was clear. When Lofty returned he nodded, talked about nothing in particular for several minutes, then shook Josh's hand, and that was that.

Now he used his phone – not the same handset, but containing the same firmware and covert-ops enhancements – and accessed GPSID via the "unofficial" portal whose URI was known only to retired operatives like Josh. Deep beneath the Chilterns, the MetaWatch team kept track of the portal's use. While Richard Broomhall's father was on a persons-of-interest list, using the portal to track Richard directly would flag up warnings; but there would be no reason to notice Josh tracking down an ordinary language teacher called Maxwell, however unusual the poor bastard's first name might be.

Having made the request, he had to wait while the verify-and-authorise procedures did their thing. Meanwhile, there were two messages waiting, and he played Maria's first.

"Hey, Josh. I know you're working, but I want us to meet. Not alone. There's– Make it the Highbury Arms, would you? Leave me a message about which day, what time, and I'll confirm."

And the second, from Mr Hammond, the hospital consultant who had delivered so much bad news already: "I'm afraid there's something not so pleasant that we need to talk about. We have some notion of your intent, but in the case of a long-term patient it would be best for explicit permission from a parent, both if possible. While stem-cell regen is the optimum choice, every week there are injured children whose organs need immediate replacement in order to–"

He wiped the message.

You fucking bastard.

So many battlefield injuries, his friends' liquefied flesh hot and sticky on his skin, and the time he pulled the trigger that blew away the, the – *don't think of it* – with the spraying red and *God he was so young,* scarcely more than Sophie's age. Not just firefights, but the desperate tragedy of men killed while hauling gear across mountains, driving or climbing far from hospitals. The reality of pain and imminent death, the necessity of triage, saving those who can survive, and there had been too many rifle salutes fired into the Herefordshire sky above Union Jack-draped coffins, the pomp and strength of military ceremony when it mattered most, keeping the survivors strong, but none of that would allow him to think of them splitting Sophie open for the organs inside her.

Something molten was roiling inside him, desperate for the blaze of violence and blood, and when the map appeared on his phone display with Maxwell's coordinates marked in red, the address in Gladwell Court, he hoped that this man had something to do with the boy's disappearance, knew information that needed to be beaten out of him, or would panic and fight so that the only option was to kill him.

No. Control.

Punch to the throat and leave him gagging as he–

There's a missing boy, and he's the objective.

Then his feelings were tight inside him once more, and he was on the move.

● ● ●

Bursting open the front door, Josh stalked straight into the living room. On the couch, a small man raised his hands, shrinking back and squeaking: "Who are you? Please don't–Don't."

"Tarquin Maxwell, three nights ago you met this boy." Josh flashed a still from the surveillance log. "What for? What were you up to, you bastard?"

"He, um, brought me. Something." Globules of sweat spread on Maxwell's forehead. He flicked his purplish tongue across his lips. "For the stress. Medicinal. It's, er…"

"Virapharm, and you know the penalty for possession, and what I want to know is where is the boy?"

"It was the first time I–Wait, no. He's from Mr Khan, but for God's sake don't use my name because they'll take my kneecaps" – tears flowed – "so don't say I told you, please."

"Tell about Khan."

"No, I–"

"Tarquin, tell me or I'll rip the information from you, so choose."

"They'll use iron bars on my kn-kneecaps. They're like that. I didn't know, before. Before I dealt with him."

"Tell me."

"Businesses, he's got businesses."

"Where? What kind?"

"Shops, a taxi service, garages. He's–"

"Where will he be?"

"I was about to… Oh, Jesus. To tell you."

"Where?"

"Corner store called, um… I can show you on a map." Fingers trembling, he tried to pull out his phone. "Sorry, I…"

"This one." Josh thumbed his own phone, and presented it face-first to Maxwell. "Tap on the places you know."

"Here's the store." Maxwell's teeth were cutting into his lower lip as he scrolled the display. "And he's got places there and… there. Don't know about the cabs."

Josh slapped the side of Maxwell's jaw, the torque producing shock. Maxwell had been starting to relax, getting the idea that he had some control in this situation.

"Describe Khan."

"He's – oh, God – dark, got a scar on his cheek here" – he pointed – "and a moustache."

"Height? Tall or short?"

"Same as you. Thin."

Asked to estimate Josh's height, Maxwell would exaggerate from the effect of fear; but then he was also scared of Khan.

"Will he have people with him?"

"Always." Maxwell's larynx worked as he nodded. "Big buggers."

"Once I've gone, don't think we won't be monitoring every word, Tarquin. You understand, right?"

"I–Right. Yes."

"Stay here, keep silent."

There was a kicked-in door that needed to be repaired, and the fear would not keep him here forever; but an hour or two was enough.

"Remember," added Josh.

A corner store, very traditional, if you didn't notice the armoured glass, the profusion of spycams. There was a possible route in through a back yard; or else through the shop like an ordinary customer. Scanning from his phone, Josh found the spycams shielded, impossible to redfang. But some part of the network would connect to the Web, and that would be his entry point, if he needed one. For now, he wanted to physically scout the shop, and see if Khan was inside.

Loading up subversion ware in case of opportunity, he crossed the street and went into the shop, accompanied by an overhead beep: a detector registering his knife. His image would be in the system; but his phone was already polling for available devices, seeking interfaces. Meanwhile, he extracted a bottle of hypercaffeinated Run! and a foil pack of Japanese chocolate. Behind the counter, a woman took his cash without comment, clearly used to doing phoneless business. Porno mags, little more than a folded poster with an embedded thirty-second movie, plus a malleable plastic attachment for that little kinaesthetic extra, were on the shelves above the cat food. Josh delayed, as though fighting an embarrassed urge to browse, until his phone vibrated silently three times. He shook his head, as if pretending disgust – a pretence of a pretence – and left the store.

There was a pub across the street. Even though it was early, when he entered the dark lounge there were fifteen, sixteen drinkers inside. Hard looks followed him as he carried his Coke to a corner and sat at a small sticky table. He got to work on his phone, following his subversion ware's progress as it mapped the network's topology. The system architecture was big, and so was the hardware net it ran on, far too extensive for a simple corner shop. Got it.

The shop was an end of terrace, a converted house, and one of four houses in a row that were conjoined: a

single building inside, while from the street you could
not tell.

They're watching me.

Shit. This was attention he did not need, as two of
the men on barstools were staring at him. Pressing a
bead into his left ear, he tapped the phone then leaned
back against the wall, eyes almost shut as though listening to music. Then, with an idle motion, he sipped
from his Coke. In his phone, a surveillance image
moved, overlaid with a transcript pane, showing their
conversation as text, in time with the audio in his earbead.

> *unknown#1:* "So who's this?"
> *unknown#2:* " This is Richie, Mr Khan."
> /** <<conditional match>>unknown#3="R" **/
> /** <<conditional match>>unknown#1="K" **/
> *K:* "You're not local, are you, Richie?"
> *R:* "Er, no, sir."
> *K:* "You know your way around?"
> *unknown#2:* "I could help him, Mr Khan."
> *K:* "Why would you do that, Jayce?"
> *unknown#2:* "Look after a mate, like."

His software had identified Richard Broomhall and
Khan, conditionally rather than absolutely, but Josh
had no doubts: this was who he was looking for. He
noted the other youth's use of *Richie* rather than
Richard. Plus, the image of Khan was clear – there
would be no mistaking him.

Now the guys at the bar were returning their attention to him. This was not good. He checked the other
drinkers. Most remained focused on their drinks or
their inner thoughts, whatever they were, while at a
small table like his, a heavy woman was pushing two

empty glasses away from her. Her makeup formed strata, emphasising, not hiding, the fault lines and general crumbling.

When she realised Josh was staring at her, she raised her eyebrows.

"Don't tell me" – Josh pointed at the two empty glasses – "you drank two at once."

"Nah. My mate Sylvia was with me."

"Well, do you need another?"

"Got a cake in the oven, going to burn. Need to get home."

Good. He had thought she was about to leave.

"I shouldn't either," he said. "Have another, I mean."

"Mind, I went to the offie last night, brought back some lagers, need finishing off."

"That sounds tempting."

Flakes of mascara moved when she batted her eyes.

"Wouldn't want to drink alone." She wiggled her soft mass. "Don't seem right."

"Damn straight. I'm Joe."

"I'm Azure."

"Nice name."

"Well. Come on then."

They left, shoulder pressed to shoulder, while the guys at the bar watched. This close to Azure, Josh kept his breathing shallow. In the Regiment, he had been through desensitisation training, able to function in heavier and heavier concentrations of tear gas; it served him well now, coping with the thickness of Azure's perfume. No doubt made from the finest ingredients in a bathtub just down the road, and flogged off a market stall.

As she made a joke and laughed, he turned to smile, checking back. In the pub doorway, both men were watching. Josh slipped an arm around Azure's massive waist.

"Up here," she said. "This door, see?"

They went into a small entrance hall. A former townhouse, now flats, and she clearly lived upstairs. Her buttocks heaved as she started the climb, starting to puff; then Josh helped push her up. By the time they reached the top, they were both laughing. They almost fell inside, then Azure lumbered into the kitchen, looking for her lagers.

From the sitting room, a window opened out back, almost without sound. Josh swung through in one motion, pushed the thing shut – it would remain unlocked, but she might not notice for a while – then crimped his fingertips into the gap between bricks, made a shuffling traverse above a twenty-foot drop, then caught hold of a drainpipe, tested it with a tug, and descended most of the way. Overstuffed, split rubbish bags littered the ground, but from the wall he leaped over them and landed, crouching. Then he went over the back wall, and into a lane running behind the houses.

Poor Azure.

But another disappointment in her life might save a fourteen year-old boy, and that was the only consolation Josh could find for acting like a bastard, using sneaky avoidance in a way that would make his old instructors proud.

An hour and twenty minutes later, he was about to resume his sneakiness. From another back lane, he had watched the row of houses until all was quiet, while his phone displayed diagrams and images of the interior. The terrace was eight houses long – clearly, buying the whole row was too much even for Khan – and Josh's chosen entrance point was the fifth house along, owned by a law-abiding widower (according to a quick scan on the Web) who had nothing to do with any of Khan's enterprises, and had on occasion complained to police and council services about the noise from next door.

The house in question was number 39, and there was no sign of the owner moving about. In an ideal penetration exercise, Josh would prepare for longer, take additional equipment, and if possible three of his highly trained mates. But sometimes you had to act quickly or not bother, so he crossed the alley, jumped up, and clamped his hands onto brick. Then he was in a kind of vertical sprinter's crouch, pushing off with one foot, swinging out then jerking in with his arms, making full use of the myotatic reflex for fast power; and he was over. Tumbling sideways, he dropped like a cat, and remained on all fours at the rear of a tidy lawn.

A check of his phone revealed his subversion ware at work, altering the logged images from four different spycams over the last few seconds. Then he slipped across the lawn, just as his phone cracked the house system, and the back door's lock clicked open. He listened, then entered, taking in controlled large breaths, knowing that the reptile brain inside every human can respond to subliminal airborne molecules, communicating with the civilised mind in the form of intuition.

Nothing. He smiled, partly because it was the same old thrill: breaking the rules for a definite good; but he no longer had the Regiment behind him if things went tits up. Then he moved through the tidy house, climbing the stairs to the upper hallway, and finding the loft door in the ceiling. Standing on the banister, he reached up to push the door aside; then he grabbed hold, palms

in, and swung his feet up, jack-knifing upward through
the opening.

He shone a thin white beam from his phone, then
gekkotagged the phone to his shoulder, freeing his
hands. Looking around the darkened loft space, he saw
neat transparent boxes, all labelled. Old comics – here,
an X-Men run from the 1970s, artwork by Neal Adams
– and hardcore fitness books: Pavel Tsatsouline, Scott
Sonnon, Ross Enamait, Matt Furey. Josh smiled, then
turned his attention to the chipboard wall that sepa-
rated this place from Khan's enterprise next door.

From his belt, he twisted free his buckle, then pressed
hard. A memory-steel blade uncurled, then snapped
into stiffness. It was sawtooth, and just what he needed.
He pressed the blade against the chipboard, increased
pressure, then doubled it. The point went through.

Got it.

There was no vibration from his phone. His subversion ware was doing its work, hiding his intrusion from
the house system. Too much reliance on high tech, and
not enough on simple materials. But then, if the partition wall had been metal or brick, he would have found
a different way in; because there always was a weakness.

He started to saw down, starting the opening that
would let him inside.

[FOURTEEN]

Khan's people had stored junk in the loft, after wiring the place with motion sensors and infrared spycams – all of them hooked in to the main system, allowing Josh's subversion ware to rewrite the data. The biggest danger was that he would put a hand or foot through the thin floor. He crawled along a horizontal beam, stopping when he reached a hatch. Here he was prepared to slow down and take his time dismantling hinges or lock mechanism; but the only lock was electromagnetic, integrated with the system, and it clicked open with a simple command from Josh's phone.

Still there might be standalone alarms he had not detected, even a simple bolt to delay his progress. Tension compressed his heart and lungs as he reached for the hatch, took hold, and raised it a millimetre, a centimetre, then stopped. Through the trapezoidal gap, grey carpet and white-painted fittings suggested a hallway or landing. The air smelled cold and tinged with chemicals. There was a steady drone of pumps, but nothing to suggest human movement.

He pulled up the hatch, scanned below, then dropped through. Hanging by one hand, he

manoeuvred the hatch almost into place, then let go.
It banged shut where his fingertips had been, but he
was already crouched on carpeting, checking the
stairway that descended beside him, the narrow door
in front, listening and sniffing.

Once through the door, he stopped and checked
again. To his left was a storage cupboard – he checked:
cleaning fluids, sponges, a bucket, and mop – and offices along the right, while straight ahead stood
another internal door. Again, system integration was
Khan's undoing, as the door simply opened, already
unlocked by Josh's code. But this time there were people, two of them heading this way, and he crouched,
spiralling back, reaching the cupboard and pushing inside. There, he exerted conscious control of his
breathing, trying to command his emotions, interpret-
ing his fear as the adrenaline surge of a soldier about
to fight; but then the voices were past, neither man
pausing. After thirty seconds, Josh pushed the door
open, scanned the corridor, then exited.

Again the internal door was unlocked, and when he
peeked through, the corridor was empty, while the
rooms on the right had doorways but no doors, emit-
ting strong white light. There was an acrid heaviness
on the air, but whether it came from here or had
slowly built up in the stairwell beyond, emanating
from the virapharm labs on the floors below, he could
not tell. If he went down here, he could wreck the ap-
paratus, destroy at least a portion of the labs – but his
phone, when he checked it, showed a small red dot
inside the schematic: Khan was in the next portion of
the building, one floor down.

There were twenty-three people in total working
here right now, several sporting shoulder holsters as

well as knives at their hips. Far too many to fight. He took a silent pace forward as–

Attack.

–a pair of brown eyes widened, too late to process the real danger because for Josh the reptile brain was in control, and this man-shaped thing in front was a problem framed in geometry and forces, and here was the objective: to shut the thing down. Josh's fist slammed into the throat, collapsing it like cardboard, then both hands cupped the man's head and ripped it down, into his rising knee; and he dropped all his body weight, his forearm vertical, elbow piledriving into the back of the neck. The corpse smacked face-first into the floor, the darkening stain in its trousers and the stench of shit confirming death.

His ware had not indicated anyone up here, so this guy had been out of camera sight, not just him but – *two more of them* – tugging guns from shoulder holsters so this was it, milliseconds before death, and the fallen corpse was a springboard he used to launch his jump, a flying knee into a face, hammering down on the other man's head. He snapped one gun away from its owner's grasp – fingers crunched – and smashed back, dropping the guy to his knees. The other was out cold from the knee strike, so there was just this man to deal with, but he was still battling, left hand going for Josh's throat, but Josh slipped beneath, whipped a ridgehand, caught his own hand – the bastard's left arm and head in the circle of Josh's arms – and tightened the arm tri-angle-choke – so-called but really a strangle – twisting as he took the guy down, squeezing the carotid artery closed, sending the brain into shutdown.

Finally he stood up, slick with sweat and maybe blood.

What have I done?

This was no military mission, and he had no mandate for murder. At least one of the guys was dead, and the other two were likely to–

You bastards.

Inside the white-lit room was a glass table, and splayed upon it was...

You fucking bastards.

...a naked teenage girl, spreadeagled and webbed with translucent tubes, connecting her to a rack of nanoviral cells. She was alive, perhaps more so than Sophie, perhaps not – but at least Sophie was no factory, no farm for viral pharmaceuticals growing and evolving by unnatural selection, because viruses in the wild, under stress from antiviral drugs, flip into a new state of accelerated mutation, call it a metamutation; and what nature can do, humankind can subvert.

There were bite marks around the girl's nipples – one of the staff obtaining added value from the goods. Perhaps one of these three lying on the floor. Josh thought he had probably seen the girl in his peripheral vision, reacting unconsciously before rationalism kicked in after the event; which meant he hadn't murdered anyone – he had saved His Majesty's courts the expense of an official execution.

I ought to kill you all.

This was more than enough for him to call in the police, let them deal with the rest of Khan's people; but Khan himself might lead the way to Richard Broomhall. Checking his phone display, he flicked from monitor view to monitor view, tracking Khan's progress, two hard-faced men in tow. Then Khan stopped, said something, and went into a room alone, a room without spycams. A toilet. Under other circumstances, Josh might have smiled.

The other two waited around a corner. They were one floor down, and in the next unit. Josh made his move, with one glance back at the abused girl. Invisible to the system – his malware continued to hack his image out of the data – he went through the next internal door, downstairs, and padded to a halt outside the toilet door, just as the flush sounded. When Khan came out, Josh whispered from behind:

"Did you wash your hands?"

"Wh–? Mmmph."

Ducking low, Josh was under Khan as he toppled, taking the weight on his shoulders, then powering upright. There had been little sound, but time was collapsing, and he needed to get out now. Running upstairs with Khan across his shoulders was easy, almost a joy, triggering memories of basic training. Then he was past the room with the girl and the three prone men – and how many other victims lay in rooms throughout the building? – and jogging along the carpeted corridor, through two more doors, until he was underneath the ceiling hatch he had entered by.

Rolling Khan to the floor, Josh undid his own belt, unravelling high-tensile cord. Then he wrapped it crosswise around Khan's body, forming an X across chest and back, and played out the tension as he swung himself up into the loft. From there, he braced his feet either side of the hatch opening, and began to pull upward, hand over hand, enjoying the hard burn in hamstrings and back, ignoring the cord cutting into his hand, thankful for the years of kettlebell swings and snatches, of barbell deadlifts and Hindu squats, feeling in control. Finally, he manhandled Khan up through the opening, and lowered the hatch in place. Now let the fuckers wonder where their boss had gone.

Khan's eyelids fluttered. Josh punched once, to the carotid.

Then he hauled Khan across the loft, pushed him through the opening in the partition, followed, and forced the cut portion back into place. Next, he lowered Khan through the loft hatch, dropped down beside him, and picked up the slack weight, across his shoulders once more in a fireman's carry. Downstairs, out through the kitchen and the back door, causing it to relock... and then Josh stopped, because a white-haired man was standing there, examining the flowers. His stance was ramrod-straight, and his eyes were clear.

"Is that the dodgy bugger who owns the shop?"

"Yes, sir. And I apologise for being in your home, but this dodgy bugger has been running virapharm labs in those four houses. Your loft was my way in."

"Virapharm."

"There's at least one teenage girl in there. And very shortly there'll be police by the truckload. I'd appreciate it if you weren't around, and had amnesia about this."

"Well." The old guy's smile gave Josh hope. "My daughter makes a tremendous curry. Think I'll go see her."

"Right. You don't want this bastard's people thinking you had anything to do with this."

"So how did you get in? My door's unmarked."

"Shit."

"Not to worry." The old guy strode up to the door, and slammed a kick forward with plenty of hip thrust. The door crashed in. "There."

"Blimey."

"Clean living."

"Right. Er… It would have been nice to meet you, sir. If I'd ever been here."

"Likewise. If you ever had."

Josh hoisted Khan over the rear wall, gave a final nod to the old guy, and went over the top. There, in the back alley, he lifted Khan across his shoulders once more.

Hope I'm like that guy when I get old.

But Sophie would never get old. Some people did not get the chance.

Twenty minutes later he was sitting in his car, with Khan unconscious in the boot. The only tricky part had been leaving Khan dumped out of sight while he retrieved his car from the car park. But now he was ready to do something about the virapharm labs. It took another couple of minutes to rework his subversion ware – it was still loaded in the building system at Khan's place, and communicating with Josh's phone – and break through additional defences, uncovering the secondary surveillance net that had to be there, the one that monitored the virapharm production, meaning the helpless teenage bodies of both sexes splayed naked across glass tables. There were twelve of them in total, none of them Richard Broomhall; but he had needed to check.

He placed a call to Petra.

"I'm on duty." Her image revealed she was in uniform. "Day shift again this week."

"At HQ? So I can talk to you officially?"

"Officially? You?"

"Sort of. Take a look at these."

He tapped his phone, then waited. Petra's expression became stone as she sifted through the attachments.

"Shit. Poor bastards. Who did this to them, Josh?"

"Some nasty fucker called Khan. Look at this map." Another attachment. "The last four houses are knocked into one. There's two dozen guys in place, maybe more, with guns."

"Really."

Bladed weapons might have become legal, but firearms remained anathema, as suspect as paedophilia. When the presence of guns was suspected, the cops went in hard.

"Don't take my word for it. Here's more from their internal surveillance logs."

"I presume there's no sender ID on this anonymous tip-off here?"

"How would I know? I didn't send nothing to no one."

"Uh-huh. Like I'm sure forensics won't find traces of your DNA inside the place."

"It would be nice if they didn't."

"Well, I'm sure they won't. Take it easy, Cumberland."

"You too, Osbourne."

He was about to end the call when she said: "Shit. That girl. I know her."

"Excuse me?"

It was the naked girl he'd found.

"Her name's Angelina Kolchek. Her father's been ranting at us about his missing daughter. He's hard to ignore."

"Someone important?"

"Only to scum. Vinnie Kolchek is a grade-A bastard, into everything, except he boasts that he never exploits kids, and any whores he runs are volunteers, not kidnap victims."

"Sounds like a lovely chap. Where would he be, if I ever wanted to visit?"

"You wouldn't." A chime sounded: an attachment arriving in his phone. "But if you did, he'd be there."

"Take it easy."

"You too. Don't let him sell you a car."

The phone went blank.

Perhaps fifty used cars were parked in front of the single-storey building. Red, white, and blue pennants fluttered, while moving posters scrolled through hyperbole – Prices slashed! Lifetime bargains here! – and cheerful music played from outdoor speakers. Josh drove past the customer parking slots, circling round to the back. Inside a cavernous garage, mechanics were at work. A welding torch was incandescent. Several men paused as Josh parked, climbed out, and walked towards them, phone in hand.

"Hey, guys. I need to talk to Mr Kolchek."

A bulky man came forward, his skin grease-stained, his hair incongruously bleached.

"Don't know no Mr Kolchek."

"Sure you don't. Take this." Josh held out his phone. "Show that to the guy you've never heard of."

"Huh?"

"I'll wait here while you do it."

The guy with the bleached hair took the phone, weighed it in his hand, then carried it inside the main building. His colleagues stopped working – apart from the welder, who perhaps had not noticed – folding their arms and forming a semicircle focused on Josh.

"You all training to be salesmen? You've got the charm thing down, big time."

"Just try us, pal."

"You mean, like a test drive?"

Jaw muscles clenched, but no one lost control. That was just as well. Josh had not taken any guns off Khan's men – he wanted the weapons to remain as evidence – but he had his own weapon now, holstered at the small of his back: a Browning PulseCloud, able to drop three or four guys at a time.

There was a bustle at the back, then a large man with a scarred face came forward, with a smaller guy behind him.

"Who the fuck are you?" said the big man.

"The man who found your daughter, if you're Vinnie. Otherwise, I'm the man who found his daughter."

"All right," said the smaller man. "Where's Angie?"

So this was Vinnie Kolchek. He should have known by the eyes.

"Safe by now." Josh held up his hands. "The police should be raiding the place about now. They'll have medics with them. Your Angie isn't the only kid Khan's people had."

"Khan." Kolchek paled, still clenching Josh's phone. "That piece of shit did this?"

"That's the man."

"So what do you want?"

"The police are raiding Khan's place, but they're not going to find him."

"Fuck that. He got away?"

"Not exactly." Josh reached out for his phone. "You mind?"

After a hesitation: "All right."

"Thanks." Josh took the phone back, then pointed it at his car. "And Merry Christmas."

The lid popped open. Inside, Khan was awake, snarling and thrashing against his bonds. Before the others could move, Josh strode to the car, pulling out the Browning.

"One chance." He aimed at Khan's head. "Either I leave you here with Vinnie boy, or you tell me what I need to know. Then I drive fast and drop you some-place, your choice."

"Motherfucker," said Kolchek.

"Shut up, Vinnie. This is my play."

"What do you want?" Khan looked up. "I'll tell you, all right?"

Left-handed, Josh brought up Richard Broomhall's image on the phone, and turned it towards Khan. It was a surveillance still from the corner shop: Richard and his unknown friend.

"Who are these two? One of them ran an errand for you the other night."

Khan's eyes narrowed. That was fast, he had already figured that Maxwell had talked.

"Strange kid, first time I used him. Don't know him."

"And the other?"

"That's Jayce. Just Jayce, no other name that I know."

Behind Josh, Kolchek's men were fanning out.

"Where does he hang out, Khan? Give me some-thing, quick."

"Shit, these kids are on the street, you know? He could be anywhere."

"Uh-huh. You know, I am kind of outnumbered here."

"There's a shelter at Zenith Place."

"Where you found him, is it?"

Khan shook his head.

"So where else?" Josh went on. "Other haunts? People he hangs around with?"

"Had friends. The Spidermen threw him out. Kid was a shit. Loner."

"You call him a shit? You're something, Khan. Gimme something more."

"That's it." Khan shrugged his shoulders. "What do you expect? Just a punk. Now get me out of here."

"Giving orders? Your world changed today, and you still haven't realised."

"Hey, we had a deal."

Josh holstered his Browning. Then he reached inside, hauled Khan out of the boot, and dropped him like a sack. He slammed the boot lid down.

"Too bad I'm a liar."

He nodded once to Vinnie Kolchek, climbed into his car, and put it in drive. There was no need to use his rear-view mirror as he left the dealership. Then he was out on the road, driving steadily, careful not to give in to adrenaline and boost the acceleration; because safety was everything. After all, he was a law-abiding citizen.

[FIFTEEN]

The pub was called the Golden Switchblade; Richard tried not to think about blades, the slitting of skin, the revealing of slick intestines. In the small yard out back – the sign read Beer Garden – Opal sat down at a wooden table, while he took a seat opposite. Brian was inside, fetching drinks.

"What did you do today?" Richard asked.

He imagined hours of gekrunning practice, or poring over educationware on screen, though she didn't appear to attend school.

Zajac, with a blade in hand–

"What's up, Richie?"

"Nothing." He should not have thought of school. "Sorry."

"Huh. Well I was helping Ciara in the market, unloading boxes of fruit, stuff like that."

Across the garden, movement made them both look up. Not Brian, but a wide-shouldered man with shaven head and rolled-up sleeves, carrying three pints of beer by their handles. A smaller man had just taken a backward step into his path, at the cost of his own beer sloshing.

"Hoy." He glared at the bigger man, not seeming to notice the guy's size. "What you think you're bleeding doing?"

"I'm really sorry, mate. I hope I didn't spill any of your drink."

"Well, you bleeding did, as it happens."

"Here, have this full one. Pint of best, was it?"

"Er... Yeah."

"There ya go then. Take it easy."

"Well. OK."

The bigger man walked on, deposited his remaining two pints at a table where his friends were waiting. The two looked at him and he shrugged.

"Looks like I lost my own," he told them. "Back in a mo."

"Be careful how you go, delicate bloke like you."

"Yeah, pay attention to where you're walking."

"Do my best."

Opal watched him go back inside, then looked at the smaller man, now laughing with his cronies as he finished off his old drink before commencing on the new one. She shook her head.

"I don't get it," she said. "How can anyone be such a twat? Can't he see?"

Brian arrived, carrying three Cokes, and put them down. Condensation glistened on the glasses.

"See what?"

"That little bloke bumped into Eddie McMullen. Gave Eddie an earful, too."

"Holy Christ."

"Look at him laughing, the twat. Got no idea how lucky he is."

"Mind your language."

Richard sipped from his Coke. It was good, cold and

with a kick. No alcohol, because that was for losers – people trying to cheer themselves up with a depressant, where was the sense in that? Father might earn money but his face looked flabbier, blotchier by the week; and whenever he locked himself away in his office at home, he invariably appeared bloodshot next morning, breath stinking, at least until after breakfast, and forty minutes in the master bathroom.

Their home had six bathrooms, five en suite. The squat had one, shared by two dozen people, give or take, and the water that came out was tepid and brownish. Paying no bills, they were lucky to have that much.

"Why's he lucky?" He meant the small guy who'd mouthed off.

"Big Eddie" – Brian gestured with his glass – "trains in four fighting systems, works the doors at Zero Point where he will not" – looking at Opal – "let under-eighteens inside, and he competes in Blade in the Cage. That's like Knifefighter Challenge, a semi-pro circuit that–"

Richard's stomach convulsed, a tsunami of acid inside. He got up and stumbled back from the table.

"Sorry…"

"Bloody hell, Richie."

"I'm sorry."

Hands clutched against his stomach, he moved as if trying not to be sick – as if a blade had pierced – into the pub, but going straight through, holding it all in, staggering through the exit and back into light. No one came after him, so he continued alone, into the hot evening, nothing in mind except to keep going until his eyes stopped burning and the acid inside him died down.

• • •

Maybe an hour later, he was sitting slouched inside a
bus shelter at the Elephant & Castle. The fear had
seeped away; now his limbs felt soft with tiredness. He
listened as two women talked.

"It isn't all bad. Look at this." One of them gestured
around the aluminium-and-plastic shelter. "Ten years
ago, there'd have been graffiti everywhere."

Some places were still covered in tags, usually where
they sprayed the streetcams first.

"Maybe, but with this heat, it's all like falling apart."

"Damn scientists and their global warming. Ozone
layer and God knows what else."

Ozone is an allotrope of oxygen, the atoms going
around three to a molecule instead of in pairs – "*Like a
saucy ménage-à-trois instead of a couple*" some chemist had
said in an online lecture. The live adult audience had
laughed. Richard had looked up ménage-à-trois at OE-
DOnLine; he already knew what an allotrope was.

"Excuse me?" he said.

"Hello, son. What is it?"

He wanted to ask them what sort of person would
have been measuring ozone concentrations high over
the Antarctic in the previous century, and exactly what
kind of people had been warning the world for decades
about climate transition. He wanted to say that without
science there wouldn't be civilisation, and the average
lifespan would be thirty-something or less. That if they
didn't get the new reactors built in time, everything
would fall apart. He wanted to say all that.

"Er… do you know how long till the bus comes?"

"Says right there, on the display. Seven minutes."

"Oh. Thank you."

Then they were deep in conversation again, this time
about taxes and what the Benbow family were up to in

SimEastEnders. They paid no attention as he slipped out of the bus shelter. How could they be so certain about things, and yet so ignorant? Why couldn't sensible people be in charge of the world?

He thought about Dr Duchesne. She'd been nice, so very calm. Perhaps he could be like her some day, far different from Father. Some day. Right now, an ache was returning to his stomach, this time from lack of food.

Later again, and still hungry, he stood at South Bank, watching from beneath a concrete overhang – out of view of cameras – while gekrunners spun through acrobatic manoeuvres, skating across paving stones, cartwheeling down stairwells, tumbling over obstacles. The interplay of movement was mesmerising, their ability to keep their nerve incredible. Several tourists looked up, and he risked peeking out from cover. On the rooftop, three gekrunners chasing each other in fun, with a series of jumps and rolls to reach the roof's edge, then somersaulting down the wall to ground level, with skilful use of gekkomere gauntlets, lethally dangerous.

"–seen him yet," a man's voice was saying.

"From his profile, he hangs out here sometimes, not every day."

They were checking images on their phones, then glancing up to check out gekrunners and the watching crowd. Could they be police?

Worse, was that his image they were looking at?

"Let's ask. Some of these little bastards might know him."

"Right, and you want them to remember someone asking after their pal Jayce?"

"Oh. See what you mean."

"He ain't around. Let's get the hell out of here."

Richard pulled right back, trying to press into solid stone. Except it wasn't him they were looking for, was it? Nor did they act like police officers; but then, how many officers did he know? I'm a criminal because of Jayce. Because Jayce had taken him to the shop owned by Khan, but maybe that was not it. Maybe if he was helpless then it was his fault, because he was as weak as Father said. And now he could never go back home, not without them coming to drag him into jail.

Laughter sounded from around the corner.

"No, I don't believe it."

The police were gone. He moved out of cover, drawn by sounds of happiness. Seven or eight gekrunners, plus a few other folk, were watching an unfurled screen. Inside the image, a twentysomething man was tearing up a T-shirt.

"He's out of his head. Carlsen will throw him off the team."

"Nah, man. Him and André will have to fight."

"No way. They're on the same team."

"Gotta happen. He's just torn up Laurenson's clothes. They'll change the rules and make 'em fight, guaranteed."

"Shit, that Knife Edge House."

"Crazy, ain't it?"

"Wish I was in there."

"Huh? Now that is insane. Spycams on you for what, three months? Can't even pull the weasel in private, so how would you survive?"

So it was here again, the world's craziness swirling around, Knifefighter Challenge and all the rest, and couldn't anyone see how insane it was? But he remembered Mr Dutton, in the calm of his classroom, explaining that we create our models of the world through perceptual filters, so people see what they focus on: "*'To someone with a hammer, everything looks like a nail.'* Anyone know who said that?"

He and Jayce and Opal and Brian lived in a different world, saw different things than–

Arches, Wandsworth, 9pm Thursday.

Jayce had got him to write the words, a reminder of someplace he had to be. Tonight. Of course. And he probably knew nothing of the men who were looking for him. Someone had to tell him.

Finally, so tired from what seemed a full day walking, Richard reached the right area. He passed a road that would lead back to the squat, but ignored it, following the railway line overhead. If he had misunderstood, then there was nothing he could do; but if arches meant railway arches, then Jayce would be around here somewhere. He looked around as a scarlet bullet bus whooshed past. No sign of... A splash of red hair. The same shirt. Blanket beneath one arm. Jayce was ambling along the main road.

Richard called out, but Jayce kept moving along, head bobbing.

"Hey! Jayce! Jayce!"

He waved both arms. Several passersby glanced at him.

"Jayce!"

The redhead turned – it was him – then turned left and disappeared behind a building.

Why did he do that?

Trying to jog, Richard moved faster, or at least with more effort – could you call it a limp if it was in both legs? – feeling the jolt in his knees. Three rats bigger than his forearm scampered across the street in front of him. Turning a corner, he skirted a bulbous pile of bin-bags, starting to wheeze, no longer with the breath to shout for Jayce. This was not a good place – sensitised now, he noted the street cams smeared with black, like congealed tar. Up ahead, Jayce broke into a run.

"Wait…"

His vision was watery, his gait a continuous stumble, unable to understand why Jayce was intent on getting away – doesn't he recognise me? – while scarcely notic-ing the silver-grey van that screeched past, heading in the same direction but an awful lot faster. Seconds later, smoke pouring from the wheel arches, tyres screaming, it swung across the road. A door banged open, three men tumbled out, and then they had Jayce. Levering his arms, they swung him inside, rolled back in, and closed the door, the van already accelerating, hurtling around a corner, and out of his world.

Jayce…

But that was the end of him. Richard took some dreamlike paces forward. Jayce had been standing right there, where the blanket had fallen.

I should call the police.

But what he imagined was heavy hands coming down on his shoulders, snapping cuffs around his wrists, and throwing him into a police van much as the strangers had done to Jayce.

He picked up the blanket.

It's Jayce's, isn't it?

Did he want to remember his sort-of friend? Or was he just keeping an abandoned item that he could use? Was this all that life was on the streets?

It's awful here.

He rolled the blanket, draped it over his shoulder, walked on.

Somehow he found himself amid greenery, sitting on grass and staring at a flowering plant, captivated by its leaves more than its yellow blossoms. He blinked, trying to remember how he'd got here. It was a tiny public garden, no more area than a large town house, encircled with tall brick walls. Rhododendrons and other things he couldn't name grew from strips of black soil, surrounding lawn grass, impeccably maintained.

During his walk here, he had passed a pub just as a door slammed open and a man flew out, launched by two large bouncers. On screen it would have looked like a cartoon, but up close the suddenness, the thump of bone on pavement, made it physical. From inside the pub came the sound of shattering glass, and the larger bouncer said: "When will this heat let up? People are going nuts."

"Keeps us in work," his colleague answered. "Got your baton? Let's get back in there."

Here in the garden, the heat was peaceful, and there was little traffic sound, though it was in the heart of London. As he thought that, a beep sounded, high up. On spycams atop the walls, orange lights were flashing, and an automated warning sounded. *"This park will close in five minutes. Please vacate. Thank you, ladies and gentlemen."*

There was no one besides Richard. No camera was turned in his direction. He moved deep beneath a rhododendron.

"Please vacate the park. Thank you."

There was only one gate, made of patterned steel bars, taller than a man. And on the street beyond–

Police!

–someone in a dark uniform was coming closer. He strode into the park, turned around and called: "Anybody there?" Back at the gate, he pressed his thumb against a scanpad and exited. Steel swung shut, clanged, then locks clicked home.

Richard was shut in.

From his hiding place, he could see a wooden bench, luminous in the sunset, a bronze plaque glowing: IN MEMORY OF JASMINE BARCLAY, 1991-2022. Had she sat here? Alone or with others? Did she take sandwiches to feed the birds? Underneath Father's headquarters in the City, as in so many corporate buildings, was a glass-lined basement containing Roman ruins, once occupied by Roman soldiers, some perhaps from Tuscany, dreaming of their vineyards, suffering in the British chill. Everything was so… temporary.

His eyelids drooped. Still crouched beneath shrubbery, he felt his shirt beneath his chin, realised his head had lowered; then toppled downward into sleep.

[SIXTEEN]

It was nearly 7pm when Josh's phone chirped and Petra's image grinned at him. He had been in a dark, quiet mood for hours, staring at the barges on the Thames, seeing the man he had killed, smelling the stench, not comforted by the memory of naked teenagers turned into nanoviral factories, and the knowledge that he would kill again in such a situation.

"Hey, lover. I wanted to give you an invitation."

"Petra. What kind of invitation?"

Earlier, he had gone to the hostel at Zenith Place, checking out the only piece of information Khan had given him. No one had recognised the pictures of Jayce or Richard. But one of the volunteers mentioned that there were other volunteers and other clients – meaning drop-in homeless people – so that if he came back later, he might get better results. What he ought to do was return now, and check again, not stand around chatting to Petra.

"The short-notice kind of invite that says, come round to my place tonight, for late supper, dinner, whatever."

"Your place?"

"With zero evil intentions on my part, tight-buns. Yukiko will be there, and she gets jealous. Bring your girlfriend, make it a foursome."

"She isn't my... Well."

Petra was a careful planner. If she were going to invite him over for dinner – which had never happened before – it would have been two weeks in advance, with detailed interrogation about allergies and preferences. But if he were to pick a list of places likely to be hardened against eavesdropping, her flat would be in the top ten.

"So you're coming, then?"

"I guess so. Can't speak for Suzanne, though."

"Come anyway. Bring her if she's free."

"I'll do my best. See you later."

"Later."

One of the barges sounded electronic chimes, for no reason he could see. He watched it move across the darkening water, against a backdrop of golden-orange radiance and the ornate silhouette of Parliament. Then he called Suzanne.

"Oh, hi, Josh. I was expecting another call. Good to see you."

"Sorry, is this a bad time?"

"I've a client coming – this is my late night at Elliptical House. Evening appointments, once a week."

"I didn't realise."

"So, if you want to talk in person, be here at eight, when my seven o'clock leaves."

"Petra's invited us to her place. For supper. And her, uh, partner will be there. Yukiko."

"You want to go?"

"I think we should."

An eavesdropper might think they were a couple, the way they were talking. He had emphasised *should* as a way of suggesting they had things to talk about, but only offline. He thought Suzanne understood.

"So you want to come here, and we can go together?"

"Sure."

"See you in a bit, then."

"Yeah. See you."

He sighed when her image winked out.

A night-time receptionist at Elliptical House made him sign in, just to wait downstairs. He hoped that Suzanne was equally security conscious. If she started to say anything untoward, he would have to stop her. As the lift door dinged open, he felt his breathing stop, and perhaps his mouth drifted open, because her presence was as amazing as he had remembered.

Her kiss on his cheek was acetylene fire, or maybe sheet lightning.

"Josh. Hey. So we're off to visit Petra. That'll be nice."

"Well, I'm hungry and she promised us supper."

"Bad Josh." To the receptionist: "Night, Bill. Regards to Shannon."

"I'll pass it on. Night, Suzanne."

Josh smiled at the guy, because if he was on a first-name basis with Suzanne, he must be all right. So how do I know that? But he just did, that was all. As they exited, he took hold of Suzanne's hand, her skin so electric, and she allowed it to happen without flinching, just like a pro, making no mention of the hard object in his palm. When their hands disengaged it was quite natural, and she waited until they stopped at the kerb on Victoria Street before pushing at her hair, a

covering gesture as she inserted the earbead he had
passed her.

With the traffic noise, it was easier to form the words
in his throat like humming, not opening his mouth: "If
you have a throat mic, the bead will tune in to it, without your phone. Otherwise, you'll just have to listen."

They reached the entrance to the Tube, and began to
descend, the mag-escalator scraping, though it was supposed to be silent. Suzanne looped her throat cord in
place, started to attach her phone, then shook her head
as though changing her mind. A disconnected throat
mic, though it had a tiny processor, would normally be
useless without a phone; but the earbead would already
be hooking in by infrared, acting as transceiver, its signal firmware-encrypted.

"Josh?" Her neck muscles moved. "How's this?"

"Good. Petra said there was a watch on query attempts, for anyone searching for Richard Broomhall."

"Yes, I remember."

"Petra's never invited me to her place. She worded
the invite as if it were natural, you know? Like she's always doing it."

"She's being watched?"

They were on the platform now, and a train was
whooshing in.

"Nice timing," Josh said aloud, then subvocalised:
"Her or us. It takes official sanction for Broomhall to be
on a watch list."

There was a vacant seat and she took it, while Josh
turned to stand by the door. As the train slid into the
tunnel and the windows went black, he stared, hoping
to look lost in thought.

"OK," subvocalised Suzanne. "What about the
Brezhinski family?"

Josh blinked. The injured boy Marek, and his parents in Swindon. He had forgotten. "You called them?"

"We talked, and I think I can help them. Where do you want me to do it?"

"What do you mean?"

"Isn't this part of the search for Richard?"

She didn't know about Sophie. "Um, not really. I just thought you could help."

"Then it doesn't matter whether they come to London or I travel to Swindon."

"No. Except–"

He shut down his mind. *Except I have to go see Maria, and the only reason she wants to see me is to make it official, because she's leaving me for good. I'm sure that's it.*

In her seat, Suzanne twitched her head, grew still. Had she heard? The problem with subvocalising was that sometimes you transmitted too much. He clucked his tongue, deactivating the mike. *Balls.* When he looked again, Suzanne was staring at the advert screens, with the bored expression of any other traveller.

She knows.

Or maybe he was wrong, because she was impossible to read and totally intriguing; and how could he be thinking like this? Petra's supper invitation was a signal to be careful, and his attention needed to be out in the world, not wrapped up in his own head. Among the other passengers, no one betrayed the signs of trained watchers: the use of geometry and reflection, or a too-deliberate attempt to ignore him.

One missing boy. That's all we're after.

But the real world was more complicated and nastier than simple missions. And it always threw surprises, his being Sophie, and the end of the future he had always imagined.

• • •

Petra grinned at them, ushering them inside her flat. Josh checked the short hallway – droplet-lensed cameras, spyballs, beaded the interior – and stopped at the edge of the lounge. It was far bigger than expected, with a sunken square in the middle, and black leather couches running along the edges. The floor was polished wood. And as part of the effect, the other occupant was beautiful, dressed in trousers and three-quarter-sleeve shirt.

"I'm Yukiko." Her voice was beautifully pitched. "Come in."

"Josh. And this is Suzanne."

"Great to meet you both. And we've got something to show you." Yukiko gestured at the blank screens on three walls. "But Petra's too squeamish, so she's going to check on the food."

"Uh, right." Petra smiled. "What she said. And the place is hardened, so we can say what we like."

"Hardened?" asked Suzanne.

"No bugs," said Josh.

"She understands." Yukiko shook hands with Suzanne, then Josh. "Make yourselves comfortable."

They settled on the couches. Yukiko pointed her phone, and a picture flicked into life: a transparent cage, scarcely visible, in which two bloodied, half-armoured fighters stood with a referee between them, holding each by the wrist, waiting for the verdict. End of a fight, going to a judges' decision. Both fighters wore fast-stick wound-dressings; the larger fighter's arm and torso were wrapped in them. This had been the rule since Switchblade Saxon died while waiting for the result: walking wounded now received emergency dressings as soon as the final klaxon blared.

The referee raised the smaller fighter's arm, as the crowd howled.

"That's a *Knife Edge* tournament," said Josh. "The guy who won is Manning. Trains with Hatchet Dawkins."

There were other promoters, smaller fight circuits, but they used different styles of cage.

"So you're a fan?" Yukiko thumbed her phone, and a lean, bearded man appeared on screen. "You'll know Zak Tyndall, then. He owns the whole show."

Suzanne, Josh realised, was looking at him and Yukiko, not the screen.

"Tyndall," he said. "Zak, son of Zebediah. Rich bastards."

"Entrepreneurial geniuses. The father is a real political power in the land, without ever holding office."

Josh stood up, turning away from the screen.

"This isn't about *Knife Edge*, is it?"

"Not really," said Yukiko. "Apart from the coincidence that the big knife-fighting final is on the night of the general election, right before online voting commences. And that Fat Billy Church has his name linked to the programme."

"Uh-huh. Thing is," said Josh, "my diary's fully booked. Washing my hair, picking my nose, important stuff like that. Maybe we can do changing the world next week? Or how about never?"

"Or you could pick your arse" – Yukiko's tone remained as elegant as cut glass – "if your head wasn't stuffed right up it."

"Whoa." Petra came out of the kitchen, salad bowl in hand. "Ding, ding, time out. Fighters, return to your positions. Suzanne, would you lend me a hand?"

"So long as you protect me from these two."

Josh spread his hands. "Sorry, Yukiko. Sometimes my mouth runs away by itself."

"Are you kidding?" Yukiko nodded toward Petra. "How often do I get to win an argument round here? I need the practise."

"Ouch," said Josh. "Also, I surrender."

"Before we eat" – Yukiko tapped her phone – "look at this. See how healthy he is?"

The screen showed Zebediah Tyndall, the father, face lined but his hair still black, his stance erect.

"Eats right, keeps fit," said Josh. "Can afford the best doctors."

"Actually, he's never been reported as athletic."

"He must be doing something right. Or is that your point?"

"Hmm." Yukiko called out in the direction of the kitchen: "There's hope for the man yet."

"Good," answered Suzanne, while Petra said: "Are you sure?"

"Jesus Christ."

Yukiko was working her phone again. A sequence of panes spread across the screen, each running a five-second loop, showing fighters in action or just afterward.

"Fireman Carlsen." Josh pointed at the first pane, then the second. "Him, I forget his name, but he's good. And that one is Serpent Sam, aka Captain Cut."

"And how healthy would you say they look in the pictures?"

"Pretty fit."

More panes opened, showing bloody wounds, fighters spinning away from flashing blades or simply falling. Date-and-timestamps popped up, labelling every picture.

"Take your time," said Yukiko.

Josh had been injured before. He knew how long and hard rehab could be.

"That's not right."

No one could recover that fast.

"The dates are correct." Yukiko dipped her head. "But yes, something isn't right."

A juddering memory passed through Josh: *Sophie, and the message from that bastard consultant, what was his name, Hammond, asking about organ donation and his baby girl still living while the machines kept her–*

"Josh."

–small lungs pumping, blood moving through veins and arteries, feeding the brain that no longer–

"Josh, it's all right."

–knew how to think, how to do anything but–

"It's OK, you're back."

–live in the moment, as he needed to do now. He looked at Suzanne's eyes, the deep chestnut shade, and her hands were soft but strong, clasping his, giving reassurance.

He was prostrate on the couch, Suzanne leaning over him, Yukiko holding his wrist to check his pulse. Then Suzanne raised his eyelid with her thumb.

"Has this been happening often?"

"Only when I think of... When I think about S-Sophie and the, the–"

"Do you like blue ice-cream or purple?" asked Suzanne.

"Wha–?"

Her fingertips came down, closing his eyes.

"Sleep."

His chin rocked to his chest.

This is weird.

● ● ●

When he awoke, it was after not being asleep, but in some other deep place where he could have moved or opened his eyes, if only he had wanted to. Suzanne's words were a warm ocean, surrounding and healing him. And then he came back into normal consciousness, feeling calm.

"Well." Yukiko looked at Suzanne. "Very nice, Dr Duchesne. I learned hypnosis at med school, but not like that."

Petra said: "I told them about Sophie's condition."

He had never discussed it with her, but they had friends in common, and her expertise was investigation.

"How much better do you feel?" asked Suzanne.

"Well enough to eat just about anything."

"You haven't tasted my food yet," said Petra.

But the scents were compelling, and when they sat around the table, there was moussaka and salad, flat bread and houmous, along with stuffed vine leaves. Petra was clearly skilled. During the meal, they talked little; it was only when the coffee came out that they returned to their reason for gathering here.

"Josh did good work today." Petra tipped him a fingertip salute. "Cracked open a virapharm facility, using runaways as incubators. Which is Yukiko's area, except hers is the legal kind."

"You're in research?" Suzanne asked Yukiko. "Not a clinician?"

"Mostly research. Time-dependent transition-capable networks are my current interest."

"Uh-oh," said Petra.

"Look, they've got brains." Yukiko raised her eyebrows. "Josh has testosterone poisoning, maybe, but Suzanne's free from infection."

"I understood every single word you said about

networks." Josh half-raised his coffee. "It was just the entire sentence that was meaningless."

"Terminal infection," said Suzanne. "But if you explain in simple words, he might understand. And maybe I will, too."

"It's just the old six-handshakes-from-the-pope kind of thing. Pick anyone on Earth, and you'll know someone who knows someone who knows that person."

"Sure."

"Look, if all your friends and acquaintances were randomly distributed across the globe – like, you're as likely to know a rice-farmer in Vietnam as your next door neighbour – then it would be quite natural that everybody seems to know everybody. But in reality, the people you know are the ones you work with, and the ones you live near."

"You're talking about nexus points."

"Right. There's a huge number of people with a smallish number of friends, and a small number of people who are hugely connected. Even Josh knows this, because it's how websites and physical servers constitute the Web. It's a straight-line graph: the more connections you're talking about, the fewer sites or servers have that number. And for disease vectors, nanoviral or not, a small number of patients are massively infectious carriers."

Suzanne said: "I've been telling Josh about complex systems, including human minds, and how they change fast, far faster than most people realise."

"Uh-huh." Yukiko nodded to Josh. "She's very fast. You understood what I meant about time-dependent networks, Suzanne?"

"I'm guessing that a person can be a natural nexus point – like a webmovie star or Zak Tyndall, with thousands of people they can call on for a favour – or have nexushood thrust upon them. If that's a word."

"Right person, right place, right time. A potential disease carrier can go through their lives free from infection, but if they happen to catch it, suddenly they're a nexus point."

Petra refilled everyone's cups.

"I'm just a simple copper. So Josh, who's going to win the Challenge? Bloods or Blades?"

"Probably."

"How many teams are in the Challenge?" asked Suzanne.

"Er, two."

Yukiko looked at Suzanne. "At least he can count above one."

[SEVENTEEN]

In the morning, Josh rolled off the couch as he came awake, landing in a crouched stance, checking the springiness in his legs.

"The warrior awakes." Petra was in the kitchen doorway. "Alert and ready for battle."

"And desperate to pee."

"Grab the bathroom while it's free. I'll make coffee."

"Deal."

To get to the bathroom, he had to pass the guest room with Suzanne inside. He paused, then entered the bathroom. Five minutes and a cold shower later, he was back out, wide awake.

In the kitchen, Yukiko, in T-shirt and baggy pyjama trousers, was staring at the coffee dripping into the pot. Her T-shirt's hologram showed a DNA double helix unwinding.

"Morning," said Josh. "How's the world's sharpest intellect?"

"Ugh."

"You want intelligent conversation from my sweetie," said Petra, "you need to wait for an hour. Longer, if we run out of coffee."

Yukiko's eyelids were almost shut. "Uh-huh."

"So this would be a good time to challenge her to chess?"

"Only if you can wait till lunchtime for her to make a move."

Once the coffee was ready, Yukiko stumbled back to the bedroom, mug in both hands like an offering. Petra put a phone on the table, then sat down. Josh sipped his coffee, strong enough to make him blink.

"The covert core monitors," Petra said, "have registers of subscribers. Apart from Special Branch, there's a bunch of subscribing officers in Thames House and Vauxhall Cross." She meant MI5 and MI6. "One particular monitor scans for querybots targeting people of interest. If it notices a suspect querybot, it notifies the listener software on each subscriber's phone."

"And Richard Broomhall's a person of interest."

"Not him. His father."

"Whose biggest corporate enemy is Tyndall Enterprises. Which is why Yukiko showed us that stuff last night."

Not just because the fighters received virapharm-based treatment when injured.

"Right."

"And Zak Tyndall has friends in Whitehall."

"Uh-huh. So the reason for the monitor doesn't matter, not to you." Petra took a slug of coffee. "Mmm. Now, if you want to search beyond the London Transport net, you're going to have to fiddle with the subscriber list, similar to your ShieldIx hack."

"Er… Right."

"You can't stop the monitor detecting your querybot intrusion, but if you hack the monitor in advance, you can empty out its address book of who to notify. Like stuffing paper under an old-fashioned alarm bell, so it vibrates but there's no sound."

"And reinstate the address book afterwards," said Josh.

"Right. The monitor only checks new stuff: processes being spawned, runtime components coming into existence. Once your querybot is up and running, the monitor won't care. Then you can put the list back in place, so no one notices."

"So all I've got to do is find a way of hacking through to the monitor. That's not exactly trivial."

"Maybe it is." Petra slid the phone across the table. "For you, lover. Take a look in Favourite Apps. Everything you need is already loaded."

"I won't ask how you got this."

"And I won't tell you how I accidentally cloned a Special Branch phone while we had spook visitors."

"Good."

"Good."

They clinked their coffee mugs together.

"There's something else, though," said Petra. "Something that worries me, although I don't think we're under surveillance."

"Which is?"

"If there are watchers outside, there's a record of you spending the night with the three hottest babes in town."

"I'll be sure to look exhausted when I leave."

"Perhaps we should carry you out."

The world was grey, and Richard was grey. Even the sunshine was grey. He sat outside the park, upturned veil-cap on the ground, with four coins inside: all he had.

"Spare any... change?"

But the busy feet had already walked past. In his listless state, he could not imagine walking that fast.

Am I going to die?

Perhaps at some point he could just let go of the world.

"There you go. Take it easy."

Coins spilling from a curled palm, a crouched woman straightening and walking on.

"Er, thank... you."

He woke up enough to check for streetcams. This seemed to be a blind spot, so he relaxed back against the brickwork. Other people walked past – workers heading for the station – and a few more coins tinkled into his cap.

Thank you. Had he said the words or merely thought them? *I have to eat.*

Retrieving the money, he jammed the cap on his head, and pulled himself up. His legs were soft, his knees painful. He made himself walk. Soon he was passing a row of shops, and in one doorway, a young woman kneeling on a grimy blanket. On her neck was a medical dressing, stained with pus. She was sobbing in near-silence.

No one was pausing to look at her.

That's not right.

He pulled out his coins, squinted as he counted, then put one third of the money back in his pocket. The rest, he carried over to her, and held out.

"Oh," she said. "Oh."

"It will get better."

"Thank you."

"Yes."

And then he walked on.

Finally, he passed a burger joint from which amazing smells drifted. He went inside, to where the fries-and-burger aroma was so strong, he wanted to cry. He stood at the counter.

"No, mate. Sorry." The woman pulled back the basket of sauce-sachets, which were supposed to be free. "Not in here."

"I wanted to buy–"

"You're disturbing the customers."

Richard bowed his head, and shambled out.

At some point in his wandering he passed MI6 head-quarters, familiar from movies: the sharp-lined ochre-and-green building, the laser turrets on the ar-moured gates. How could it be a Secret Intelligence Service if everyone knew where they worked? Then he stumbled on, passing beneath an old steel railway bridge, and found a stallholder who sold him a bar of Cadbury's and a bag of locust-flavoured crisps. The salt and sugar tasted fantastic; but afterwards, his back-ground headache worsened, filling his skull, dampening his vision.

At some point, as he crossed a dirty park away from the shops, a girl's voice sounded. The effect was like a giant hand swatting him, making him stumble.

Opal?

"–that way," she was saying. "Like this. When your hands hit the wall, your hips are still well back, so there's time to get your knees up to your chest."

It was a big rubber-coated block she was vaulting over, not a wall. Other blocks stood around the grass, along with crash mats. Opal made it look easy, going over with her legs passing between her hands, landing in a quarter-crouch.

"If we had gek-gloves–" someone started to say.

"Freerun first, gekrun later." Opal slapped the rubberised block. "If you can't do a Kong vault freehand, you'll never manage the gloves and skates."

She looked around her small group of trainees. A couple looked about fourteen, her age; some were younger, some older. One lad might have been seventeen, starting to bulk up with muscle; but he stared at Opal with awed concentration.

"All right," she said. "Next we try to push our legs out into a pike, right? It's like a Kong, but you double-slap and kick through into a Kash." She took several steps back. "When you start your run, make sure you're looking at– Richie?"

Faces turned towards him.

"Uh. Hi."

"Richie, you *idiot*." She was in front of him and grabbing his upper arms, as if she had teleported from where she had been. "What happened to you?"

"I don't… They got. Took. Jayce."

"He was bound to get arrested sooner or–"

"Not police. Someone else."

"Forget him. Have you been eating?"

"I–" He shook his head.

Her arms were holding him up. When had his legs grown so soft, unable to take his weight?

"Paul?" she said to the seventeen year-old. "Take over."

"Me?"

"Show 'em Cat, then dismount from Cat. Then a three-sixty Cat, all right?"

Paul's lips moved, and he nodded.

"Got it," he said. "Maybe a TicTac afterwards?"

"If you like, for fun. Only keep 'em safe. Everything

on the equipment, nothing on the street."

"OK. All right, everyone…"

As Richard left, guided by Opal, the group began to jump at the upright blocks and cling like a kitten on a curtain who suddenly doesn't know what to do. It was a feeling that he knew inside out. But Opal's thin body felt strong as stone as she half-carried him towards the squat that suddenly was home.

In her consulting room in Elliptical House, Suzanne used her phone to contact the Brezhinski family. It was Mr Brezhinski who answered, his image brightening in the small display. He was probably thirty-something, made older through the facial lines of stress.

"Mr Brezhinski," she said. "Did you come to a decision yet?"

"If you could come here tonight… my wife will be home, because her bridge club cancelled the usual meeting."

"My expenses will–"

"We're not rich, but it doesn't matter. Please help her."

"Then I'll be there."

"Thank you. Thank you so much."

After a moment, his image cleared.

"Call Josh," said Suzanne.

In seconds, Josh was smiling at her in the phone. But there lines on either side of his mouth that reminded her of Mr Brezhinski.

"Hey," he said.

She remembered that she'd been given this phone by the police, and someone might be monitoring. Perhaps she should not have called.

"I'm glad to see you, Josh. So what's up?"

"Mindreader."

"If you like."

"Maria called again. That's my… wife. Wants us to meet up."

"And how do you feel about that?"

"Like I don't want to be psycho-interrogated, cheers."

"Sorry. But I've just arranged to meet the Brezhinskis tonight. At their home."

In the phone image, he looked at her, then his gaze flicked across to his right.

"Can I call you straight back?"

"OK, if you–"

The display was dark.

Why am I doing this?

She looked around at her consulting room. Perhaps the ambience needed to be warmer. Maybe throw some kind of cheerful fabric over the magnetometer. Or perhaps what she needed was to let go of her feelings for a married man.

But his marriage is in trouble.

Closing her eyes, she breathed in through her mouth and out through her nose, a deliberate reversal. Her mind stilled. When the phone chimed, she was calm.

"Hey, Josh."

"If you want a lift to Swindon, I can take you."

"Why? I mean, great, but–"

"I'm seeing her tonight. Maria. It's all arranged."

She should not be doing this, not even contemplating it.

"All right," she said. "Pick me up here, in Victoria?"

"One hour."

"See you then."

His image was gone.

Josh Cumberland.

Just the way his face vanished from her phone made her feel bereft.

You're a dangerous man.

But she was smiling.

Sitting in his car, parked near Grosvenor Square – if anyone detected him, they might think he was CIA, working out of the US embassy – Josh worked the phone's illegal app, hacking the monitor system long enough to slip his querybot into place, then restoring the register. None of the intelligence officers interested in Broomhall senior would know that someone else was searching using parameters that concerned them. This was not the most illegal thing he had ever done; but it was close.

He would have liked the querybot to notify him straight away if it found something; but a direct callback was dangerous. Instead, it would post its reports to an anonymous website, and he would check in, via cutouts. Now, with everything set up, he put the phone away, and thought about his travel plans for tonight. If the bot found something straight away, he would have to cancel everything else. He should not have said anything to Maria, or Suzanne.

"So why am I doing this?"

At the arranged time, he was parked by the kerb outside Elliptical House. Suzanne tapped on the door, and he opened it from inside.

"You had it locked," she said, sliding in. "Is that habit?"

"In an urban environment, I don't want people ripping open the door while I'm stopped at a red light."

"Oh."

"And before I get in, I check the car's unoccupied, with no one in the back seat. From a distance, I can see that there's no one hiding underneath, or behind other obstructions, like concrete pillars. It's habit, not paranoia."

"He said defensively."

"Shit." Then he laughed. "I give up."

He put the car in drive, told the navsys he wanted to get onto the M4, and let it pick the route. It diverted him away from heavy traffic, then back along the Thames, past Olympia and onto the Hammersmith flyover. Were it not for the blue road surface, this would have looked the same fifty years ago. But there would have been no trains or trizeps in the sky.

During the drive west, Suzanne talked a little about growing up on the northern outskirts of Paris, and he related his experiences as a young soldier, drying up when he came to Maria and the problems of a military marriage, the spouse at home and the soldier anywhere and everywhere, abroad for months at a time. Finally, he dropped Suzanne off outside the Brezhinski house and arranged a pickup point – a nearby pub, easy for her to walk to – in case she finished before he did.

Then he drove on to the pub where Maria would be waiting. It was called the Silver Dagger, and if he had been there before, he did not remember. He parked the car, unclipped his sheathed knife and stowed it in the glove compartment. From the upscale look, it would be a check-in-your-weapons establishment, the kind of place where they politely refused to return the weapon on exit if the person was too drunk.

Inside, the counter was polished copper, the lighting golden. Some of the drinkers were in business clothes. Two games of pool were in progress, all very casual. And Maria was sitting beside a narrow-faced man who wore an Italian-cut suit. Boyfriend or lawyer?

Lawyer.

The man offered a slender hand.

"I'm Charles Little, representing Ms McLean."

"You mean Mrs Cumberland." Josh shook hands.

"It's a difficult situation, and I sympathise. Would you like a drink?"

"I don't think so." Josh pulled out a chair, then sat square to them both. "We can dance around for hours or you can tell me what you want. In a single sentence."

Little looked at Maria, who nodded.

"Just show him," she said.

She was as beautiful as the day he had met her. Funny how it was obvious now, when so many times recently he had been unable to look at her, seeing only Sophie's body worked by machines, while her mind was software that no longer ran, the hardware brain a lifeless thing.

Little unfolded a wide-view screen and touchboard from his phone, and turned it to face Josh.

DECLARATION OF FORMAL SEPARATION.

Beneath the title, bullet-point summaries preceded the separate clauses, all clickable for the full legalese, to any depth required, with sideways links to any part of British law or beyond.

"Just tell me what it says about ownership of goods and shit."

"That's a separate addendum, which can be filled in now or later." Little pointed to the link. "If you don't fill it in, ownership defaults to a fifty-fifty split on pretty much everything. For a fast-track, er, culmination–"

"You mean divorce."

"–it's best to keep to a simple formula."

"Uh-huh. Interesting that we're meeting here instead of your office, Mr Little."

"I asked him," said Maria, "and it is evening."

"Actually, I don't really have an office." Little smiled. "We're a twenty-first century firm. Online anywhere, that's where we work."

The City banks would have disagreed, but they had tens or hundreds of thousands of employees, plus the need for physical security on their tens of thousands of servers. A small law firm with maybe a dozen people might entrust their entire business to cloud computing in the Web; Josh's clients could not.

His fingers flicked fast across the touchboard. There were input fields allowing complex specifications, or simple radio buttons for easy options. Tabbing rapidly through the document, he speed-read bullet points, clicked into two of the detailed pages, then shut down the auxiliary panes, returning to the beginning.

DECLARATION OF FORMAL SEPARATION.

After a long exhalation, he looked at Maria.

"No doubts? That's what you want?"

Curves of tightening muscle around her mouth.

"Yes."

Josh looked straight into her eyes and pressed his thumb down on the reader. He kept his gaze there as Little turned the screen back, sucked in a breath, then said: "You both need to authorise it."

Maria stared back, pushing her own thumb down. Then she broke, looking away, sniffing, not wanting to cry.

"Duly witnessed." Little pressed down. "Thank you. Your generosity is–"

Josh stood up.

So it's over.

He had seen too much to fantasise about might-have-been. Too many dead soldiers who should have lived. Perhaps his eyes revealed his thoughts, because the lawyer's voice croaked into silence, and he pulled back, looking frightened.

Over.

Pulsing with the need for violence, Josh stalked out of the pub, praying that someone would get in his way, knowing it would be disastrous. Then he was by his car, shaking, the sky a deepening turquoise touched with sunset gold, pure beauty, while down here a rat rustled beneath the bushes, on dark soil containing a seething biomass of warring beetles and desperate worms, insects eating the babies of other insects, billions of organisms dying every second, some beneath the fangs and mandibles of predators, others killed and then sucked dry by their own kind.

It was a long time before he could get into the car and drive.

[EIGHTEEN]

Josh pulled in to the car park of the Red Stiletto, found the last slot, and parked. The pub's sign had once been a scarlet shoe – in the days when strippers worked here – but now was a glistening, stained blade. Inside, its main attractions were massive wallscreens tuned to sports channels. But there was no need to go in; Suzanne was outside, standing with folded arms.

"Hi," he said, failing to sound relaxed.

Her voice was nearly as tight as his. "What did she do?"

"Her and her fucking lawyer waiting for me, how about that? With a fast-track divorce, online and legal."

"What did you do?"

"Signed the agreement because… When it's over, it's over."

Saying it, he relaxed a little, though he was still sweating as if after a workout.

"My friend Miriam," murmured Suzanne, "went through something like that with her partner, and when it was over she said to herself: 'Now it's time to let it go, remember what was good and accept the rest.' And she also said: 'You kept hold of someone who lasted for years successfully, so you can do it again, and maybe next time do it better.'"

Josh rubbed his face, and breathed out tension.

"Well, good for her."

Suzanne touched his arm.

"Yes, she knew how to accept what you can't change, as the old saying goes."

"Right." Josh gestured towards the pub. "You want another drink, or something to eat?"

"Maybe at the motorway services."

It was quite a drive to the Reading service area, but he assumed she knew that.

"You want to start heading back?"

"Let's do that. You're OK to drive, clearly."

He held open the passenger door for her, then got in behind the steering wheel, inserted the key, slid his phone into its console slot, reached for the ignition button – then stopped.

"I was pissed off," he said, "when I entered the car park. Now I'm not."

"You look more relaxed."

"Yeah… You're quite the witch, aren't you?"

Suzanne's smile was enchanting. "Possibly my ancestors practiced voodoo."

"Mine painted themselves with blue dye and mud, but you don't see me doing it."

"Hmm… You know I can make you laugh, right?"

Josh looked at her.

"I'm feeling better, but not that m–"

She touched his arm and he tipped his head back, laughter bubbling up inside him.

"Jesus," he was able to say finally. "How did you do that?"

"Like this."

Another touch, and a paroxysm took hold, matched by Suzanne's laughter. Soon he was laughing so hard that the tears were coming. At last, she settled back in her seat, giving a final giggle.

"That," said Josh, "was the weirdest thing I've ever experienced."

"Voodoo."

"With the greatest respect, bullshit. How did you do it?"

"That spot I touched on your arm. That exact spot?"

"I don't see–"

But she merely stared at the spot, and he laughed. Her gaze went back to his face, releasing him.

"Hypnotism?" he asked.

"Simpler than that. In Petra and Yukiko's flat, I created an association between pressure on your arm exactly there and laughter, between the gesture and the mood. All I did was press that point when you were laughing at their jokes. You never noticed."

"You're kidding me."

"Maybe I'm joshing you."

"Oh, please…"

"Honestly, it's that easy." Her chestnut eyes seemed to deepen to chocolate. "But the timing has to be perfect, at the height of the mood. It's one-shot learning, and it's a physical skill to create the associative link."

It seemed impossible; but his own reaction was compelling proof.

"This stuff happens unconsciously?"

"Very much so. Most of what happens inside our heads is below conscious awareness. There are sixty muscles in your arm, and you're not aware of orchestrating their movements when you put the car key in the slot."

"Yes, but–"

"What's three times three?" she asked.

"Nine."

"How do you know?"

"Er..."

Suzanne smiled. "Right then, you could have gone into trance – with a little encouragement – during that search for internal meaning we call a *duh* moment."

"Bloody hell."

"You can know an answer without knowing how you retrieve it. Every conscious decision you think you make, your brain started to create that thought three hundred milliseconds earlier. At least. End of lecture."

"Jesus Christ."

He went quiet, contemplating this. Then he sniffed in a breath.

"Will you teach me how you do it?"

"Maybe." Her smile looked surprised. "Maybe I will."

At the roundabout where he should have exited to join the motorway, he continued turning, into a second rotation.

"I need to do something," he said.

"Visiting hours must be over."

It was scary how she understood what he intended.

"I'll manage to get in."

"Then let's do it."

He took the Swindon road, and continued on to the hospital. Suzanne said nothing until he pulled in and parked the car. Outside, the night was darkening.

"Do you want me to come in with you?"

"No. Thanks."

Reaching over to the glove compartment, he became sensitive to her warm proximity, and the fragrance she was wearing: airborne molecules propelled by the heat of her flawless creamy chocolatte skin. Swallowing, he extracted a dull silver ring from the compartment.

"Fake ID?" asked Suzanne.

"A dummy, to make me look genuine." Josh extracted his phone from the console. "This is what will get me past the scanners."

He walked to the main entrance, nodding to the security guard beyond the glass doors, then held his ring close to the door, and faced the cameras. What should happen was a three-way check among data stored on the ring (including fractally compressed facial images), the camera scan, and the staff database; what actually occurred was fast intrusion from his malware, a false recognition code, and the clicking open of magnetic locks.

"Hi," he said to the guard.

"Evening, doctor."

Beyond reception, he walked corridors now half in shadow, conserving energy and helping patients sleep. The wall signs glowed, but he did not need them to find his way. At the nurses' station outside the coma unit, he stopped, opening up his senses while remaining still inside. From the sounds and other subliminal cues, he understood there were two nurses inside the open office, drinking lemon tea – he could smell it. Their chairs creaked as they rotated them, one leaning close to murmur something to the other; and as they naturally faced away from the doorway for a moment, Josh slipped past.

Inside Sophie's room, machines sucked and hissed, susurrating as they worked her small lungs. Medicinal smells were strong. Monitors glowed and beeped, tracking her physiology and rendering a clear message in steady coloured graphs: no change.

Sophie's face was delicate, luminescent grey in the half light. He brushed a curl, fine and wispy, away from her forehead. Then he took her fingers in his, remembering her as a baby, grasping a single finger, smiling her heart-splitting smile.

My little girl.

For a long time he held still; then he leaned over, kissed her forehead, and stepped away.

"Good–"

I can't say it.

A complete farewell was impossible.

His exit route was irrational, perhaps from the need for physical action. He raised the window of Sophie's room – he was three floors up – went through, pulled the window shut – the automatic lock clicked home – then spidered his way down in the dark. Brickwork was hard and gritty against his palms. His shoe soles made scraping noises as he descended. Then there was ground beneath his feet: an anticlimax that came too soon.

Everything people do is for unconscious reasons. Wasn't that what Suzanne had been trying to tell him? He knew symbolic logic, could design software in Evolutionary Z, but it seemed to have little to do with the way his mind worked, or the way Sophie's image remained in his mind no matter what he was doing.

When he opened the car door, Suzanne flinched.

"Where did you come from? I was watching the entranceway."

"Sorry."

He slid in and closed the door. And sat there.

"What happened, Josh?"

"I... I tried to say goodbye."

"What stopped you?"

He closed his stinging eyes as his mouth turned down. Then he blinked a few times.

"It's too late, because she's gone. It was too late the moment the car hit her."

Suzanne's hand was on his forearm. No psych trick, just a human gesture.

"That's not Sophie," he went on. "It's a remnant, like a fingernail or a – a lock of hair."

"I'm so sorry."

He nodded.

Time passed. Epochs or minutes, he could no longer tell the difference. Then he slid his phone back into the console, and turned on the engine.

"Let's get you home."

Once they were on the motorway and cruising, Suzanne told him how things had gone with the Brezhinski family.

"The parents are less stressed, and young Marek will be practicing healing visualisation."

On the battlefield, Josh had seen men who gave up and died from survivable wounds, while others fought, living against horrific odds. The worse the physical injury, the more vital was the mind controlling the immune system. Many soldiers developed a form of autohypnosis to cope with small combat wounds.

"Good." He forced his attention outward, onto the dark motorway, for the sake of Suzanne's safety as he drove. "You calmed them down."

"Actually, I got one of them sputtering with confusion as I tied them up in verbal knots, showing the contradictions in their behaviour. Sometimes you need to be outrageous and almost aggressive." She smiled. "Rapport can be overrated."

"So no hypnosis."

"Well, maybe a little."

"But you can't hypnotise someone against their will."

"Uh-uh. Look, pay attention to the road right now, but in the past, have you ever drifted off while driving… then come to your senses, and wondered who the hell was in charge for the past fifty miles?"

"Oh. So it's not just me."

"Everyone who's been lost in a good movie was in a trance, because that's all it is, an altered state. We drift through dozens of different mental states every day."

"Mind control," he said. "Tell me about the mind control."

"Bad metaphor. People want to learn how to hypnotise others but not go into trance themselves. Wrong, wrong, wrong. It's more like a dance, leading someone into a state where they're more resourceful than usual. The fastest way to induce a trance is to go there first."

"You're joking."

"I go into a different state from theirs, because my eyes are open, my attention on the client while they go inside themselves. But I'm still in a kind of trance. The fMRI proves it."

Josh was not sure whether he was impressed or disappointed.

"You say it's like a dance. There are links between martial arts and dance, you know."

"What I use is not a weapon."

"Oh."

Clearly she could read his mind.

Later, still driving, he tapped the phone, then told it the URI to connect to. Ghostly outlines in blue, red, and green popped up on the windscreen: a translucent heads-up display. Via proxies, he had the postings list from his querybot, with two hits registered, both recent.

"What's that?" asked Suzanne.

"High-probability sightings of Richard Broomhall." He tapped for a map-pane, which he dimmed. "London, south of the river. We can check the video footage when we stop."

"How far to the services?"

"Ten minutes. Perhaps we should go on. I've had to control my bladder before."

"Do you like watching waterfalls? All the water splashing down, splish-splash."

"Jesus, you *are* a witch."

"No, I'm not telling you to think about a flowing tap, the ripples of running water down a channel that—"

"All right, I'll stop."

"I promise to use my powers only for evil," said Suzanne. "Er, I mean good."

"Witch, witch, witch."

At the service area they pulled in, plugged the car in to recharge, used the facilities then carried cappuccinos back to the vehicle. Inside, he put music on. After ten seconds, it was replaced with a shushing sound.

"That's odd," said Suzanne. "Has the channel gone offline?"

"No, it's anti-sound in the chassis and windows. There's one-way silvering on the glass as well, now that I've changed the polarisation."

"Er... Are there onboard missiles? Machine guns?"

"I think that's next year's model. And your phone's blocked, by the way."

"Oh." Suzanne had velcroed her phone around her wrist. "Right, it's dead."

"Standard anti-surveillance. I don't want you flagged as of interest, or no more than you already are, by associating with Broomhall."

"Associating?"

"Or whatever. Anyway, let's see the footage."

Both segments were short, and he set them up to loop simultaneously in two panes. In one, the pinpointed youth walked along a street past piled-up bin bags – a moving shadow might have been a rat – while in the other segment, a youth in a green sweatshirt – maybe the same person – crossed a road to avoid a group of larger teenagers.

"That's him." Suzanne kept watching. "In both loops, that's Richard."

"Right." Josh blanked the display, then called up the map. "Depending on how far he tends to move at night… if he's settled in somewhere, he's in Wandsworth, maybe Brixton."

"Settled in. Asleep in a doorway. Poor Richard."

"Maybe not asleep." Josh did not want to mention nocturnal predators. "But trying to keep out of sight and warm."

"So you're not likely to find him if you start looking now."

"But if we–"

"We both need sleep."

"OK, but we make an early start," said Josh. "Or at least I do. Richard might sleep until noon, but he might have to clear out from where he's hiding before people start work."

"Is the car charged yet?"

"Not quite."

"Take me home, so I can sleep in my own bed. Since I haven't been home for two nights."

"You're wearing different clothes," he said.

"Very observant, for a man. Pardon the stereotyping. My clothes are different because I went shopping."

"Speaking of gender stereotyping…"

"Uh-uh. I own four pairs of shoes and two handbags, no more."

"Whereas I made a whole career of firing big guns. I mean really massive."

"In order to make up for…?"

"Oh, that. Well" – Josh held thumb and forefinger a centimetre apart – "we are talking tiny in other departments. Minuscule."

Suzanne was laughing.

"You are a bad man, Josh Cumberland. Take me home."

[NINETEEN]

At 5.30 am Josh was out running, past Earl's Court and through the Gothic cemetery, making a long loop back to his hotel, a white-painted cheapish place he had used before. There was parking for guests, and he thought he might leave his car here today. Back in his room, he showered fast, drank protein shake, and left ten minutes later. Soon he was riding a bus to Vauxhall, sipping from a take-away cappuccino. A few minutes before eight, he walked past the first place where Richard Broomhall had passed through surveillance. Which way would the lad have gone?

Up ahead, a group of grimy-looking individuals stood with cardboard cups and rough-cut sandwiches in hand. They were on a gravel lot in front of a dilapidated concrete cabin, some small business long gone to ruin. Several volunteers were setting out plastic chairs. One was a thickset, square-jawed woman with short grey hair. She looked capable.

Josh called up his clearest image of Richard Broomhall, and held out his phone as he advanced.

"My name's Josh. And this is Richard, in the picture."

"We don't talk to the authorities, didn't they tell you?" The grey-haired woman continued unstacking chairs. "Not about individuals."

"Sure." Josh picked up a chair one-handed and set it down. "I'm not exactly official, just helping the family. The kid could be in trouble."

"They all are. So what kind was he in before? What did he run away from?"

"I... don't know. Not completely."

"So why would you drag him back there?"

"Look, the streets are hardly safe. He comes from a well-off home, good school."

"And your point is?"

"Shit." Josh looked at his phone. The kid was four years older than Sophie. "If it was my daughter, I'd tear the city apart to find her."

"So what's the boy's father doing right now?"

Josh blinked. This was his week for being off-balanced by strong, knowledgeable women. "Counting his money, I should think."

At this, the woman gave a snort and a half-laugh. "Show me the picture again."

"Here."

"Couple of days back, he came around. I gave him a sweatshirt."

"A green sweatshirt?"

"Actually, yes. Why?"

"It's all right, nothing's happened. Someone spotted a kid wearing green, might have been Richard." He did not want to discuss hacking into surveillance data. "You don't know where he's hanging around?" he went on.

"No, I don't."

"Shit."

"Look... they disappear," said the woman. "Run-aways, they always stop showing up, sooner or later. But recently, it seems to have hit the young ones more, you know?"

"Is this something the police are aware of?"

"Not so you'd notice, officially. But some of the offi-cers who work the streets are good people, including my partner. They know, for all the good it's done."

"Does your partner work locally?"

"Sometimes, but not as a rule. You wanted to give me a copy of that picture, is that it?"

"If you think it would do good," he said. "Unofficially."

"Meaning you don't want it on the system."

"That might cause questions for your partner."

"My partner is honest and good at the job."

"I'm sure she is," said Josh. "I'm on Richard's side. There's nothing dodgy in that."

The woman blinked.

"You're pretty sharp," she said.

"My best friends are lesbians and witches."

"Huh." She held up her own phone. "Give me the details. And I'm Viv."

"Pleased to meet you, Viv." He redfanged the data. "And I'm making you a promise."

"Which is?"

"I won't put him back in danger."

Viv looked at him for almost a minute, then held out a thick-fingered hand.

"Good to meet you, Josh."

"Likewise, Viv."

Her grip was dry, solid and strong.

Carol Klugmann was waiting in the coffee shop, larger than life, with the staff already in thrall. Suzanne shook her head as Carol called out: "Harry, my friend'll have a latte, full-fat and big as you can do it. None of that skinny shit, all right?"

Behind the counter, one of the baristas grinned, then nodded to Suzanne. "I'll bring it over," he said. "Just for you."

"You mean, because you're frightened of Carol."

"Not so much frightened," he said, "as terrified."

She sat down, opened her handbag, took hold of Carol's phone and popped it inside, then snapped the bag shut. After putting it down on the floor between her feet, she smiled.

"This has been an education," said Suzanne, "in police procedures."

"You got something to hide, honey?"

"I don't think so, but I don't know what you're about to say. My phone is in Elliptical House, but there's spy-cams here, like everywhere."

"Conspiracy theories now?"

"No. Broomhall senior is high-profile. People want to keep an eye on him."

"So why haven't the police found his son, if he's that well known?"

"Maybe because he hasn't murdered anyone," said Suzanne. "I don't know. So why did you want to talk? Am I suspended yet?"

"Broomhall's lawyers made the petition. No one's doing anything without a hearing, and that's not even scheduled yet. Early days."

"Wonderful."

"He did get a private investigator on the case. Cumberland. Did you met him yet?" A smile made Carol's face even rounder. "We got ourselves a private dick. A gumshoe."

"Josh isn't a–"

"Oh ho." Carol stopped as Harry came over with Suzanne's latte. "We'll settle up later, OK, big boy?"

"You got it."

"And no wonder," said Carol when Harry was gone, "you want to talk in private. What's he like, this Josh? Show me pictures."

"It's not like that."

"Uh-huh. Your pants are on fire, Dr Duchesne, but not cause you're a liar. I think the incendiary reason has the initials JC."

"Jesus Christ."

"Really not who I was thinking of."

"Carol…"

"What's he like at undercover work? You have been under the covers, I take it?"

"For God's sake."

"Oh, you haven't. Well, maybe it's best to keep your minds on the job." Carol's eyes flickered up to her right. "Keep focused on finding Richard."

"So I am in trouble."

"Let's just say, it would be better if he came back with a reason for running away that's nothing to do with you."

"Back up, Carol. If it was my fault he ran, then what are you saying? That it's best for him to be found, or stay missing?"

"That depends on whose viewpoint we're looking at it from. Right now" – Carol patted Suzanne's hand – "if we can maintain enough doubt, show possible reasons beyond the scope of what your session was to address, then you might get away with it."

"And from the viewpoint of a fourteen year-old runaway with no street survival skills?"

Steam hissed from the big espresso machine. It was solid and dependable, as you would expect in an old-fashioned coffee shop, never thinking about the pressure building up inside, or its scalding potential. Harry worked the device with practiced skill.

Then Carol answered, "Someone needs to find the poor little bugger."

In theory, Richard was back working in the bicycle and gek gear shop; in practice, he was sitting somewhere that Brian could keep an eye on him, and whether he got any programming completed seemed to be irrelevant. He worked with a gek-gauntlet plugged in to a non-phone workstation, the gauntlet's source code open in half a dozen display panes. Two panes were stepping through instructions in debug mode. Even so, he could not see the problem's cause.

"You all right?" asked Brian.

"I guess."

"You need a break."

Actually, he had achieved nothing to take a break from. There was no sign of Cal, the owner, who perhaps would have expected more.

"So, let's see what's happening." Brian pointed his phone at the wallscreen, taking over the display. "Maybe Fat Billy has resigned as prime minister. Or maybe he's made himself pope."

News item thumbnails formed a snowflake pattern around a central article, their distribution representing their degree of interest for Brian, grouped by subject. One pie-slice portion represented local news. Brian tapped a link, zooming in.

"Well," he said. "Greaser Khan, imagine that."

"What is it?"

"Something nasty happened to a nasty man. Never mind." Brian made the article disappear. "He probably deserved it."

"Is he dead?"

"Well, yeah… You don't know Khan, do you?"

"I thought he… I thought he took Jayce."

"Maybe he did. Police shut down a virapharm house the other day, which is why Khan was on the run. Except he wasn't running anywhere. He'd already been chopped into pieces, like meat in the butcher's shop. Nasty."

"Vira–"

Something expanded inside Richard's throat, while a huge invisible hand squeezed his heart and lungs into stillness.

Skin, beneath the cases, the metal slab, masked spectres and the scalpel glistening as it comes down, slicing flesh so it falls apart, with the sucking sound from hungry tubes–

"Hey." Hands, Brian's hands, holding him upright. "Richie, what's wrong?"

"Can't. I'm… sorry."

Puke came bubbling up from inside him.

Not again.

And spattered on the floor.

"Bloody hell," said Brian. "Cal's going to kill us."

The incoming call was anonymous. Josh accepted it as read-only, sending nothing back, until he saw that it was Petra. Grinning, he enabled full comms.

"Nice to see a friendly face," he said. "I've been walking the streets for hours. Not getting anywhere."

"I'll bet you're loving it. Met any interesting characters?"

"Well, there was a young lad working in a newsagent's who's lived in seven different countries in the past six–"

"See what I mean? You always find interesting people to talk to. You're the only person I know who can do that."

"Uh, if you say so. So how are you doing?"

"Fine. I like to watch the local news. A bad guy called Khan made it big in the newsworthy topics list. A couple hundred pieces of him made the news, in fact."

"Nasty."

"We narrowed it down to three possibilities: a pissed-off supplier, a pissed-off customer, or a pissed-off rival."

"So you're closing in." Josh hoped his voice was level. "You've ruled out everyone who didn't know him."

"Anyway, it's just a professional tip I thought I'd pass on, that little habit of mine."

"Say what?"

"Reading the news. Did Suzanne keep you up all night, lover? You're a little slow today."

"The news."

"Sometimes it's the business section that's interesting, believe it or not. Give that girl a hug from me. And Josh?"

"What?"

"Be careful. Really careful."

"That's a strange thing to–"

"With Suzanne, be careful with her."

"She's not dangerous, for God's sake."

"No, but you are. Hurt her, and I'll have your balls for earrings."

"That doesn't–"

The display went shiny black.

What the hell?

So much about Suzanne Duchesne was a mystery. Was he truly fascinated with her, or just reacting to Maria and Sophie and everything? Was he spinning out of control? Enough of the Regiment guys, whether from Ghost Force or other squadrons of the SAS, had ended their lives in spectacular ways after Army service, trying to find meaning where they had been taught to look for it: right on the edge, the more risk and adrenaline the better.

In the Regiment, you learned to accept what your comrades told you, because sometimes they can see a problem that you don't. Petra's brother Andy had been particularly good at it, just one reason why he'd been such a great troop leader, before the Siberian debacle. Good times, spent sipping tea around campfires and–

Forget the history. Look for Richard.

There was a greasy spoon on the corner. Josh went in. There were workmen polishing off great plates of sausages and chips, others with falafel or locustburgers. Josh was tempted to ask for a lightly tossed salad and Dom Pérignon, but maybe not today.

"Cheese bap and a mug of tea," he said. "And have you seen this lad, by any chance?"

The guy behind the counter was young and dark skinned. Unlike some others, he took care checking the image; still, he shook his head.

"Sorry, man."

"Never mind."

"Eat in or take away?"

"Here, please. I'll sit in the corner."

His table was at the rear. Incense smells drifted from out back. He sat leaning against the wall, pulled up the business news and searched for Broomhall. A tiny overlay pane checked for new sightings of Richard, finding nothing. The main pane showed thirteen recent items, none mentioning Philip Broomhall directly, all featuring companies he owned. Every one of them was facing a shareholder revolt or some other indication of possible hostile takeovers. Put together, it was an all-out corporate attack on Broomhall's interests.

Shit, I hate this stuff.

There are salespeople whose idea of aggression is to sell things more cheaply than their competitors. Business writers couch their narrative of corporate manoeuvres in the language of battlefield and military strategy. Without limbs being blown off in boardrooms, AGMs being rife with sucking chest wounds, and seventy percent burns on voting shareholders, the analogy was an insult. Or perhaps he was one with the limited viewpoint.

A related comment piece, one that did mention Philip Broomhall, described him as looking "unusually self-absorbed." Worried about his son?

Maybe he loves Richard and just can't show it.

"Cheese bap. Tea." It was a young woman who delivered the food. "Here you are."

Her gaze was dull and her shoulders slumped, and she shuffled back toward the kitchen with little interest in what was going on. Congenital, or worn down by her situation? But saving the world was beyond him: witness his inability to find a single fourteen year-old boy.

The bap tasted dry and floury. Chewing, he scrolled through his phone's contacts list, found Viv, and pressed. He forced down the food as her image appeared, with the homeless shelter in the background.

"Hi, Josh. I haven't heard anything definite, before you ask. But there was something I was going to follow up before calling you."

"What kind of thing?"

"Just a maybe… The lad might be friendly with some gekrunners."

"Any particular location?"

"No, sorry."

"Viv, you've given me the only piece of meaningful information I've had today, maybe this week. So thank you."

"Well, you're welcome. Look, we're busy at the–"

"Sure. Take it easy."

"You too."

So, gekrunners. He could fire off querybots to re-search their movements locally, see which places they haunted, perhaps even backtrack to where they lived.

His attention snapped outwards as seven young guys, aged around eighteen, filed in and sat around the win-dow table. The large workmen had departed; only two solitary men were left, finishing their lunches. The gang – all white, some with motile tattoos: a swastika rotat-ing on one guy's neck, or flowing lines of tears from eye to jawline – ordered tea, then sat waiting for every-one else to leave.

The dark-skinned man behind the counter shuffled his feet. His gaze kept moving towards the gang, then sliding away, while his hand repeatedly went to his phone, drew back.

Josh shut down his own phone.

First guess: five were armed.

"Tea tastes like piss," one of them was saying.

"We need to ask for our money back."

"With cash interest, like."

"Fuckin' dark skin cooks their brains, don't it? Absorbs heat, right?"

They sniggered.

"Need a piss," said one.

"Got a magnifying lens you can borrow. Help you find it."

"Fuck off."

It was Rotating-Swastika Guy who went past Josh, heading for the small toilet at the back. Meanwhile, some of the others were on their feet, slapping each other's arms, all part of the ritual. The two men who'd been lunching both drained their cups and left, heads down, trying to maintain a fiction: that nothing was about to happen, that what went on around them was none of their business. Finally, Rotating-Swastika came back grinning. Chairs scraped as the remaining gang members stood up. Rotating-Swastika stopped at the till.

"You got cash in there, intya?"

"That's nothing to do with you."

"Seein' as how you served us piss, it fuckin' does, pal."

"Please leave now."

The others were gathering in a semi-circle, one-deep, behind Rotating-Swastika. When Josh stood up, all seven of them were in front. The tables on either side would make it hard for anyone to outflank him. They thought they outnumbered everyone; in fact they were lined up, targets for him to drop.

"Oh, sorry, mate." One of the guys with dripping-tears tats had noticed him. "After you."

The thug's sweeping, ushering gesture, encouraging Josh to leave, was not courteous: it was passive-aggressive. In court, he could claim he was being polite; uneducated witnesses would find it hard to describe the intimidation.

Except I'm not playing.

As Josh breathed from his diaphragm, his voice came out deeper than normal.

"I'm in no hurry to leave."

Dripping-Tears Tat and five of his mates straightened, eyes widening. Only Rotating-Swastika Guy failed to react, immersed in mouthing off to the lad behind the till. But the others were frozen, their brains processing unconscious alarms, primal senses re-evaluating the violent potential here.

One of them grabbed hold of Rotating-Swastika and yanked him back.

"Come on, you dick."

Those nearest the door were already leaving.

"What–?"

"Police officer, come on."

Then they filed out, and were gone.

Good.

Except that part of him thought the opposite, that it was an aching shame they had denied him the opportunity of the dance, to let loose the reptile inside, the lizard-brain that fought with logic, and the primate layer that knew the joy of blood because a smile and a scream are predator's expressions, the baring of teeth and the spurting ecstasy of ripping and rending, hitting and twisting, smashing knee-joints, slamming skulls into red oblivion.

He wanted to tear them apart.

[TWENTY]

The guy behind the till was called Gopan. After thanking Josh, he called out all his family so they could give thanks, too. Three people came out from the kitchen: a large man called Uncle Rajesh, skinny brother Sanjeev, and the tired girl who served the food: Gopan's sister, Mina.

"You're all welcome," said Josh. "And look, you've already got spyballs. Why don't you get two more cams, and rearrange them there and there."

"Ah." Sanjeev's eyes were bright as he nodded, understanding the geometry. "Very good idea."

"Add an alarm that you can trigger," Josh pointed at Gopan's phone. "Then buy a monthly call-out plan from one of the local security firms. Except check at the police station before you deal with anyone."

"Will you be there?" asked Gopan.

"I'm not a police officer. They were mistaken."

"Ah. But you were looking for someone."

"I'm working for the boy's father, who's worried."

"Oh. Would you show us the picture again?"

Josh brought up Richard's image, and turned the phone to Gopan. This time Gopan frowned for a long time before shaking his head.

"I'm really sorry. Uncle Rajesh?"

The big man took a look. "No, sorry."

Sanjeev had been peering at it over the others' shoulders. "I don't think so."

But Mina gave a tilting nod.

"You recognise him?" said Josh.

"With Opal." Her voice was less dull than before. "Walking with Opal."

"Who's—?"

"Local girl," said Sanjeev. "Comes here sometimes, not often. Chats with Mina."

"When did you last see Opal?"

"Days ago." Mina looked down at the floor. "A few days."

"You know where she lives? Or which school she goes to?"

Mina shook her head.

"Sanjeev?" asked Josh. "Any ideas?"

"Sorry."

"That's OK. I've got a name. You probably don't know her surname?"

"Afraid not."

"OK. Thanks, everyone."

"Thank you!"

Smiles and nods and waves carried him to the door. He went out onto the street grinning, remembering to check for signs of the gang waiting in ambush, but seeing only a clear ordinary street, safe to walk along. After some eight or ten paces, he stopped, remembering Viv at the shelter, and what she had said just a few minutes back: *The lad might be friendly with some gekrunners.*

He turned and went back in. The family were still standing among the tables, discussing what had happened.

"Mina, I don't suppose this Opal is a gekrunner, is she?"

Mina's smile was big as she nodded.

"Jumps," she said. "Somersaults and things. She's brilliant."

"So are you," Josh told her. "So are you."

Uncle Rajesh hugged her, and her grin reminded Josh of Christmas and getting just the present you wanted, and had thought you would never have.

Josh waved a salute and left.

Richard looked up from the floor, sponge in hand, as Opal entered the shop, unhitching a backpack from her shoulder.

"Whoah, bad smell," she said. "Who threw up? Cal told Brian to keep out the winos."

"It was me. Again."

"Oh."

"Brian's getting some sort of spray, says it'll clear the air."

He rinsed the sponge in the bucket, and wiped some more. There was nothing left to clean up, nothing visible, but Opal was right: the stench remained.

"Hey, Opal." Brian came in from the back, a huge yellow aerosol in hand. "Stand by for some biochemical warfare. This is powerful stuff."

"Maybe I should open the front door."

"Probably." Brian looked down at Richard. "You must have started wearing a hole in the floor. It won't get cleaner than that."

"Sorry."

"That's the seventy-seventh time he's apologised," Brian told Opal. "I've been counting."

"Not that many," said Richard.

Opal asked, "What did Cal say?"

"He hasn't been in, thank God." Brian waved the aerosol, sloshing the contents. "Let's keep him none the wiser."

"Oh, right. He's probably at South Bank."

"And you're here about tonight." Brian pointed at her backpack. "Equipment check, right?"

"Uh-huh. So, you want me to open this door? Cause I'd like to breathe."

"Sorr–" Richard stopped himself.

"I've a better idea," said Brian. "Opal, close up, and we'll go in the back room."

She locked the shop door and tapped the buttons on the door frame. The glass shone with the word CLOSED, in reverse.

"Come on." She took hold of Richard's sleeve. "Let's get out of here."

He picked up the bucket, dropped the sponge inside, and let her lead him out of the room. From behind came the sound of Brian sucking in a breath, followed by the prolonged hissing of the spray. Then Brian was pushing him into the back room and slamming the door shut.

"That is evil, evil stuff. But when it blows away later, it'll take any other stink with it."

Opal tapped Richard on the forehead. "Don't say sorry again."

He grinned and shook his head.

"All right," said Brian. "Take out your gear, and let's take a look."

Around the workshop stood several wooden workbenches with clamps and tools, covered with bits of bicycles and other equipment, not to mention sawdust, metal filings and the heavy smell of oil, currently contaminated with sharp chemical scents leaking through the door. Opal made room on the least cluttered bench, then laid her backpack on top. From the pack, she extracted a pair of goggles and what looked like an ordinary white sweatshirt.

Brian used a clamp to hold a spyball camera in place behind the goggles. Then, even though there were four wallscreens in place, he unfolded a small display and positioned it in front of the goggles. Then he tapped his phone, and the screen lit up, showing a rotating abstract pattern.

"Test pattern. Opal, let's have the blackout cloth."

She rummaged on a shelf, then backed out bearing a folded black cloth. It looked flimsy as she opened it out, spreading it with Brian's help over the workbench, forming a tent over spyball, goggles, and the screen with the test pattern.

"The cloth's one hundred percent opaque," said Brian. "Lightweight but optically dense."

"Oh." Richard looked at the wall screen. "You're testing the goggle's response."

"Bright lad." Brian pointed his phone at a wallscreen, causing it to show numeric data plus a copy of the changing test pattern. "Now we cross-check the calibration."

"It's all right, isn't it?" said Opal.

"Your long-wavelength response is a little skewed." Brian pointed. "So it ain't perfect. But safe enough to use."

"Good."

Richard looked from one to the other. "Use for what?"

"Night run," said Opal.

"Tonight." Brian grinned. "You'll see."

"And the shirt." Opal laid the sweatshirt on the bench, clipped a thin cable to the fabric, and held out the other end of the cable. It had a phone connector. "You got the downloads ready?"

"Uh-huh. How's it working at the moment?"

"All right, I think."

"Let's see."

Opal did something, then star-shaped splashes of sapphire blue and glimmering emerald radiated from the centre of the shirt, pulsing over and over. After a moment, the red outline of a gekrunner began tumbling through extreme gymnastics across the blazing background.

"Wow," said Richard.

"It's so old." Opal looked pleased anyway. "Need something new for tonight."

"I've got just the thing," said Brian, taking the cable. "Switch it off, and I'll run the download."

"Lots of bright colours?"

"Absolutely."

"None of your political slogans?"

"Not for you."

"But no pink, right?"

"Wouldn't dream of it." Brian looked at Richard. "I hope you're memorising all this. If you buy her a present, it can be anything but pink."

"I don't–" His face was warming. "Er…"

"Maybe a pink *face* is all right."

"You're both stupid," said Opal. "I'm going. I'll be back later."

She started towards the main shop, then stopped, perhaps remembering the noxious aerosol spray, and headed for the back door, which she slammed open, stormed through, and hooked backwards with her heel.

"–ing boys," floated back as the door banged shut.

"Something I said?" asked Brian.

Bright sunshine. Stinking black bags filled with household refuse, stacked outside houses, waiting for services that would not come until the strike was over. That would mean the union and management sitting down to negotiate, pulling their thumbs out of their butts and talking to each other like actual human beings, abandoning the chip-on-shoulder resentment that was the national pastime. Josh had fought in Zimbabwe, in the former Somalia, and on the ice-covered steppes of Siberia. Every conflict was awful; each had provided glimpses of ordinary people, sometimes working heroically to keep their families or neighbours from starving, often amid surroundings that made Britain a paradise in comparison, every house an imperial palace.

People should have some fucking gratitude.

In a small park with pollution-stained grass, Josh sat beneath a tree, working his phone. His new querybots were popping up a richness of data, hits tagged gekrunning, freerunning or both. Among the surveillance data, none crossmatched exactly with the search argument Opal, but among the myriad currents of microblogs, he found something related – an avatar called OpalKid273, who had posted today:

nite run *2nite* ru up 4 it? nu route nu shirt nu trx!!!

Most of her subscribers were in the *run_gek_run* forum. Hyperlinks had been bidirectional since Semantic Web, but few users realised the ease with which querybots could heuristically backtrack. Philip Broomhall had asked how it was that Josh Cumberland could do more than the police; the truth was that it did take many eyes to search for a missing youth, but Josh had an army of observers – they just weren't human, they were code.

In the gekrunning subculture, night runs were a feature; and tonight's run, according to the forums, was an unofficial part of the Mayor's Festival, set up years ago by some politician called Boris Livingstone, or something – he didn't bother checking. Perhaps, if OpalKid273 was the right person, she would have Richard Broomhall in tow tonight. His best inductive-reasoning bots were searching for links between the avatar and real images, ready to notify him in near-re-altime if she appeared.

Bringing himself back to the real world, he scanned the park, the stunted trees and rust-patched playground, noting shadows and geometry, angles of movement, and the thirteen people currently here, none paying attention to him or close enough to attack. Then he raised the phone.

"Call Big Tel."

"Hiya, mate," Terry answered in a second. "How's tricks?"

"Usual. Are you free tonight?"

"Had a busy morning, loads of legit fares, plus a little observation job at the same time. Putting my feet up now."

"So if you and your taxi were on standby for a call-out, that'd work?"

"Depends where it is you're talking about."

"South Bank, or close to it."

"Easy enough from the Old Kent Road. Give us a buzz and I'll be there. Prep for trouble?"

"A fourteen year-old lad. I might be able to handle him."

"Watch out for him squeezing zits at you. The old pus-in-the-eye trick."

"Jesus, Tel. You were a kid once yourself."

"Yeah, I had a strong right hand and poor eyesight, from all that puberty."

"And look how you turned out."

"Suave and sophisticated. A gentleman, like."

"Pretty much what I was thinking."

"Later, pal."

"Later."

He wanted to phone Suzanne, but her phone was bugged. Except that he could always introduce a little misdirection. In his phone's Favourite Apps, he opened a hotel and pub guide, then tapped an improbable series of keystrokes on the pad, stared at the lens so it could read his retina pattern, and placed the call. His signal now carried sneakware that subverted the GPSID system, changing the coordinates of his phone as logged in the data tier. So long as he and Suzanne were careful with their words, it was safe.

"Hey," he said.

"Josh. You're doing OK?"

"Yeah."

"Any luck on… you know." She was being circumspect, but if the police were monitoring the case, they knew what he was working on.

"Maybe Richard has a friend, maybe not. If I can find this person, it might help."

"That's good."

"Suzanne? Are you OK?"

"Disciplinary hearing. I've been served notice."

"What do you mean, disciplinary hearing?"

"Mr Broomhall has taken legal action through the

professional association I belong to. Apparently, that does not preclude the possibility of further action through the courts, it says here."

"Shit. Are you suspended?"

"No, but they tried for that. The review board agreed that the case was serious, but not that the initial evidence was so strong that I needed to be kept from seeing clients in advance of the hearing. They advised me to let my insurance company know what was happening, and not take on any new clients."

"You'll be all right. I'm sure you will."

"Thanks, but Broomhall has expensive lawyers, and I don't. The army with the biggest guns wins, isn't that how it works?"

Josh stared at her in the phone.

"You know, when Thatcher was prime minister forty years ago, a full-blooded Marxist coup clamped down on the Gambia republic, taking their prime minister's family hostage. Said prime minister was visiting Britain at the time – he was an ally – so old Iron Maggie didn't take too kindly to that."

"I know where the Gambia is. I don't know this story."

"Three – count 'em – three Regiment guys went in country to investigate, and discovered that the rebels were holding the family in a hospital. The guys went in openly and without weapons, knowing they would be searched."

In the phone, Suzanne nodded, though her expression remained unhappy.

"But they didn't need weapons," he went on, "because once inside, they beat the bejesus out of some of the guards, took away their guns, and proceeded to extract the family. Spirited them away in the night. In and out like ghosts."

"You mean like ninjas?"

"Yeah, like that. The thing was, that was all it took for the coup to collapse and the government to reinstate itself. Three quiet guys."

Suzanne bit her (very kissable) lower lip.

"You're an interesting man, Mr Cumberland."

"And you're not so bad, Dr Duchesne."

"You want to meet up for lunch tomorrow? In Victoria would be best for me."

"If I can. I'll ring you in the morning to confirm. Say, ten-ish?"

"Yes. Good luck."

He rang off, checked the surrounding park again. Three people had left, none had entered, and all appeared quiet. A boomglobe played music. Outside the railings, a group of youths was passing. Suddenly, one guy leaped up, hit the railings and flipped over backwards to land in a crouch, then threw himself into a shoulder roll and came up to his feet. The others laughed, one clapped his shoulder; then the group continued onward, joking about something.

The gekrunners are gathering.

Or maybe they were freerunners, but two of them wore backpacks that might contain gek-gloves and boots. He could jog after them, catch them up and ask about Richard or Opal, but it might have the opposite effect to what he wanted. They looked like lads who would be suspicious of the law, or someone who acted halfway official – witness the thugs in the café who had assumed he was a police officer, simply because of the way he stood and used his voice.

His fingers seemed to tap the phone by themselves.

What the hell am I doing?

His now-ex-wife's image appeared, eyes widening.

"I didn't expect you to call."

"Come off it, Maria. We can still talk."

"Yes, but will we actually say anything?"

She was there in his phone in miniature, the woman he had slept beside – when he was at home – for so many years, who had shared the unglamorous intimacies of farting in bed, of peeing while the other showered, of doing each other's laundry, the deep sharing of everyday life that goes beyond romance; while the miracle they had created in collaboration was one day to become a woman in her own right, except of course that would never happen, not now, because the mind was gone and the body-shell would not last, not even with the machines; because humankind can build electronic bellows to work the lungs but not rekindle the fire of a living mind.

She knew him deeply, this stranger. There were no secrets. They could say anything to each other. Yet there was a disconnect: a severed cable that had once linked two human souls in the ultra-high bandwidth, two-way transmission of love; a gap in the hardware; a break in the signal that might be only centimetres but might as well be lightyears, too wide for the spark to leap across.

"If you need anything, you can call on me for help."

"All right."

"How's… ? Have you been to the hospital lately?"

From the webcam recordings he could check, but he usually just peeked in at the realtime image whenever he had to, at whatever random time the urge arose.

"Yeah. Hammond talked to me today. With our, er, new status… it will only take one of us to consent to, ah, you know."

"Turning off the machines."

"Right."

"Because he wants the organs for donation."

"I told him to keep Sophie alive. God decides when life ends."

He did not believe that. But if Maria's belief system helped her through this, he would hold back on attacking it.

"Whatever your decision, I'll back you up."

"Are you sure y–? OK. Thank you."

"Take care of yourself."

"Yes. What are you doing right now?" In the screen, she blinked. "You're outdoors, with voices and music. A party?"

"I'm working."

"Ah. I should have guessed."

"I'm sorry, I've always been too focused on–"

"Josh, it's all right. We're on different life-paths, that's all."

Perhaps they were, but if so it was his fault. And it was too late to go back, so what he ought to do was accept it and let the situation go.

"You're correct. You always are."

"Ah, Josh. Take care."

"Yes. Take care."

He stared at the black display.

I'm an idiot.

Then he put the phone away, checked the knife on his hip, and got moving.

[TWENTY-ONE]

The Millennium Wheel was wired for light. Each ellipsoidal car, wrapped in a smart plastic lamina, rippled with scarlet, indigo and white patterns, shining even in sunlight. The struts, braided with optic fibres, shimmered with a thousand colours, shifting in time to the music's beat – atop a tall pedestal stage on the Embankment proper, a band was playing, their instruments redfanging the lights: a visual kaleidoscope phase-locked to the beat.

"It's brilliant," said Richard.

"Yeah, watch now." Opal pointed. "That's Hammerfeld, from Norway, you want to talk about brilliant."

The grassy square next to the Wheel contained a complex arrangement of scaffolding towers, some with tough lightweight sheeting to form walls, plus ramps and outcrops of hard plastic with minimal padding. The competitors were doing their thing two at a time, partly because this was a friendly competition for little prize money, a demo showcasing the participants of next week's Xtreme Run championships. Most of the foreign competitors were already here in London.

Richard knew all this because Opal had explained it

several times over. He even remembered some of the nicknames.

"That's Mjolnir, right? Aka the Hammer?"

"Not bad, Richie."

People were swirling all around them. Brian had gone off somewhere with some older guys his own age.

"What are the towers for? They're too smooth to climb up."

"Only for the freerunners. No gloves, no skates, see? This is the freerunning; the gekrunners come afterwards."

"And old Hammer up there is a freerunner."

"He does both, actually, unlike most of them. In competition, leastways."

Brand names and mottos of clothing and equipment companies scrolled down the ramps and slides and towers. Opal and the other squatters, gekrunners or not, despised the System, meaning banks and ordinary jobs and all the rest; but they accepted companies promoting their gek-gear, because otherwise there would be no events like this, no money to pay for people to come from abroad, or to hire in the massive stands, and whatever else it took.

Of them all, it seemed only Brian saw the contradictions in their views.

And me.

At least Brian had a place among them.

What can I do?

Athleticism was alien to him. If he were at home now, he'd be up his bedroom, reading a book on his widescreen, drinking a Diet Coke or milk, pretending not to hear Father downstairs swearing as he got deeper into the whisky, or the rows with the in-house staff, the screech of wheels if Father set off for a drunken, too-fast drive in his ElectroBentley X.

"Richie, did you see that?"

"Uh, what?"

"He went from like a Lache into... Never mind."

"Sorry."

"You all right?"

"Sure. Yeah."

There were smells of roasting food, nuts and cicadas and chicken, and the sweetness of candy floss; but the pain in his stomach was familiar now, a constant hard pressure. His lack of money was a reality. But Opal was with him.

She was focused on the freerunners cartwheeling and leaping around the competition stage: absorbed, lips apart and eyes alight, perhaps seeing herself up there one day, feeling how it would be to flip through the air like that, enjoy the attention of the crowd. At least, that was what he thought was happening in her head.

The music was a piece he knew, Everyone Runs From Something, and he would normally remember the name of the band but tonight it wasn't there in his mind. Despite the crowd all around and Opal beside him, he felt more lost than he had ever imagined he could be. People jostled and cheered the freerunners' performance, which to him was a montage of senseless movement and confusion.

None of this was right.

Josh followed the stream of people. At intervals, he checked his phone, then, after finding no search hits, he randomly accessed the footage his software agents were analysing. Around the Embankment and further east at South Bank and Waterloo, the flow of faces and

bodies along the streets formed an organic river, so hard
to dive inside for individuals, especially when they were
kids, shorter than the throng of adults. If they were
here at all.

More people passing meant a wealth of video data,
more possibilities – counterbalanced by the difficulty of
seeing someone clearly enough for recognition. All
around was a press of individuals caught up in the tidal
motion of the crowd, though each of those thousands
was a self-aware individual, a human being with success and failures, loves and disappointments, a family
past and an unknown future; while he himself could
drift with his thoughts or come back to reality: a fourteen year-old boy needed to be found, for his own sake
and Suzanne's.

Josh bought a pink candyfloss, so he looked like
someone here for pure enjoyment, and held it in his
right hand, keeping his fingers away from the wispy,
sticky sugar-cloud.

On the grass area by the Eye, gekrunners were
warming up. He moved closer, protective of his candyfloss, finding a place to stand. Ignoring the
competition spectacle, he looked around the crowd,
trying to spot a girl or lad matching the images in his
mind. Meanwhile, his phone was in his sealed shirt
pocket, ready to vibrate if one of his querybots found a
hit.

Around him, some wore their phones velcroed to
sleeves or on bands around wrist or biceps. Though the
fabric would make a noise if pulled, this place was
crowded and the music was loud – wearing phones that
way invited theft. That was why Josh's was in his
pocket.

A strange hand took hold of his knife hilt.

He reacted as trained, slapping his hand against the attacker's, pinning his grip and knife, dropping his weight as he spun, free hand hammering down, still with the candyfloss – impale the eyeball – but the attacker was small – *pull back* – eight or nine years old – *Jesus Christ* – and he diverted the strike in time. He twisted the trapped hand, and the kid went to his knees.

"I should snap every bone in your arm. If I sneeze it'll happen anyway."

"S-sorry."

"Get up." He unpinned the hand. "Come on."

"All right. You didn't have to hurt me."

"Sod off."

This was a child with a story as intricate and emotive as Richard Broomhall's; but no one could solve every problem in the world, and dragging the kid to the police would do nothing to achieve what he was here for. After a moment, the kid started to slide off through the crowd.

"No. Stop," said Josh.

The kid froze.

"Take this." Josh thrust the candyfloss at him. "Take it."

A shaking hand closed on the stick.

"*Now* sod off, and think how different things might have been."

The kid went.

Shit. Suzanne would've handled that better.

Maybe it was because he worked best with a single focus, a clear mission objective that–

"I saw you manhandling that boy."

"What?"

A tubby man, his convex belly straining his polo shirt, pointed a short finger and said: "You're a bully and a bad parent, and I've half a mind to report you to–"

Josh's hand whipped out, thumb hooked, the web of skin striking the idiot's throat.

"Chh–" The guy rocked in place, panicked and frozen.

Fuck it.

Josh walked away, knowing the idiot could not follow, would not be able to speak for a time. Swallowing food was going to be a bitch as well. Call it the Cumberland diet.

He didn't deserve that.

The voice inside his head was Maria's.

On the periphery of the crowd, freerunners were tumbling in a loose, lighthearted fashion. None of the competitors were up on the competition stand: some kind of break between events. They all looked to be in their teens. Josh wondered if he could match them, then realised he had no chance.

Good discipline.

It looked impromptu, and free format was obviously the name of the game, but they all had techniques in common and knew how to perform them. Josh might not be trained in what they did, but he understood how the body moved, and these guys simply flowed.

"Very nice," he said, as one of them jumped from the riverside railing, performed a vertical spinning crescent kick – at least that was how Josh thought of the move – and dropped to the ground, into a shoulder roll, and came up with a hands-free cartwheel to land in a crouch.

"Cheers, man," said the freerunner.

One of the others, a white guy with dreadlocks tied in a topknot, nodded.

"I hear you guys are doing a night run," said Josh.

"Yeah, we're part of that, all right."

"It's a bit crowded here."

"Not after dark," said Dreadlocks, "but we're not starting from here. Down at South Bank, outside the old theatre, then down the underpass ramps and up around the station."

"You're going to freerun through Waterloo?"

"Through it, under it, and over the top," said one of the others. "Gonna be good."

"I'll be watching," said Josh. "Take it easy."

"You, too."

He wandered away, heading east alongside the river, staring at the crowd and food vendors. Across the darkening waters, the stately turbines were slowly rotating, their vanes' leading edges rippling with electrophosphorescent red, glowing like blood on a blade.

Suzanne. I wish I'd invited you.

But she might be with a client now, and if she were free and came, his attention would be on her. He was here was to find Richard Broomhall, and everything else was secondary.

Reaching the South Bank complex, he stopped. There was a jumble of grey concrete blocks and ramps, the old theatre building with its balcony patio where the clientele were drinking wine spritzers, while down below some twenty young men and women were wandering among the people and the architecture, doing pretty much the same as Josh: taking in every aspect of the geometry, internalising a model of the surroundings in three-dimensional detail.

It felt strange to be among kindred spirits. But their goal was different from his, because they were mapping vectors of movement across a 3-D urban setting for the sheer flowing fun of it; while he was planning to snatch a kid – Richard, or else Opal, if only she appeared.

The incident with the idiot had made him realise that if Richard or Opal called for help, there would be dozens of athletic helpers all around. While he might be able to beat them in a straight run on barren land, in this cluttered city world, with a struggling kid in hand, he would have no chance of getting away.

Suzanne, if she were here, would find some way of explaining to the gekrunners that it was for Richard's benefit; but for Josh there was too much risk. And there was something else, because of the promise he had made to Viv, the woman at the shelter who had helped him – he would not drag Richard back to his father against his will. And that meant no police.

He circumnavigated the boxy building several times, then moved along the nightrunners' probable route, towards the Imax Ruin in Cardboard City, and up to the Victorian-looking sculpture of Waterloo station's entrance: stone flags and banners, memorials to former railway workers who fell during wartime, defending the country against an implacable enemy.

Had there been a single conflict since then that made as much moral sense?

Forget it. Look and concentrate.

In the station he drank coffee and ate a yoghurt-coated flapjack, used the facilities, then left via the pedestrian skyway over the EuroLev terminal – if Suzanne were here, they could be in Paris within the hour – and descended to ground level. He followed the streets and underpasses back to South Bank, made a final looping circuit of the theatre complex, and found a place to sit near the riverside railings.

Waiting was one of his best skills.

• • •

When it was dark, they began to congregate. All wore shirts that gleamed with light – some with blazing white backgrounds across which moving figures jumped and tumbled, while slogans scrolled down the garments, many reading: *Le Mouvement, C'est Moi*; others with shining kaleidoscopic patterns that lit up the night in a sea of shining colours.

It was terrific, a spectacle Josh had not expected. It was also horrific in terms of identifying a solitary kid. There were non-gekrunners among the throng, but at least two hundred wore the shining animated shirts, rendering the surroundings darker by contrast, as much a problem for the omnipresent cameras as for human vision.

French voices sounded among them. Gekrunning came from and coexisted with parkour, as created in the northern suburbs of Paris. Josh knew that, though the closest he had come to freerunning was swarming over endless assault courses.

Shit. Where's this Opal?

He was trying to zero in on the smaller figures among the gekrunners, but their relative shortness would mean they were hidden by the shining shirts and other gear. This was a nightmare of a mission that should have been straightforward: look for a kid and find him.

"Listen up, everybody." The speaker was a Frenchman, standing on one of the concrete blocks that served as seat or sculpture. "We start the main run in twenty minutes. For now, have fun around these structures" – he crouched down to slap concrete – "and in twenty minutes, we will meet our Waterloo!"

Two hundred people cheered, and even Josh laughed.

Then the night exploded into brilliance as movie-image garments shone and their wearers leaped in all directions, tumbling and spinning, performing running jumps, vaulting over seats and off railings, while others skated at high speed across the flagstones, boots set to near-zero friction, and some began to spider up the theatre's external walls, using gek-gloves.

All those moving images were an absolute–

Idiot.

–golden opportunity for anyone who thought of himself as a tech-head, a warrior-geek from the Regiment's Ghost Force, who ought to know better than to feel stymied when he was surrounded by technology that was waiting to be subverted. From his pocket he took out his rolled-up touchboard, unfurled it and clipped his phone on top, the tiny current causing his touchboard to snap into useful rigidity.

Come on, Cumberland. You can do it.

Well, of course he could, but the question was whether he could do it in time, because in twenty minutes – less now – these buggers would be gone, running over the buildings as well as past them. If it was hard enough to spot a missing kid now, it would be impossible when the night run was in full flow.

The time to have had this idea was an hour ago, maybe two, when he could have dawdled over his coffee and flapjack and worked the way an old coder knew best. But his fingers were already flowing across the touchpad.

Here we go.

This was the true Zen, the immersion in a task so total there was no bandwidth left for self-conscious thought. He went deep, very deep, out of necessity; so that when he finally sucked in a breath and came out of it, his task completed, there were runners all around getting ready for the off. Twenty minutes had passed. His opportunity was almost gone.

But in his display, several panes were blinking red, code was ready to be loosed, packages anxious to be broadcast. Compiled and zipped, loaded and ready to go.

"So, everybody" – it was the French guy standing on the same concrete block – "we count down, ten… nine… eight… seven… six… five…"

Sound disappeared from Josh's awareness as he focused on the display, letting the code fly. Then he brought himself back.

"…two… er, what is–? I mean, let's go!"

Every shirt blazed the exact same shade of pink, then mutated to a sapphire blue, while in the centre of each garment, front and back, a picture of Opal (retrieved by backtracking from her avatar) appeared. Beneath it scrolled a message in scarlet:

HAVE YOU SEEN THIS GIRL?

No one could transmit to every shirt through the web at once, but Josh's phone redfanged to those nearest, and those shirts redfanged to their neighbours, and the whole cascade took place in under a second. Now, every shirt appeared synchronised as Opal faded out, and an image of Richard appeared.

HAVE YOU SEEN THIS BOY?

The runners' concentration was broken. Some faltered in their first manoeuvres; others simply turned inward, congregating with their nearest neighbours, all voicing some variation of "What the hell is this?",

"Qu'est-ce qui se passe?" or "C'est merde!"

There was a ripple in the pattern of light, and that was all he needed. He redfanged the abort, and every shirt resumed its normal display.

"Everyone, come on!"

Freerunners and gekrunners flowed into motion, tumbling and running over obstacles, some of the gekrunners ascending the theatre walls like gymnastic spiders, their shirts pulsing with light, a beautiful spectacle for anyone with time to watch, but not Josh. He broke into a run, trying to catch the eye of the storm, the centre of the rough circle of disturbance: the reaction of people near Richard or Opal. From the way that centre had moved, he thought it must be the girl: someone capable of running with the rest.

In the gloomy dark no one paid much attention to a solitary runner wearing unlit clothes who chose to run along the ground without gymnastics. All around were vaulting, wheeling, flick-flacking urban athletes. For a moment, as he sprinted around the side of the theatre, he lost his target – light and movement, runners everywhere – and then he poured on the speed – there – and in a moment he had her.

Come on, run.

Her motion matched the gait of the figure in the surveillance logs, and she appeared to be doing the same as him: running without worry about spectacular moves, in her case because she was fleeing. Pointing his phone like a gun as he ran, he redfanged the target code – got her – and immediately the back of her shirt began to pulse pink like a strobing Barbie, a beacon impossible to miss.

Tumbling figures were all around and someone must have guessed what he was up to because – "Got him!"

– there was a grip on his sleeve – no – and he slammed into the gekrunner instead of pulling away, twisting and using momentum, and then he was free – run hard – as another grabbed and Josh's kick scythed low – "Ah shit!" – taking out the knee, tipping Josh forward but he fell into a sprinting step and continued – faster – then he was pouring on the speed – push it – as his assailants fell behind.

The concrete ramp sloped into darkness, the pedestrian underpass leading to Cardboard City, its walls alight with gekrunners in sparkling shirts. Josh looked up – move – as one of them dropped like a hunting spider, arms clamping hard around him – roll out – so he dropped forward as if falling, clasping the gekrunner to go with him, managing to hook an ankle – got it – and they went over together, a combat sambo classic, concrete-nightsky-concrete filling his vision – move on – hearing the cry and soft crunch, then he was rolling up from the prostrate body, running once more, looking for his target.

Flashing pink, ahead.

Sprint now.

Still on the downslope with the girl further below, obstacles everywhere, dodging homeless folk and gekrunners, gaining on her now because this was fell-running of a kind, the art of accelerating where other runners would slow to avoid injury, definitely gaining – getting close – and into the underpass, tearing past cardboard-box homes, faces open or blank with confusion at the blazing, lit-up gekrunners bounding and somersaulting all around. Then he was into the circular plaza that was below ground level, open to the night sky, dominated by the cracked and blackened cylinder of the Imax Ruin.

The girl jerked left, altering course.

Spotted me.

Possibly, but this area was more open, and by turning a right angle she opened up the possibility that he would follow the hypotenuse of the triangle, cutting her off, and perhaps she did not understand evasion, but she was a gekrunner and they had good instincts and – there he is – because the boy Richard was up ahead, and Opal had changed direction to draw pursuit away, but it wasn't going to work. He poured on the speed, reaching to grab the stumbling boy.

"I'm a fr–"

Something massive barrelled into him as he twisted, arcing back with his right elbow – a thud of impact – continuing the spin to slam a knee into the liver, then haul the head down to concrete – no, not to kill – and redirect the flow, spinning the attacker to ground as – another one coming – and the second gekrunner was fast, a woman, whipping a kick toward him – no – as he slammed his palm-heel into her spleen and spun her aside, leaping forward and hooking his hand to grab – got you – and then he had the boy, his target.

The gekrunners were not finished because three of them were making a spectacular run sideways along the curved wall – you have to be kidding – and he got ready for their hurtling approach as a foot slipped, a gek-gauntlet struck concrete at the wrong angle, and then the gekrunner was tumbling, arms flailing, striking another, arcing through the air and trying to twist out but too late as her head struck concrete with a crack of sound, stopping everything.

No.

Everything but the second gekrunner toppling, her balance thrown off, shirt pulsing pink as she dropped, hitting sideways and rolling to stillness.

Next to Josh, the boy was frozen, not running anywhere; and the third gekrunner, a male, had halted, clinging to the wall. Beyond, on the far side of the circular atrium, a beautiful flow of light continued: the majority of the gekrunners into their night run as planned, oblivious to the chase, the tragedy splayed upon concrete.

A dark puddle spread, slow and viscous, beneath the first gekrunner's head.

Blood looks black at night.

Then Josh's phone was out, and he was stabbing the emergency icon. "Ambulance, this location, now. One probable fatality, one possible. Gekrunners, made a long fall. There are others injured."

He disabled the normal misdirection, so they could read his coordinates in clear.

Shit. So stupid.

As the third gekrunner inched down to the ground, others drew closer, switching off their shirt displays, congregating around their fallen friends. All were silent. One knelt to check pulse and breathing, taking care not to shift the head. Beside Josh, Richard was trembling.

Within minutes sirens burped and whooped. Green strobing light preceded the arrival of a paramedic motorcycle, manoeuvring with care amid the makeshift cardboard homes, rolling down to the flat ground. Overhead, more lights reflected off the Ruin, as an ambulance circled the roundabout, looking for a way in.

Richard whispered: "Opal."

A gurney came rattling down a ramp, pushed by the ambulance crew. Their motorcycle colleague was

already snapping support-braces around Opal, and
spraying fast-foam to stabilise her. Then the ambulance
guys slid a thin pallet beneath her, before raising her
onto the gurney. As they turned, the back of their
jumpsuits revealed a cheerful bulldog symbol and the
slogan "Timmy Is Your Friend". From some children's
hospital.

Richard gave a cry, then shuddered into stillness.

What the hell?

Josh kept his hand on the boy's shoulder.

The paramedics conferred. Then the ambulance guys
pushed the gurney, now with Opal, back the way they
had come. The motorcyclist returned to the other fallen
body. After less than a minute, the siren whooped overhead as the ambulance sped into motion.

So the other gekrunner was dead.

Perhaps Richard made the connection, too, because
he slumped, and Josh had to move fast to catch him.
Then, carrying the fourteen year-old in his forearms,
he backed away. Soon the police would arrive. Moving
softly, he circled around the back of the Imax Ruin,
took an exit ramp directly opposite the accident site,
and went up to ground level, checking for spycams, his
phone polling and disabling, getting him clear.

Finally, down a narrow street behind an ornate Victorian red brick building, he put Richard down, feet
first. The lad swayed then stood there, like a window
mannequin.

Josh thumbed his phone and raised it.

"Hi," said Suzanne's image. "How are y–?"

"I need you now."

She might have blinked.

"All right."

[TWENTY-TWO]

Big Tel's taxi came to a halt, and the nearside passenger door opened, the interior light revealing Suzanne. Josh swept Richard up and lifted him inside. Suzanne settled Richard in place, strapping him in. Tel's hands flickered across the dashboard, checking surveillance.

"He's almost catatonic," said Suzanne. "What happened?"

"Bad accident, one fatality, another hurt badly. She's a friend of his. He saw it happen."

"The fatality?"

"The injury. Could be serious."

Suzanne's fingertips fluttered across Richard's head and neck. "He's not physically injured? You're sure?"

"Certain."

"Then let's get him to a–"

"Your place."

"What?"

"Let's get him to your place. Please?"

Up front, Big Tel was craning around in his seat, watching through the clear partition.

"*Merde*," said Suzanne. "All right. My place."

"Terry, would you–?"

"I've got it, Josh. Hold on."

They pulled away from the kerb with hard acceleration – Big Tel once flew armoured Vipers in Sudan –
then hauled out onto the roundabout, swinging north
along Waterloo Bridge. Soon they were heading along
Shaftesbury Avenue, then Tottenham Court Road
where the tech shops and convenience stores blazed
with light despite the hour.

"Terry?" Suzanne tapped on the partition. "Can we
stop here for a moment?"

Big Tel, in the mirror, looked at Josh.

"Whatever she says."

"Then I'll pull over here."

Richard continued to stare at nothing. Suzanne
slipped out, crossed the street and went into a Libyan
store. In minutes she was back, with bags of shopping.

"Supplies," she said, getting in. "That's everything."

Big Tel swung the taxi back into traffic. Josh leaned
past Richard to see what Suzanne had bought. Gro-
ceries, plus T-shirt and shorts, it looked like. *Ah.*
Richard's body odour was ripe.

Soon enough, they were stopping in front of the flats
where Suzanne lived.

"You'll be all right?" asked Big Tel.

"Yeah. Cheers, mate."

"Keep your safety off and brain switched on."

"I owe you one."

"No one's keeping count. But if they were, you owe
me seven."

"Is that all?"

Suzanne helped Josh manoeuvre Richard on to the
pavement. Then Big Tel gave a half salute, put the taxi
into drive and moved off. Richard wavered a bit, then

took a step as Josh encouraged him, then another, to the front door.

They ascended the stairs step by careful step, an improvement on having to carry the lad. Finally, when Suzanne opened the door of her top-floor flat, Josh was glad to see she had left the lights on, a dim and cheerful orange, the lounge a place of restful reds and browns. Suzanne closed the door.

"Sit down, Richard."

Josh settled him on a soft couch, and waited. Suzanne went into the kitchen. A minute later, she returned with a steaming mug, honey-sweetened milk, and placed it in Richard's hands.

"Take hold, that's right. Now drink."

Richard took a sip, shuddered, then relaxed.

Suzanne worked with him, encouraging him to drink. When the milk was all gone, she said: "Time to get clean, now. And Josh will help you."

Richard's mouth formed an arch of misery.

"Soon you will feel better now and safe because… everything is all right here… you can relax, deeper, that's right."

Josh found himself blinking. But the focus of Suzanne's ambiguous syntax was Richard, who received the full effect of her reassurance, growing calmer. Then he allowed Josh to help him to his feet, and escort him to the bathroom – Suzanne showed them where it was – and even helped remove his gritty, pungent clothes.

After switching on the shower, Josh stepped back and encouraged Richard to get in, prepared to manhandle him inside if necessary, thankful when Richard stepped under the spray and stood there, eyes closed and swaying. Finally, Richard used the shower gel, washed and rinsed and did the whole thing again, then a third time.

He came out clean, smelling of pine, but still not talking. When Josh told him to, he dried himself with one of the big bath towels.

Josh opened the bathroom door halfway to call for Suzanne, but she was already there, offering the new T-shirt and shorts for Richard to wear. Afterwards, dressed in fresh clothes for the first time in days, Richard seemed revivified.

"Do you want something to eat?" asked Suzanne.

He nodded.

A stomach unused to food could rebel; but Suzanne appeared to know that. She made soup for Richard, then gave him a small sandwich to eat. After a few bites, he stopped.

Tears welled up.

"You're safe," Suzanne said.

When she was sure that Richard had finished eating, she nodded to Josh, and they helped him stand up. She led the way to a small guest bedroom that held shelves of hardcopy books. The duvet was blue and smelled newly laundered. Richard slid into bed.

Then Suzanne began to speak to him in a lilting voice, and Josh crept from the room, because this was for Richard alone. Suzanne seemed to think of herself as a scientist and healer; but there was something magical about her work.

Finally she came out. "He'll sleep now. For a good eight hours, I hope."

"Well done."

"If his father doesn't come barging in to interrupt things."

"He won't."

"How do you–?"

"Because I haven't told him about Richard."

"And you're going to do that when, exactly?"

Josh stared at the bedroom door. "When he's happy about going back to whatever scared him off."

"So you haven't told the police, either. Legally, we're probably guilty of kidnapping. You know that, right?"

"*Mais oui.*" He deliberately anglicised it: *may-wee.* "We probably are. While I'm facing suspension and worse, you're disregarding your employer's wishes."

"Client. Broomhall's my client, not my boss." He could have added: I'm freelance, just like you.

"Like that makes a the difference."

"Actually, it does."

"Hmm." Suzanne glanced toward the door. "One of us needs to make sure he doesn't just wander out. I don't think he'll wake up, but nothing's certain."

"The couch looks fine." Josh pointed. "I'll wake up if he moves."

"You sound certain."

She was standing very close to him now.

"Confident," she continued. "Not to mention capable."

When he kissed her, the explosion of sweet electricity slammed through his body, swirled up and down, beyond anything he had experienced.

"My God," he whispered, holding her upper arms. "Suzanne."

"I've never done this before, Josh Cumberland. Not this fast."

"Done–?"

"Can your ninja senses detect someone sneaking out beyond a closed door?"

"I don't…"

"Come on." Her hands pulled him as if he were weightless. "Come on."

Inside her bedroom, she pushed the door quietly shut. The room was lit by a small bedside lamp, which she tapped, switching it off.

Only faint silver moonlight illuminated her form as she pulled her blouse off over her head, then undid her skirt and let it slide to the floor. Time slowed as she removed bra and panties, and stood there, a perfect goddess, the long scars glistening like moonlight inside her arms.

Josh blinked eyes filled with grit, with salt, with the overwhelming knowledge that he deserved nothing, and certainly not this. Then he removed his clothes with a Zen exactness, his gaze never deviating from her face.

They embraced standing, her skin incandescent, smooth and warm, and then she was pulling him to the bed where they lay down, his mouth finding her throat, working slowly down, to her nipples like black cherries, to the smoothness of her stomach, her soft inner thighs and the sweet surprise within, burying himself until she arced back, giving a low cry; and a shuddering sob as she took hold of his head and pulled him up to her face.

"In me," she said.

Then he was riding to the stars, expecting it to be immediate, but silky, soft strength enclosed him, prolonging the voyage, every nerve juddering; and then the atomic fireball cascaded outwards, bursting with nova energy until he was done, lying on her and in her, holding her forever, only her name in his mind and on his lips: Suzanne, Suzanne, Suzanne.

After a time, she said "Sorry, you're squashing me."

"Sorry." He rolled sideways, and she turned with

him, so they remained embraced though he popped out of her. "Oops."

"Shame," she said, then burped. "Oh."

They shook together in shared laughter.

"Now what are we going to do?" Josh stared at her in the darkness, amazed at the world.

"We could sleep."

"I guess."

He continued to stare, wonder seeping through him, with no awareness of the moment when he drifted downwards into restorative sleep for the first time in an age, with a sense of correctness, of security at last.

Everything paused.

They awoke still embracing, with no trace of cramp, as though their bodies fitted together exactly. Their kiss was soft, on the lips, and then she had him pulled inside her and they rode together, for longer this time, grinning, staring into each other's eyes at the moment of explosion, his before hers but only by seconds; and then he collapsed beside her.

"I need to brush my teeth," he said. "And did I mention you're beautiful?"

After taking it in turns to use the bathroom – a quick trip each, then a longer sojourn in the shower – they dressed and went into the small kitchen area. Suzanne put coffee on, then turned to him.

"You realise I'm not white?" she said.

"My God. And did you notice I'm not black?"

"I noticed everything."

"Me too."

The world was at peace as they kissed again, very soft and very still. Then they disengaged and got ready for breakfast, putting out bowls and cereal, occasionally glancing at the door to Richard's room, neither mentioning the boy's name.

"You're going to work with him today?" Josh kept his voice low. "Or would that get you in trouble with the disciplinary board?"

"Probably, if it gets that far."

"Ah. Let's sort out his problems, then maybe nothing will happen. It's his father who–"

The guest room door clicked open, and Richard was standing there. "Can I use the–?"

"It's over there."

He nodded, then shuffled past them to the bathroom, and went in.

"The poor lad looks awful," said Josh, "but not as bad as last night."

"No. The first thing I need to deploy is a powerful psychophysical technique for integrating body and mind for the day ahead."

"Cool."

"It's called breakfast."

Afterwards, while Suzanne did more work with Richard, Josh went into her bedroom to use his phone, checking the hospital for Opal's condition. He could have hacked into the watchcams, but the always-present memory of Sophie stopped him. A nurse told him that Opal was in post-op recovery, no further details available. The earliest she might possibly receive visitors would be tonight at 7.30, but he should call in advance, in case she was not ready. Thankful to have talked to a human being, Josh closed the call.

When he entered the lounge Richard was in an armchair, apparently in a light doze.

"I'm going to talk to Josh now," Suzanne told the

boy. "And when I talk to you again directly, you'll know the difference. For now, just rest."

As she turned to Josh her tone changed. "He's all right."

"Good." He said nothing about Opal. "That's good."

Suzanne nodded. Somehow they were on the same wavelength – if there had been positive news from the hospital, it would have been OK to share it; otherwise it was best to say nothing. She reached out her hand; when he took hold, it felt wonderful. With a smile, she led him into her bedroom – their bedroom? – and this time he knew it was only to talk. They smiled, holding each other's hands, as though about to start some old-fashioned dance.

"So what are we going to do?" she asked.

Josh let go of her hands and sat on the bed.

"You've no idea how warfare" – *remembering fourteen years old and the rifle coming up and his head exploding* but that was not the worst of it – "screws you up."

"We can deal with this later," said Suzanne. "And I mean it – we will deal with it."

"Maybe there are things that shouldn't be... but it's Richard we need to think about. Sorry, my l... Sorry."

Her lips twitched.

"Everyone," she said, "has the resources they need to deal with their life and make it better, and I mean everyone."

"What if I want to learn Chinese, and I have no materials and no ability? There's positive thinking and there's delusion."

"I didn't say you could learn the language in ten minutes, but that's more than enough time to dissolve whatever holds you back, like the false belief that you can't learn a language. I worked with a webmovie writer who'd been blocked for three years. Freeing up the block took five minutes. It still took him a year to write the next script, but he did it, that's the point."

"And you didn't discover what caused the block?" he said.

"Actually, the guy knew precisely what had caused it, but if he hadn't, I wouldn't have tried to find out. I didn't need to know. It's a form of brief therapy, and that's a technical term."

This was what he did not understand about her work. Despite the counselling he had been through, he still thought of therapy as uncovering hidden pasts.

"So treating traumas, you don't need to know the details."

No heads exploded in his memory. Her presence kept him calm.

"It depends. If someone was in a traffic accident, not their fault, just something dreadful they had experienced... then all I need do is recode the memory, so they don't re-experience anguish whenever they think of it. Not amnesia, but no overwhelming emotion, either. Delving back into their childhood and how they related to their parents would be nonsense, because it's not the problem."

"All right."

"The old opponents of that approach called it treating the symptom instead of the cause, but sometimes treating the symptom is all you need. For example, sweating is a symptom of bubonic plague. During the Black Death, if the victims had been given more fluids, many would have lived, because it was the dehydration that got them."

This was not what he wanted to hear, because there was something odd about young Richard's reactions, and not just to witnessing his friend fall.

"On the other hand, if the trauma patient is a victim of violence" – Suzanne glanced down at her own inner forearms – "then recoding the memory is not enough, because two-thirds of such people become victims again within eighteen months. Their behaviour patterns mark them out as soft prey for predators, so then I do have to explore their world, use the psychodynamic approach, and help them get more freedom in their lives."

"So maybe you need to uncover Richard's past."

"Ah. That's what you're after."

"Look, obviously my first sight of him was when he's under stress. But he gave this strange reaction..."

He described the soft cry that Richard emitted, seeing the bulldog logo on the back of a paramedic's jumpsuit. And how his catatonia – if that was what it was – started then, not at the moment Opal fell.

"I'll ask," said Suzanne. "But when the moment is right."

"OK."

"So what are you going to do next?"

"I thought I'd take a drive to Surrey."

"To Richard's father?" She glanced at the closed door.

"Yeah, but maybe I should do it after you've talked with Richard some more."

"That would be wise."

"Why don't I go fetch my car from the hotel, and bring it back here?"

"To take Richard home?"

"Only if he's ready."

"All right. I may not have anything for you. Uncovering memories is delicate, because it's too easy to implant false ones, vivid hallucinations of things that never happened."

"I have vivid memories of last night. Something I must have imagined."

She leaned over, and their kiss was fire.

"A shared hallucination," she said.

"Relax now, in trance everything is fine, and my voice will go with you as you go deeper still into the trance-inside-the-trance, and go back in time to a moment when..."

Richard felt himself floating in a vast, star-filled cavern, totally calm; and when the memory rose up, he held still instead of screaming, knowing he was strong enough to watch.

It is a world of giants, the adults, and they do not seem to realise how confusing it all is. The plane travel is wonderful, then boring, seeming to last for days. He plays games on his pad, sleeps, eats food he does not like, knowing Father will shout if he leaves any behind.

"Twenty-one countries," says the lady in uniform, "in twenty-five days. Even I don't do that."

He has no idea how to reply, or quite what the words mean, but at least she is friendly. Then there is–

A ripple moved through him, a tightening of his stomach, but then her hand was on his shoulder and he relaxed, calm again.

"Tell me. Go back to just before the time you were afraid."

–Father's presence, big and comforting however much it frightens, because this is Father, strong and unbeatable, around whom the world revolves. The whole trip has been a chaos of dislocating sights: corridors and rooms, smiling faces looking down on him, fake-cheerful voices, adults chivvying him along, their words without sense.

There is the clinic and the grinning dog on the wall, the cartoon dog called Timmy he has seen before. Big hands press his shoulder blades, urging him forward, and he feels the grown-ups might trample him like the elephants they saw yesterday or the day before, those legs longer than he had expected for such round, heavy creatures with amazing trunks that Father said were prehistoric or something like that, and if only Father would hold his hand while the smiling men and women showed them round all these places but there was grown-up work to do, Father said so, which was why everything was a jumble of adults who–

The hand on his shoulder.

"Closer to that time, Richard. To just before the fear started, and you can tell me about it now."

–do not notice when he slips away by sort-of accident, staying behind when they turn, continuing into the shining white place they had partly explored. Somewhere a toy had squeaked, so perhaps there are other children here, boys and girls he can talk to and maybe play with. He goes through the big doors that slide back with a whoosh, the air feeling very cold as he steps further inside.

There is a chair beside the raised – thing – that looks like a metal bed with a curved glass casing over it. Climbing up, he is able to stare inside.

She is very pretty, the sleeping girl beneath the glass.

For a long time he wonders whether he should try to waken her, but if she's tired or maybe sick then that would be a bad thing. So he climbs down, and moves to the next one in the row, wondering if it's a boy or girl inside and whether they'll be awake. He is just about to climb up when voices sound and he crouches down, shaking, wondering what will happen if they catch him, and how much Father will shout when he finds out.

There are six of them, two of them sort-of white–

Her fingertip made him pause. Then her question came.

"Tell me more about sort-of white."

His voice seemed to speak by itself: "Like Chinese, but I was young."

"And the others were white?"

"No, the other doctors were black."

"Like me?"

"No. They were dark. So were the others."

"What others, Richard?"

"In the big rooms. Offices. Wearing suits."

"So… Tell me about the doctors. What happened next?"

He returned to the star cave, then the dream.

–and the glass raises up, one of the bed-things, and he can see the boy inside has no clothes, which seems funny, and he's lying there while the doctors get things ready, a trolley with metal stuff on it, and those tubes from the ceiling dangling over the boy, and something is not right which is why he is frozen and his mouth opens wide in a scream as the first doctor raises his hand and it's shining when he, when he, when he–

Hand on his shoulder.

"Just breathe, and breathe, and step outside yourself as if you're watching a movie of what you did,

watching yourself in the scene, that's right, and tell me
what happened next."

I am watching crouched down, trying to hide, screaming without sound when the shining metal descends
and the skin splits open, everything inside so liquid
with globs of stuff and twisted things like pipes inside
his body. I stumble away, knocking against a bed or
something but the monsters, the doctors, are too busy
to notice as I run, too scared to say anything, swearing
I will say nothing if only I can get back to Father because otherwise they will cut him as well as me chop
him up slice us up cutting and slicing and cutting and–

Hand, the dream fading, only the star-filled cave and a
feeling of soft ease.
   "Sleep now."
   Drifting.

[TWENTY-THREE]

Josh travelled by Tube, smiling at fellow passengers. Back in his hotel room, he exercised and showered, got changed, packed a few clothes and toiletries in his gym bag – but leaving the rest, making no assumptions about Suzanne wanting him to stay the night again – and carried the bag out to his car. Then he drove into the heavy traffic, feeling relaxed: he was in a travelling armchair, when you thought about it, and the speed he moved at was irrelevant. The slow stop-start progress made him calmer by the minute.

Wow. Suzanne.

Some forty minutes later, he pulled up in front of her place, used the keychip she had lent him to get through the ground floor entrance, then jogged upstairs to her flat. There, the door opened, and she smiled at him.

"Hey."

She hugged him. There was a tremble inside her, different from before.

"What is it?"

"I'll tell you in the bedroom."

Not a lover's promise.

"All right."

Richard was sitting in the lounge, watching a straightplay movie, interactive decisions set to default paths. He looked up.

"Hi," said Josh. "You feeling better?"

"I think so."

"OK… Er, I need to put my bag away."

"Come on." Suzanne tugged him.

In her bedroom, he put down the bag.

"The kid looks calmer."

"He doesn't consciously remember what he talked about in trance. I'm inclined to leave it that way. But if it surfaces by itself, then that's all right too. So long as the emotion isn't overwhelming."

"Emotion?"

"He was younger, so there are missing details, things he didn't understand. As near as I can make out, he accompanied his father on a trip to Africa. I'm not sure whether his mother was still alive at that time. I am certain she wasn't with them."

"Africa."

"He was in a lab. There were local and Chinese doctors. What he saw them do to children… it's been buried deep by fright, fear for himself and for his father, because of what he saw. All his anxieties… it was never really a fear of weapons."

"It wasn't?"

"Call it a generalised fear of scalpels."

"But scalpels aren't…. Oh."

"He saw them slice open living kids."

"Virapharm labs?" His fists trembled, forearms becoming bands of tension. "Broomhall's running virapharm labs?"

"There was a bulldog symbol on the wall. It comes from Tyndall Industries Medicales. Hence Timmy, for the children's wards and drugs."

"Tyndall? But virapharm... Outright criminality isn't their style. The kid's confused."

"Not about what he saw," said Suzanne, "however little he understood. One country's illegality is another's *modus operandi*. Did I mention there were Chinese doctors among the Africans?"

"Chinese influence... That does sound like Africa. You're not sure which country?"

"No. Poor Richard was flying all over the place with his father. It was a confusing time, even before he... saw what he saw."

"Shit."

He was shaking, unable to help it. *Soft flesh splitting open and the boy's head exploding into mist because he was swinging the rifle up and Josh had to shoot* and he hated himself for the way he—

"Tell me, Josh."

"It was the kid," he said. "Same age as Richard is now, and the bastards had armed him with a rifle. I was first into the house and he turned towards me and I – fired."

"That's right."

"But—" Tears were in his eyes as he turned away. "I enjoyed it. That was... that was the thing. The boy's head blew apart and inside I was laughing. Triumph, because I was alive and he was dead and he was fourteen years old, Suzanne, fourteen and they put him where I had to, had to—"

"Yes, you had to, and euphoria is part of the reaction when you save yourself from death. It's the way we're programmed, nothing more."

Josh remembered soldiers laughing hysterically after tragedy, surrounded by the bodies of their comrades as well as the enemy.

"Maybe, but he was only a—"

"Stop." Suzanne touched his face. "Tell me. What do we do next about Richard?"

"I… Sorry. Give me a moment."

He turned away, rubbing his face, knowing she must hate him now.

"All right," he went on, forcing himself. "I'll go talk to Broomhall senior. This Tyndall thing… They're the ones trying to take his corporation down."

"If you're taking Richard, I need to come with you. Whether I go inside the house is a different question."

"It's better for me to go alone."

"Josh, I care about Richard, but I'm thinking about you. Holding Richard here without telling anyone—"

"You want to back out?"

"No. But I don't want to cause you trouble that we can avoid. Richard might do better if he stays here, but he might not."

"That's not the way to play it."

"He needs to—"

"I'm thinking tactically, not like a therapist, Dr Duchesne."

"Oh."

"The first thing I want to talk to Broomhall about is virapharm. How he answers that will determine what I do. You're OK looking after Richard?"

Virapharm. Nanoviral engineering. There were rumours that Chinese state orphanages were oddly clustered around car manufacturing plants, that there were uses for organic substrates in engine control production that Western countries had not explored. Those rumours were not substantiated; but the use of poor Africans for virapharm research, children's bodies used to evolve and incubate new drugs? That was almost a tradition.

"Yes. Let me go through the Africa trip, as I put it together. And his current situation at school, because there's a boy called Zajac…"

She related all she had learned.

"Now go see Broomhall." Her hand on Josh's arm made everything bearable. "I'll be here when you get back."

"And I'll be wherever you want me to be."

"You'd better kiss me, Josh Cumberland."

"Come here."

No drug on Earth could compare to the sensation of holding her, kissing her lips. He carried the sensation out with him, scarcely seeing young Richard, floating out of Suzanne's flat and down to the car, which he put in drive.

Time to see the father.

The big gates rolled back, and he drove forward a car's length before stopping again, this time at foot-high metal barriers. They had not been here on his previous visit. Only when the main gates were shut did the inner barriers descend into the ground. It was a good way of controlling the entry of one vehicle at a time. Josh put the car back in drive and continued up to the house. The man who opened the front door was new, his stance erect and solid.

Once inside, another man took over, and then another, leading him through the clean, polished house. All was wood and glass, rich and impersonal. Their destination was an office at the centre of the house. Inside, Broomhall was sitting behind his desk in what should have been a comfortable chair, but his posture was a web of mismatched tension, his face blotched.

This was a different room than before. Leather hard-copy books, African masks on shelves. *Interesting*. Small bronze sculptures, all of them ugly.

Even before the door closed on them, Broomhall said, "I'm not paying you indefinitely, I hope you re-alise. Time and materials are a fine basis to work on if you deliver results."

"Yes, I know."

"Well, I was half hoping you'd turn up with Richard in your car. I guess that was stupid of me."

"Do you want me to agree or disagree?" Josh pulled his phone out of his pocket. "The boy's still missing and I'm sorry, but if I continue to spend time on it then eventually something will... There."

Blue lights flashed one at a time, chasing each other in a loop around his phone display. He placed the phone face-up on the desk.

"Your spycams" – he gestured at the ceiling corners, at one of the African masks – "are now showing static. What's the procedure? Do your men burst in after–?"

The door clicked open. The assistant who stood there was dressed in a good suit, his haircut expensive. Plus, his knuckles were swollen and hard, and his gaze was flat.

"Everything's hunky-dory," said Broomhall.

"Sir."

The man backed out and closed the door once more.

"I presume," said Josh, "that a different phrase, like 'Everything's fine,' would have caused him to make a move?"

"What is this? I want to know what the bloody hell you're doing to find my son. If you're just here to milk me for more money, then I suggest you fuck off now. In fact you're fired, so get out."

"The security company is professional, coming up with the code phrase. Probably they gave you a button or pad to press, something out of my sight, maybe even inside your shoe."

Broomhall's blotched face altered, his mouth coming open, then closing.

"It's a good setup, outside and in," Josh went on. "And I like the camera-in-the-mask thing, rather classic. I'm interested in Africa, so why don't you tell me about it?"

Now the blood drained from beneath Broomhall's skin, leaving only a spiderweb of alcoholic's veins around his nose, like a dried-up river delta somewhere in Africa, where neither rain dances nor silver iodide cloud seeding had any effect, for there were no clouds any more.

"Get out, or I'll–"

"Something happened to your son in Africa. I'm wondering if you even know that, and what exactly you and Tyndall Industries were up to." Josh gestured towards the door. "Why those guys out there? A falling-out between good buddies? Are you really a long-term rival of Tyndall? Or was it all a cover until now?"

"What happened to Richard? What do you mean?"

Josh looked at him, wishing he could see with Suzanne's eyes.

"He has a fear of scalpels, hence all blades. Also, his teachers at school failed to tell you about the knife duel he was due to fight, or the bullying that made his life a suffering hell, or hadn't you noticed?"

"I–" Broomhall's mouth worked. "Scalpels. And... the school?"

"Your trip to Tyndall's virapharm labs in Africa. Richard got lost, and saw some nasty stuff. What I wonder is, why was he too frightened to tell you about it, Broomhall? Was it because he knew you were a sick bullying bastard, someone who didn't care what happened to a bunch of helpless kids, far away from European law?"

Finally Broomhall's face hardened. He used his hands to push himself to standing.

"I didn't see any kids but I worked out they were there, which is why I've done everything I can to take down that bastard Tyndall, for all the good it's done me. And now I'm going to lose the lot, so what does it matter?"

"You're not working with Tyndall Industries?"

"I was until I realised how they operated, then I severed every connection. And Richard saw–? Why didn't he tell me?"

Josh saw misery, Broomhall's sudden insight into his depth of failure as a parent. Yet Josh's own situation was worse than Broomhall's, because Sophie was gone but Richard Broomhall might be saved. Did that mean fighting the father or saving him as well? That was not yet clear.

"Do you talk much to your son?"

"Well, of course we... Maybe. Maybe not." Broomhall lowered himself back into his chair. "If you've not found anything, at least Richard is probably... I mean, the worst hasn't happened."

"Whether you fire me or keep me on," said Josh, "I'll be invoicing you up to and including yesterday, no more, because I'm focused on results."

"I'm not going to– Oh."

"That's right. Result."

Everything about Broomhall's face and body changed. *"You've found him!"*

"He's safe, well, and I have him protected."

"I need to see–"

"No, you don't," said Josh. "Not if you have enemies watching. I'd expected you to be the target of corporate manoeuvring, not physical danger. Richard's well away from this, and you don't want to lead people to where he is."

"They wouldn't harm him. They're not monsters."

"Aren't they? You've hired these guys for a reason. Something frightened you."

"Oh, my God."

"Your opponents think you're cracking up, which is why they're moving against you, subverting your shareholders and mounting takeover bids. Am I right?"

"Just who are you, Mr Cumberland?"

"Perhaps one of your security folk can tell you about Ghost Force, and the kind of people it turns out. I mostly do corporate training, including system security, not hunting for runaways."

"My friend Adam recommended your associates, but how can I know whether to trust them?"

By associates, Broomhall meant Geordie Biggs and his freelancers.

"This Adam was the person who introduced you to Dr Duchesne?"

"That bitch. Yes."

It would be better for Josh's plans to say nothing about Suzanne, for Broomhall to assume there was no connection between them. That would be good strategically. But the battlefield was one thing; how he felt about Suzanne was something else.

"She gave Richard confidence to leave a bad situation. She probably saved his life, since he was about to go up against a blade. In St Michael's, I mean."

"But the school... No, they wouldn't allow it."

"Don't you remember being a kid?" said Josh. "How much of what went on around you was hidden from teachers and other adults? How much, Broomhall?"

"I... Christ. Oh, Jesus Christ."

Josh smiled. "I believe your son is an atheist. Did you know that?"

"What do you mean? He's too young to have any... Oh. Are you a father, Mr Cumberland?"

A stillness curled around Josh; a silence coalesced.

"My daughter's lying brain-dead in a hospital bed. Your son is safe. Don't think you're the worst parent in the world, Mr Broomhall, because you're not."

Josh hadn't expected to reveal anything about himself. That was not how the game was played.

"I'm sorry." Broomhall rubbed his eyes, then held out his hand. "My name's Philip. Pleased to meet you."

It took a moment.

"I'm Josh." He reached out. "Good to finally meet you, Philip."

"Just don't ever call me Phil. I hate that."

"I promise I won't."

The physical attack had been a botched kidnapping, not an assassination attempt, and it had taken place near Moscow. Josh had known something must have happened, and that was it: a failed snatch on Russian soil. But the problem had not been local.

"I've done nothing to piss off the Russians," Philip told Josh. "If anything, I'm making a great deal of money for everyone."

"No victims? No one losing their jobs, their land polluted by waste, compulsory purchase orders on their homes so someone can build corporate premises?"

"Actually no. Not as far as I know, and I do investigate."

"So you think it was someone employed by Tyndall, taking you out on foreign soil?"

"It would be the final straw. My whole group of companies would collapse, while Tyndall and his friends would plunder the remnants."

"You'd never prove a connection," said Josh. "There'd be so many corporate layers and cutouts, the trail would break long before you could prove that Tyndall said something to someone that resulted in a criminal act."

"That's what Adam told me."

"This Adam, do you trust him in your gut? I mean, free of doubts, straight from instinct?"

"Yes."

"All right. Without Dr Duchesne's help, I could never have found Richard. If you agree he's unharmed, I want you to drop the lawsuit action."

"I... She helped?"

"If Richard needs saving, she's the one to do it."

"Christ." Philip curled his lower lip beneath his top teeth. "So my atheist son needs saving. You want to know something funny?"

"What?"

"I thought of going to see her myself. You know, making the appointment for Richard, but then I would show up myself. Because ever since Elena died... Well."

"Maybe you can do that later."

"Yes, maybe." Philip looked down, then up at Josh. "You didn't like it that I insulted Dr Duchesne, did you?"

"No."

"All right. So you think I shouldn't see Richard. But I want to talk to him."

"Of course." Josh reached inside his pocket, and pulled out another phone. "We'll call you on this."

"Look, Mr... Josh. I believe you have Richard and he's safe, although exactly why I believe you, God knows. But why keep him away? This place is a fortress."

"Yes, and inside it all alone, you could easily be cracking up, hitting the booze and going nuts, worried about your missing son."

"That's not far from the–"

"Or you could clean up your act and mount a little counteroffensive, all from inside these walls, with no one to observe."

Philip was very still. His smile began slowly, like the shoot of a new plant.

"What kind of counteroffensive? These are security guys, not an army."

"I mean your kind of warfare. The kind with accountants and lawyers, balance sheets and contracts. Alliances and plots with employees, associates, clients, suppliers. Whoever."

Now the smile grew.

"I'll need to work round the clock," said Broomhall. "Talk to people very privately, all sorts of people, especially key shareholders."

"The kind of thing a distraught, drunken father couldn't manage?"

"Exactly that kind of thing."

"Good," said Josh. "Then we're getting there. That's your part settled."

"My part?"

"I can't let you have all the fun."

"Your job is to guard Richard."

"His street friends call him Richie. I wonder if it'll stick."

"Street friends?"

"One of whom is in hospital now, badly injured, because she wanted to protect him."

"My God, just how did you find him?"

"He'd moved into a squat, joined a community, and believe it or not they look out for each other. He did have some nights sleeping rough, but after that he was pretty well looked after."

Philip shook his head, as if trying to shuffle information by physical movement. "You'll call me? So I can talk to him?"

"Yes. From a friend's place, where he's safe."

"Thank you."

"You're very–"

"But you haven't told me what you're up to. I can save my companies from Tyndall, and by God I will."

"And what about Billy Church, our wonderful prime minister?"

"The PM? The government supports Tyndall, because Zebediah's been around a long time and knows everybody. I happen to believe that most civil servants are honest, and some goodly percentage of politicians. But between Tyndall and Church's cronies, an awful lot of dirty work gets buried away. More than you'd imagine."

Ever since Yukiko had shown those pictures of Knife-fight Challenge, and Josh had thought about the blatant manipulation of public sentiment, the coincidental timing of the *Knife Edge* final and the general election, with Billy Church linked to the sporting event… ever since then, a part of him had been searching for a target, someone or something to take down, some way to destroy the corruption that appalled him.

"So there's your answer."

"What do you mean?" said Philip.

"You're going to save your companies from the Tyndalls. I'm going to save everyone else."

"How can you possibly do that?"

Josh felt his mouth pull back, his voice go soft.

"Violently."

[TWENTY-FOUR]

At night St Thomas's looked bleak. Some twenty minutes before visiting hours were due to end, Josh wheeled into the car park, and found a space. A few drops of rain spotted the tarmac and his clothes as he crossed the open space. Inside, the receptionists were helpful, and told him he needed Springfield Ward. After he had ascended two floors, a nurse pointed him in the direction he needed. When he reached Springfield, Suzanne and Richard were still there. She was at the foot of the bed, while Richard stood at the side, gazing at Opal's bandaged face.

"Hey," he said, keeping his voice low. "How's everything?"

Suzanne probably saw how tightness spread through him. How he had to struggle to look at the girl in the bed.

"Opal was talking earlier."

Right now the girl's eyes were shut, bruised purple. Tubes and bandages were everywhere. No twitch of movement from her hands. Yet somehow – from the rise and fall of her chest, from the colour of her skin – she transmitted a sense of impending animation, a potential for health and aliveness. Not like Sophie, whose form held absence, not promise.

"She was talking coherently?"

"Yes. And she can wiggle her fingers. Oh… Look."

Richard had reached forward to hold Opal's hand. He remained there, not even blinking, his face intent as though trying to force telepathic healing into her.

Josh reached for Suzanne's fingers, and gently squeezed.

"Did you talk to the doctors?"

"Yes, and read the notes." Suzanne pointed at a screen on the end of the beds. "See that little abbreviation? SBA?"

"In the comment field." Free-format text. Hardly the best way to enter codes.

"Private notation among the medics. Should Be Alright. As opposed to BAP, Bloody Awkward Patient, or WOO, Waste of Oxygen."

"You are joking."

"No. They have alternative meanings for everything, just in case someone asks. But everyone on the job knows the truth."

Spatters on the window became washing rain, then hissing jets of water as the flash storm intensified. Josh nodded toward the glass.

"Good job you don't need the Tube to get back."

"They're getting better. It might be OK."

Most lines had overground sections which flooded during flash storms. London Underground had spent millions of euros on drainage tunnels and elevating barriers, with some success. But every summer, the storms grew more frequent.

"Come on." Suzanne tapped Josh's upper arm. "Let's take a break."

They walked out to the corridor, leaving Richard at the bedside.

"He needs to tell Opal how he feels," she said. "I'm not sure how she'll respond later, because for now the drugs are dulling her mind. But Richard needs to verbalise his thoughts."

"What do you mean about responding later?"

"Once she's a bit more *compos mentis*, she'll remember his words. I've no way of telling what they'll mean to her. Maybe she'll blame him for her being here."

"If it's anyone's fault, it's mine. But won't she be more worried about social services carting her off to some home? I mean, she's young and living in a squatters' commune."

"Maybe." Suzanne looked back toward the ward. "I'm not sure what we can do for her."

"Are you trying to save the world, Dr Duchesne?"

"One person at a time. Fractal salvation, my new theory. Save one, save all."

"You have an interesting mind, Doctor."

"Whereas you're a thug whose major assets are physical."

"I may not be intelligent, but I can lift heavy weights. That's the Navy Gunners' motto."

"It's not so much your muscles I was thinking of."

"Dr Duchesne. Tsk, tsk."

"Hmm." Once more she looked back at the ward. "What are we going to do about Richard and his father?"

"Philip and I had an interesting chat."

"Excuse me? Did you just refer to Broomhall senior as Philip?"

"Actually, I did."

"Tell me. All of it."

• • •

Richard felt someone tapping on his shoulder.

"–are over," she was saying.

"I'm sorry?"

"Visiting hours," said the nurse. "All done. Our patients need their rest, you know?"

"Yes." He touched the back of Opal's hand, avoiding the inserted tube. "They do."

"Your folks are waiting out on the corridor."

"My–? Oh. Right."

He walked alongside the bed, touching the warm metal of the bedframe as though it could keep him linked to Opal; and then he went out. Dr Duchesne, Suzanne, was there.

"Josh is checking his car and the roads. It's quite a storm, isn't it?"

"Storm?"

"Look, there's some kind of waiting room for patients' families, just round the corner. Shall we go in and sit down? Hang on for Josh?"

"OK."

White-and-blue corridors and a sharp chemical tang: this was a strange place, almost dreamlike. In the waiting room, Suzanne sat him down, then took a chair at right angles to his. If she was going to put him into trance again, that was all right with him. Anything to forget the bruises on Opal's face that were all his fault; except that was wrong, he needed to keep her in his mind, every detail.

"You know," said Suzanne, "when I was a student, a friend asked me to cure her phobia of snakes. She lived in the middle of Paris, so I asked her if it really was a problem."

There was a pause. Some distant part of him wanted to hear the rest of the story.

"Well," Suzanne went on, "she said if she just walked into a room where a screen was showing a scene with grass, she'd have to leave the room – in case she saw a picture of a snake. So she really did need to feel comfortable about what used to be a problem."

His eyelids were blinking.

"In this country," she continued, "arachnaphobes used to be in no danger at all, but over time things change, and you know about copperlegs being sighted in London?"

"Um, Ms Cole in biology showed us a newsclip from Kansas, this church guy saying copperlegs are another sign of the, er, apocalypse, is that right? The Final Days."

"Not Josephson, President Brand's pastor?"

"Yeah, that's him."

"So what did you think?"

"She also showed Sharon Caldwell saying that visible speciation, black widows turning into copperlegs, is evolution in action, right before our eyes."

"So do you think the TechDems can win the general election here?"

"I guess."

Father thought otherwise. He had said he would support the TechnoDemocrats if he thought they could win, but since they couldn't, he was forced to work with Billy Church's LabCon cronies.

"Tell me about visible speciation."

"You get pure black widows in Arizona," said Richard. "And pure copperlegs in Illinois. They're a new separate species, the copperlegs, and they can't, er, mate with black widows."

He was beginning to blush, but carried on.

"The thing is, if you start around Phoenix and travel

up to Chicago, you see the black widows slowly becoming different. Like halfway along the journey, you get spiders that can mate with black widows *or* copperlegs. They're kind of a transition, you know? Ms Cole said speciation is analogue, not digital, if you look close enough."

During his days on the streets, he had not been able to think like this, not even in the workshop with Brian.

Suzanne touched his shoulder, and he felt calmer.

"There can be things in the world," she said, "that are safe so long as you take care, like some spiders that you have to handle carefully, while others you can do anything with. You can feel safe without overconfidence because you can relax…"

Here came the trance, and he slid into it with a smile. He drifted, allowing the process to happen, for what seemed like days. Then it was time to leave the imaginary star-cave and ascend to the normal world, the real world. He rose to the surface and opened his eyes.

"Welcome back," said Suzanne.

Josh was standing inside the doorway.

"Interesting," he said. "What was that about copperlegs?"

Richard answered: "They're proof of either Armageddon or evolution and climate change, depending on who you talk to."

"Are you sure you're only fourteen?"

"I'm sure."

"Good. So, look." Josh pulled out a phone. "You're staying with Suzanne for as long as you want. You know that, right?"

"Er…" Richard looked at Suzanne.

"You're fine." She touched his shoulder. "See?"

"Yes."

"I talked to your father today," said Josh. "In person. He was—"

"Is he all right?"

Suzanne smiled at him. So did Josh.

"Yes," he said. "Now he knows you're safe, he's much better."

Richard looked down. The floor design seemed to swirl, matching the feeling inside his stomach. Finally, he raised his chin. "But he's worried about me?"

"Yes. Unfortunately, he doesn't know how to say it. Not to you."

"Oh." Richard looked down at the floor again. "Maybe…"

"What?"

The words just seemed to creep out by themselves. "Perhaps I should talk to Father."

Suzanne was smiling.

"Well, perhaps you should."

Josh found **PB** in his contacts list and made the call. As soon as Philip's image appeared, Josh said: "Someone to talk to you."

He handed the phone to Richard.

"Richard? Oh, my God, Richard. You're all right. You're really all—"

"I'm sorry, Father," said Richard, and began to cry.

Josh looked at Suzanne, who nodded. He assumed she meant *leave them to it*.

So this was what reconciliation looked like. But in his case it would never happen: Sophie was not coming back, and Maria had nailed down the coffin of the marriage that he had killed through neglect, and that was that. He left the room, knowing Suzanne would remain, in case she needed to intervene.

"I don't know what the fuck I'm doing," he said to the wall.

At the far end of the corridor, a nurse glanced at him, then walked through a doorway and was gone, used to visitors in odd states of mind.

I know what I want to do, but not how to do it.

Forget the flash storm outside. His nerves were dancing, electrified, like every op before the start, but there was no Regiment to back him up; and just because he needed to fight, that did not mean he could succeed.

He prowled until the waiting room door opened, and Suzanne waved. Inside, Richard was finishing up his conversation with a soft "Goodbye, Father."

"Well," said Suzanne. "You won't believe what Richard just did."

"What was that?"

"Er, I got Father to show me his knife. In the phone."

"Bloody hell," said Josh.

His own weapon was in the glove compartment. Wandering around a hospital armed was not the done thing.

"We can test your being confident again." Suzanne pulled out her phone. "What was that thing that Yukiko showed us the other night? Oh, yes..."

She tapped commands, calling up movie panes, then turned the phone towards Richard. Josh wondered if the smallness of the images helped him deal with seeing things he feared. Or had been afraid of, more like.

"Knifefighter Challenge," said Richard. "That thing."

In the panes, there were fighters in training armour, some in actual combat, and a garish webviral – 20TH JULY glowing across fight scenes – whose audio track sounded from the phone: *"Live from the Barbican Centre, the ultimate clash of warriors begins..."*

Establishing shots followed, showing the venue, and then from last year's final, the championship belt being handed over.

"... *handed over by the Godfather of Violence, president of Bladefight Inc., Zak Tyndall, along with his*–"

Richard's face whitened.

"What is it?" Suzanne muted the sound. "Richard? Richie?"

"That's them," he whispered.

"Who?"

"The ones in... in Africa. In the labs."

"Holy crap," said Josh.

Suzanne was holding Richard's shoulder, steadying him.

"Where were they, exactly?" she asked.

"In the... When I slipped away from Father."

"They were in the virapharm lab? Those two men?"

"Yes. Talking to the, the doctors. When the two of them walked away, the doctors turned and I slipped in behind their backs, you know?"

"And where did you go?"

Richard's chest heaved and tensed, as if in the throes of asthma. "The room with the... with the children on the slabs and the, the–"

"You're safe." Suzanne pressed on his arm, then tapped his collarbone and beneath his eye, some kind of acupressure thing. "You're safe and everything is fine."

Both Tyndalls were in the picture, Zebediah and Zak, father and son. Tyndall senior was the architect of the Blade Acts, while his son was the public face of Bladefight, owners of the *Knife Edge* reality show and the Knifefight Challenge circuit.

"Bastards," said Josh.

"Look, I'm not talking about the disciplinary thing," said Suzanne. "But you'll remember what I told you about confabulation, and the installation of false memories."

"I remember it." Richard was calmer now. "You know I do."

"Yes, Josh and I know it. What we don't want to do is try to prove it legally."

She meant in court, with her and Richard treated as hostile witnesses by lawyers intent on tearing their story apart.

"I'll get the evidence." Josh took the phone from Suzanne. "These bastards are recognisable. There'll be footage, and I'll find it."

"Don't do it. Leave them alone."

"Why would I do that?"

"They've got power, and you haven't." Suzanne touched his arm. "Please."

"Is this another of your emotional triggers? That point on my arm?"

"Josh?" She pulled her hand back. "I'm not trying to manipulate you."

"I... Shit. I know that."

Richard was watching them, holding very still.

"Look." Suzanne tapped the phone in Josh's hand. "Whatever you try to tell the world, they'll find a way to bury it. You should know that better than me. Government disinformation, burying the truth. You've probably participated, in your time."

Josh forced a breath out.

"We call it regime engineering, when we do it abroad."

He stared at the pictures of the Barbican, the montage of knives arcing through air and fighters training, and the webviral message once more: *Live from the Barbican Centre, the ultimate clash of warriors begins.*

Then he remembered what Yukiko had said about right people, right place, right time, the ones who found themselves massively connected in a complex system balanced on a tipping point, ready for phase transition. It worked for tracking diseases and managing economies; it should work for other things.

Like toppling a government.

Josh smiled at Richard and Suzanne.

"Time to change things, don't you think?"

[TWENTY-FIVE]

Josh drove carefully along a shallow-flooded street, foam washing from the wheel arches. He was intent on the road, checking for signs that the road dipped, leading into deeper water. Behind him, Richard pointed out swimming rats, making the journey from one island of refuse bags to another.

In its dashboard slot, his phone chimed. He popped the caller's image up on the windscreen at half brightness. It was Tony.

"Hey, Josh."

"How're you doing?"

"Well, I'm clean. I walked ten metres in the rain from my car to the apartment building, so I got well and truly washed. Shoulda took shower gel."

"That's nice. Listen, I'm just driving some friends home."

"In what, a submarine? Good luck, pal."

"Cheers. If we start floating, I'll send up flares. How's the training course going?"

"Really good. I was hoping you'd chat with a couple of the newer guys, give Vikram a heads-up on some of the security modules."

"Uh… well, so long as you weren't thinking of tonight."

"Vikram's crapping himself on quantum triple entanglement, tell you the truth."

"Don't tell me, he's teaching it tomorrow. Afternoon or morning?"

"Morning."

"Jesus."

"So what time do we expect you?"

"Exactly when I get there."

"Fair enough. Out."

"Yeah."

He drove on.

"So who's Tony?" asked Suzanne. "Besides an old friend, clearly."

"Tone runs the outfit that gives me most of my work." He glanced back at Richard. "Not this kind. Corporate training."

"So where are they based?"

"Right now, the basha's in Docklands."

"Basher?"

"Basha. Base of operations. Military jargon, but it's just a corporate flat. Short-term hire, kind of thing."

"You're kidding."

"It's close to the investment bank where the programme–"

"I mean, you're kidding about driving to Docklands tonight, through this. It's going to take long enough to reach Kilburn. Assuming you *are* taking Richard and me home."

Up ahead, a classic internal combustion car, owned by someone rich, was stranded in water. Josh's car lacked the low exhaust that made old vehicles vulnerable; but the water looked deep, so he stopped and backed up anyway. Then he hooked a right, taking a detour.

"Your place first, then I am going to see Tony, because that message wasn't what it sounded like."

"Ah." Suzanne's tone was knowing. "I wondered why you tensed up. That's why I was curious about Tony."

"His phone and mine should be secure, but perhaps he was standing someplace where his voice could be heard. The thing is, he talked about Vikram as though he was one of the newbies, needing advice. But Vik wrote the book on quantum crypto, knows it better than me."

"What's the Barbican?" asked Richard from the back seat.

"A big jumble of buildings," said Josh. "There's a waterway, theatres, and really expensive apartment towers, all in one kind of estate. You've never walked through it?"

Richard shook his head.

"So that's where they film *Knife Edge*?"

Suzanne's eyebrows were raised, and she was smiling. Josh could understand that.

Phobia cure: job done.

She was amazing.

"Only the finals," he said over his shoulder. "They seal the place off and make it look like a bad urban landscape. There are running fights, some between rival teams, pairing off the fighters. Some are fighters that left the show in earlier rounds, brought back after online voting from the audience. If they've healed up, that is."

He thought about that, still driving.

"Can I take this out?" Suzanne reached for the phone. "Josh?"

"Sure."

"All right." She extracted the handset from the dash-board, and handed it over the seat-back to Richard. "Look it up, if you like. The Barbican."

"Oh, thanks."

Josh continued to mull over the logistics. As a nexus point, it would be ideal. That was why security would be massive.

"Are you OK?" asked Suzanne.

"Thinking things over."

But he kept most of his attention outside, as the car surfed across a dip, then ascended to wet but unflooded tarmac.

"It used to be owned by the City of London," said Richard. "Now the Barbican Centre is owned by... by Tyndall Industries."

Josh felt his mouth move.

Tyndall. Who'd have guessed?

"Says here," Richard went on, "that the architecture style is something called Brutalist – honestly, that's what it says – and it stands on the old ward of Cripplegate."

He sniggered, not a pretty sound.

"Good name for a knife-fight venue," said Josh.

"Yeah. Cripplegate was destroyed by German bombs during World War II, so they had a whole district to re-build."

Complex systems change fast.

Josh glanced at Suzanne, then winked.

Including fourteen year-old boys.

Richard continued to give them commentary, saying more in a few minutes than in the previous twenty-four hours.

Here, the road was clear, allowing Josh to increase speed.

• • •

Nearly two hours after he dropped off Suzanne and Richard, Josh pulled up by the Docklands apartments. Then he called Suzanne to tell her he had arrived safely, an odd pattern to have slipped into so fast. Outside, sheet lightning whitened the sky, followed by darkness and floating purple after-images.

Tony opened the front door before he could ring.

"Hey, my friend. Right on time."

"I didn't give you a time."

"So you're not late."

There was a long hallway with bedrooms on either side. At the far end, the lounge looked empty. From one of the bedrooms, as they passed the door, soft music floated, something classical.

"Vikram?" asked Josh.

"Uh-huh. And Sheena's in that room, prepping for tomorrow."

"I'm glad someone's doing what you pay them for."

"Yeah, well, wait till you see who's in here." Tony tapped on another door. "Hey, Matt. How're you doing?"

"Good."

The man who opened up was hugely muscular and square-jawed. It took Josh a second to place him.

"You're Haresh's oppo from Epsilon Force," said Josh. "I saw you in the Bunch of Grapes."

"Right, I remember."

They shook hands. Matt held back on the tension, careful not to splinter the bones of a lesser mortal.

Tony said: "A Sabre Squadron is shipping out. Nigeria, strictly covert. Matt was supposed to go with them."

"Depending how you regard supposed. I'm here for training and observation."

"I know how that goes," said Josh.

It was practically a spec ops tradition, visiting soldiers joining host country operations their own governments could never sanction.

"But if I go missing now," said Matt, "then the guys back home will assume that's where I've gone. Darkest Africa, out of contact, because I'm not officially deploying."

Josh looked at Tony.

"What's going on, my friend?"

It was Matt who said: "Things back home… It's getting bad. In a total breakdown kinda way."

"What does that mean?"

"President Brand," said Tony, "has taken the first regulatory steps to dissolve the triumvirate. The enemy for the coming Apocalypse isn't in Africa or Asia, it's the creeping darkness in his own continent."

"Oh, shit." Josh normally kept track of things, but this was new.

"Meaning other Americans," said Matt. "He's going to secede. Possibly he's going to declare war on CalOr-Washington. Maybe the eastern seaboard, too."

"Holy fuck."

"There's talk of senior officers being shot inside the Pentagon. But exactly who, and by who, and what for, no one's saying. It's the kind of mess maintaining a unified army was supposed to prevent."

"You're talking civil war."

"Yeah, well, we only had the one so far, which makes us even with you Brits. You know us, always like to go one better."

"Actually, we had two," said Tony. "If you count the War of the Roses."

None of this explained why he wanted Josh here.

"So what are your plans, Matt?" asked Josh.

"Well, this is a message for my cousin Carol." Matt tossed over a memory flake. "If you could deliver it for me, that'd be great."

"Your cousin?"

"She's a friend of Dr Duchesne," said Tony. "Also, she's the reason that Broomhall got in contact with Geordie, which is how you got the job."

"And you" – Josh nodded to Matt – "are the reason that your cousin knew about Geordie Biggs and his amazing operatives for hire. Is that it?"

"That's about the size of it."

"So why the secret message?"

"Well, I've lodged a time-delayed resignation from the Army." Matt frowned at the ceiling, and the lights flickered, while the window's magnetic locks clicked open, then shut. "But I'm aiming to skip the surgical removal, if you know what I mean."

Epsilon Force soldiers were filled with implants. On returning to civilian life, they were supposed to leave their little extras behind, courtesy of a military hospital.

"I'll be all right if I can get to my folks back home," added Matt. "But I've got a tiny problem flying like a regular passenger."

The implants again. This was why Ghost Force didn't use them, preferring to operate covertly, often posing as civilians.

"We've got friends flying out from Norfolk in the morning. Private flight." Tony raised his eyebrows. "Since you're dragging your heels or whatever, we kinda hoped you'd help out as a chauffeur for Matt."

"What do you mean, dragging my heels?"

"Hey, just kidding. I mean, since you haven't found the boy–"

"How do you know I haven't?"

"Jesus, his old man is reported to be losing the plot." Tony pulled out his phone and turned it around. "See? Rumours of nervous breakdown, senior employees leaving his home looking worried. All sorts of shit, while his companies look about to go under."

It was the nearest that business journalists got to the soap opera dramatics of their showbiz counterparts. Was it concern for a distressed Josh Cumberland that had Tony checking those stories, or was it something else?

"You got any shares in those companies, Tone?"

"Er… No. Why?"

"Cause if you did, I'd recommend you hang onto them."

Matt suddenly laughed.

"Now I feel better. You guys are the sneakiest hard cases I've ever met, you know?"

"Thanks very much," said Josh. "It's cause we're shy."

Gone midnight, Josh pulled out into the quiet roads, only the hiss of tyres sounding. The storm had passed; the air was cool and exhilarating. For a while, he drove with his window down. In the passenger seat, Matt Klugmann sat like some animatronic figure used to advertise a muscle movie, huge even when relaxed.

Regretting the loss of storm-fresh air, Josh raised the window, so he could talk surveillance-free. "If I swing past a building complex, you think you could do an infiltration scan? Broad sweep, whatever you can manage."

"Paying my fare, is that it?"

"Actually, no." Josh turned left. "I'm taking you to Norfolk because I said I would."

"Fair enough."

"Although if you do me the favour, I'll give your cousin Carol your love, as well as the memory flake."

"Jeez, it's your loving she'll be after, good buddy. You wait till you meet her."

"Bit of a man-eater, is she?"

"The way a starving great white shark is a bit peckish."

"I'll go in armed."

Windscreen and window were lined with refractive laminae, while the chassis resonated with anti-sound generated onboard to cancel out conversation inside. It was one of the reasons that Tony had wanted Josh for the job, because the car was not just surveillance proof – it slid past watchers in a way that seemed innocuous, rather than the result of illegal mods.

Deep in the City now, Josh turned along London Wall.

"There's a whole estate." He pointed. "Those tower blocks, and inside there's a jumble of what-you-call-em, promenades, and a long pond that's like a canal."

"Huh." Matt's eyelids fluttered. "That's heavy duty. Slow down."

Josh decelerated as if afraid of deep water, though the extended puddles were shallow enough. Beside him, Matt's eyes began to shimmer.

Nice.

He had heard of these: contact lenses acting as displays, eyes-only information at its purest.

"All right." Matt blinked the glow from his eyes. "I've seen what I need to."

Josh pointed the car north.

"So they're broadcasting a live event in a few days, right?" Matt continued. "Because there's a permanent, wired-in security system, multi-tiered and hard-shielded. Plus, they're setting up a top-of-the-line webcast studio for the production."

"A Knifefight Challenge event," said Josh.

"Which is also the season finale of *Knife Edge*, right? The two teams leave the fighters' house for the last time. Man, I've been loving that show."

"Oh."

"Shame I won't be around for that. But I don't suppose it matters. It'll be morning where I am, when the evening festivities start here. I can still watch."

"I'm hoping it'll be a good one."

"Uh-huh. So who lives in those tower blocks? I mean, we're talking luxurious, like some exclusive deal in Manhattan, right?"

"The ones who are fans" – Josh glanced up at a tower, then returned his attention to the road – "get to watch from their living rooms and throw big parties. Others fasten their shutters or disappear for a few days. All of them are rich already, and they all get paid a tidy bundle for having their homes turned into a movie set."

"Nice deal. So are we talking signals or bodies, Mr Cumberland?"

"Say what?"

"Your insertion op. Are you infiltrating their software, or sneaking actual physical people inside their perimeter? Maybe with actual physical weapons for hurting other folk? That's the question, my man."

Josh hooked his lower lip behind his front teeth.

Then: "Could I possibly have both?"

"I like your style." Matt chuckled. "You sure you're not American?"

• • •

It was twenty minutes before dawn. At the edge of a wet, fresh-smelling field, Josh leaned against his unlit car, watching a black, jagged shape climb into an indigo sky, its mutable wings twisting as it arced through an improbable angle. Then its trajectory levelled off as it whispered into darkness, and was gone.

"Good luck, my friend."

He thought of the fractured ruin that had been an idealistic country and a symbol of freedom to the world, of self-destructive illusions that became self-fulfilling under a mass belief in Armageddon, a consensual chaotic hallucination perhaps no different from the final days of Mayan greatness or the ending of Rome, a frightening signal that civilisation is and always has been a fragile beauty, a delicate construction.

Then he climbed inside the car, tilted the seat back, and closed his eyes. Sleep was waiting for him: cold, uncomforting, but necessary.

[TWENTY-SIX]

They met at 5 pm in the British Museum, Suzanne arriving to find Carol in the Stone Age section, before a worn stone carving of a voluptuous, large-bellied woman.

"The original sex goddess," Carol said. "My role model."

"You think she was addicted to chocolate, too?"

"Allow me my one and only vice, why don't you."

They walked on, stopping at the ancient tablet that contained the world's oldest written story, the tale of Gilgamesh. They paused again at the Rosetta Stone.

"Incredible. When you think how we went from tree-hugging apes to this" – Carol pressed her fingertips against the glass, then waved at the high airy surroundings – "and on to all this. It makes you want to... eat cake and drink coffee, quite frankly. Where's the café again?"

"Downstairs," said Suzanne. "Same as the last time we were here."

"Well, let's go."

At the café entrance, they came to a halt amid a press of Parisian schoolchildren, their voices tumbling

Suzanne back to childhood – but not enough to prevent her from pressing the memory flake into Carol's hand, and winking. Amid the hubbub, pretending to blow her nose, she murmured: "From Cousin Matt."

Carol nodded, before noticing one of the French teachers accompanying the party. She gave him her broadest, sexiest smile. The teacher tilted his head toward his charges, and shrugged an eloquent apology: *Je suis désolé.*

Her answering shrug said: *Your loss, pal.* Then the sea of kids parted, allowing Suzanne and Carol to walk through.

Once installed at a table with coffee and snacks, they relaxed. Suzanne broke off a tiny piece of her pain au chocolat, while Carol attacked a large slice of carrot cake.

"Just cause you were raised in France," said Carol, "doesn't mean you have to nibble croissants, not when there's cream cakes on offer."

"This pastry is not crescent-shaped," said Suzanne. "Only an American barbarian would call it a croissant. Even the English know this is a pain au chocolat."

"Jeez, there's cowflap on my boots yet again."

"Yee-hah. So how are things in Austin? You've been in touch?"

"Well, shit." Carol stared down at her cake. "You know the city's like a bit of San Fran or maybe Seattle, smack in the middle of good ol' Texican cowboys."

"It must be tense right now."

"They closed the university, pretty much. Curfew on campus, kids arrested and beaten by armoured police."

"Oh, no."

"Meanwhile," said Carol, "rioters over the state border decided to protest the water rationing by going wild and *setting fire* to downtown Phoenix. How's that for clear, logical thinking?"

"I'm sorry."

"Yeah. Still... Good news here is, looks like you're off the legal hook."

"What do you mean?" asked Suzanne.

"Mr Broomhall his own self is going nuts, speaking as one professional to another. Acute asshole-itis being my diagnosis."

"He's withdrawn his complaint?"

"Not exactly. Mr B did everything through his lawyers, except that since yesterday they ain't his lawyers no more. He screamed and shouted, then sacked the lot."

"Oh," said Suzanne.

"Yeah." Carol went quiet for a moment. "This city's going to fall to plague or drowning, so who cares? My street is piled with garbage, or rubbish as you Eurotrash put it. Plus, there are rats everywhere, some of whom aren't guys I've dated."

"At least we still have cake and coffee."

"Yeah." Carol raised a finger smeared with cream. "That we have, thank God."

She popped her finger in her mouth, then looked over at the French teacher, who was now standing at the counter, paying for the kids' soft drinks. He looked at Carol – who raised her eyebrows, still sucking her finger – then turned away.

"You've made him blush," said Suzanne.

"I'd rather make him whimper."

"You are a bad person, Dr Klugmann."

"And your point is?"

Outside her front door, halfway through the automatic motion of reaching forward, Suzanne paused.

Something in the atmosphere felt different, yet reassuring. Perhaps it was the intellectual knowledge that Josh and Richard were inside; or perhaps it was more visceral. This was her nest, where normally she was alone, and she felt almost elated by the new situation as she opened up and went inside.

"–nice," Josh was saying. "Let's have more like that."

I don't believe it.

Rugs and furniture were scrunched against the edges of the room, leaving clear space. On the polished wooden floor, two figures were manoeuvring barefoot, their trousers rolled up at the calves. They moved fast and sure, and it took her a moment to realise that the knives were rubber.

"Trap my hand." Josh hooked his blade upward, his forearm banging against Richard's left wrist. "Good."

And Richard's free hand whipped past Josh's throat, blade across skin.

Oh, my God.

"Again, but without the knife."

"All right."

Tossing his practice weapon onto the couch, Richard spun away barehanded, waiting for Josh to attack once more. This time the uppercut stab was faster, but he blocked it as before, left wrist against bone, while his right fist pumped punches into Josh's throat, holding back from contact but only just, then rammed in his knee and twisted away, ripping the knife from Josh's grasp.

"Good," said Josh again. "OK. From that angle, come in closer next time, use a fast knee, more a snapping motion, less hip." He demonstrated. "The long thrust is harder, but I might have tried to grab your leg. Not that I'd be able to after those punches."

They did it again, Richard moving with a coordination that seemed at odds with the gawky, scared boy Suzanne had first met. But wasn't she supposed to be the one preaching rapid change?

This isn't what I imagined.

It was disturbing. The point of empowering clients was for them to set and achieve their own objectives, not hers. But all the same…

"Excellent." Josh raised his left fist. "We're done."

Richard reached out his own fist, and they touched knuckles. Clearly a ritual, a trigger to change state and calm down from practice. Did Josh understand the significance of these things, or was it just automatic? On balance, he probably did know what he was doing.

She felt warm inside her clothes.

"Hi, Suzanne." Richard's smile was easy. "Josh is teaching me eskrimaga."

"Is that some kind of needlework?"

"It's a mixture of krav maga and escrima. Dead cool. It's what the special forces use."

"Well, isn't that interesting."

Josh rubbed his face.

"I got bored of losing at chess to our resident genius" – he tousled Richard's hair – "so I thought we'd go for something different."

"It's brilliant," said Richard. "I know I'm rubbish at it, but–"

Suzanne blew out a breath, deciding.

"The first time you tried to walk, you fell over, you know? But you just keep doing it, and from what I've just seen, you've picked up coordinated movement" – she clicked her thumb – "just like that."

"I didn't know girls could snap their thumbs," said Josh. "Did you, Richard?"

"Er, no." Richard grinned. Then his features descended into seriousness. "Opal's really fit, and she does all these gymnastics. You wouldn't believe it."

"She will be leaping around again." Suzanne slowed and lowered her voice tonality. "The doctors feel confident."

"Yes, I guess." Richard put his hands in pockets, and stared down at the floor. "After I go back... will I still be able to visit you two?"

Suzanne was astounded by the assumptions in his words, accepting that he would return home, presuming that she and Josh could be visited at the same time, because they would be together.

"Of course," she said.

"Too right," said Josh.

Then Richard produced the final surprise.

"Perhaps I should call Father again."

She took hold of Josh's hand – he grinned – and led him into the kitchen, leaving Richard to make his call.

Sunset was glowing strawberry and gold when Josh pulled up before the main gates of the Broomhall home. They opened. He rolled the car inside, and stopped before the inner barrier.

"Get ready," he said.

"OK," sounded from the rear footwell.

One of the security guys walked up, and Josh lowered the window. "Evening," he said. "I rang ahead, to see your boss."

"Please open the boot, sir. And step out of the vehicle."

His colleagues approached, stone-faced, betraying no clues to outside observers.

"All right."

The guards moved in as the rear of the car popped open, and Josh stepped onto gravel. No one looked at Richard as he rolled out of the car and crawled three metres to the foot of the hedge, keeping to the blind spots, and stopped. From his crouched position, he grinned.

"You can go up to the house," the first security guy said.

"Thank you."

Josh got back in, waited for the barrier to sink into the ground, then drove to the massive front door. A stern-faced woman opened it: Lexa, the driver. She waited until he was inside and the door was shut, then she grinned.

"You've stirred things up. Whatever the old man's up to, it's all your doing."

"I have no idea what you're talking about."

"Sure you don't. Anyway, I've got to go out for a drive and get some shopping."

"Good."

"Richard will be able to slip in while I'm waiting at the gate. They've arranged a little delay." Lexa paused, then: "He is all right, isn't he?"

"Sure he is. You'll see for yourself."

"Good. Nice work, soldier."

"Thank you, ma'am."

"The boss is waiting for you. You remember the way?"

"Sure."

He walked through to the same massive office as last time. The house might be the same, but Philip Broomhall was transformed. His hair was greasy, and his jowls unshaven; but when he stood, his eyes were clear and his back was straight.

"I've got the bastards on the run," he said. "They just don't know it yet."

"Ah." Josh found himself smiling. "That's always the best way."

"Africa's proving more of a problem, though. You don't have conclusive data yourself, I suppose?"

"I've deployed query agents in the Web," said Josh, "and combined with what you've got, we should build up a picture of how they work."

"But it's not the killer blow, is it?" Philip was fleshy and unused to physicality; his notion of killer blows was the manipulation of stock interests. "What we need is a picture of what Richard saw. Virapharm labs growing product inside children. Bloody Billy Church and the Tyndalls looking on."

"So far we've got facts and figures. Pictures of Church and the Tyndalls at premises which we can show are virapharm facilities."

"It's not enough," said Philip. "They'll spindoctor us to oblivion. Bury the facts with fiction and false figures."

"Suzanne Duchesne has taught me something profound."

Philip's eyes tightened. "What is that?"

"It's not what you say, it's how you say it." Josh grinned. "Not to mention, where and when."

"I so hope you're right. All right, let me show you what my people have ferreted out." Data blossomed on half a dozen wallscreens. "Here we have Tyndall Industries owning a hundred percent of this Nigerian facility, although you wouldn't know it from the stockholder list. It's all cutouts and proxies. You realise none of what they do breaks the local laws."

"It'll still cause outrage here. All we have to do is get the data in front of people."

"Well, that's the challenge, isn't it? Anyway, over here you can trace the interrelated–"

A door clicked open, further down the hallway. Then the office door opened.

"F-father?"

"Richard!"

They stepped toward each other, then stopped, as though held back by a force field. Behind Richard, Lexa frowned. Philip seemed unable to move.

"Are you all right, son?"

"Yes, Father. I was... I was very lucky."

Then something broke as Philip stumbled forward first, Richard falling against his chest; and they were hugging each other, crying and not caring. Seeing Philip's tears, Josh finally decided he could like the man.

Lexa led Josh into the hall, and closed the office door behind them.

"Looks like you did good," said Lexa.

"I just found him," said Josh. "Suzanne fixed him."

"Ah, that'll be Dr Duchesne. You and her, you're together? It's the way you say her name."

"Er, yeah."

"Figures. All the good ones are taken." She shrugged her muscled shoulders. "Never mind."

After a while, the office door opened. Philip came out, arm around Richard's shoulders.

"I'm going to do some work, otherwise I'd be letting Mr Cumberland down. And we can't have that, can we, Richard?"

"No."

"You three go on, and I'll join you shortly."

"OK. Father?"

"What is it?"

"My thing about blades..."

"That doesn't matter. You're safe, and you're home."

"But Josh taught me eskrimaga. I mean, he started to."

Philip was puzzled.

"Combat skills," said Lexa. "So, you want to carry on learning, Richard?"

"Josh is staying here?"

"Wouldn't that be nice." Lexa raised an eyebrow. "The answer's no, but why don't you all come see my bedroom?"

"Without dinner first?" said Josh.

Richard said "Josh has a girlfriend."

"I figured." Lexa winked at him. "So, are you coming?"

"I'll tag along, if I'm welcome." Philip glanced back at his office. "It'll keep for a few minutes."

"Sure thing, boss."

She led the way to a ground-level room that overlooked the rear lawns. There was a brass label on the door reading Estate Manager.

"He got the sack." She grinned at Philip. "And I got a room upgrade. Come see."

A huge office had been transformed into a more-than-bedroom. The bed itself was small, tucked against one wall. What made Josh smile was a vertical plastic-and-ceramic cylinder, man-high and waist-wide, from which several stiff rods poked out, representing limbs. In China they were made of wood, a mainstay of wing chun fight training.

On the bed were two rattan canes – escrima sticks – and a coiled skipping-rope. Under a chair stood a kettlebell.

Josh tapped Richard's shoulder with a half fist. "Looks like you have a new trainer."

Richard looked at his father. So did Josh and Lexa.

"You mean it's my choice?" Philip's voice was mild. "I'm happy if you do, and happy if you don't. All right?"

"Thanks, Dad."

Philip blinked. Perhaps it was the first time Richard had called him anything but Father.

Josh felt a soft punch on his shoulder.

"Like I said, soldier." Lexa leaned close. "You did good. Now go home to your girlfriend, before I show you my restraint holds."

"Yeah. Take it easy."

"You, too."

[TWENTY-SEVEN]

Josh stormed out of the Broomhall house, slamming
the front door and muttering "Fuckin' arsehole..."
clearly enough for spycams to pick up the image, if
not the sound. Getting into his car, he yanked the driver's door shut, switched on the ignition while
snapping his safety belt in, released the hand-brake
simultaneously with flicking the car into drive, gun-
ning it into a sharp, gravel-spraying turn, and
accelerated for the gates.

There, the security guys remained blank-faced while
the gates opened; save for one man, standing in a surveillance blind spot by the hedge, who dropped Josh
an exaggerated wink. Then Josh drove out onto the
road, moving too fast, acting enraged though his mind
was cold. He was already working on mission prep.

Once on the motorway he drove more reasonably.
Tapping his phone in its console slot, he queried vlogger
sites.

"Command: select keywords America, political situation, Brand, coup, secession. Command: spelling
disambiguation, coup equals C-O-U-P. Command: display top ten, most viewed."

He lowered the brightness on his heads-up as ten static panes showed low down on the windscreen. Then he tapped the console below the rightmost image.

A shaven-headed man in what looked like an expensive suit, shirt and tie began to speak.

"In Samuel, King David says: 'He traineth my hands for war, so that my arm may bend a bow of bronze.' The conflict you have been training for is here. Too long have we put up with Islamist jihadists, but at least they had the guts to declare war, unlike the left-wing godless liberals who have weakened this country for so long. Now we move to cleanse the Earth in the final crusade, the triumph of—"

Josh shut it off, changed lanes to slow down, then tapped below the next pane. Here the speaker was maybe twenty, his hair in braids, glancing off to one side every few seconds as he spoke.

"President Brand is threatening democracy, let's be clear on that. You don't agree, tough, because the police will kick your door down and drag you out as a threat to homeland security. That means no trial, no lawyer, no limit to how long they—"

He tapped that pane, also, to stillness. Then he wiped the display.

"Hell. To. Handbasket. In, a, going. Make a sentence out of that."

The phone chimed its do-not-understand tone.

"End voice commands."

After some twenty minutes driving in silence, he tapped again. Tony's image appeared, ghostly on the windscreen.

"Hey, Tone."

"Josh, my man. Are you OK?"

"Always. Are you still in contact with Taffy C?"

"Is he still alive?"

"That'll be a no, then."

"Actually, I think he's in London. I'm surprised you want to see him, though."

"If you're talking about the time I interrupted him with three rent boys and a blindfolded donkey, I think he's forgiven me for that."

"And I thought Vikram was the potty-mouth round here."

"Call me back?"

"After I've washed that image from my mind."

"Cheers, mate."

A car cut in front, and Josh braked, slowing right down. He shook his head, continuing at reduced speed; and it was only when the idiot turned off at the exit that a memory returned: dragging a hapless suicide jockey out of his car and throwing away the key.

All I needed was something important to work on.

If the situation here were as bad as the not-so-United States, there would be nothing he could do about it. But for now, so long as general elections took place and public opinion mattered, he could spread the word about corruption in the prime minister's office, hopefully to more effect than some student vlogger trying to warn his fellow citizens about a near-silent coup among the upper echelons of government.

Tony's image popped back up. "Park in Sainsbury's in Richmond, walk out here" – a secondary pane flicked into existence, showing a map – "and Big Tel's taxi will pick you up. RV is seventeen hundred."

"Got it. Where's Taff?"

"Centre of London, Shaftesbury Avenue. Tel has drop-off details."

"OK. Thanks, Tony."

"Give Taff a kiss from me."

"Only if it's no tongues."

He killed the comms.

He was in Richmond with nearly five hours to spare, so he parked as close to the great park as he could, changed his clothes in the car, and went running. The highlight was a magical face-to-face with three young deer, who watched him as he crept past, before continuing his run.

A sponge bath at the back of the car – when there was no one around to watch – and he was back inside the vehicle, working with the heads-up, poring through the schematics and interface definitions that Matt had pulled from the Barbican.

"You guys are paranoid," Josh said aloud. "I'm impressed. Unfortunately."

Finally, he shut everything down, and drove to the supermarket for the rendezvous. At seventeen hundred hours and two seconds, he climbed into Big Tel's taxi cab.

After the usual banter, he said: "You free for an op on the sixteenth? By free I mean available, because I'll pay you for it."

"What do I get, like?" Tel manoeuvred the taxi out onto the road. "Straight fee or percentage?"

"Your choice, pal."

"Well, how much are you earning for this gig?"

"Somewhere between zero and nothing."

In the driver's mirror, Tel smiled. "If we're in the big leagues like that, then I'm in for five per cent."

"You fool, you could have twisted my arm for twenty."

"Uh-huh. We're talking heavy duty logistics, are we?"

"Solo insertion, maybe some of Tony's crew for distraction purposes only. I'm working on the details. The infiltration is just me."

Tel navigated a junction, then: "And exfiltration afterwards?"

"Not needed."

"I don't like the sound of that."

"No, it's OK. If I do the job all right, I'll walk out on my own two feet."

"And Plan B?" asked Tel.

"I've reason to believe there'll be medics nearby. With luck, they might help me. Otherwise it's Plan D for dead, so it won't matter."

"Hmm." Tel drove on for a bit, then: "So where's the location, boss?"

"The Barbican."

"The–? You know, the big final's there on the twentieth."

"It is?" said Josh.

"Yeah. But security will be tighter than a duck's rectum, so if anyone was going to like sneak inside, they'd want to lay up early."

"I imagine so."

"Maybe four days in advance."

"Sounds good to me."

"So long as they wasn't thinking of going up against, like, thirty of the country's best professional knife fighters, that would probably be all right."

"Probably."

"Not to mention," said Tel, "close-protection teams with guns galore, on account of the PM visiting and all."

"Not to mention."

"Well." Tel swerved into a side street, one of his famous shortcuts. "You remember Mad Jock, right?

Legend of the Regiment?"

"Sure."

"Wait'll I tell people I've had Mad Josh riding in my cab."

"Shit."

"That's what they'll do when I tell 'em."

Just before seven, Josh climbed out of the cab on Shaftesbury Avenue, directly by a side door of the old red-brick theatre. Big Tel drove off, and a male member of the theatre staff, dressed in black, opened the door from inside, and nodded to Josh.

"Alwyn is upstairs." The young man gestured to a narrow flight of wooden treads, darkened with age. "I'll lead the way."

He pushed the door shut – it would only open from inside – then started up the stairs.

"Don't you think this is a wonderful production?" he added. "It's the most fabulous I've worked on."

"Say what?" Josh kept pace as they ascended.

"*Nine Princes in Amber*. You must have seen it."

"I'm not really into musicals."

"But that's dreadful. Never mind."

At the top of the fourth flight, they turned left, and passed into a huge, high-ceilinged room ringed with dressing-tables and clothes racks... and some three dozen actresses who were naked or near-naked, changing into costume, or applying make-up while their pert, bare breasts bounced with the motion.

"Bloody hell."

Josh had twice known paralysis in the face of lethal danger. This was not quite the same but – there was the most perfect female arse he had ever seen, bending over to pull up her voluminous skirt from the floor. Awe and lust washed through him.

"Oh, dear fellow, do come on."

Looking back, Josh allowed himself to be led into a side room. When the door closed, hiding the beauties outside, he thought he might weep.

"Alwyn, I've brought your friend."

Blinking, Josh turned round. "Hey, Taff. How's it going?"

Taff rolled his eyes, then shrugged to the young man. "I apologise for my philistine friend."

"Oh, I find his rough edge rather a thrill. Or dare I say *alluring*?"

"Out with you, Freddy. I need to talk to my friend alone."

"Never mind. Ta-ta."

"Yeah," said Josh. "Cheers."

Once young Freddy was gone, Taff grinned at Josh.

"Did the ladies outside bring a lump to your throat? Or somewhere southwards?"

"How can you work here and not turn straight?"

"Dear Josh, you haven't seen the *boys'* dressing-room."

"Uh-huh." He looked around the shelves stacked with jars, the polystyrene heads on which rubber masks were draped, and empty gloves in the form of grey-skinned hands bearing long, curved spurs. "From the show?"

"Of course. Demons, sort of. Makes for a rather nice dance number, their big fight in the first act."

"Er, right." Josh sometimes worked with the sound-track of *Bladefight* 7 pounding in his earbeads. That was the nearest he came to associating blood and pain with music. "So I was looking for something to change my appearance."

"That's the only reason you lovely lads ever invite me to Hereford, isn't it?"

"How could we resist you?"

"Excuse me, but what makes you think everyone there rejected me?"

"This, I don't want to know."

"Ah, well." Taff waved at the shelves. "What are we talking about? Meeting up close and personal? Or just smiling for the spycams?"

Josh rubbed his face, trying not to think of perfect breasts. From next door, female laughter sounded.

"Er, mainly cameras, but I'll be in view for some time. I'd like not to be recognised later."

Assuming he survived so there would be a *later*.

"Are we talking lo-res from a distance? Or state of the art with close-ups?"

"The latter. Imagine I appeared on a webcast watched by millions, and wanted to be anonymous."

"Wouldn't that be a lovely thing? I don't suppose you could wear a demon mask? I could do you with or without horns."

"I'd rather look normal."

"My dear boy, normal? That sounds so boring."

"And I'll be taking the stuff away with me. I won't need it for days yet."

"So you remember all my lessons in artistry? How to layer it on so it's undetectable? Of course not. Now sit down in front of this mirror, and be a good boy."

"Yes, Taff."

"And pay attention, because I assume your taut arse will be on the line again."

"Isn't it always?"

It took over twenty minutes – interrupted when a bra-clad beauty poked her head around the door and called Taff out to help with something. If Josh hadn't been half made-up, he'd have offered to help – but finally he was staring at a different face in the mirror. It was like seeing a distant cousin for the first time.

"You're a genius, Taff."

"Aren't I, indeed."

"So…"

"The boy wants even more from me?"

"I was wondering if you could supply light disguise for up to seven, no, make it nine guys. Just in case. They'll be on the periphery as a distraction."

"Hmm. Skin colour?"

"Whites and browns" –Josh thought of Vikram – "quite dark, no orientals."

"I'll prepare a selection. Did you bring a bag of some sort with you?"

"Er, no."

"Aren't you supposed to be master planners, all of you?"

"With all those girls outside, master something springs to mind."

"Tsk, tsk. Well, let's see… Oh, why don't you pop next door, while I'm getting things together."

"You got some kind of secret setup going in here, Taff? Something I shouldn't see?"

"No, but it's almost curtains up. You want to catch the last few titties before they disappear, better take the opportunity now."

Josh looked at the door.

"If it's necessary for the mission," he said, "I guess I can manage it."

[TWENTY-EIGHT]

With his backpack slung over one shoulder, Josh got through the ground-level entrance, despite its being locked, climbed up to the top-floor hallway, and knocked on Suzanne's front door. Then he stood waiting, unable not to smile.

The door opened. Suzanne looked at him.

"Hello?"

He said nothing.

"Look, who are you and what do you–? *Josh*? My God, Josh."

"You're not supposed to recognise me."

"I almost didn't. That's so spooky."

"You want to make out with a stranger? We could switch the lights off."

"Come in. For God's sake, come in before Mrs Arrowsmith sees you."

After he was inside and Suzanne had locked the door, he said: "Who's Mrs Arrowsmith? The neighbour?"

"Yes, and I've got a reputation to uphold, Mr Cumberland. Strange men coming in and out at all hours would not be much help."

"Well, I'm certainly strange."

"You are, in fact. You weren't thinking of not taking that stuff off, were you?"

"I wasn't... Was that some kind of psych trick?"

"What do you mean?"

"The way you said something about what I wasn't thinking of."

"Ah, so you have been paying attention."

"To you, definitely."

"Then go in the bathroom and remove that disguise right now."

"Yes, ma'am."

Afterwards, he came out looking normal but smelling like turpentine. He went out to the kitchen.

"Hi," he said. "What are you doing?"

"Cooking us supper, because you're staying the night, in case you hadn't realised."

"Ah."

"So what have you been up to? And where did you get that disguise?"

"A friend of mine, works in an interesting place."

"What kind of interesting place?"

"Do you know" – he stared at her brown eyes – "I forget. Really. When I'm looking at you."

"Hmm. So why the disguise, if you won't tell me where?"

"So no one recognises me afterwards. After I confront Zebediah Tyndall on camera."

"In the middle of this knife-final thing?"

"In the middle of this thing" – Josh blew out a breath – "that millions of people will be watching in realtime, yes. On the day of the general election, when a large chunk of the population are expected to vote online in the evening."

"Right. And that will help how?"

"Well, you know, when people are watching sports events, they have all sorts of secondary panes popped up: fighter stats, you name it. Panes that could show any number of interesting things instead, to do with political corruption."

"And how many people will be with you?" asked Suzanne.

"Like I said, millions of folk watch the–"

"No, how many people are helping you to carry out this insanity?"

"I'm still ironing out details. Six to nine, probably."

"Is that enough?"

"The tighter the perimeter, the fewer people you use to infiltrate."

"All right." Suzanne placed peppers and an onion atop a chopping-board, then picked up a kitchen knife. "And no one's going to stick one of these in anyone?"

"I hope not."

"Does that mean you'll have guns?"

"Probably not. Gunpowder gives off a detectable signature when you–"

"And you'll have nine men with you. They are men, I'm guessing. No women?"

"Women are far too sensible." Josh stared into space for a moment. "Apart from my friend Hannah, maybe. She's probably up for it."

"They'll be inside with you all the way?"

"Er… Inside, it'll just be me."

"No." She put down the knife. "No, Josh Cumberland, that's not good enough. You cannot go in there by yourself. I won't allow you to."

The obvious response was: *How can you stop me?* But she looked serious.

And she was pulling up her sleeve. Beneath the kitchen lights, the long scars were white-and-silver, and very bright, with a near-liquid sheen.

"That's what happens when someone leaves me alone."

"Suzanne…"

"My brother Gérard went out to check the banging sounds from outside, thinking the neighbourhood toughs were setting light to cars again, and he was supposed to come right back but he never did. I never saw him again, only his coffin which they kept sealed. They wouldn't let us look at him. Not after what had been done to him."

"Oh, Suzanne. But if you never… What happened?"

"You mean these?" She stared down at the scars, her mouth turned down. "They're all about fighting back, cutting deep, causing hurt because it's the only way to be alive."

"Who cut you? Who were you fighting?"

Because if they still lived, he would hunt them down; and they would suffer slowly.

"Don't you get it, Josh?"

Things turned inside his mind.

"Oh, shit."

I should've seen it.

"Right. When you're helpless, there's only one enemy you can turn on, and that's your own weakness. Only one person who's soft and weak enough to deserve the way it cuts into your muscle, the skin stinging but the insides feeling weird, more than anything, and the little globules of grey fat soaking in your own red blood."

It happens in prisons, among prisoners who lack the ability to fight the others off.

"You cut yourself?"

"It was the only thing I could do."

"Oh, my dear Suzanne."

"I'm sorry." She sniffed back tears. "I'm really sorry. But that's why I'm going in with you. Why I can't let you walk out, promising you'll come back, when maybe you won't. And I couldn't stand that, Josh Cumberland. I could not stand that."

He didn't know what to tell her. Observation posts were not made to be comfortable, and few people could remain still and undetected for days on end.

Once, he had set up an OP in the loft of a family home, keeping watch on a house across the street, while using plastic scent-absorbing containers for bodily waste, spending most of his time holding still. And all during the five-day op, a boisterous family went on with their lives in the house underneath, never once suspecting the presence of Josh Cumberland in their attic.

Was this the kind of person Suzanne wanted in her life? The kind of person she could act like, even for a short time?

"You'll need to remain a non-combatant. They set the thing up as a sort of street scene, the final. A bit of urban chaos. Women don't fight if they're not carrying, and don't have to fight even if they are. Carrying a knife, I mean."

"What happens when you make your move?"

"Once it kicks off… it'll get crazy."

"So. In that case" – she looked at the inside of her forearms, then at him – "I may need to protect myself, once you kick over the rules. How long do we have before going inside?"

"Twenty-two days."

"That long?" Her smile was like a child's, shining from inside. "You've heard of accelerated learning?"

"Training is my business, and it's a large part of what the Regiment does: teach élite groups around the world."

"So you use intensive techniques?"

"Sure we–"

"Josh, my lover. You ain't seen nuthin' yet."

On the first day of preparation, Josh cleared the lounge floor as he had with Richard, then he faced Suzanne in the centre of the room, and told her to put her hands out in front of her, keeping elbows bent. Placing his wrists against hers, he pressed gently.

"So, here's the game. As I move my hands, you keep your wrists pressed against mine."

"You said you were going to teach me how to fight."

"Trust me. Here we go."

He began moving his hands independently of each other, in slow motion at first. An observer would have seen a kind of tai-chi waltz, initially with feet static, then with slow footwork as he began to move and Suzanne reacted. There was no need to tell her to pivot rather than backstep: with this low intensity, the reaction was natural, coming from a place of calmness.

"This doesn't seem much like–"

"Let me up the pace a little."

His hand pressure became harder as well as faster, increasing by increments so she kept pace. And then his hand motion became more directed, left and right still moving independently, but occasionally curving or thrusting toward her face or ribs, liver or spleen. All the while, her wrists remained glued to his, absorbing and redirecting the force vectors, protecting the vulnerable parts of her anatomy.

Finally, he called a break.

"That's amazing." Suzanne was breathing. "Suddenly, it clicked, and I understood what we were doing."

"Wax on, wax off."

"I beg your pardon?"

"Never mind. Do you do much dancing? Because you handle your bodyweight pretty well."

"Yoga," she said. "I do a bit of yoga."

"Hmm. You know the Salute to the Sun?"

"Of course, but I'm surprised you do, Josh Cumberland."

"All right, we'll stretch and get warm with that, followed by some Indian wrestling exercises that sort of come from yoga. Then we'll *chi sao* a bit more."

"*Chi sao*?"

"With the wrists, sticking 'em together. Chinese term. The Okinawans call it *kakie*."

"All right. What else are we doing today?"

"How about I show you how to break a person's neck?"

"Oh, goody."

On the third day of preparation, it was nearly noon when Suzanne turned from the coffee machine and stood with hands on hips.

"Josh? Weren't your friends supposed to be here an hour ago?"

Leaning against a wall cupboard, Josh answered, "The RV was your place, right here, at eleven hundred. Fifty-seven minutes ago."

"RV?"

"Rendezvous. I believe that's a French word, cherie."

"*Ouais*. I had the impression your punctuality was a professional habit."

"We're never late for an RV. On operations, a few minutes late can mean disaster, so we learn to be on time."

"But fifty-seven minutes late, and you don't look worried, Josh."

"I'm not."

"I don't–"

At that moment a shape unfolded itself from behind the couch, and another rotated around a corner from the bedroom door.

"*Merde! Qui êtes-vous? Espèce de–Josh?* Who are they?"

Suzanne backed up against the cooker.

This handsome reprobate is Tony." Josh gestured. "And the lady over there is Hannah."

"I…" Suzanne's hand was at her throat. "That's not… How long have they been there?"

"Since 11 o'clock," said Hannah. "Like your boyfriend says, we're never late for an RV."

"*Merde*," murmured Suzanne.

"Sacred blue," said Josh. "Cause I'm too polite to say shit."

"You know, you're sensitive and intelligent and over-whelmingly observant–"

"Ta lots."

"–and there's a part of you that's incredibly creepy. Did you know that? All of you?"

Tony advanced, holding out his hand. "Sorry. Professional habit. I'm really pleased to meet you, Dr Duchesne."

Behind him, Hannah said: "I'm looking forward to hearing about Josh's creepy part. Is it as small as everyone says it is?"

Suzanne giggled and Tony laughed, failing to shake hands; then the four were in hysterics like schoolkids.

"Even smaller," said Suzanne eventually, and set them off again.

On the fourth day of preparation, Suzanne taught Josh, Tony and Hannah how to put each other into trance. They took it in turns, two sitting at right angles to each other, while the third observed.

"Remember to synchronise your voice with their physiology," said Suzanne. "And use tonal marking as I told you."

Hannah was the best with voice control, leading Tony into a deeply altered state.

"That was amazing," he said when he came out of it.

"It's a slow process, this trance induction," said Josh. "I mean, there might be uses in preparing your mates for a contact – a firefight – and for the post-traumatic stuff. But you can't sit an enemy down and talk them down like that."

"If you think of them as an enemy," answered Suzanne, "you'll never lead them into trance. Hannah, did you realise that you were going into an altered state along with Tony? Actually, ahead of him?"

"Er… Yeah. My vision went a little weird, yet I was totally focused."

"Exactly."

"But Josh is right, "said Hannah. "It takes a while, doesn't it?"

Yet there were other approaches to combat than fast and hard. Josh remembered the single aikido class he had trained in, where most of the people practised exaggerated sweeping attacks, and when grabbed, they went with the flow of every technique instead of wrenching away. Few looked as if they could stop an angry ten year-old; but the instructor had forearms like a bear, and an attitude that was implacable. He stepped straight into the centre of rotation when his students attacked – the concept of *irimi*, entering the heart of the whirlwind – and slammed them in all directions.

It was strange that he thought of aikido with its wrist-grabbing techniques, because just then Suzanne reached for Tony's hand as though about to shake it, but when Tony started to respond she twisted his hand, pushed it against his face and said one word:

"*Sleep.*"

Tony's head rocked back and he was under.

"Holy fucking shit," said Hannah.

Josh looked at her; she stared at Josh. In the automatic choreography of amazement, they all turned to Suzanne.

And you thought I was scary.

On the seventh day, Vikram came to visit, wearing a thin raincoat and mild disguise. Tony had taken the disguise kit back to the Docklands apartment, and this was the result. Suzanne led him inside.

"I thought you were just going to materialise like a ninja," she said. "Isn't that what you guys do?"

"Not me. I'm a tech-head." Vikram grinned. "And a mere mortal."

"But he's OK, all the same," said Josh. "So what goodies have you brought us?"

Vikram opened his coat. "I feel like a flasher."

"But I like what you've got, darling," Josh told him. "A rather beautiful pair."

Under each armpit hung a small, neat handgun.

"I thought you said…" Suzanne stopped. "Something about gunpowder being detectable, wasn't it?"

"That's right." Vikram removed his coat, then struggled out of the shoulder holsters. "These electromag babies are strictly illegal. All ceramics and superconductors, no gunpowder involved. You'll want to use them only if necessary."

"We're going to be in front of cameras," said Josh. "I don't want viewers having any reason to think of special forces."

"Uh-huh. Cop hold of these." Vikram gave Josh the weapons, then turned back to his raincoat and pulled open the lining. "Here's your shirts, neatly folded. Hannah guessed your size, Suzanne."

"That's nice. Dark blue, not black?"

"So you could pass for an innocent person and still hide in the shadows." Vikram held up the shirt by the shoulders. "See those nice buttons?"

"Sure."

"They're fake. Josh?"

Josh took hold of the shirt-front and ripped it open, accompanied by the sound of Velcro.

"Very stylish," said Suzanne. "But what's the point?"

"You'll wear the shoulder holster under the shirt," answered Josh. "If you need to use it, you'll tear open the shirt and whip out the gun."

"Oh."

"So wear a bra," said Josh. "Unless you really want to distract them."

"I'll never remember how to do that. Not under pressure."

"Sure you will." Josh smiled at her. "I'll teach you."

• • •

On the eighth day, Tony returned. Josh got him to hold up an impact pad on each hand as a target, while Suzanne whipped palm strikes and punches into them, using plenty of hip twist.

"Whoa," said Tony. "That's what I call power."

"She's doing all right." Josh winked at Suzanne. "Really good."

"Thanks to my teacher here."

Josh wasn't so sure. She had deconstructed what went on inside his head when he fired off techniques, then reproduced his state of mind inside herself.

"When I hit the pads," he said now, "I hear Lofty's voice inside my head telling me to hit harder. Though I'd not been properly aware of it."

"So…"

"So Suzanne does the same thing, hears someone encouraging her on."

"Auditory hallucination," said Suzanne, "if you like."

Tony looked at the pads he was holding.

"That sounds nuts, except I've never known a beginner hit that way. There must be something in it."

Suzanne smiled at him.

"Josh tells me you were one of the best shots in the Regiment."

"*One* of the best?"

"He also said you were modest."

"Ah."

She picked up a coffee mug, walked to the far end of the room, and held it up.

"Imagine you were going to shoot this."

"All right."

"Really imagine it, as if you were holding a weapon."

From nowhere, Tony drew a real gun and pointed it. Josh remained relaxed.

"Interesting," said Suzanne. "How big is the mug?"

"About ten inches. But my wife would say three and a half."

"Yes, but how big does it really look?"

"It... Jesus." Tony lowered the gun. "It looks about four feet tall, but only in my head, you know? My mind's eye."

"Hmm. That's a common strategy among top marksmen," she said. "But I'd only read about it. You actually use it. Hallucinating – visualising – the target bigger than it is."

Tony looked at Josh.

"And you've been in this woman's company day and night for how long now?"

"I've lost track."

"When Amber moved in with me first, remember how she rearranged my furniture?"

"Er, yeah."

"At least she didn't refurbish the insides of my head. On the other hand, I didn't need it, whereas you clearly did, old mate."

Josh looked at Suzanne, whose reply was a beaming smile, full of innocence and wicked intent, all at the same time.

"Have you tidied up my mind," he said, "just cause you're a neuropsych and you can?"

"Oh, no."

"Well, thank God for–"

"It's because I'm a woman."

Tony laughed.

"She's well and truly got you, mate."

On the tenth day, after laying anti-surveillance kit throughout Suzanne's flat, Josh popped schematics up onto the wallscreen. Tony, Hannah, and Vikram watched from the couch, while Suzanne fetched coffee.

"There are five different possible OPs," Josh said. "We could lay up here, this crawlspace, which is the closest to the action, but the hardest to keep quiet in."

He had analysed the hiding places in various ways: ease of access – getting in without tripping alarms even he could not subvert – and ease of exit on the day, to get close to the action; the acoustic properties, for silence was going to be key; ventilation and the amount of room available. All were part-way reasonable; none of them was perfect.

"Not bad." Tony leaned forward, pointing. "What about going in through the–?"

"Hold on." Hannah looked at Suzanne. "Didn't this all start with your friend Philip Broomhall? And isn't he stinking rich?" "I don't think Broomhall considers me a friend," said Suzanne. "But he is rich, yes."

"Well, what kind of person lives in the Barbican?" asked Hannah. "It's your city financiers, and a bunch of rich actors, all that kind. That's who."

"So–?"

"So what kind of friends does Broomhall mostly have? You think maybe rich ones? Could be, he knows someone who lives there."

"That's not bad," said Josh.

"Come off it," said Hannah. "It's fucking genius."

"Yes, you are." Tony saluted her. "We bow down before you, oh great one."

"Good. Just keep that adulation coming, minion, and we'll get on fine."

On day thirteen, amid the greenery of Hampstead Heath, Suzanne ran five kilometres straight for the first time since schooldays. Back at her apartment, Josh used so-called pattern interrupts for rapid hypnotic inductions, dropping both Tony and Hannah into trance in less than a second.

"We're getting there," Josh said.

"Yes, we are," said Suzanne.

The fifteenth day was a nightmare for Josh, in contrast to everyone else, who performed superbly on the assault course.

"What's up?" asked Tony afterwards.

Suzanne said: "He didn't come to bed last night. At all."

"Josh?"

"Call me a geek." Josh shrugged. "I went through the subversion ware from start to finish, and re-edited the data archives. Philip came through with good stuff."

Combining Philip Broomhall's corporate awareness with Josh's tech knowledge had paid dividends in triangulating on footage that neither the prime minister nor the Tyndalls would want the public to see.

"So it's going to make an impact?"

"Oh, yes."

On day seventeen, they were in a converted Georgian house, surrounded by its own grounds, in the heart of Herefordshire. It was a training facility, normally rented out to companies teaching management techniques; but occasionally the people who hired it were ex-Regiment, and the training that took place was light-years removed from anything an MBA would expect.

When a dark-clad figure grabbed Suzanne's shoulder from behind, she spun and slammed a palm-heel into a visor-protected chin, slammed a shin-kick into a padded thigh, and knocked the man down with a curving elbow strike.

"Nice," said Josh.

Suzanne looked down at the half-prone man.

"Not now, Kato," she said.

They spent the rest of the day either springing out on people to ambush them or else being the target, reacting to random attacks as they wandered through the building. She called it Clouseau training, a reference that Josh failed to catch, which meant an evening of watching old Pink Panther movies when the day's work was over.

Her viewing was interrupted by a call from Peter Hall, her client who had cancelled on the day she met Adam and later Philip Broomhall. Peter was distraught, and she calmed him down, taking him to a more resourceful neurophysiological state, able to cope with the sudden loss of his job that had triggered the reaction. By the end of it – including a trance induction over the phone – Peter had coping strategies in place. He would be ready for jobhunting tomorrow, while managing his emotions.

Finally, she closed down the call and looked at Josh, Tony, and Hannah.

"That wasn't just a wandering conversation, was it?" said Josh. "We sort of appreciate how you did some of it, at least. Now we know the basics, that was a bit of a masterclass."

Tony nodded, while Hannah said "You rock, girl."

"Thank you."

On day twenty-two, in darkness, in front of the training house, Suzanne hugged the others farewell, Tony, Hannah, and the others she had met only five days before,

Raj, Brummie, Ron, and Morio. Josh's way of saying goodbye was more in the way of wry smiles, punches to the upper arm or touching fists, and a final inventive insult that was returned in kind.

There were four cars, already packed with kit. Josh and Suzanne climbed into the first together, and drove off. The others would leave at intervals, dispersing rather than forming an obvious convoy. They would rendezvous tomorrow morning, coming together from different directions.

"Three days left," said Suzanne. "And yes, I know. We've got to get through tomorrow first."

"Good job we're ready," said Josh.

[TWENTY-NINE]

And so, the Barbican.

It was a jumble of architecture, a long promenade by a wholly artificial rectangular lake – American visitors called it a pond; the locals thought it too big for that label – with its own straight-edged waterfall to a lower level, leading to a pool that partly undercut one of the towers, which was supported on stilts.

On the promenade, under normal circumstances, chairs ringed parasol-covered tables for al fresco dining. Now, the area was covered with jagged-looking obstacles that looked like massive fragments of shattered concrete, though they were rubberised and soft to the touch. Graffiti marked them: symbols of urban breakdown and destruction, props for the coming show.

In total there were three towers, including the one undercut by water, all of them filled with apartments overlooking the promenade-turned-urban arena. The building walls at one end formed a hollow curve, like some Circus Maximus of old. There, the apartments' silver-shuttered windows offered perfect views of the action to come, while keeping the residents far removed from the real urban dangers beyond the estate's high walls.

In previous decades a music college had enjoyed premises on site; now that building was occupied by a blue-sky research campus owned by an Eastern European consortium, part of the Web 4.0 Initiative. It was just one more accidental by-product of the wealth pouring into Poland, Slovakia and the Czech Republic, now that their natural uranium deposits were growing ever more valuable in the ongoing rush to throw up reactors as fast as possible. In contrast, the alternative programmes were years behind schedule and/or underfunded by billions, depending on who you asked.

Under other circumstances, Josh would have been tempted to break into the W4I labs, just to see what they were up to.

Silvery membranous sheets were draped shroud-like against walls and over awnings. In ambient daylight, they were translucent; but later, when the smartroof drew over the promenade arena, casting shade, the sheets would come alive with rippling, motile patterns of light, turning the post-apocalyptic setting into something eerie and modern. Background music would pulse throughout the estate. The same music that would form the backing for the webcast, with state of the art audio mixing.

Men and women in dark blazers and sharp-creased trousers were patrolling the grounds, the stairwells and colonnades and corridors, and the theatre complex that was the Barbican Centre at the heart of the estate. They paid no attention to the spyball cameras dotted everywhere; they did watch the cleaning staff and webvision roadies moving along the promenade among the props. This was despite the hoops everyone had already jumped through simply to come on site, three successive security checks, taking an hour in total.

For the most part the residents were staying away from the promenade, for the few days it formed a webvision set under construction. But some walked their dogs or strolled according to habit, and the security personnel were careful both to observe the walkers and keep their distance. The residents were rich or they would not be able to live here, and the security objective was to keep them safe, not annoy them.

By 9am, many residents had long departed to go to work, though others worked at home, while some – several actors and at least one luxury-class prostitute – would still be sleeping off the previous night's activities, ready for a late start to their working day. Few families with children lived here, because it was not that kind of place: it was for the go-getters, the well-off or those thirtysomethings who were too busy fighting in the corporate jungle to create for themselves an actual life.

Casual visitors, for the next few days, would be turned away with unswerving, implacable politeness. Some would walk outside the perimeter proper, taking in an external view of the jumbled, purplish architecture, all hard edges and curves, with neither the plentiful glass of more modern creations nor the gracefulness or playful details of classical design. A few of the visitors might be envious, wishing they could live so close to the City – which is not the city, not London itself, but only the calculating financial centre with both the bustle and the heartlessness of Wall Street or the Beijing Bourse.

Most of their co-workers rode packed commuter trains to and from their air-conditioned offices that bore all the warmth of a locker room, and spent long days stressed

by violation of their personal space, by verbal sniping and
turf wars fought over imaginary corporate territory. All
the while, their workplace constraints forbade the physical movement or verbal release that might dissipate the
built-up hormones of freeze-flight-fight that were crying
– on the strength of a four-billion-year evolutionary history – for free expression.

Rats in a cage.

Outside the estate proper, the security firm had no
presence, relying on normal police spycams to pick up
anything suspicious. For today and tomorrow morning,
that would remain sufficient. But tomorrow afternoon,
and all through the big day itself, there would be extra
security: uniformed and plainclothes officers, plus specialist close-protection units, working the streets in
vehicles and on foot, and patrolling the skies in heli-
copters. When the prime minister ventured out from
Fort Downing Street, this was the kind of coverage he
required.

That was standard, but the forthcoming event was
even more crucial, because any mistake would poten-
tially be webcast to millions of viewers. It was
near-realtime transmission, with a five-second delay
which was supposed to be long enough for the produc-
ers to pull the switch if necessary. Otherwise, if things
went as normal, the event would be watched with that
five-second lag by nine million households at least, and
would be picked up later from the amorphous Web at
people's leisure.

Inside the Barbican Estate, high buildings and early
morning combined to create cooling shade. But on the
streets outside the temperature climbed towards un-
comfortable intensity as the bustle of pedestrians began
thinning out. Everyone who was working had reached

their destination, grateful for their job or cursing the day ahead, whatever the case might be.

By 9.45 am, when a white-and-blue van marked Quantum Cleaning Services (motto: Teleporting grime away) drove along London Wall, and slowed to a halt at a pedestrian crossing, the street was almost deserted. An exception was the bent-over man limping across the black and white striped crossing, while the cleaning-van driver shrugged at his mates, and none of them noticed the dark-blue car pulling to a halt behind them. Nor did they notice a silvery balloon accidentally released by a thin woman, just as she passed the pole-mounted yellow globe that marked the crossing. Surely she could not have known that her balloon would pass in front of the mounted spycam, obscuring its view.

At that moment, two shapes dropped from beneath the car, wriggled forward, and disappeared beneath the cleaning van. Then the old man reached the end of the crossing and waved his thanks to the van driver, who nodded and put his vehicle into drive.

The van pulled away, followed a second later by the blue car. At the next junction, the car turned into a side street and was gone, leaving the van to continue slowly forward. Soon it drew up before the heavy metal doors of a service entrance leading to the Barbican Estate. The doors rattled aside, and the van drove into a covered entrance bay, echoing with engine sounds bouncing back from concrete. Then the doors clanged back into place, followed by the dull thudding counterpoint of mag locks ramming home.

Vibration and soot, the tremor in his eyeballs making it hard to see, and the cloud of carcinogenic crap turning his respiration into wheezing, the underneath of the van pressed against his face, hard and caked with grime and oil, all of it unpleasant, his thoughts slow and difficult. The webbing harness bit into Josh's body everywhere, pinching his inner thighs, constricting his balls into aching compression, dug into his back below his shoulder blades, and bounced him against hard metal with every unevenness in the road.

Poor Suzanne must be having a hard time of it. For him, this was business as usual. He twisted, careful not to let a jolt damage his neck, and squinted at Suzanne. She was clinging, knuckles pale, using all her strength to assist the harness. They had planned this so they would be under the van only during the last part of its journey, when it was moving slowly; but for her this was probably a high-speed ride more dangerous than she had ever attempted.

"Scan coming up." Tony's voice sounded in his earbead. "And you're over it."

In the old days, guards used mirrors on castors, pushed on long poles, to check underneath vehicles. Thank God for modern systems, relying on cameras and intelligent software, just waiting to be subverted by those with the right technology and attitude.

The van rolled to a halt beside a loading platform, the engine whining down to stillness, the suspension rocking. After a moment, the guys inside dismounted.

"Check-in with security is through there, right?"

"Yeah. Bring the gear, it'll save time."

"OK."

Thumps and swearing meant they were unloading their cleaning equipment. Loud trundling accompanied their exit from the loading area, ending with the dull bang of a heavy steel door. Then silence.

Webbing dug into Josh's back and hamstrings as he hung there.

"Get ready," came Tony's voice.

Josh looked over at Suzanne. Her mouth was tight with strain as she nodded.

"Release in five seconds, four, three, two, one, go now."

Gekkofastenings tore free, and Josh and Suzanne dropped to the ground. They rolled sideways as if spilled from a carpet, the loading bay a blur of oil-stained concrete and corrugated roofing. Then he thumped against brickwork, and Suzanne rolled into him.

"Internal bay is clear. Go for next stage."

The spycams around the loading bay would be transmitting an ongoing still image.

Josh vaulted up onto the high platform, crouched into a squat, and hauled Suzanne up. Then they flung themselves either side of a utility doorway, not the one the cleaners had left by. In the centre of the door was a pane of armoured glass, revealing distorted outlines of blazer-clad men moving on the other side. From that glimpse, it appeared they were walking and looking, a roving patrol. With luck, they would rove off out of here.

"Hold position."

Suzanne was swallowing. Josh gave her a wink.

"Move in three, two, one, go now."

The door clicked open – Tony's handiwork, conducted remotely – and they went through. The security personnel were gone.

"Third door on the right."

Josh gave a tongue-click acknowledgment, then nodded to Suzanne and led the way, half jogging to the target doorway. His boot soles were rubber, therefore silent, as were Suzanne's.

"Clear to go through."

Suzanne was staring at him, eyes huge. It took a moment, then he realised: a hunter's fang-revealing grin was stretching his mouth.

"Go now."

Filled with electric aliveness, he went through, every action magnified and excited by surrounding danger, like a stage performer thrilled by the onset of showtime, coming fully into his own. His movements were exact, exquisitely controlled, because these were the conditions he had learned to operate under, against role-playing opponents using live ammunition and out in the field, against real and lethal threats; and that made all the difference.

This was home, where he did more than operate: he came alive.

On the edge.

Ten minutes later, they were just inside a door that opened onto a quadrangle. Once through the threshold, they would move into the domain of another tier of the surveillance system, where security personnel wandered in greater numbers. At this point, it was no longer possible for Tony to edit over the images. Deep inside the system, the software observer-components *were* subverted, failing to report on two individuals whose gaits and features had not been logged on entering the estate. But for human security staff watching monitors, there was no way of hiding Josh and Suzanne. It was time to move openly.

From their pockets, they pulled out squares of lightweight fabric that unfolded parachute-like into bright, billowing jackets: his, fluorescent orange and silvery grey; hers a blazing lime-green. Suzanne wrinkled her nose. At the training house, she had made remarks about how ugly it looked, how it made her appear fat.

Josh blew her a kiss.

She gave a sick attempt at a smile, then pulled out a silver cylinder from her pocket. A twist of her wrist, and it blossomed into a heart-shaped helium balloon, floating upward on string until it bounced against the ceiling. Tugging it down, she nodded to Josh.

Josh triple-clicked his tongue, signalling Tony.

"Raj, ready for your big fight scene, and… do it now."

In the earbead, there was a muted, distant sound of shattering bottles and hostile shouts. Suzanne swallowed.

"Go now."

They slipped through.

Josh pulled a big smile, a deliberate tensing of facial muscles, nothing amused about it. Taking hold of Suzanne's free hand, he walked forward with her, while she let the balloon rise a little on its string, bobbing as they progressed.

"Natural looking. Very nice," came Tony's voice. "Ready in five paces, Suzanne."

As they walked, water was to their left, where one of the towers stood partly on wide brick-covered pillars acting as stilts, the building's underside forming a watery cavern lit by rippling reflections. Only one spycam was trained directly on them, and the timing needed to be exact. Suzanne's hand felt sweat-slick in his. He gave her a squeeze, then released her.

"Ready to let go, two, one, go now."

Suzanne's fingers opened and the balloon rose, just as Josh tore open his loose jacket, ripped a package from the small of his back and tossed it into the water.

There was a plop, an attenuated ripple, and it sank from sight. They walked on.

The main security sweep had been yesterday. As the protection teams tightened up the system, they had scoured everywhere, including underwater. Secondary sweeps would follow, but they would focus on telltales of weapon technology, the spectroscopic signatures of airborne and waterborne molecules that might indicate explosives, the inductive resonance of electronic devices. Even if they found the thing, they would consider it an oddity, perhaps from a party balloon similar to the one Suzanne had just let loose.

They passed among the rubberised "concrete" slabs, along the promenade. In the blues and reds of spotlights, the fragments would look menacing; up close and in daylight, they seemed like toys. Josh used the time to memorise the layout, so that he could pass this way with his eyes closed or with commotion all around. He imagined crashing sound, the detonation of flashbangs, like the Killing House in Sterling Lines where they taught him first to operate in chaos, then to cause it.

Past the restaurant and the entrance to the Barbican Centre, the showpiece theatre at the heart of the complex, they walked hand in hand, observing all, appearing casual. Doors were propped open, allowing roadies to wheel props into place. Spotlights and cables were everywhere. One such doorway led into the curved apartment block at the far end of the promenade, where Josh and Suzanne were headed.

As they went inside, he squeezed her hand. Along the carpeted corridor they went, pausing at the first intersection until Tony's voice said "Clear."

Following his directions, twice making detours that

took them out of their way but avoided other people, they reached the fifth floor. Here they had to wait in the stairwell, because cleaners were at work. It would be possible to simply walk into the open corridor and go past; but right now the spycam over their heads was showing an empty staircase, at least in the central logs. The sudden appearance of Josh and Suzanne in the corridor would look like teleportation, and while Tony could deal with threat-recognition engines in software, a human who happened to catch sight of the anomaly would bring everything crashing down.

Finally, the cleaners were inside an apartment, and Tony gave the signal to move.

From his pocket, Josh drew a spectacles case, took out a pair of glasses and put them on. They stopped outside the designated apartment, and he peered at the fish-eye lens. While the system read the false retina pattern, he pulled on a latex glove, and pressed his thumb and fingertips against the reader. Suzanne muttered something, guttural French he could not understand.

Then the door clicked open, and they were in.

The apartment was plush, rich, and insulated by deep carpet, therefore quiet. He had taught Suzanne the rules of maintaining an observation post: no chatting, careful movement, and in their case no intimacy, although it was the no-flushing bathroom etiquette that disturbed her most. Besides her presence, which made this different from every other OP he had been in, there was this overwhelming feature: he was on a mission that was likely to bring down the government of his own country, an act that by most criteria was treasonous.

However instrumental the Regiment had been in changing regimes elsewhere, that had been under political control, however indirect, from Whitehall: covert warfare as an instrument of policy. Without such sanction, when the military took it on themselves to alter governments, it was generally considered a coup, and the result was typically tyranny. When a single, embittered former soldier attempted such an action, that was more correctly seen as folly.

Sophie. I'd let the world go hang if it brought you back.

And of course that was the point. Sitting here amid soft furnishings, it was so easy to give in, to back out and take the sensible course, meaning to do nothing. With an effort, he crawled to a shuttered window, and stared down through the slits at the promenade below. After a while, he pulled back, and sat back against the wall, legs outstretched on the carpet.

Suzanne came over slowly, and sat next to him, shoulder touching.

"What's wrong?" she whispered.

All he could do was shake his head. He was used to following standard operational procedures, but whether SOPs would carry him through this crisis, he no longer knew. The thing was, self-doubt before the climax of a mission was rarely seen as a good thing. When the crunch came, as it soon would, what he needed above all else was one thing: focus.

What if I'm wrong?

Or worse: *What if I'm right, and it's pointless anyway?*

In the past he and his fellow Regiment members had sometimes railed at the political decisions underlying their operations. They, far more than other soldiers, maintained deep understanding of the countries they were operating in, the indigenous history and the current issues faced by citizens. They had to, whether it was to win a hearts and minds campaign or simply to pass for natives. But this time, the political decision was purely his own, and how could he possibly trust that?

He had often been scared, but he had never doubted everything.

Not like this.

In the end, he decided not to decide. As with any op, he would shut down all considerations besides the mission at hand. Then, at 17.30 the day after tomorrow, he would go into action or hold back, however his instinct demanded.

Shoulder to shoulder, he and Suzanne sat. From time to time she used a secure phone he had given her, sound off, to check the news channels. He had not wanted to pay attention; but when she handed him the phone and pointed, he had to look and wonder how Matt was doing, whether he was fighting or simply looking after his family as his country went to hell.

President Brand had moved his troops to the borders, both east and west. Commentators speculated about long-range reconnaissance missions into New York state and Oregon. The formerly united armed forces were splitting along regional divides. But for all Brand's apocalyptic rhetoric, could he truly be thinking of simultaneous invasions against both seaboards? It was strategic insanity; but cultural madness had already subsumed political intelligence, when the president talked of "*smashing the legions of Satan,*" and "*taking back the country which is ours.*"

Flicking back to the London news, for what seemed like almost light relief in contrast, an unidentified infection had broken out in Brixton, while ongoing streetfights-cum-riots were igniting across the capital, against a backdrop of continued white sheet lightning from storms that would not break.

I'm trying to save the world.

Everything was grim; everything was hopeless.

Maybe there's nothing left to save.

He wanted to laugh and scream. Instead, he pulled everything inside himself and waited.

In the morning, the news was no better. The PM publicly deplored the deliberate anarchistic violence, and the civil sabotage that was crippling normal services – from refuse collection to electricity. Power outages were likely, purely as a result of the riots. Despite all this, he finished with an upbeat, jocular message:

"I, for one, will be voting right after Knifefighter Challenge, because whoever wins the final, what we need is a champion for this country. Someone with the strength and daring to cut down those who would steal our way of life from us. I'll be running on a platform of increasing the people's power to change things, by letting us slice through red tape and hack away bureaucracy, once and for all!"

Afterwards, Josh pulled up his contact list, scrolled through the URIs, and selected **Sophie2**. Then he sat and watched, with Suzanne beside him.

A small, near-unmoving image. Monitors ringing a white bed, and at its centre, all his vulnerability, the next generation that should have been; and why did he want to save the world when the one who should inherit it was like this? How could any of it matter?

They watched the picture in silence.

That night while Suzanne slept in the master bedroom, Josh lay on the carpeted lounge floor, drifting in and out of almost-sleep. It was always like this the night before a mission, and he knew that sleeplessness would count for nothing tomorrow, because the preparation had been in the weeks leading up to this; and tomorrow would be a day filled with adrenaline.

Discrediting a prime minister on Election Day: it would be a classic op, one for the history books, to be taught to the neos at Hereford, if only it were officially sanctioned and on foreign soil. But here and now, it was a stressed-out, possibly insane ex-soldier – accompanied by his therapist girlfriend, how about that for irony – with a mission to take out a corrupt fascist bastard only because he consorted with those using children's bodies as drug factories; and it could be argued that every country's leader oversaw activities that were equally bad but never saw the light of day – including the leaders that most would consider heroes.

Insane, insane, insane.

At some point in the hours before dawn, he decided he was going through with it. For the remaining short time, he slept.

[THIRTY]

At 4 pm on the twentieth, the preliminaries began. The smartroof polarised to winter dusk, belying the bright heat outside. Blazing scarlet and iridescent blue ran across the membrane-hung arena walls while music pounded, the high notes keening, the bass track deep and visceral as a pounding heart.

On the promenade, women as well as men moved among the faux concrete shards, the fake urban landscape whose graffiti glittered beneath ultraviolet. These people were the extras, bit players in the drama to follow; but for some of them, this evening would be mortal drama, life-changing or life-ending, because they were semi-pros and skilled with blades, most wearing only half armour; and they would skirmish against each other or even against the Blades or Bloods, provided they issued challenge within the rules, at the locations and times when the team fighters were obliged to respond, or face their comrades from their own side.

In this sport, being cut from the team took on a new and literal meaning.

Josh's phone showed near-live views from the separate changing areas for Blades and Bloods, the warm-up routines of the fighters, the priests giving blessings. And then the preliminaries began.

From the window he watched in reality, while casting glances at the five-second-delayed pictures in his phone, as a female Blade stalked into the outer arena – the transformed promenade – and saluted the glittering entrance to the inner arena, the theatre whose imminent production was an affair of sweat and whipping limbs and the sweet slick spurt of blood. Then she yelled out to the female extras.

"Which one of you needs a piece of me?"

There were fists pumped in reply – and some swallowing – but one young woman, lightly armoured, leaped out from the rest, ripping out her knife as she screamed "Challenge accepted!" and then they were into it. Blades flashing, they spun and closed distance, each making good use of the free hand for slapping escrima blocks, nicks on skin marked in red, then the Blade shin-kicked her opponent's inner thigh, slammed right wrist against right wrist, and reverse-hooked her blade point, stabbing shoulder muscle first, then the rubber-protected throat, hitting the carotid artery without penetration.

The challenger dropped. Across the land, pubs would be filled with cheers.

First casualty.

"This is awful," whispered Suzanne.

"I know." He touched her pale milk-chocolate cheek. "It's because we're waiting, not moving."

She shook her head, because there was more to it than that, and they both knew it.

Over the next hour, first Blades and then Bloods ventured among the non-team fighters, issuing or responding to challenges. One of the semi-pros took out two Bloods and a Blade, scoring with accumulated minor cuts. In return, he received a crimson waist sash, while medics escorted him to the Bloods' changing area for patch-up, because he had just gained a place on the team.

But that was a reward for competence more than spectacular fighting. Other combat took place among the rubberised concrete slabs, group confrontations that swirled across the artificial landscape, the fighters squinting against the pulsing red-blue lights, music reaching crescendo at the height of action. Some of the fights bordered on the acrobatic, including one high-jumping fighter who kicked against a slab to reverse direction while airborne, spinning behind his opponent to deliver a downward diagonal slash, scoring full victory.

Then, at 5pm, the first Blade-against-Blood one-on-one confrontation began.

Reilly was the Blood's name: a whipcord-thin fighter who in training had shown blinding speed such as Josh had never witnessed. And it wasn't just the explosiveness from static posture; his ability to switch and even reverse directions was unparalleled. He was long-limbed, preferring to dominate from the outside range, edge rather than point, taking out his opponent's arms and legs before closing for the final strike, the unnecessary but dramatic coup to complete his victory.

The Blade was called Richler, heavily muscled and powerful, fast but not tricky, preferring to slam aside his opponent's arms and thrust hard to the body, sometimes smashing his fist into the other guy's face, before hammering back with the hilt, then slamming the point home to win.

At first the fight was Reilly's, as he curved around Richler, keeping the distance, drawing blood from

Richler's forearms – but only the outer muscles, not the vulnerable inner flesh. Then Richler powered in–

"Kick," said Josh.

–and slammed his heel into Reilly's hip, knocking him back and folding him, then Richler's hand thundered down as if with a mace, hilt to skull, and Reilly was already unconscious when Richler kneed him in the face, followed his falling body to ground, and knelt on him while forcing his point under the chin, holding back from ramming it in, because he had already won.

Suzanne wiped a layer of moisture from her face, sweat that ran like tears.

Medics wrapped bandages around the victor's arms, while others carried Reilly away on a stretcher, stumbling fast, rarely a good sign.

Two more Blood-on-Blade fights followed, the first conservative and boring for distant spectators, though probably not for the fighters themselves who risked death right here and now, in the moment. The second was chaotic, a dance of abandon, with a spectacular in the moment. The second was chaotic, a dance of abandon, with a spectacular hamstring cut from a downed fighter who had looked to be beaten, followed by a stab to the Achilles tendon as he rose and performed a blistering hand and blade combination, chaining sequences together propeller-fast, overwhelming his crippled opponent and cutting him down.

The prone man died, blood gushing from a severed femoral artery, before the medics got to him. Josh continued to watch from the window; in the bathroom, Suzanne was throwing up.

At a slower pace, the next confrontation was among the semi-pros, a three-against-four duel, decided on points, the fighters finishing soaked in blood but all from surface wounds, including a slashed face: capillaries and smaller arterioles spilling blood but not at pressure.

Three more one-on-ones, and the last was Blood-against-Blade once more.

"Time for us to move," said Josh.

The corridors were deserted, making it easy for Tony to override the surveillance from afar. They went down fast, Josh's chest filled with the hot emptiness that always replaced his heart at moments like this, the void before action; and then they were at the doorway on ground level, ready to go through.

"Clear to go," sounded in his earbead. "And give 'em hell."

He inhaled from his diaphragm, then tightened to exhale as he sank his body weight an inch, centring himself. Then, straight-backed as a samurai, he stepped through.

Three guards turned to look at him, hands reaching for the firearms on their hips.

As they did so, Suzanne slipped from behind him, smiled at the men and spoke a series of confusing words – inaudible to Josh, his ears filling with the surf-like rush of blood that accompanies combat stress – then three pairs of eyelids fluttered, Suzanne passed her fingertips downwards, and three chins tipped forward onto chests.

Slowly, they slumped to the ground and curled sideways, eyes closed and deep in slumber. Then Suzanne looked at Josh and smiled.

Oh, my God.

Phase one complete.

• • •

Josh walked out onto the promenade. A football player on the turf at Wembley must feel like this; but the walls, hung with sheets of membrane rippling with patterns, replaced the live thousands; while it was music, not cheering, that deafened. As he advanced he pulled up his sleeves, revealing unprotected forearms: a provocation. Several fighters turned, eyes narrowing.

A Blade and a Blood were facing off against each other, preparing to fight. If Suzanne had taught him anything, it was the power inherent in unexpectedness, interrupting automatic behaviour to spin minds into confusion.

This is it.

Off to one side, someone called a warning. "There's a renegade!"

I'm worse than that.

He drew closer to the pair.

You just don't know it yet.

Drawing his blade, he said, "I challenge."

The crouching fighters paused.

"Which of us?" asked the Blood.

"Both of you."

Unlike the semi-pro extras, all of their training for months had been geared toward one-on-one confrontation with varying degrees of armour. Now he was going to take them into new territory. It was his only tangible advantage.

Sophie, my sweet girl.

She was his intangible strength, his sorrow and rage and love combining to produce determination beyond mission focus, beyond military discipline: the purity of Zen with purpose.

Then he was into the fight.

He whipped a low kick across the Blood's leading knee, driving him back, and continued the spin like a discus thrower, releasing – now! – and his knife flew at the Blade's face, straight for the eyes, and as the man reacted Josh used a sprint step forward to launch the jump, through the knife defence and bringing up his thigh, power in the hip and his knee ramming into laryngeal tissue, a flying knee-strike to the throat; and then the fighter dropped, still living only because of the protective gear. But there was another fighter behind Josh – move fast – and he shoulder-rolled straight over the downed Blade and came up on his feet, spinning to face the pursuing Blood, his own right hand held high.

In it shone the knife he had stripped from the fallen man.

Now, you start to realise.

He cut twice, fast and downward, and the Blood was on the ground, eyes open and unable to move as Josh's knee dropped, a crack as the sternum broke, then he hammerfisted hilt into temple and the Blood was out of it.

"Who's next?"

"I challenge," called a Blade.

Beyond him, two other fights were in progress – the show must go on – with a Blood against a semi-pro, and a two-on-two between semi-pros only. The music grew louder, and Josh wondered whether any of the viewers were watching him yet, or if all the webcast camera angles were on the official fights. Time to steal the attention.

He broke into a run, then dodged behind a near-upright rubberised slab, hooking his left behind a support and running up it, parkour-style, before rolling over the top and dropping. The Blade, realising the danger, spun as Josh closed on him from behind; but Josh used a backfist to knock the left arm, and hooked a cut inside, tearing the left biceps, then he elbowed the ribs and twisted back up, corkscrewed his body to stab beneath the chin then disengage, whipping sideways and out of range.

The Blade's face was red with blood from beneath his chin, but he came for Josh regardless, whipping figure-eights through the air, as Josh dodged sideways, then went low.

To the Japanese this would be a *sutemi-waza*, a sacrifice technique designed to win or die. It was a variant of *kata-ashi-dori*, known in the West as a single-leg take-down; but Josh came from the side, rolling down the shin he had hold of, spinning the man down, continuing to roll across the fallen man's body, and stabbed downwards once before twisting away and staggering to his feet.

That had been a hard one.

"Behind you 7 o'clock high."

Without Tony's warning he would have died, but instead he spun, a high arcing kick hooking to the rear, heel across the bastard's face – he was aiming for the temple – but he followed with a left hook, collapsing to a downward elbow strike, then reversing the spin with a diagonal slashing uppercut and then to the other side, an X drawn with upward strokes, and blood spurted from beneath the fighter's arms, his hips giving way, dropping onto both knees, cracking them on the flag-stones.

The final blow was an uppercut punch that Josh powered upward from the ground, smacking the guy straight back. Beyond him, all along the promenade, the other fighters – Bloods, Blades, and semi-pros alike

– stood frozen, their other fights forgotten, the focus only on Josh.

I've got the limelight now.

Phase two accomplished.

Then phase three became insane.

First up was a Blood but affiliations were irrelevant now, and so were surprise tactics, as Josh blitzed forward with forehand and backhand cuts, his left hand creating a dance of independent movement, parrying and distracting, like the chi sao with Suzanne taken to another dimension: desperate to keep the other's blade from him, feeling a momentary sting, then he powered a right roundhouse kick to the thigh, stabbed down into the leg while his left arm was a shield, then he whipped the blade left-right and pushed the falling man aside.

Faster now.

These were pros, drilled to fight in certain ways, proven in sport, but his style used different angles and distancing; and they were fighting for money and perhaps the love of combat, while he was defending Sophie and the world, and that made all the difference.

He dodged left-right-left moving forwards, swept a Blade's forearm to deliver a lunging thrust with everything behind it, and then the Blade was down, wounded or a corpse, and he was onto the next challenge.

Faster still.

A blitzkrieg, two at once, and he elbowed one into the other, tangling them both, kicking down to shatter a knee, punching the side of a neck, stab-parry-stab and he was free of them.

Yes, like that.

Both arms up to defend, and he dropped into a bouncing squat, skewering the next man's foot with his blade, then leaping clear, because he was not here to score a contest victory on every fighter: he was here to plough through them while staying alive.

A group of semi-pros was rushing him and he did the only thing he could, surrounded as he was by obstacles and no time to get behind them: he plunged into the centre of the attackers, *irimi* his strategy, deep in the heart of the whirlwind, and then he had a knife in each hand – one of the men no longer had need of a weapon, and never would – and he became a blaze of movement, twin blades cutting in all directions, and then he was through the bloodied group and out the other side.

None looked about to pursue him.

Good.

But there were plenty still ahead.

Keep going.

Next was the deadliest enemy: two men approaching on different diagonals, keeping the angle when he shifted sideways. They were coordinated and watchful, a greater threat than a mob-handed group, advancing at a pace to suit them. Facing them was dangerous, so he decided not to.

He turned and ran...

There.

...as far as the nearest tall slab, where he leaped high, left hand in an ice-pick grip, slamming the blade into the rubber, the knife forming a piton, hauling himself up, then throwing himself away from the slab, over the head of one of the incoming fighters, and he kicked downward before dropping, arms like cobras hugging the guy's waist, rolling him to the ground – Josh's blade was point up beneath the liver as they went over – and then Josh was standing, his right hand slick with blood, his blade glistening a metallic red.

His left hand was empty – the other knife was still in the slab, high up – so he took the downed man's weapon. Now he had two blades against the other fighter's one, and whether that was sporting he no longer cared, as he fell on the guy with criss-crossing attacks chained seamlessly, leaving no openings as he cut the right arm open, then sliced the face.

For a moment, the guy staggered back and looked about to quit; then he swung toward Josh–

Oh, for God's sake.

–who stamped down hard enough to shatter the instep, smacked a headbutt into the guy's face, then whipped him over in a good old-fashioned hip-throw, because he could.

The double downward stab was unnecessary. He did it anyway.

Then a muscular man, one of the Blades whose name Josh actually knew – Foster, known as Mad Mick and one of Fireman Carlsen's protegés – stepped in front of him, and brought matters back to a formal footing, as though this were still a normal Knifefighter Challenge, and the *Knife Edge* finale.

"I issue challenge."

Josh really did not want to face this one.

"Accepted."

Everyone else fell back because they knew Foster's reputation, and his other name was Wall of Death because the air around him came alive with danger, every limb a weapon, not just the blade. At least one fighter had gone down when Mad Mick bit in hard, tore away a chunk of the guy's carotid artery, then spat it out and grinned.

In that case, the medics had kept the loser alive. They might not try as hard to save an unknown renegade who had gatecrashed the party.

Josh zigged and zagged, attacks that he dared not push to completion, setting up a rhythm only to break it, and then he was charging from the outside, almost behind his opponent; but Mad Mick was fast, a hooking cut and a massive kick knocking Josh back. His chest felt caved-in as he rolled, then straightened, feeling vulnerable as Mad Mick charged in with a crushing attack.

There was a semi-pro nearby, purely a bystander, but Josh twisted and lashed out, cutting deep, pushing the whimpering guy into Mad Mick's path. A long punch travelled over the guy and rammed Josh's head back, green spots fluorescing in his vision. But his cut had hit target, the injured fighter spurting arterial blood, and as Mad Mick stepped into a scarlet puddle his balance wavered, which was all Josh needed.

He stabbed high, kicked low, half-parried a burning thrust along his ribs, cupped blood in his left hand and scooped it into Mad Mick's eyes, because if ever there was a fair fight, this wasn't it. He punched hard, and again; then Mad Mick was on hands and knees, so Josh dodged past him and continued his advance.

Must keep going.

Then the mêlée fell upon him.

His limbs were a blur and so were theirs, the attackers, their number unknown, while time slowed down in the paradox of violence, his body flowing – a double slap, left-right against a weapon arm, a backhand slice across the cheek, a stab-and-throw designed to tangle two men together – and for a while he had no weapons save his own body but everything was useful, his chest a pivot point as he hooked a leg with his own, ducked

and pushed, came up inside someone's arms, close
enough to smell sick-laden breath, hooked his thumbs
up along the nose and ripped outwards. For a moment
his opponent's scream stopped everything as Josh flung
his arms wide, an eyeball spattering to either side.

They fell on him again, but he had a knife once more
– there, a liver shot, and the man folded, unable to drop
because of the fighters pushing from behind – and now
Josh was double-bladed again, and the thing that happened next was strange.

Awash with blood, he laughed.

Again they closed but there was a difference now, a
hesitation, and he hook-blocked with a blade while
ramming his knee into a thigh, then groin, a downward
elbow to the back of the neck, slicing backhand to spin
away through a group of three men, the others falling
back, and he kicked long to break another knee, cut the
falling man's face, piled onward, momentum carrying
him through the last few fighters, and then he realised:
he had fought his way through, from one end of the
promenade to the other.

"Three seconds," sounded in his ear.

Two fighters approached and suddenly tiredness
clawed at his arms, but he would not give in to it as he
flung himself forward and down, using the last-ditch
technique that fighters consider a circus trick and im-
practical, save for the Russian Spetsnaz special forces
who developed their own way for the battlefield, and
that was what he used now.

Focus. There is only the…

On one knee, he threw the knives–

…target.

–and they spun through the air to strike home with
meaty thunks in the same moment the lights went out.

• • •

Phase four was the waiting.

Below water, he lay in coolness, staring up at the kaleidoscope of light rippling across the surface, hiding him from the world. The darkness had lasted only seconds, long enough for him to roll over the edge and slip down into the water. At the bottom, he had felt for and found the tiny breathing cylinder, the device he had tossed in earlier.

Breathe.

It was about remaining calm.

Control.

From the world above, the music was an attenuated, eerie thump, while the fighters and webcast crew regrouped, commentators talking with excitement about what had occurred, and the renegade who had disappeared. It would take time for them to finish up the preliminaries, and proceed to the bouts in the inner arena, with the final four fighters from each team, along with the two iconic pros, Carlsen and McGee, while all around them the dignitaries sat at their plush tables, flushed with champagne and the sick excitement of watching others face what they themselves could not.

For some twenty minutes, until Tony gave the signal, he would remain here, submerged, hidden by the surface reflections.

Breathe.

And then the signal.

"Phase five. Go now."

He rose through the water, flowed up over the brick-work edge into a crouch on the edge of the promenade. Before him, starting some twenty feet high, a wide strip of red carpet marked the way to the indoors auditorium. There were civilians standing with the semi-pros, whose part was over. None looked in Josh's direction, not at first.

Heads began to turn as he advanced, dripping.

The fabric of his clothes was water-repellent, living up to its name as it shed liquid, so he felt light rather than sodden, with a new mental clarity, as if a wide space had opened up behind his eyes. People stared, and then drew back, as he walked along the carpet strip.

Four guards stood shoulder-to-shoulder across the entranceway, facing him. They had the bulk of power-lifters, the stare of snipers, and each hip bulged with a holstered firearm. These were the real deal, a barrier of determination.

"Down on your knees," one of them said. "And put your hands on your–"

Josh ripped his shirt open, tore his gun free, and fired eight times.

Always bring a gun to a knife-fight.

It was an old dictum, sort of a joke, and he remembered it as he blasted across the row of thighs, shooting the legs, to wound and because they looked to be wearing body armour. The rounds contained neurotoxins designed to incapacitate, not kill; and the men were lying stunned, mouths working, when Josh jumped over them and stalked through the entrance.

Phase five complete.

Showtime.

Raised platforms stood like plateaus above a forest, in the brilliance of spotlights rather than the sun, while below were not treetops but linen-covered tables and the smart coiffures of guests, while the river-like glitter came from polished silverware. At the far end, atop a yellow dais, stood the two team coaches, Fireman Carlsen and Ice Pick McGee, who would face off when the remaining pairs of fighters had finished. To one side of them, in plush red throne-like seats, Zebediah and Zak Tyndall flanked the prime minister, Billy Church.

All around, massive wallscreens replicated in realtime the pictures being webcast to the watching world. Those millions of remote viewers were five seconds behind the action; and the authorities believed that gave them the ability to cut transmission should the unexpected occur. They were yet to learn who was in control here.

Someone grabbed Josh; he struck them down.

"Holster the gun."

Hiding the weapon he continued down the red-carpet ramp, among the richly-dressed diners who more and more were turning to look at him. There were bodyguards everywhere, but he was headed for Carlsen and McGee, and that made them hold back – that and the knowledge that their every action would be seen by millions.

Someone shouted, and hands grabbed both his sleeves.

Shit.

He twisted, one hand rising as the other descended, both circling, his torque and body weight stronger than their arms, and two men spilled to the floor, rolling against two more who had been closing in, and if he continued like this then their weight and number would bury him, and none of this would work.

So he sprinted, focused from beneath his lowered eyebrows only on Fireman Carlsen.

You're a runner.

His thighs were springs, pumping. The carpet was a blood-red blur, arrowing ahead.

So run fast.

Pumping hard.

Faster than ever.

More hands reached, table knives and forks stabbing in his directions – spectators getting into the spirit – while he sprinted on.

Yes, faster.

And then he was paces from the dais.

Go.

Fingers tried to hook him but his leap was massive, an antelope escaping from a lion, but that was he wrong because he was the hunting cat, the predator, and in that moment something changed in Fireman Carlsen's eyes, as Josh spread his arms and stopped.

"It's a shame about the elephant," he said, "since I prefer pink gardenias–"

"Huh?"

Josh's movement became underwater-slow, un-threatening like a tai-chi master.

"–since it doesn't matter whether you blink now or in a second – that's right – while the more you wonder what it's not worth wondering about and don't wonder what is worth wondering" – he gestured downward with his hand, his voice growing mild – "is no wonder you're feeling sleepy and my voice goes with you as you wander deeper... and deeper... into a state of deep... relaxation, that's right... all the way... and... soften as you..."

Carlsen's chin dropped to his chest.

"...sleep now."

Success. He hoped Suzanne could see.

"All cameras are on you, Josh."

"Good."

Off to one side, Ice Pick McGee was blinking. The prime minister, Billy Church, sat with his mouth beginning to open. The elder Tyndall, Zebediah, was struggling to rise from his chair; while the younger Zak was on his feet, snarling.

At least someone understands.

But this was the PM, not just a couple of entrepreneurs, and his close-protection teams were élite. Four men in suits were already moving into position between Josh and his targets. All four had guns drawn; and if his own weapon had been visible, they would have gunned him down already.

"Freeze. Do *not* move!"

"I'm doing it," said Josh.

"Down on the–"

"Everyone's watching." He stared straight at Zak Tyndall. "Game over, you bastard."

"–floor."

Palms at the back of his head, Josh knelt, then sat back on his heels.

"This is it," said Tony. "Smile for the cameras."

On the giant wallscreens all around, secondary panes blossomed. In them were images of labs, children on slabs, shots of cash changing hands, displays of bank transfers, and lists of names and dates, amounts and descriptions, and overlaid diagrams of corporate structures, the false identities linking legitimate companies to crimelords. The scenes from Africa were the most harrowing.

"Virapharm labs." Josh's face was huge on the screens, his voice echoing as the system picked it up, magnifying his words. "Children, living children, used as factories, incubators where the Tyndalls' employees force-evolve new drugs by unnatural selection. Zebediah and Zak Tyndall, supporting and supported by the great and the good... and up on the screen, isn't that our prime minister going into one of those torture labs?"

Zak was muttering urgent questions, using a throat mike and earbead, then glancing up at the screens, teeth baring, and shouting: "That's not good enough! Cut it now!"

"The world," said Josh, "can still see everything."

Zebediah put a clawlike hand over his chest.

"Relax," added Josh. "You don't have a heart. And just think of the ratings."

In his earbead, Tony chuckled. "I got rid of the five-second delay. You wouldn't believe the numbers logging in. It's a microblog cascade."

More tables and graphs flicked across the screens. Later, when people analysed their downloads in detail, these would clinch the evidence, the minutiae of unethical and outright illegal transactions, following the complicated routes of money. Everything he and Philip Broomhall's people had uncovered was here.

All of it.

Let's see you whitewash this, you fuckers.

Fat Billy Church was pale and red at the same time, blotching as though his body could not decide how to react.

For Sophie.

Whatever happened now, he had done what he had to do for her.

"You bastard," said Zak Tyndall. "You can't manufacture false data and expect–"

"Let the people do the digging. They'll find out what's true."

"You–"

But Tyndall's father took hold of his arm, shushing him.

Wise, but too late.

Behind Josh, something moved.

"Hold still." A woman's voice.

A ring of coldness on the back of his neck. Gun barrel.

"Lower your hands. Keep them behind you."

He did, and plastic bindings locked home.

"Now stand–"

And that was when the change occurred.

"They're trying to force a cut-in," came from his earbead. "All-channel webcast."

"Stop them."

"I'm sorry, mate. Not this time."

The screens blossomed with new pictures.

Plumes of smoke.

A ruined cityscape.

And a voiceover relating destruction.

"–of the San Andreas Fault at dawn this morning, eruptions taking place across California, spreading north. Los Angeles is destroyed, repeat, LA is gone. In Washington State, Mount Rainier's eruption is orders of magnitude greater than predicted by–"

Great clouds were covering California: a whole string of locations along the Western Seaboard. Grainy footage that might have come from someone's phone showed the moment of Mt Rainier's eruption in a single massive fireball.

A blaze of energy that curled down as it grew.

No. They… couldn't have.

Rose and curled to create an iconic image that had not been seen for so long.

A mushroom cloud.

"–from President Brand, who is quoted as saying 'The Sodom and Gomorrah that infested our sacred land are now burned from the Earth. For the moment, we have no more to say.' The whole world will be wondering the exact meaning of those–"

Pandemonium encircled the tables. Atop the fighting platforms, the competitors had put down their knives. Everyone stared at the screens.

Behind Josh, several men and women in suits were gathered, firearms trained on him. One held out ID to the PM's close-protection team.

"Special Branch," she said. "We've got this bastard."

The CP men glanced up at the unreeling disaster on screen.

"Take him."

"–bigger than a hundred Hiroshimas combined, or a hundred Tunguska meteorite strikes. While the immediate death toll must be in the millions, no one knows if further–"

Rough hands tipped Josh off balance, dragging him away.

It's all gone wrong.

Not just his plan, but the world.

[THIRTY-ONE]

The "Special Branch" team had a large, nondescript van parked in the loading bay. They bundled Josh inside, then climbed in themselves: Suzanne first, then Raj and Hannah, while Vikram went up front with Tony and Big Tel, who was driving. Raj undid his tie.

"I hate wearing suits," he said.

"Really? I think you look handsome, all dressed up," said Hannah.

"Well…"

The van swung into motion.

"Did you all see?" Vikram held up a phone, showing aerial views of cloud cover over California, ash falling from the sky. "You saw the mushroom clouds?"

"Not even Brand is that fucking insane," said Tony.

"Are you sure?"

"Well, no."

Josh opened his mouth, found himself with nothing to say, and just sat there, letting the motion of the van take him where it would. Everything had changed, and whatever would happen, would happen, *que sera, sera*, while he no longer had the energy to do anything but watch.

His arms, he noticed from a distance, were trembling all by themselves.

"Oh, Josh." Suzanne was holding him. "Oh, my God."

"You did good," said Hannah. "Amazing."

Josh blinked.

I feel nothing. It's all over.

Both tiredness and energy were gone, leaving him in a state of nothingness, of neither-nor. His brain seemed to be floating.

How very strange.

"The only amazing thing," he said, "was that I didn't get cut."

Hannah and Raj looked at each other.

"What?" said Josh.

"Darling." Suzanne's eyes were wet. "They cut you to pieces. Can't you tell?"

He looked down at himself, soaked through with what he had thought was water.

"Oh, God."

"Josh, you're going to be all—"

Oh, God.

Blackness grew inside him like a mushroom cloud.

[THIRTY-TWO]

Monday, and Richard's first day back at St Michael's. He sat in the back seat for several minutes after the car had stopped outside the gates.

"You sure you're all right?" asked Lexa.

"Yeah. Dad's going to have an interesting day, isn't he?"

"I should think so."

Shareholders to confront, legal coups to make public, revelations that he had already – in secret, via proxies – regained control of his corporations, even before the nose-dive in Tyndall shares across the globe. It would be a day of triumph, muted by the general geopolitical shock of the ongoing disaster in North America, none of which seemed real.

Here, as Jags and Bentley Electros pulled up at the school, everything was weirdly normal. Perhaps the sky was greyer than you might expect, but that was all.

"See you later," said Richard, climbing out.

"Later." Lexa winked goodbye.

Some of the other boys glanced his way, but no one said anything as he walked through the gates. Ahead were the proud old buildings, and he realised he had missed them.

He thumbed his phone, selecting **Opal** from his contacts.

"Hey." A bandaged face smiled at him. "Are you
OK?"

"First day back. I'm just going in."

"You'll be fine. Call me later?"

"Sure."

Her image winked out.

Boys jostled him, not deliberately but because he was
in a bottleneck. He let himself be carried by the flow,
into the old corridors where the parquet floors shone
with polish. For some reason, the beeswax smell made
him smile. He went through into a quadrangle.

Here, some of the boys were on a bench, comparing
notes on homework. Others were moaning about the
Knifefighter Challenge being ruined, or talking about
the rogue fighter who had done so much before bringing the event to an off-kilter end.

"My father says it's the election that's the important
thing."

"There was no election, dummy. They cancelled it.
Nothing happened."

"That's what I'm talking about."

Richard thumbed his phone again, selecting
Suzanne.

"Hello, Richard. You must be at school by now. Feeling good?"

"I'm fine. Really fine."

"I did feel confident on that score."

"How's–?"

"Take a look." The image swung to another bandaged
figure. "Here's the man himself."

"Hey, Josh."

"Hey, Richie."

Richard grinned at him.

"Can I ring you again tonight, and talk for longer? I've got to go class now."

"Sure you can. We'll talk later, pal."

"Bye."

He put the phone away, still grinning; and that was when the mood changed. The sky above the open quadrangle seemed to darken, but perhaps that was an illusion, caused by the other boy's bulk, and the hardness of his voice when he spoke.

"Well, fuck it," said Zajac. "Little turd's come back, two days *after* we was supposed to meet. How about that?"

From the far side of the quadrangle, Mal James called: "Leave the poor bugger alone, why don't you?"

Richard – no, from now on he was Richie – looked at Zajac from beneath his eyebrows, his chin lowered and his shoulders hunched. Zajac was sneering and smiling at the same time.

"Think you can get away with it, do you, little turd?"

Richie straightened up.

"Not really," he said, his tone light.

Something changed in Zajac's expression, as though the ground had shifted.

"Just because there's gym class today don't mean–"

"Forget it," said Richie.

"Ha. I was right about–"

"Let's do it now."

All voices stopped. Faces grew pale.

"Without armour?" said someone.

"What's the matter, Zajac?" Richie stared into his target's eyes, aware of the pulsing throat, the solid body, even the position of the feet. "Are you scared?"

"No, I–"

"Back off," called Mal.

"No." Zajac ripped his knife free. "You've had it now, Broomhall."

"Richard," said Mal. "Run inside to a teacher."

"My name is Richie." He drew his own blade, scarcely hearing the gasps. "And I'm fine here."

This is it.

He began to circle Zajac. Around them, boys formed a perimeter, defining a fighting arena. From the distance, Richie might have heard Mr Dutton's voice calling for them to stop; but he could not be sure, because his hearing was filled with a hiss like surf. This was a sure sign of stress, and he knew it was natural, so he could continue.

Zajac leaped forward and Richie spun away.

"I knew it," sneered Zajac. "Cowardly little f–"

Richie's blade sliced open the back of his hand. Zajac screamed.

It's called defanging, you bastard.

Then Richie slammed his hilt inside Zajac's right wrist while slapping the back of the hand with his left. Zajac's knife spun away and was gone, clattering to the flagstones. Then Richie's foot stabbed into a knee, and Zajac was down.

Got you.

Richie held his blade against Zajac's throat, preternaturally aware of how soft the skin looked, how easy to slit open, and what it would look like if he did.

"This," he said, "is the carotid artery. One and a half inches to penetrate. Five seconds till loss of consciousness. Twelve seconds to die." He shifted the knife to Zajac's arm. "Brachial artery. Penetration, half inch. Fourteen seconds, unconscious. Ninety seconds dead. Radial artery–"

A third of the way through the Timetable of Death, Zajac fainted.

Good.

There was a long, extended pause; then everyone in the quadrangle cheered.

"What's this?" Two teachers finally pushed through. "Broomhall? What's happening?"

"Nothing, Mr Dutton."

"It doesn't look like–"

"Hush, Jack." The other teacher, Mr Keele, touched his sleeve. "It doesn't matter."

"What do you mean, it doesn't matter?"

Mr Keele stared upward, then down at Richard.

"You're off the hook this time, Broomhall. Just this once, all right?"

"Yes, sir. Thank you, sir."

On the ground, Zajac, bizarrely, had begun to snore.

"Cool," murmured someone, and several boys laughed. But Mr Dutton was looking up, just as Mr Keele had.

"You're exactly right," he said.

The two teachers stared at each other. Then Mr Dutton addressed the boys.

"I'd say global cooling is here."

"Salvation?" said Mr Keele.

"Or a different kind of doomsday." Mr Dutton smiled. "Maybe a cup that's half empty or half full."

Now everyone's attention was on the lead-grey sky. And then...

It's not possible.

... Richard held out his hand, and felt the specks descend upon it. They were so soft, when they touched his skin, that he felt nothing, nothing at all.

What does it mean?

The air was hushed as the sound-deadening, soft cascade intensified like thickening snowfall, darkening the world, changing everything.

Black snow.

Acknowledgments

The late Bob Bridges (aka Rob) formerly of 22 SAS, software guru and teacher par excellence, gave me one of the key events in this book, and with it the character of Josh Cumberland. May you walk among the stars, my friend.

Ghost Force is the title of a blistering and controversial history of the SAS, written by Ken Connor. It is also the name of his proposed replacement for the Regiment, the hi-tech special forces operatives of the future. In acknowledgment, I have used the same name, although my fictional Ghost Force is an addition to the world's most famous military élite.

I gained insight into covert operations from *The Operators*, James Rennie's terrific account of life in 14 Company, aka 14 Int, aka Det.

The bodyweight exercises used by Josh are from Matt Furey's Combat Conditioning system. I use the system myself. (So, apparently, do instructors from the US Marine Corps Martial Arts Program.) Josh's groundfighting drills come from MMA coach (and fighting legend) Steve Morris. Petra's combat class derives heavily from the Morris Method and from Geoff Thompson's reality-based training.

The fictional fighter called Mad Mick Foster bears absolutely no relation whatsoever to my good friend, sensei Mick Foster, fourth dan. Ahem.

Scary but true: the Timetable of Death was devised by a surgeon on the prompting of WE Fairbairn, founder of WWII commando training and co-inventor of the Fairbairn-Sykes commando dagger. The figures are in Fairbairn's classic book *Get Tough!* I got the term "Timetable of Death", along with the historical background, from Pat O'Keeffe's excellent *Combat Kick Boxing*.

Suzanne's therapeutic techniques are real, though I've omitted certain details, particularly from hypnotic inductions. They derive from NLP, and are currently used by medical doctors that Suzanne would approve of (and by less scientific practitioners too).

Nexus by Mark Buchanan is a great description of complex networks and small-world connectedness. Check out books by Steven Strogatz, and (for complexity theory) Stuart Kauffmann, and the incomparable Jack Cohen and Ian Stewart for further reading.

I owe an immense debt to all my martial arts teachers over the decades, in particular the late Enoeda sensei, ninth dan. He truly was the shotokan tiger.

Finally, endless thanks and unbounded love to Yvonne, who has suffered through all my books, whichever name they appear under.

Oh, and I have a view on edged weapons...

The place for a knife is in the kitchen.

About the Author

Thomas Blackthorne is the pseudonym of science fiction writer John Meaney, author of *To Hold Infinity*, the Nulapeiron sequence, *Bone Song*, *Dark Blood* and the Ragnarok trilogy. His works have been shortlisted several times for the British Science Fiction Award, won the Independent Publishers Best Novel award (in SF/Fantasy), and been one of the *Daily Telegraph* Books of the Year.

Now a full-time writer, in his time he has taught business analysis and software engineering on three continents, and is a black belt in shotokan karate, cross-training in other arts. A trained hypnotist, he remains severely addicted to coffee. He is currently finishing *Point*, the even darker sequel to *Edge*.

www.johnmeaney.com

An extract from
POINT

Coming soon from Angry Robot

His hands were claws because they had to be. Josh hung in shadow beneath the bridge, like a frozen bat on the underside; but he could not flit away: he needed to wait.

"–happened to him?" said a voice overhead.

Police officer.

You could tell from the tone.

"Disappeared," someone said.

"Like a bleedin' ninja, or one of them magicians, like."

The sniffling kids were gone, led away by murmuring adults. You might call them traumatized, but not if you had seen what Josh had seen: in Africa, in Siberia, in post-Deathquake Japan.

Like claws.

He could not let go, that was the thing.

Like steel.

Only failure of will could stop him now, but the stubborn aggression that had kept him alive so many times before was active again. If only it had neared the surface earlier, he might have avoided the despairing stance on the bridge, hands on the rail as if contemplating the jump – *was I really thinking of it?* – leaving it to the emergency response centre of the brain, the amygdala, to react when the hand clapped his shoulder, and that was it: the craziness that could have turned worse, into murder.

Black Thames beneath; but he would not let go.

Like steel.

Entering endurance-trance in order to survive.

There were voices in Suzanne's head, howling self-accusation. She was a neuropsych therapist and supposedly good at her job. It would not have taken expert verbal technique to short-circuit Josh's reaction, then lead him into a psychological space where he could grieve as he needed to.

Où es tu, Josh?

When her thoughts reverted to her native French, she was in trouble.

Calme-toi.

She needed to breathe, to calm down. There must be some way she could help Josh.

Call Tony.

She paused, thinking it through. Tony Gore had helped during last year's infiltration of the Knife Edge final. If the authorities were targetting her for surveillance… but she was not engaged in illegal activities now, and neither was Josh. She needed to make that call.

When she picked up the phone it showed a message waiting, but the pane read **Message from: Adam**. She minimized it.

"Call Tony," she told the phone.

"Which Tony, please?"

Merde.

"Call Tony Gore, urgent."

While she waited, she pointed the phone at the wallscreen, transferring the display. When Tony appeared, his face was larger than lifesize.

"Suzanne. Hey, doll. What's wrong?"

"I don't know for sure that it's bad."

"But you're ringing me at three in the morning, flagged urgent."

"It's Josh…. Sophie died today."

Yesterday, technically. Was it really three a.m.?

"Hang on." Tony turned to one side. "Am? Josh's daughter died."

There a swing of motion, and Amber, Tony's wife, was on screen, rubbing her face.

"Josh? Oh, Suzanne. Awful news. How is he?"

"He's distraught. It's why I needed to talk."

Amber blinked. As an ex-soldier's wife, she was used to hearing about tragedy and people going off the rails. The image tilted, then Tony was back on.

"What's he done, Suzanne?"

"Ran off into the night in thin clothes. Hours ago. Without his phone."

"Shit."

Civilian phones were DNA-tagged and GPS-linked, but people like Josh and Tony were not so easily found. Their handsets broadcast subversion code that altered the data inside the surveillance nets. Ordinary police could not have found Josh, even if they tried – which they would not, unless Suzanne used her authority to declare him at risk of self-harm.

Irrelevant. Josh had left his phone behind.

"Running is therapeutic," said Tony.

"It's been five hours."

Josh might still be running. During Tony's time in

the Regiment, he had been able to run for longer than that. Josh had kept the discipline on leaving the army, that was all.

"What about his state of mind?"

"He was on the edge of losing it," said Suzanne. "Presenting all the signs. But how that might manifest, I couldn't tell."

Five hours ago.

"I'll call you back." Tony's face tightened. "Try to rest, sweetheart. Our Josh is a survivor."

"Yes…"

"Out."

The screen blanked out, as did her thoughts, leaving only feelings: sadness and fear, swirling together, corkscrewing through her body, unnerving her.

The Regiment was not perfect, but they had soldiering skills that others lacked for two reasons: training and resources. They could spend hours firing the latest weapons, using ten thousand euros worth of smartshells or nanoflechettes in a session. They could slip through enemy forces, because guile was a primary focus of their discipline, along with extreme physicality.

With hands like steel claws, he remained beneath the bridge.

Listen.

No one remained above, no humans, but spyballs and motion sensors were something else. He had escaped immediate capture; now it was time to evade the enemy.

Police. Not hostiles.

For his own sake, he needed to get clear, to think. Treat it as an exfiltration exercise through enemy territory, provided he remembered not to harm anyone who tried to arrest him. Things were bad enough already.

How could I screw up like that?

The answer was: reflex-fast, no conscious thought involved.

Shut up.

Pressing his tongue against the roof of his mouth, he stilled his mind.

When he moved, screams sounded, but only along his sinews as they cracked into motion. Then he was crawling to the end of the bridge – avoiding spycams – where he hung in place for minutes, before using counterpressure to climb around the end struts, then clamber onto the stairs.

He was in a surveillance blind-zone.

An automated street-cleaning drone moved like a giant louse along the kerbside, its lights strobing orange. It would have anti-vandal countermeasures, but for urban infiltration the Regiment's training was all-inclusive: he knew how to avoid tripping the detectors.

Pre-dawn was smearing turquoise to the east. There was no foot traffic, no vehicle in sight besides the drone.

Now.

Two lunging steps and a shoulder-roll, and he was inside the carapace, clinging once more, squeezing his eyes to slits against the grit and noise.

Phase one of his evasion was under way.

There is an insomniac state of mind where someone thinks they are awake, while in fact tumbling through a series of micro-sleeps: undetected, unsatisfying, a safety mechanism for avoiding breakdown. Suzanne flitted in and out of grey drowsiness, worrying about Josh, her knowledge of neurology no help at all.

When the door chime sounded, a rush of acid filled her stomach.

Josh!

But the wallscreen, switching to building surveillance, showed three bulky men on the landing outside her door. They had already passed through the locked ground-floor entrance. Two wore police uniform, while the third was dressed in a suit and overcoat.

"Adam?"

He had left a message on her phone, hadn't he?

"Oh, God."

She pressed the release, and electromag locks clicked open. When she pulled back the door, she blinked her sore eyes, unable to read their expressions.

Bad news?

Adam said: "Can we come in, Suzanne?"

"Of… course. Yes."

She was panicking, but she could not speak freely in front of the uniformed officers, not unless she could be sure they knew who Adam Priest was: not a civil servant in the Department of Trade and Industry as his ID declared, but a serving officer in MI5.

"I'm Inspector Edwards." The larger officer held up his phone, showing the official sigil. After a second, it echoed on the wallscreen. "And this is Inspector Calvin."

The smaller man showed his ID the same way.

"Is Josh all right?" said Suzanne.

Inspector was a high rank; she was almost sure of it.

"Ma'am?"

"My… boyfriend. He's in a state of distress – his daughter died – and he went out running. I'm worried about him."

"And his name is Josh?"

"Josh Cumberland." She nodded towards Adam. "You can tell them, can't you?"

"I already have," said Adam. "I could tell you I'd just bumped into the officers by chance, but you probably wouldn't believe me."

Suzanne had no answer. There were implications here, but she was too tired to unravel them.

"Coffee, ma'am?" asked Inspector Calvin. "I could make some all round."

Suzanne said, "I'll just–"

"I'll do it." Inspector Calvin nodded towards the kitchen alcove. "No problem."

"Do you think he's in danger?" asked Adam.

"I'm afraid–" Suzanne blew out a breath. "He might turn that violence inwards."

Then she wondered whether she had heard correctly. Had Adam said he's *in* danger, or he's *a* danger? She closed her eyes, her nostrils feeling odd as she inhaled, dragging alertness into her mind.

Something was wrong, but not what she had feared.

"Where would he run?" said Adam. "Any particular place?"

Inspector Edwards was checking his phone. He was behind Suzanne, a gloomy reflection in the now-dark wallscreen. He looked up – at Adam? – and shook his head.

Adam's eyes gave the tiniest flicker.

Do they know each other?

"He likes exploring new routes," said Suzanne. "No special place."

"So is Josh very fit?" asked Adam. "I mean, the way he was in the military."

There had been a time, after last year's *Knife Edge*

final, when Josh had been recuperating from cut- and stab-wounds: a snarling patient who was hell to live with as he forced himself back to full activity.

"He ran fifty kilometres last Sunday," said Suzanne.

"Some kind of marathon race?" Inspector Calvin was working the coffee machine. "I've always wanted to try that."

"Longer. But just a training run."

"By himself?" asked Adam. "That's disciplined."

"He is," said Suzanne.

From the micro-expressions on the three men's faces, they disagreed. Their reactions were out of kilter, unless… unless Josh had done something. Not self-harm. Something else. Something not disciplined at all.

Josh. Please.

Vast reservoirs of energy inside him made Josh an electrifying athlete and lover; but the same energy could detonate as violence. Her memories of him fight-ing would have been awful, had she not used therapeutic techniques on herself, so that the images were distant, flattened and blurred, losing their impact.

"Here you are, Dr Duchesne." Inspector Calvin had brought two mugs. "Mr Witten."

"Cheers," said Adam.

Suzanne looked. There were no other coffee mugs.

"Aren't you and your colleague–?"

"We'll leave you in peace, ma'am."

Inspector Calvin smiled at Adam, and said: "Steve."

"See you later, Ron."

The two men left. When they were gone, the flat's security system caused the electromag locks to snap home.

"Do police inspectors wear uniforms?" asked Suzanne. "I thought they were plainclothes."

"That's only the detectives," said Adam.

"Oh. But one of them called you Steve. Is that, what, a cover identity?"

"It's my real name. It's 'Adam' that's my cover." Steve/Adam gave an asymmetric shrug. "Sorry."

"I thought Philip Broomhall was your friend."

"He is. He also knows me as Adam Priest, and I'd be grateful if you allow him to continue."

"But you're really… Steve Witten, is that it? And you don't work for the DTI."

"I think you knew that already." His face was lean, his grin cheeky, like a kid's. "You know, in China, it's no big deal. People change their names throughout their lives."

She realized there was no ring on his left hand.

Don't look at his finger.

Last year the wedding band had been white gold. Now there was only a depression in the skin.

"What's happened to Josh?" she said.

Adam – no, Steve – sipped from a retro mug labelled PSYCHOLOGISTS DO IT THOUGHTFULLY. When he put the mug down, he kept his face blank.

"As far as I know, he's alive, uninjured, and somewhere on the streets of London."

"And what else?"

"I have a lot more to say, Suzanne. The thing is, I came here to ask for help. My timing may be awful, but I have to show you this."

He raised his phone and angled it towards the wallscreen.

"If this is official," said Suzanne, "then shouldn't you be checking for eavesdroppers, or something?"

"We already did." Steve/Adam's mouth twitched. "You're clean."

Dead people showed on screen.

"Oh, no," said Suzanne.

"Right," said Steve.

Sprawled, limbs angled and twisted, all of them teenagers, arranged in what might have been a circle before they slumped at random and died. Those with long-sleeved garments had the left sleeves pushed up, revealing inner forearms and the longitudinal gashes in soft flesh.

The pool of blood they lay in was almost black.

"Suicide pact." Suzanne felt phlegm in her throat. "Thirteen teenagers. With drugs or alcohol in their systems?"

"That's what the experts expected," said Steve.

"Oh. The post-mortem's been done?"

"A while back."

Suzanne could not look away. There was movement in the image, only because the camera's operator was alive and changing angles. The dead things on the floor would never move again, not of their own volition.

"Thirteen," she said. "Possibly a significant number."

"Besides being unlucky, are there any associations or meanings you know of?"

"I don't think so." Her face felt strange, tightening as if to weep, while her eyes were dry but stinging. "Thirteen dead kids. Awful."

"No." Sad and soft, Steve's voice lowered. "Not thirteen."

"I make it–"

"One hundred and sixty-two," he said. "We thought when it reached thirteen times thirteen, the deaths would stop. Today we found out we were wrong."

"Oh my God. Oh no."

So many teenagers, unaware that their isolation was shared by billions, including every adult in the past, for everyone lives through it. Or takes the despairing way out.

"We've done everything to keep this quiet," said Steve. "That's why, if you agree to help, you'll need to sign the Official–"

"Keep it *quiet*?"

"Yes. To stop it spreading."

Suzanne blinked at the awfulness on screen.

"That's impossible. Burying news like this."

"You'd be surprised, but it's not easy."

Awful, awful, awful.

"Thought contagion," she said. "Memetic cascade. A crazy idea that spreads like a fad."

"That's what we think."

"Spreading even though you've buried the news."

"Right." Steve's voice was like grating bones. "And when it gets out, what's going to happen then?"

That was the worst thought of all.

"An epidemic," said Suzanne.

Whenever a suicide is reported in the news, fatal traffic accidents increase, because they are not truly accidents. Even the death wish is contagious.

"Exactly."

"A suicide epidemic."

Steve said nothing.

I didn't even know your real name.

And now this, when Josh was gone, and surely needed her.

Yet you expect me to help.

Their flesh was white-grey in the image. Every eye was opaque, creamy with death as proteins decayed.

"I'll do what I can," she said.

Because she did not have a job – she had a calling, and helping people was it.

I have to.

For the first time in years, the silver scars inside her arms began to burn.

Go deeper.
POINT

Coming soon from Thomas Blackthorne and Angry Robot Books

**ANGRY
ROBOT**

Teenage serial killers
Zombie detectives
The grim reaper in love
Howling axes **Vampire
hordes** Dead men's clones
The Black Hand
Death by cellphone
Gangster shamen
Steampunk swordfights
Sex-crazed bloodsuckers
Murderous gods
Riots **Quests Discovery**
Death

Prepare to welcome
your new
Robot overlords.

angryrobotbooks.com